<u>ALSO BY AMBER BOUDREAU</u>

The Dragoneer

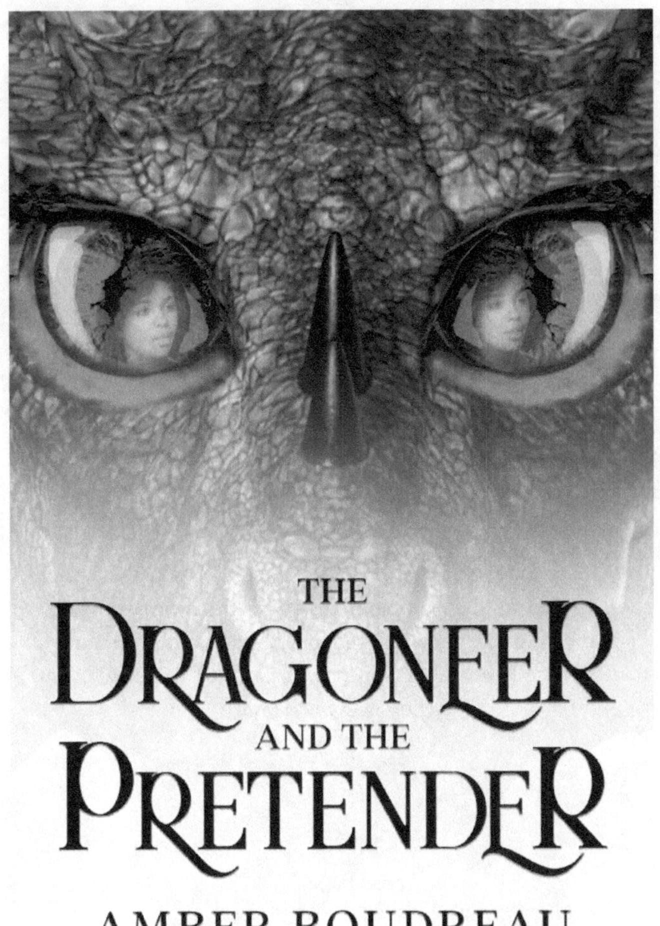

THE
DRAGONEER
AND THE
PRETENDER

AMBER BOUDREAU

A Dragon Street Press Book

PRINTING HISTORY
Published October 2022

This is a work of fiction. Names, characters, businesses, places, events, locales, and incidents are either the products of the author's imagination or used in a fictitious manner. Any resemblance to actual persons, living or dead, or actual events is purely coincidental.

1 3 5 7 6 4 2
Trade Paperback
ISBN-13: 979-8-9867714-0-3

Cover art provided by MiblArt

Printed in the United States of America

For my mom, Beverly.

I would have made a terrible nurse, Mom.
People would have died.

1

Moira Noble stood rooted in place, afraid to turn around. Her hand on the knob, she stared at the wood grain of the hospital room door in front of her. A second ago she'd been ready to leave, convinced she'd done everything she could, and it hadn't worked.

Had Bertram just said her name?

Maybe she was hearing things, her hopes manifesting themselves as an auditory hallucination. There was a first time for everything. But if it wasn't an illusion, then she could very well have willed her comatose high school teacher into waking up. Bertram had been unconscious for a week, ever since the captain of the trolls got his hands on him and forced his way into Bertram's mind to find out what Bertram knew about Zephyr and his dragoneer.

That would be her. Zephyr's bite, the night before her fifteenth birthday, had imbued her with certain abilities.

And one of those abilities might have just awakened Bertram.

In the stillness, her urge to turn around warred with the one to stay put. Another rustle of fabric and the slap of plastic tubing against steel reached her ears.

Moira swallowed, bent her knees, and braced herself. She twisted her head millimeter by millimeter to peer over her shoulder.

In the hospital bed, Bertram eased himself forward onto an elbow, a hand to his temple.

Moira sucked in a huge breath that raised her shoulders and shed a weight she'd carried ever since she'd sworn a promise to help Bertram get the book out of his head.

Bertram heard. "Ms. Noble?" he repeated her name, his voice raspy from disuse. "What happened?" His gaze shot to the darkened window. "What day is it?"

Moira stood there, her jaw slack. "It worked." The words came out in a whisper.

He squeezed his eyes shut tight, blinking them open again a moment later. "What worked?"

"Nothing. Never mind." Moira faced the bed and stuffed her hands into the back pockets of her jeans, staring, heart thumping. As the weather grew cooler, she'd added a long-sleeved checked flannel to cover her arms. With her coat on, ready to go, the layers worked to make her sweat.

She swallowed. "You've been out of it for a week. Since last Friday."

Bertram blinked at her. Thanks to her anonymous phone call the night of Homecoming, EMS workers found him in the library. She knew he must be weak, but he was awake. The part of his face not covered by a dark beard had some color and his eyes were bright. He wasn't the same teacher she remembered from freshman year chemistry, but for the first time she could picture him teaching again. That wouldn't have been possible if he still had a book stuck in his head. Now the book was gone. The Librarian had assured her Bertram could return to a normal life, though his mind might bear some scars. Meanwhile, *The Book of Wyverns* now lived in her brain for the time being. She bore it better than Bertram had, having sacrificed part of her personal memories to make room for it.

Confusion and worry took turns flashing across Bertram's features. He didn't look at her but through her, perhaps thinking that if he peered hard enough, he would see into the past and what had happened. "I... I remember. You were there. How... why were you there?"

He remembers the top of the hill. That was good.

"Zephyr came and got me." Sort of. Zephyr had reached out to her through the connection they shared. "We saw what happened."

Bertram fell back against the raised head of the bed, pressing the heels of both palms into his eyes. "So you know... everything."

Moira took a step closer to the side of his bed. "That man... with the cape? He gave you the book. You were supposed to kill Zephyr, but you didn't. He found out you'd been lying to him and that Zephyr had a dragoneer. He was going to kill you and then hunt us down to take care of us himself. I shot him with an arrow before he stabbed you and he went back to wherever it was he came from."

The breath shuddered out of Bertram. He lowered his hands, peering up at the ceiling. "Thank you. For saving my life."

A bolt of lightning outside the windows lit the room like a flashbulb. Bertram's head jerked toward the window, wide-eyed.

It was edging past dusk into night, but Moira didn't turn on any more lights. She crossed the room, stopping at the side of his bed. "Who was that guy? What did he do to you?"

She remembered how the man had clapped his hands on either side of Bertram's head and then knew things only Bertram could have known. Her stomach churned, recalling how Bertram had fought against it, his body arching to get away from whatever the man had been doing to him.

His gaze fixed on the window. "I'm sorry. I tried to help. I tried to keep your secret. To keep you safe. I just wanted... " One hand flew to his head, his fingertips pressed to his temple. He shut his eyes and, just as quickly, opened them again. "Where is it? Where's the book?"

Moira squinted. "It's gone. The Librarian... " Bertram winced at the name, "... got it out. It's somewhere safe." She didn't think it was the time to burden him with details, like how the book that had caused him such misery was now in her head and didn't cause her any trouble. Not unless she tried to remember something specific from her past. Then things went wonky.

Another flashbulb of light. Bertram gasped. "No. You have to go, Moira."

His telling her to go put her on edge as much as him using her first name. "What are you talking about? You just woke up."

Bertram looked at her. "You're not safe." He swallowed and licked dry lips. "I tried not to... not to show him," Bertram stared at her, his eyes welling. "I don't know what I've done, but he's coming back. There's always a storm." He shuddered, looking toward the window again. Rain splashed against the pane of glass at a sharp angle.

Moira's hands came out of her pockets. There was no doubt in her mind who Bertram was talking about. "I shot him. Right in the middle of his chest."

Bertram shook his head. "He's not dead. I can feel him. He was inside my head." He blinked. "And now he's coming back."

Bertram knew more about the captain of the trolls than anyone. If he thought he was coming back, then she believed him.

He appeared to be searching his thoughts, his gaze unfocused. "He's back. But not for you."

Moira frowned. If he wasn't after her, who could be there for? "Zephyr?"

"He'll kill him too, if he can, but no." Bertram swallowed. "It was dark. He couldn't see you, Ms. Noble. He only saw what was in my head." Bertram stared into her eyes, trying to tell her something, urging her to make the connections and understand what he had done to keep her safe.

Moira blinked, working it through. If Bertram had suppressed his memories of her and Zephyr, who else would the man have seen out in the woods with Zephyr?

"Ansel." Her friend's name came out in a whisper.

"Hurry." Unsettled, Bertram's legs churned beneath the blanket as if he wanted to get up and run. However, the movement alone exhausted him. His head fell back against his pillow, his eyes closed.

"Are you sure? This could just be a regular storm."

He groaned. "I wish it were, but it's not. Go! Go!"

Moira backed away from the bed.

"Run, Ms. Noble."

Moira rushed out of the room. In her haste, she ran into Aunt Paige just outside the door. Her aunt, a nurse, worked at the hospital and had already been in to check on Bertram once that evening before the end of her shift. She was coming back to collect Moira so they could head home together.

Aunt Paige stumbled backward, gripping Moira by the upper arms. "Moira! What is it?"

Moira gripped her aunt in return. "He's awake. Bertram's awake. I have to go. I'm late... for that thing. I'll see you later." She pulled herself away from her aunt and took off down the hallway.

Her aunt spared the door to Bertram's room a glance, but called after her. "What thing? Where are you going?"

Moira didn't answer. She didn't wait for the elevator either, swinging into the stairwell, pounding down the steps to the first floor. Outside, rain still fell, but it was already tapering off, the storm winding down and passing on.

She ran, her feet slapping the pavement. The hospital was across town from her house. Ansel's place sat between the hospital and the high school. She knew how to get there by car, but on foot, roads wouldn't restrict her. She raced through unfenced yards and around obstacles in as much of a straight line as possible. But she still had a lot of ground to cover. One hand pressed to the stitch in her side.

She kept moving. She couldn't stop.

She had to watch for a break in traffic, though. Once across the road, she hit the sidewalk at a sprint. From there, she cut straight through a small abandoned lot. She projected her feelings and thoughts as she ran, hoping Zephyr would pick up on what she was trying to tell him. She tried to convey a sense of urgency and danger, thinking in pictures of the man she had shot and then an image of Ansel. Then she thought in pictures of the way to get to

Ansel's house. How would the captain of the trolls even search for her friend? She didn't know, but Bertram didn't seem to think that a little thing like not knowing exactly where to find Ansel would stop him.

The rain stopped.

She pulled her phone from her pocket as she came around a corner. She and Ansel hadn't spoken since before Homecoming, when he tried to stop her from going to the dance with his brother Aaron and asked her to go with him instead. They'd seen each other around school, but they hadn't talked, Ansel always letting his gaze skip past her as if she wasn't there. He didn't know what happened at the top of the hill on Homecoming, or in the library afterward. But he probably knew Bertram was in the hospital. She pressed the icon to call Ansel. It rang once and went to voicemail. She hung up and tried again. Voicemail again. One more time. Voicemail. She sighed and tried to slow her breathing so she could speak in complete sentences. Her message still came out in fits and bursts. "Ansel... call me when you get this... I have to talk to you. Bertram's awake. Be careful. And call me." She disconnected. What else was there to say? He didn't know about the captain of the trolls because she'd never told him because he wasn't speaking to her. Her anger gave her a burst of speed, but it didn't last.

She tried another number. Aaron didn't answer either. She left a message after the first try, huffing and puffing as she ran. "Aaron... do you know where Ansel is? If you see him, tell him to call me."

Unlike Ansel, she and Aaron had talked despite her having rushed out on him at the Homecoming dance. He'd been disappointed she had left, but he seemed to have understood that whatever she'd needed to take care of was important. The next time she saw him, he had a blackened left eye. He didn't elaborate on how he got it. However, she'd spotted Ansel's split lip and bruised knuckles across the hallway the next time she'd seen him. How much of their fight had to do with her and how much of it had to do with Aaron and Ansel letting off steam, she wasn't sure. She knew they'd argued in the past, but she wasn't sure how physical those arguments got. Aaron and she were supposed to be getting together later. She might have asked him about it tonight.

As she rounded the end of Ansel's block, she knew something was very wrong.

Every light was out. Darkness reigned.

2

Moira scanned the homes on either side of the road. Her dragon-enhanced sight allowed her to see more than she otherwise could have. Not just the street lights were dark, but every house. The electricity for the entire block appeared to be out. Sweat trickled down her back, but the chill in the night air chased a shiver down her spine. A hum in the air made it sound as if the current was still running but with nowhere to go. It didn't reach any electric lights. Moira's pace slowed as she approached Ansel's house cautiously, her breathing harsh.

The weeping willow in the front yard at the end of the lane stood silent and silvery in what light there was from the next block over and the skies overhead. Moira's thoughts turned to Zephyr. She parted the curtain-like limbs of the tree and passed through them. The tire swing underneath swayed back and forth.

Wrapped around the trunk of the tree, the scales on his back like an extra layer of bark, Zephyr watched the front of the house through narrowed lids. The top of his head was at least eight inches above her own and twice as wide. Zephyr rested both talon-tipped hands against the tree as he stood motionless, his tail wound around the base.

Moira bent over, hands on her knees, and when she was sure she could speak, asked in a whisper, "When did you get here?"

Zephyr's head tilted toward her, but his attention remained fixed on the house. "A minute before you."

Moira followed his gaze.

The garage door stood open.

Aaron and Ansel often worked with their dad in the two-car garage, but she didn't know why the door would be open with no one around. She thought of all the dark homes she'd passed on the way. *No one's even bothered to light a candle? Something is seriously wrong here.*

A thump and a crash erupted from inside the garage.

The growl of a motor reached her ears. It roared closer. Moira expected it to drive by.

Zephyr held out Moira's bow and quiver. She took them and slid the container of arrows over her head.

The rumble of the motor came to a stop as Ansel's truck parked at the curb.

Moira did a double take and slipped out from beneath the willow.

The headlights flicked off and Ansel climbed out of the cab. "Moira?" His gaze dropped to her bow. "What's going on?" He sounded worried.

They hadn't spoken in over a week. He looked well. His bruises were fading just like his brother's, but he looked tired. The shadows under his eyes were darker than when they last spoke. His sandy hair was still longer and shaggier than Aaron's, but otherwise, the two remained identical.

"Did you get my message?" Moira asked.

"What mess… "

A deep voice interrupted. "Amazing. Another."

Moira jerked, facing the leader of the trolls, their captain, as he stepped out of the darkened garage very much alive. He looked a lot healthier than the last time she'd seen him, when her arrow sprouted from the middle of his chest. His renewed health was inexplicable. When she put an arrow in something, she intended it to stay down. He'd replaced his ruined armor with a new metal breastplate, but otherwise appeared unchanged, his long red cape flowing from his shoulders. Did his close-cropped hair have a hint of gray to it that wasn't there before? Were those lines etched into the skin around his eyes new? She couldn't be sure.

Another movement in the shadows caught her attention. A large troll emerged from the garage behind the captain holding a semi-conscious Aaron by the arms. The troll stopped next to its commander.

Aaron's gaze was unfocused. He didn't appear to be bleeding or physically hurt, but considering what the captain had done to Bertram, she didn't know for sure.

Moira's jaw clenched so tight it popped.

Ansel stormed around the front of his truck. "What did you do to my brother?"

"Do I have the pleasure of addressing the dragoneer?" the captain asked without a glance in her direction.

Ansel's gaze, however, flicked to Moira and back. "You do."

The captain flicked a hand toward Ansel. "Bring him to me."

The troll released Aaron, who slumped to his knees on the ground. Moira thought it could have been the same troll that had helped spirit the captain away after she'd shot him. It was over six feet tall, one of the largest she'd seen, with an orange tint to its skin, and armor made of thick leather. The troll didn't bother to unsheathe any weapons as it stalked forward. Perhaps it expected Ansel to come quietly.

If anyone else saw the branches of the weeping willow part, they said nothing. Moira remained silent.

Zephyr stabbed the troll through the middle before it was halfway across. Moira noted the turbid swirls of color settling across Zephyr's scales as he dispelled the camouflage that made him invisible to everyone but her. The troll toppled to the cement driveway.

Moira allowed herself a moment's satisfaction when she saw the captain's eyes widen at Zephyr's sudden appearance. Unfortunately, that was all he did. Moira had hoped the captain might go into a freeze. That didn't happen. The captain must have spent enough time around dragons that Zephyr's appearance didn't faze him. Instead, he reached down and hauled Aaron to his feet by his hair.

Aaron didn't make a sound.

The captain grabbed Aaron by the arm, drawing a dagger. He pressed the point of the blade into the flesh of Aaron's neck above his shirt collar. "I expected you to be smaller. Your kind are always so much easier to get rid of when you've just hatched." He spat the words. "But why take a dragoneer?"

Zephyr raised the sword Bertram was supposed to have killed him with after he hatched. The troll's blood, still wet on the blade, caught the light. Zephyr's only answer was a rumbling growl so low Moira felt it in the hollow of her chest.

Moira drew and nocked an arrow. "Let him go."

The captain sneered, but only glanced in her direction, his gaze never leaving Zephyr for longer than that. "Who are you?" He pulled Aaron by the arm, dragging him to the side.

Moira's gaze fixed on the spot of blood that welled up at Aaron's throat, where the dagger broke his skin. "Let him go. He doesn't know anything."

The captain pulled Aaron around in front of him, using her friend as a shield. No way she could hit the captain without hurting Aaron. "Answer my question. You look familiar. Leave now and you won't get hurt."

Moira fired.

The arrow sank into the frame of the garage.

The captain flinched.

Moira quickly drew and nocked another arrow. "Stay and answer the question, or leave? Which is it?" she asked.

The captain glared at the still quivering shaft before turning back to Zephyr. His lips drew upward in a joyless smile as he muttered something under his breath.

The blade flashed silver in his hand before he threw it straight at Zephyr.

Her dragon jerked to the side to dodge, but the dagger was faster. The blade hit him in the shoulder. His roar split the air.

Zephyr's sword hit the ground.

The echo of his yell reverberated through Moira's head, making her gasp, her throat raw as if she had been the one to yell. A quick glance showed her the handle of the dagger stood perpendicular to Zephyr's scales. Blood trickled down his arm. Anger flashed through her in a red-hot wave. She steadied herself, ready to draw more of the captain's blood herself.

The air around Aaron and his captor blurred.

Moira twisted toward Ansel.

From one heartbeat to the next, Aaron and the captain materialized beside Ansel. He didn't have time to react. With Aaron in one hand, the captain grabbed hold of Ansel with the other. Ansel shuddered at the contact and tried to throw him off, but the captain wouldn't let go. He muttered, low and indistinct.

Moira saw her opening. She gathered her will, took careful aim, and fired. Her arrow came to a dead stop a foot in front of the captain's throat before it dropped to the ground.

The air grew thick, pressing down on them in an unseen fog, making it hard to breathe. Sound grew muffled, affecting Moira's ability to focus. She raised a hand, convinced the air was so thick she could push it aside. Her movements were slow. The captain, Aaron and Ansel still in his grasp, faded from view. She stared as their edges lost sharpness, their colors growing dull. She struggled to nock another arrow.

Stupefied, Aaron hung in the captain's grasp. Ansel's gaze went from the man who gripped his arm, to his brother, to Moira, eyes wide with fear. His lips moved. He might have said her name. He might have yelled it. There wasn't enough Ansel left to make much noise. All three were now transparent.

She fired. The arrow passed through the captain's head, now no more substantial than a wisp of steam. As the arrow sailed harmlessly through him, the captain's gaze met hers while he continued to fade from sight. His eyes narrowed into a sinister glare, and Moira got the impression that he was finally seeing her for the first time.

Moira fought to grab another arrow, fumbling through the thickened air.

A bright white arc of static electricity flashed through the air where the captain had been standing, releasing the caught-up tension in the air. Moira closed her eyes against the burst of light, and staggered, her feet carrying her forward suddenly.

The light faded. They were gone.

3

Moira stumbled to where Ansel and Aaron had stood not a minute before. Nothing remained to show they had ever been there. As suffocating as the air had been, it was clear now. And quiet, save for her halting and gasping breaths.

They were gone.

Her heart pounded, the edges of her vision growing dark. She pushed back her rising panic as she turned to face Zephyr. Across the driveway, her dragon slumped, his eyelids half lowered. He reached up to grasp the hilt of the dagger still buried in his arm.

"Wait," Moira said, rushing to his side. "The blade is keeping you from bleeding out."

"Yes, but it also keeps me from healing." With a grunt, Zephyr pulled slowly on the hilt, hissing. As the blade cleared the edges of the wound, a rush of blood welled up and over, running down his arm, but it immediately slowed.

Though bloody, the edges of the wound were already knitting themselves together.

"I am sorry, Moira. I was of no use," Zephyr said.

Moira glanced at the dead troll sprawled on the ground at their feet. "I wouldn't say that."

Around them, crickets chirped anew. Whatever the captain of the trolls had done was fading now that he was gone.

"Are you going to be okay?"

Zephyr flexed with a hiss, but the gash had stopped bleeding. "I will recover."

She pointed her chin at the dead troll. "We've got to do something about that." She wasn't strong enough to move the troll on her own.

"We could bury it."

"Not here. I've got another idea. Can you drag him around the house?" Moira knew the Idlewilds had a huge fire pit in their backyard and hoped it would suit their purpose.

While Zephyr moved the body, she searched the garage. Their other car was missing. She assumed Aaron and Ansel's parents were out for the night.

Moira went from the workbench in the back of the garage to the shelves, seeking an accelerant and something to light it with. She worried the flames might draw attention to the lights being out. Perhaps the troll and his master had blown a transformer. Her nose told her there was already another fire going in the neighborhood. Their fire wouldn't be the only one, and the six-foot privacy fence would help keep what they were doing, well, private.

Having something to do, a task to accomplish, helped. There was no time to go to pieces. Her hand gripped the shelf as she searched, her knuckles turning white. Events played themselves repeatedly in her head, a few distinct moments resolving themselves in her memories, like pictures developing on film. The snapshots would stay with her. She could take them out and look at them whenever she wanted. Knowing she could do so, she pushed them from her mind and found what she was looking for.

In the backyard, Zephyr laid the troll in the firepit. It was a good thing the Idlewilds had used the pit for bonfires in the past, otherwise, the troll might not have fit. A brush pile sat nearby, ready to be lit.

Moira squeezed the bottle of lighter fluid over the body, lit a match, and dropped it. The liquid ignited with a tiny *whoomf.*

Zephyr stepped back. "We are going to need a bigger fire." He slipped away, only to return a few moments later with the sword and dagger, but nothing to feed the flames.

Moira spread her hands open in front of her as if to warm them. She focused on the flames as she walked the perimeter of the fire pit, injecting her will with every footfall, imagining as she did she enclosed it, walling it off from its surroundings. This invisible cylinder she imagined as the tip of a funnel, drawing oxygen from the air overhead down into the pit, a harder task to accomplish considering the air they breathed contained only about 21 percent oxygen. She silently encouraged the flames to consume the troll, watching as they changed color from orange to blue, the smoke dying down. To discourage anyone from getting near the pit while the fire burned, she urged others to stay away. It was a complicated message. She walked the circle several times, pouring her will into the magic to get it to work. An acrid smell hit her nose, so she attempted to wall that off as well. Then she stepped back and stood next to Zephyr, staring into the pit, watching the fire without seeing it.

His frustration was a palpable thing. "I am sorry," he said again.

"There's nothing to be sorry for, Zeph. This wasn't your fault."

He stretched his neck forward, lifting his chin. "This is all my fault."

"Stop." She peered at him in the dark, blue firelight flickering across his scales. "Do not blame yourself. Not for any of this." Anger crept into her tone, but she wasn't mad at him. She was angry with herself. He'd taken a knife to the arm while she stood there and watched.

"Likewise," Zephyr said, catching her eye, their empathetic connection telling him how she felt.

She nodded once. If there was nothing he could have done, the same went for her and there was no sense in blaming herself either. The blame lay with the man who had hurt Zephyr and taken her friends.

"Do you still have that knife?" she asked.

Zephyr opened his hand. The double-edged blade lay flat across his palm about ten inches long, still smeared with his blood. Light from the fire bounced off the red gem embedded in the hilt.

"Hold on to it. I'd like to return it to the captain of the trolls myself." She turned back to the fire. "Bertram woke up."

Zephyr's head jerked to the side, watching her as she watched the flames.

"That's how I knew there was trouble. He told me something was wrong." She met his gaze. "The captain's going to figure it out eventually. Ansel's either going to tell him, or he'll find out another way." She swallowed, thinking of what exactly that could mean for Aaron and Ansel. "I don't know what he's going to do when he realizes he got it all wrong and I'm the dragoneer."

Zephyr dipped his head once in agreement. "What do we do?"

Moira turned back to the flames, willing them to burn hot and fast. "We get them back."

***

With the additional oxygen and her magic, it didn't take long for all biological traces of the troll to be erased. A buckle or two remained from its armor. Moira buried them. Then she held out her bow and quiver to Zephyr. "Can you take these back to the clearing? I'll meet you there."

"Where are you going?"

"Home. I have to grab a few things. We can't wait around here for the captain to realize he made a mistake." Her eyes met his.

Zephyr accepted her bow and quiver and slipped away without a word.

At home, her aunt wasn't back from the hospital yet. Moira rushed to gather what might come in useful for a trip she wasn't even sure she and Zephyr could make. Out of her backpack came schoolbooks and notes. Into the bag went her rock hammer, flashlight, and a few provisions for her and Zephyr. She didn't know what to expect, did not know what would come in handy or not, but there was no time to waste. She grabbed everything remotely dragon-related and was about to rush downstairs when she heard a noise.

It couldn't be her aunt. She would have sung out when she came in the door. Who or what had followed her home? Her heart beat double-time. She focused on controlling her breathing as she slipped downstairs, avoiding the steps that squeaked.

There, the sound of metal sliding against metal. It came from the kitchen. She inched down the hall, her breathing shallow, her heart pounding. How could she have been so stupid? She should have brought her bow home with her. Now she was unarmed, potentially going up against an assailant in her own home who was already in the kitchen, home to all the best weapons. Moira backtracked to the hall closet and grabbed an umbrella. It was better than nothing. She raised the curved wooden handle overhead, inching toward the kitchen. In the doorway, she came to an abrupt stop.

Her aunt Paige stood at the stove watching the kettle, waiting for it to boil, a faraway expression on her face. Then she saw Moira and blinked.

Too late to make a hasty retreat, Moira froze.

"Hey." Aunt Paige's brows drew together in a frown. "What are you going to do with that?"

Moira lowered the umbrella and set it against the wall. "Defend myself against a home intruder, obviously. I didn't know you were home."

"Sorry, I didn't mean to scare you. I didn't know you were home either."

Moira pressed a hand to her sternum, trying to get her heart to slow its frantic pounding.

"Are you okay?" her aunt asked.

Moira waved at her, then bent at the waist to catch her breath.

"You're kind of jumpy tonight, aren't you?"

More like paranoid.

Her aunt grabbed a cup from the cupboard. "What happened to you earlier? Why'd you run out of the hospital?"

Imagining her ribs expanding with every breath, Moira took a moment to answer. "I had to go. I was late to meet Aaron."

How was she supposed to get out of there now that her aunt was home? Moira couldn't just mosey out the back door without telling Aunt Paige where she was going.

Her aunt's hand went to her hip. "What did you and Aaron get up to?"

Moira swallowed, thinking fast. "We went for a drive."

Her aunt's hand left her hip and wrapped itself around her middle. "Did you eat?"

"Yep. Did you talk to Mr. Bertram?"

Her aunt's gaze refocused on the kettle. "Yes, I did. He's very agitated. Not making sense. That's not unheard of for a patient coming out from whatever had him under for so long. We eventually got him to calm down. I might... " She cut herself off.

Moira's breathing was almost back to normal. "What?"

"I might head back. He asked me to stay, but I already put in twelve hours today. I needed to take a break and come home. Make sure everything's okay here."

"Everything's fine. I'll probably head to bed soon." She stretched her mouth wide in a fake yawn she covered with one fist.

The kettle sputtered a raspy whistle. Her aunt killed the fire and made herself a cup of tea. "Sit down for a second?"

Moira slid into a seat at the table.

Her aunt spoke as soon as she sat down. "Thank you for going to the hospital and helping Harold."

"I didn't do anything... "

"Just your being there helped, I think."

Oh. That was good. Her aunt didn't suspect she had anything to do with waking Bertram, though she was pretty sure the only reason he had woken up was because of what she did, willing him to regain consciousness.

"I know it couldn't have been easy for you," her aunt was saying. "Going to the hospital." She blew across the surface of her tea before taking a tentative sip.

Her aunt was right. Moira hadn't been a fan of hospitals since panic attacks landed her in the emergency room on multiple occasions. That was a long time ago, though. Therapy had given her the tools she needed to cope, and she was doing much better — dragons, trolls, and murderous kidnappers aside. How soon before she could slip off to bed and then away? Aaron and Ansel were gone. She had to get them back, and she didn't know how long that was going to take.

Aunt Paige set her cup down. "I'm proud of you, kiddo. And you should know that I trust you, even if I give you a hard time about school and curfew. You're an excellent student and I know I can always count on you to do what's right."

Moira's breath caught. Her aunt trusted her. How could she be thinking of sneaking out of the house? She met her aunt's gaze, her lips parting, but no words came out.

"Your dad would be proud of you, too. I know he would. Remember when... "

Moira exhaled in a rush.

Whatever her aunt was about to say, Moira would not remember. A picture of her and her father hung upstairs in her room. She knew what he looked like, had memorized his features again since the Librarian took the book that was in Bertram's head and put it in hers. Her father died when she was eleven. But... everything from before she turned twelve was gone. She'd sacrificed her childhood memories to make room for the book so she could function more or less normally with no ill side-effects.

"… we would go camping? We would go for a hike, but we would have to stop every ten feet because your dad would see a bird and want a better look." Aunt Paige shook her head and took another sip of tea.

Moira swallowed. "I should go to bed. I'm exhausted."

"Okay. Get some rest. Any plans for tomorrow?"

Moira could barely think beyond the next hour, so she went with the universal backup answer. "Probably just studying. What about you? Are you headed back to the hospital tonight?"

Her aunt glanced at the kitchen wall clock. "I might. I'll stick my head in and let you know if I do."

Moira stood. "No. Uh, don't bother. I'll probably be asleep. I'll just see you in the morning. Good night."

"Night," her aunt called after her.

Moira stopped in the hall to collect the umbrella, peering over her shoulder one last time to witness her aunt staring into her cup of tea. Then she put the umbrella back in the hall closet and headed back up to her room. There she made up the bed to look as if she were asleep in it. She'd told her aunt not to check on her, but there was no guarantee she wouldn't do just that if she headed back to the hospital.

Moira went to her desk and sat. She couldn't just leave. Her aunt trusted her. Maybe she and Zephyr should stay put. When the captain realized he'd made a mistake and didn't have the right person, he would come back. They would be ready for him when he did. That was one option.

Then she remembered the night of Homecoming and how she saved Bertram from being run through.

No. They couldn't wait. They had to take a more proactive approach. The captain of the trolls would not be happy when he discovered he'd made a mistake. Aaron and Ansel were counting on her and Zephyr. She and her dragon were the only ones who knew the twins were missing. Her aunt trusted her to do what was right. Going after Aaron and Ansel was the right thing to do.

She still couldn't just leave, though.

Grabbing a pen and a blank piece of paper, Moira chewed the inside of her bottom lip. Best to keep it short and to the point. *Aunt Paige*, she dashed against the paper, *there's something I have to do. I might not be home for a while. See you soon. Love, Moira.*

Cringing at the vagueness of the message, she laid the pen down on her desk. If she didn't come back, her aunt would find it when she searched her room. With one last long look at the four familiar walls of her bedroom, she strode to the window and quietly thrust up the sash. Using a ball of string, she lowered her backpack to the ground outside and tossed the ball after it. Ducking low, she sat on the edge and studied the branch of the sturdy oak that grew near her window ledge. It was the same branch Zephyr used when he was smaller, the night he bit her.

She stretched one leg out over empty air until she could step onto the limb. She did the same thing with her other leg, turning to brace herself against the house, sliding the window closed from the outside. With a heave, she pushed away from the house and grabbed another branch to steady herself. Then she climbed down, collected her backpack, and set off into the night.

She met Zephyr in his clearing. He had her bow and quiver ready and waiting for her. Moira contemplated the size of the quiver versus the capacity of her backpack with a shake of her head.

"I can take the bag," Zephyr said.

"Are you sure?"

"Yes. That way you can carry your arrows."

Moira slipped her backpack from her shoulders and lifted the quiver over her head, carrying it alongside her bow. The sword definitely wouldn't fit in the backpack, but the dagger did. Zephyr had cleaned both weapons of blood. She zipped the bag closed, loosened the shoulder straps as far as they would go, and helped Zephyr into them. The bag's seams stretched to the max across Zephyr's broad back. As long as he didn't flex, she thought the straps would hold.

"Let's go," she said.

At the edge of the clearing, Zephyr paused and glanced back. The waning gibbous moon overhead barely crested the treetops and offered little in the way of illumination. Not that there was much to see. Moira's night vision was excellent, but the meadow was empty save for the pile of medium-sized boulders and smaller rocks mounded in front of Zephyr's alcove. There was no sign anyone had been there. Not since they'd taken down Bertram's tent and stowed it out of the way, unsure if he would ever need it again.

Zephyr's shoulders slid up and down as a sigh escaped him. Perhaps Zephyr saw more than she did. Moira wasn't sure, but she thought his night vision was even better than hers.

They approached the high school from the rear, as they had the night of Homecoming. There were no security cameras there that she knew of, but a glance at Zephyr revealed the turbid swirls of shifting shapes over his scales, which meant he was using his camouflage. With no one around, they crept into the school through the loading dock, Zephyr ducking through the door to the hallway, and headed to the library. Administrators had turned most of the lights off to conserve energy. She held both library doors open for Zephyr and they stepped inside.

Moira didn't expect to run into anyone so late on a Friday night, so she wasn't trying to be quiet. Too late, she saw a desk lamp aglow in Ms. Haven's office. What was she doing in the library so late at night?

The sound of a chair rolling across the floor reached them.

"Hello?" Ms. Haven's voice rang out from her office. "Jerry, is that you?"

They froze. They were in front of the circulation desk, too far away from the stacks to dodge behind them without making a noise. Thankfully, the rest of the lights in the library were off. Moira thought Zephyr's camouflage would hold up, but that didn't help her.

A moment later, Ms. Haven appeared in her office doorway. She was wearing the same button-down blouse tucked into a pair of trousers she had worn during the school day. Her long, dark hair fell straight from the top of her head, past her shoulders in a wavy haze. The librarian held her reading glasses in both hands as if she'd just taken them off.

Moira squeezed her eyes shut, hoping that by blocking the sight of Ms. Haven, she would herself become invisible. Childish, she knew, but she couldn't stop herself. A second later, she blinked her eyes open, expecting Ms. Haven to call out her name. Ms. Haven would want to know what she was doing in the library at night, and with a bow and a quiver full of arrows no less.

To her surprise, Ms. Haven remained in the doorway, not coming forward. "Is anyone there?" she called, head turned to the side, listening.

Moira and Zephyr remained silent. She wondered if the light was playing tricks on the librarian's eyes, coming from her well-lit office to peer into the dark library.

Ms. Haven tutted to herself. Then she slipped her glasses on, turned away, and disappeared back into her office.

Wide-eyed, Moira turned to meet Zephyr's gaze. She raised a finger to her lips. Zephyr nodded, and they moved as quietly as possible to the far corner of the library, away from Ms. Haven's office. Only then did Moira's shoulders relax a fraction.

The last time she got the Librarian's attention... not Ms. Haven, but the scary one who took the book out of Bertram's head and put it in hers... she didn't have to be quiet. She might have yelled. She might have had to push entire shelves of books to the floor. Moira pressed her lips into a line. Now, what were they going to do?

She looked at Zephyr and shrugged. "Librarian?" she whispered.

"Yes?" came the reply at full volume next to her ear.

4

Moira jumped away from the Librarian, who stood next to her in the dark. Her hands curled into fists, her nails biting into her palms.

"Would you stop doing that?" she said, keeping her voice low.

The Librarian raised one brow in an imperious manner. "You called me." He spoke at full volume.

"Shhh," Moira warned him. "Please," she added.

The Librarian lowered his brow, relenting. "What do you want?" he asked, his voice quieter than before.

He appeared as flawless and polished as usual in his sharp black suit and crisp white button-down shirt without a hair out of place. But there was something off about him. She'd noticed it as soon as he transferred the book to her, but she couldn't put her finger on it then and she still couldn't.

His weight shifted from one foot to the other, as if he didn't have time for whatever it was she wanted. But he was there. He'd shown up when she called the first time without having to knock any books off their shelves. She'd have to think about that one later. Of course, he probably resented being pulled away from whatever it was a being such as he did. That was why she came to him. She couldn't think of anyone else powerful enough to assist them.

"The man who hurt Bertram... he took my friends and he disappeared. Can you help us find them?"

The Librarian stepped back, scanning her from head to toe as if it were the first time he was seeing her in a long time, evaluating her in a way that creeped her out more than his usual manner. He took in her bow and quiver full of arrows and turned to Zephyr, who carried the sword at his side.

Her dragon stood silently by, but she knew better. Zephyr was already on alert, ready for whatever the Librarian had in mind.

The Librarian spoke. "I suspect he's taken them to the world your dragon hails from."

Zephyr grunted. They had surmised that much on their own.

"Can you help us get them back?" Moira asked.

"I cannot, but I will tell you this: to travel from one world to the next, you must pass through the spaces in between. It's easier to leave one world behind than it is to gain access to another." His gaze met Moira's. "However, you possess a key."

His gaze lost focus then, his fingers smoothing the lapel of his jacket. He glanced down, as if surprised to find he was wearing one. Then he closed his eyes and tipped his head back. There had always been an element of otherworldliness to him, but now he appeared almost approachable, which just wasn't right. He turned away.

"Wait," Moira said. "That's it?"

The Librarian turned back. "Yes?"

"I've never traveled between worlds before. I was hoping for a little more to go on." Moira pointed to her temple. "And what about the book? How do I get it out?"

The Librarian rocked back on his heels. "You do not 'get it out.' Once you have it, you bring it to me, and I attempt to reverse what has been done. The good news is that the physical copy of the book will want to be reunited with its content."

Moira frowned, not liking his use of the word 'attempt'. He was the Librarian. If he couldn't transfer the book out of her head, she didn't know who else to turn to.

"As for traveling between worlds,"... he shrugged... "You have all you need."

As if that explained everything, he turned before she could respond, and melted into the ether.

Zephyr recoiled.

"I hate it when he does that." Moira huffed out a breath. "Did you hear him say something I didn't? Any idea of how we're supposed to get to wherever it is you came from?"

Zephyr lifted a shoulder. "I heard what you heard. He said something about a key."

Moira patted her pockets. "I'm fresh out of... oh." Her head snapped up.

"What?"

"I might have something. Come here." She stepped around the end of a bookcase to a table. "I need the backpack."

Zephyr slid the straps down his arms and off. Moira opened the front pocket and dug through it. A flash of white caught her eye. She snatched up the piece of shell Zephyr had given her after she'd brought him the fire rocks that gave him a jump start on his growth spurt. She hadn't taken it out when she was emptying her bag earlier. Zephyr's shell was mottled black on the outside with a bright white interior curve. Could it be a key? She zipped the pocket shut. Zephyr picked up the bag and slipped it back over his broad back.

"The Librarian said we had a key," she said.

Zephyr eyed the shell, nostrils flaring. "If it is a key, how do we use it?"

She set the shell down on the empty table, concave side up. "I have no idea."

They bent their heads over it.

The shell wobbled.

Moira reached out with a finger and pushed the edge of the shell. It spun like a top before it slowed to a wobble again. She stood up straight. "I'm confused. Why do I need something from your world? I have you." She raised both hands, palms up, motioning to Zephyr.

He raised his head. "But I hatched here. Perhaps I am… tainted."

Moira chewed the inside of her lip. "I don't think tainted is the right word." Soon after he hatched, Zephyr snuck into her room while she was sleeping and bit her on the ankle. There had been a time she wanted to know why, but he couldn't put his reasoning into words other than he needed someone like her. Moira's past issues with her anxiety were part of it. She was stronger for having suffered so much, but she still had potential, whatever that meant. He'd injected her with his venom and she'd survived, but he'd gotten a taste of her blood. Perhaps he was less tainted and more… altered. She wasn't sure. The Librarian said they had a key. This was the only thing she possessed related to Zephyr's world, besides Zephyr himself, that she would consider a key.

She bent forward, hovering over the shell again. "What if... " Moira reached out a finger and flicked the shell again. Except this time, she added a pinch of her will. The shell spun, but instead of slowing down, this time it spun faster. She straightened and caught Zephyr's eye. They stepped back from the table.

The shell spun faster and faster, becoming a blur. Then it shot off of the table and struck the end of a bookcase with a thump and disappeared. It happened so fast, Moira didn't know where it went, but thought it must have rolled under the table.

"I'll grab it and we can try again," Moira said, crouching down. Nothing. She went to the floor on her hands and knees.

"Moira," Zephyr nudged her with his foot.

Nothing under the table. Where could the shell have gotten to?

"Moira," Zephyr said her name again, louder.

Her head snapped up.

Zephyr stood in front of the end of the bookcase the shell had ricocheted off of. A poster hung from it. She stepped up beside him. His gaze didn't leave the unframed single sheet of paper. Moira recognized it as one of those encouraging types of posters with a large tree that had something printed on it about planting the seeds of learning or having the courage to branch out. She couldn't remember, but it didn't matter because there were no words. Not anymore. Now there was just the tree. Moira stared hard at the poster and could have sworn she saw a leaf float down from one branch.

"Did you see..." Zephyr's voice trailed off.

"Uh-huh."

The branches of the tree swayed as if stirred by their breath.

They shared a glance. Moira swallowed, reaching a hand out toward the tree.

Zephyr caught her arm. "Wait. Together."

Moira nodded. Her quiver and bow snug across her back, she gripped them tight to her shoulder with one hand and snagged Zephyr's free hand with her other. His leathery palm pressed against hers and squeezed tight. She leaned forward.

Her face did not smack into the end of the row. She took that as a good sign and focused on the tree. The branches waved, and another leaf twirled freely. Then the tree moved. It didn't pick up its roots and stalk away, but receded into the distance. Moira lifted one foot, but both feet left the ground. Then she felt a tug somewhere behind her navel that sent her tumbling forward into an abyss.

Zephyr grunted as the air rushed past them. A slightly more terrified shriek left her mouth. She clung as hard as she could to Zephyr's hand, but could feel her grip slipping. The tempest they stepped into swept them forward and jerked them apart.

Moira screamed.

Zephyr shouted her name as her hand left his. His voice grew distant, and faintly echoed in her ears as she tumbled forward into a steep fall.

5

The world bent and stretched around her, leaving the taste of copper-tinged cotton in her mouth. Her arm, the one not keeping a grip on her bow and quiver, swam through thin air, her feet kicking and getting her nowhere. The world went dark. Not because Moira passed out, but because she squeezed her eyes shut, terrified. She could only hope it ended soon, and yet, not too abruptly.

She willed herself to slow down.

She could not recommend this interspatial travel, or whatever it was.

The landing wasn't anything to write home about, either.

It was better than it could have been. How could she tell? She was still alive after she hit the ground, albeit with the wind knocked out of her. She blinked her eyes open, sputtering, cheek pressed into the dirt, surrounded by tall vegetation. With one hand, she pushed herself up to her knees. Her stomach churned and she retched. She pulled at the leaves of whatever tall plants she'd landed in and used them to wipe the vomit from her face. She kept her other hand clenched against her shoulder, her fingers wrapped tight around the string of her bow and the strap of her quiver. She loosened her grip, but she had to uncurl her stiffened fingers one at a time before she could flex them.

All she could see from where she sat was more tall grass. A breeze stirred the plants, along with her hair tangled around her shoulders. She combed her fingers through her curls, her hair tie lost with all the flailing and thrashing.

When Moira was sure she wouldn't be sick again, she poked her head above the top of the plants and saw... more of the same, everywhere. Rolling hills surrounded her, broken up by an occasional stand of trees.

No Zephyr.

She reached out with her extra sense, the dragon-o-meter, which told her which way to go to find Zephyr.

Nothing.

Her head whipped around, right to left, and back again. Where was he?

When her dragon-o-meter didn't point her in any direction, that usually meant he was nearby, but he wasn't. There was no dragon-shaped depression in the ground anywhere. Just rows and rows of whatever crop she'd landed in. She couldn't find him, which was a problem because she couldn't do this without him. She could not be here on her own, could not do this alone.

In an instant, her heart-rate doubled. *Oh, no. Not now. Not now.* Telling herself it wasn't a good time for a panic attack didn't do any good. Moira put one foot in front of another. The physical act pushed back her anxiety. She struggled to deepen her breathing and closed her eyes.

Raising her right hand, she pressed it to her chest, imagining a circle opening and closing, breathing with it. Her foot caught on a clump of dirt and she tripped. Startled, she opened her eyes, the urge to panic thankfully passing.

The rows were a good sign. Someone had cultivated the field, so they must also tend to it. Perhaps whoever handled the crops had seen Zephyr. She shook out her limbs and kept walking.

The wind picked up, turning the field into an undulating sea. Moira started downhill, swallowing against the growing lump of fear in her throat. Zephyr had to be there somewhere. She just hadn't found him. *Yet*, she told herself. She just hadn't found him… yet.

Ten minutes passed until, her face turned into the wind, she heard voices. High-pitched and excited, the words were indistinct. Perhaps someone had found a stray dragon roaming the hills looking for his lost companion? Moira hurried forward noting the crops thinning as more trees took their place.

The excited chatter reached her ears again. Near a stand of trees at the bottom of the hill, two dirt roads crossed each other at a shallow angle, forming a wide spot.

What got her attention, though, were the large round metal cages. Three of them hung near the crossroads, suspended by heavy chains wound around the stout limbs of the trees overhead. Two were empty. The occupant of the third cage wasn't making the ruckus. The group of men surrounding the cell was doing all the talking. However, the glint of a sword told her it wasn't all talk.

Moira's feet started moving faster. Before she knew it, she was running.

To her knowledge, people got stuffed into cells because they did something wrong and someone decided they needed to go away. They did not get stuffed into cages to be run through.

Three armed men stood outside the cage, but only one had his sword unsheathed. That one harried the unarmed man behind the bars with his blade. "How does it feel to know your luck has run out, half-breed?" The man sneered.

The prisoner crouched at the back of his cage as far away from the end of the sword as he could, but it was quite a small space. For all that the cell was round, the man was cornered. There was a rent in his shirt, edged in blood and a long scratch down one forearm. Beyond that, he appeared unhurt, albeit scared if the whites of his eyes were anything to go by. Moira couldn't tell how long he'd been in the cage. Besides the tear in his shirt, his clothes were clean. There was no way of knowing what he'd done to land himself in his cell, but she could not have misread the situation, either. The man standing outside the cage took the hilt of his sword in both hands, bracing himself, ready to run the unarmed man through.

Moira pulled an arrow free and had it ready to fire before her feet stopped moving. She skidded to a halt and aimed. "Stop!"

Four heads turned her way.

No one spoke.

The man with the sword was younger than she thought, maybe only a few years older than her. The youth relaxed his stance at her intrusion, but didn't drop his sword. His head was the first to turn away. He drew back again, his intent clear: ignore her and kill the man in the cage.

Moira fired.

The arrow struck the sword from his hands, although she couldn't be sure. His expression when he realized she'd fired on him was full of such incredulousness, he might have dropped the sword in surprise.

His jaw fell open as he sputtered at Moira. "How dare you interfere?" He stooped to pick up the sword.

Her next arrow sprouted from the ground beside the hilt before he could lay a finger on it.

A look passed between the other two men. They must have decided it would be a good time to back up their buddy because they reached for their swords.

Moira drew two arrows and nocked them both. "Don't do it."

"Who are you?" The youth turned to the man in the cage. "Who is she?"

The prisoner shrugged with a shake of his head, looking no less fearful.

"This is some fae trickery." The youth backed away, edging behind the cell. The other two backed away as well. When all three of them were far enough away, they turned and ran toward a trio of tied horses.

Moira and the man in the cage watched them mount. The horses' hooves stirred a storm of dust as they fled.

When they were out of sight, the man in the cell turned to Moira, his blue eyes wide. "I thank you. I do. But who are you?"

Moira relaxed and stowed the arrows back in her quiver. Then she collected the arrows she'd fired, moving around the cage but keeping her distance. "My name is Moira Noble. And you're welcome, but I'm not letting you out of there." Saving him from being run through while pinned down, unable to defend himself, was one thing. Freeing him would be another. Someone had put him there for a reason. She didn't think she had time to work out why. She had to find Zephyr.

"That's quite all right," the man said. "I have a feeling my luck is changing." He shifted to the center of the cage and straightened as far as he could. The bars at the top of the cage were bent inward and would not permit a person over five feet tall to stand up straight. "Did Herron send you?"

"Who?" Moira asked.

The man pulled his belt from around his waist. "No matter. My name is Urion, and I am well met by you who call yourself noble."

"It's my name," Moira said.

He shrugged. "No judgment. Most people around here name themselves after what they do. Then again, I just go by Urion." He pulled his belt nearly all the way through to the buckle, so it left him with a loop on one end. The loop he dangled through the bars of his hanging cell, fishing.

Moira turned in a circle, in search of Zephyr, reaching out with her extra sense, but there was still nothing. And no sign of her dragon. "I guess my name would be Moira Dragoneer, then."

The man, Urion, paused in the middle of what he was doing. "Dragoneer Moira, you mean."

Moira shielded her eyes, staring into the distance. "Sure. You haven't seen a dragon around here, have you?"

Urion shook his head. "I would have noticed." He worked the loop over the tip of the sword the youth had dropped and raised it into the air. The cage swayed. The bars were maybe five inches apart. With his arm between them, he lifted the end of the sword high enough to grab it with his free hand. Then he dragged the sword through the bars and set it aside. He loosened the loop and redid his belt.

"I assure you this was all a misunderstanding and I shouldn't be here. These things happen to me sometimes.

I owe you for saving my life, though." He angled the sword and used the point to pry at the lock. It was shiny and new, but what the jailer had secured it to was not. The latch, lock and all, popped off and dropped into the grass.

Urion opened the door of his prison. Moira's grip on her bow tightened until he tossed the sword away. Then he stepped out and his knees hit the ground. She wondered if he was too weak to walk, but then she saw his hands move through the grass. He gave terra firma a pat and a kiss, whispering something she didn't catch before he stood and stretched himself, arms overhead, reaching as far as he could. He wasn't as tall as her, but being in that cage must have been a torment.

"How long were you in there?" she asked.

Urion smiled, showing rows of even white teeth. He kicked the latch, sending it flying. "A day and several hours too long. I was beginning to worry." He shook himself as if the need to worry was worse than having been in the cage. "We should go. Those fools will return, and I'm afraid they'll bring friends."

Moira held up a hand. "Hold on. We?"

6

Urion smiled with a shake of his head, evidently confused by her question. "You saved my life. I am indebted to you and am at your service." He stuck one leg out straight and bowed deeply from the waist, his wavy brown locks flopping forward.

"You don't have to do that," Moira said.

He didn't straighten up. "Do what?"

"Repay your debt, or whatever. You don't have to do that."

"Yes, I do."

"No, you don't."

"Dragoneer Moira, I am only telling you what I must do."

It was clear he wasn't standing until she relented. She lifted both hands, fingers curled, in a gesture of frustration before letting them fall back to her sides. She didn't have time to argue. "Fine. But I'm not going anywhere until I find my dragon."

Urion straightened, his face flushed. He eyed her with a quizzical lift of his brow. "How do you lose a dragon?"

She sighed. "We're not from around here."

His head tilted as he took in her appearance. She hadn't dressed for interspatial travel, so she was wearing the same thing she had at the hospital. Dirt and mud caked her sneakers from running through the field. In contrast, Urion wore a light green linen tunic with a banded collar over a pair of dark green trousers and tall boots.

"I believe you," he said.

She nodded, glad she didn't have to convince him. "Where are we?"

"A few miles outside of Farrago. Where did you want to be?"

"I'm looking for a man... "

"I thought you were looking for a dragon."

Moira took a calming breath and said, "My dragon and I are after a man. He took our friends. We're here to take them back."

Urion's eyes narrowed. "Describe this man."

Moira huffed. "I'd rather describe my dragon."

"Is he a common brown leatherback?"

"A what?"

Urion pointed with his chin at something over her shoulder.

Moira turned.

Fifty yards down the track, a full-grown wyvern stepped out of a field, head raised as if taking in new surroundings and smelling the air. Could it be?

Then she saw the sword, which now looked tiny, and the tattered remains of her backpack.

"Zephyr!" Moira ran towards him.

His massive head jerked at her call. "Moira!" His shout filled the air between them. When he saw her running toward him, he rushed forward.

Moira raised both arms and skidded to a halt several yards away because she decided running into a full-grown dragon at speed would be like running into a wall, with teeth. "What happened? Are you hurt?"

"No. You?" Even his voice was bigger, or at least deeper. So deep it rumbled.

"No." She lowered her arms. "You got big."

Zephyr stood at least ten feet tall now and twice as long from his head to tail tip. With his increased height came a proportional increase in girth. He flexed and his tail whipped through the air.

Zephyr's head bent forward as he studied his new self. "I woke up like this."

Moira shaded her eyes and stepped around him, mindful of his tail. She closed her eyes and rubbed her forehead, thinking back to the first time she'd met Zephyr. He'd been about the size of a large dog, still going around on all fours. Then she'd fed him fire rocks, and he'd grown as tall as her. He'd kept growing steadily since, but their travel had further accelerated his growth. Moira blinked her eyes open. Now the top of her head barely reached his elbow. His scales shone with a dull luster and varied in size as they always had, larger and more plate-like over his belly and torso, smaller on his limbs and even finer on his face, hands, and feet. What had Urion called him? A common brown leatherback. She knew it was just a type of classification, but she didn't find him common at all. From where she stood, he looked damn spectacular. Some of his scales were what you might call brown, but their color varied over his entire self from black to dark green, and in the right light she caught an iridescent sheen along the edges of some scales which turned them purple.

The thrill of having him back chased a shiver down her spine as she finished walking around him. She didn't know where their friends were or how they were going to get them back home, but she had Zephyr. Together, they could figure it out.

As his big head turned one way and then the other, she checked his shoulder. Only because she knew where to look did she notice the lighter shade of scales where the dagger had pierced his hide.

"Who is this?" Zephyr asked, looking over her shoulder.

Moira turned to watch Urion approach in a cautious but relaxed manner.

"This is Urion," she said.

Urion heard the introduction. "Dragoneer Moira saved my life."

Zephyr glanced from Urion to Moira and back. "Already?"

Moira shrugged. "Urion, this is Zephyr."

Urion bowed as deep a bow for Zephyr as he had for her and waited.

The spiny ridges over Zephyr's eyes arched. "I am well met."

Urion straightened. "As am I, Master Zephyr. Excuse me." With a nod to both of them, he turned his gaze toward the road.

Zephyr turned to Moira. "What now?"

"How's the shoulder?" Moira asked. Just because there was no sign of injury didn't mean it wasn't causing him pain.

Zephyr curled his arm and made a rolling motion with the joint in question. "It is good."

Moira picked up the remains of her backpack. One strap was torn, but the fabric was intact though unzipped. The webbing had been no match for a rapidly growing dragon. The flashlight and food were gone, but the rock pick and dagger were still inside. Reluctant to discard the bag, Moira zipped the pick and dagger away inside and looped the one good strap over her head with the quiver, making sure she could still reach her arrows. "I don't think that sword is going to do you much good anymore." In Zephyr's full-grown wyvern hands, the sword looked more like a large knife; not all of his fingers fit on the grip. A dagger would be a toothpick. "I'll take it."

He was a full-grown wyvern now, Moira reminded herself. She wouldn't be leaving him defenseless.

Zephyr took the sword by the flat of the blade and held it out to her. As she reached for it, her hand brushed his.

She snapped back as if scalded. A searing pain started in her ankle and rolled through her from there. "Ow! Ow, ow, ow!" Sharp pins and needles raced up her flesh. She jumped and stomped her foot against the ground.

"What is it? What's wrong?" Urion asked. He turned from scouting the road, alarmed at her shout of pain.

"Take my hand." Zephyr held his open.

Moira didn't hesitate to slip her hand into his as if to shake, though his palm was more than twice the size of hers. The pain dulled to a throbbing ache that spread up her body. She grunted and held on tight. Zephyr didn't flinch. She could chart the progress of the pain inch by inch. Behind it came a cooling sensation that made her shiver. The two opposing forces worked their way up her body, the second gaining on the first so that by the time the fire reached her head, it throbbed for one hot second before being soothed away.

Moira gasped. "What was that?"

Zephyr frowned down at her, still holding her hand. "We have a connection once more. I am sorry, I could not prevent the pain, but I could soften it now."

"I couldn't find you earlier," Moira said. "I tried to and I couldn't."

She recalled a similar event after she named Zephyr back in his cave. They'd shook on it and a similar sensation had knocked her out. At least she had remained conscious this time. "So, we're good?"

"I believe so."

Moira took a steadying breath and slipped her hand from his. "You're not gonna bite me again, are you?" She shook her hand out as Zephyr's mouth curled, displaying his fangs and a good number of other pointy teeth.

Urion inhaled sharply.

Moira shot him a look. "What?"

"Nothing... I just... you were bitten?" He turned to Zephyr. "You bit her?"

Her dragon straightened. "It was necessary," Zephyr said, and there was an extra rumble to his words, as if he resented having to explain himself.

Urion took a step back. "When you called yourself a dragoneer, I assumed you were a squire, but you are dragon-bit, which is... a good deal more." Urion stopped talking, his gaze going from her to Zephyr and back. As if his thoughts were bigger than his brain could handle, he blinked and pushed a hand through his hair. The movement exposed the tip of one ear, which came to a noticeable point.

"What are you?" The question slipped from Moira's lips before she could stop it. He had been called a half-breed by the young man intent on running Urion through while he'd been a sitting duck in the cage.

Half-human, half what?

7

Urion finger-combed his wavy locks to cover the tips of his ears. "You can worry about what I am later. For now, I think it's best if we get away from here. Those fools will return." He spared the deserted road a glance. "Come with me. In the city, we can find food and shelter, and you can tell me more about this man you seek."

"What city?" Zephyr asked.

Urion dipped his head in the direction he had been scouting earlier. "Farrago. It's to the north of here."

The name sounded strange to Moira, as if the city was far away. But Moira didn't think she and Zephyr had another option. Not really. They had no supplies and no idea where they were going. They needed help. How else were they going to get Aaron and Ansel back?

"I swear no harm will come to you while I am with you. You saved my life. I owe you," Urion said. He glanced in the direction from which they had fled, his head jerking in a double-take. "But you should make up your mind." He pointed in toward the crossroads. A cloud of dust rose above the treetops.

"Zephyr?" Moira's feet were already moving.

"Right behind you," Zephyr said.

Urion bolted down the track, passing her. Moira followed him until he ducked down a row into the nearest field. She jumped clear of the road and tried to follow, but lost him in the tall plants and had to stop. Zephyr pulled up short behind her and must have realized she couldn't see Urion anymore because he pointed with the sword he still carried, the one she'd failed to reclaim, ahead and to the right. She ran that way and glimpsed Urion's back between the rows of cultivated stalks as he headed for the trees.

They reached the forest and Urion stopped and held a hand up for quiet. He wasn't even breathing hard. A minute passed with Moira gasping for air while Zephyr stood by quietly, not out of breath at all.

Urion spoke just above a whisper. "They didn't know you were traveling with a dragon. If they saw Zephyr, they may have thought he was working in his fields. We should be able to make it into the city by dark." He waved a hand and set off at a slower pace, careful to make as little noise as possible. They didn't speak again until they topped the first rise and were on the other side. The wooded hills offered them some cover. Not for the first time, Moira was glad she wore sneakers, but spent a moment longing for her hiking boots. Among the long shadows under the trees, she zipped her jacket closed.

Urion slowed until he walked next to her. Zephyr, silent as ever, followed just behind them. "Tell me more about this man you seek."

Moira watched her step, but her focus turned inward. The details of what happened since she left Bertram at the hospital were still fresh, but she would have to go further back. For a moment, she got carried away. Homecoming. Aaron. The dance.

Too far. She couldn't think about that now.

She sped her memory forward to the woods when she and Zephyr had first seen the man who'd taken her friends.

"Tall guy. Taller than me. Crooked nose. Short dark hair. Like really short. Cropped close to his skull. Mean. He had thick leather armor and wore a long red cloak. He ordered the trolls around. Like he was in charge of them. One of them called him their captain."

Urion slowed but he didn't stop. "Go on."

Moira glanced back over her shoulder. Zephyr kept pace with them, the sword in his hand no burden at all. "He stuck a book in the head of one of my teachers and gave him that sword to kill Zephyr." She tipped her head toward Zephyr and faced forward, letting the memories roll over her until they were a jumble, watching for things that stood out. Something else he had said sprang to the forefront of her mind. It hadn't made little sense to her at the time, but he had mentioned someone else. "He said the imp general was tired of waiting."

Urion stopped.

Moira tore her gaze away from the ground she was trying not to trip over and waited. "Does that mean something to you?"

Urion turned to face her. "Are you certain that's what he said?"

"Yes. He said the imp general was tired of waiting and so was he."

Urion's gaze grew unfocused in the gathering twilight, but she thought she recognized the expression. He was putting something together, perhaps trying to decide how much to tell them. His eyes met hers. "I have an idea of whom you speak, but if what you say is true, we are going to need a lot more help. And you say this man took your friends? Why?"

The memory of Aaron and Ansel fading away in front of her was still as clear as glass. Her jaw clenched. "He thought my friend Ansel was Zephyr's dragoneer, but he caught up with Ansel's twin brother Aaron first. He didn't know I was the one he wanted, and seeing as how they're identical, he didn't know which one of them might be the one he was after. So… he took them both."

Urion said nothing for a minute. "For their sake, I hope they can tell him something. If your friends are smart, they'll make themselves useful."

Moira swallowed. "That's what I'm afraid of. I'm afraid if they stop being useful, they'll stop… being."

Zephyr growled.

"We've got to find them," Moira said.

Urion cleared his throat. "I might know where he took them."

"Where?" Moira asked.

Urion held up a hand. "Don't get excited. It's not anywhere nearby, but the man you described… I think I know who he is."

"Who?"

Urion turned. "Let's keep going. I'll tell you what I can on the way."

They descended into a bowl-shaped hollow. Urion's steps didn't slow, and Moira pushed to keep up. Zephyr slipped along behind them, ducking to avoid the lower-hanging branches.

"The man you described fits the description of a man I've heard of. This man used to be the High Magician in the lands to the west of here until the king died, or was murdered, depending on whom you talk to. That was years ago. Now there's an argument over the rightful heir to the throne. Well, not an argument. The Regent doesn't want to return it to the king's heir, and that's created some... " he stopped, squinting into the distance, "... tension," he added at last.

Moira's eyes narrowed. "What kind of tension?"

"Halt! There they are! I've found them!" A voice shouted.

They froze.

Urion's head jerked to look over his shoulder as he crouched, muscles tensed, ready to flee. The young man who had tried to run him through reined his horse through the trees. "Gods, you have got to be joking," Urion muttered.

Moira slipped her bow free.

The youth had indeed done as Urion said and returned with friends; the same two from before and three more besides, each with a horse. In moments, the pursuers surrounded the trio, the men climbing down from their horses.

With nowhere to run, Urion relaxed and glided away from Moira, placing her behind him on his left, with Zephyr next to her. Urion had no weapon, having left the sword he used to pry his cage's lock at the crossroads. The youth had already replaced his weapon and brandished the new blade. All five of the other men kept their swords sheathed. For now.

The youth's lip curled in a sneer. "You stay out of this, whoever you are," he said to Moira. His gaze moved upward to meet Zephyr's, his tone changing completely. "We do not mean to keep you from your labor, Master

Wyvern. I will dispose of this filth, and we will be on our way."

Zephyr glanced at Moira and settled back, saying nothing.

No one mentioned the sword he held. Maybe field dragons carried swords with them when they worked. She didn't know.

Urion let out a disgusted sound. "Stow it, Kaidence. You don't know what happened."

Kaidence pointed his sword at Urion. "I am going to do what that fool judge was too afraid to order. You have befouled your last fine lady."

"Fine ladies decide for themselves to whom they wish to speak. Not you."

Kaidence charged. Urion jumped clear.

At the same time as Moira drew and nocked an arrow, Zephyr let out a soft, "Hey-o," and tossed the sword by its handle to Urion, who grabbed it out of the air.

Kaidence came to a stop, gawking at Zephyr.

"There is no honor in fighting an unarmed man," Zephyr said.

One of the other men's hands twitched on the pommel of his sword. Moira put him in her sights ready to fire at the first glimmer of a blade, hoping no one would call her bluff. She didn't want to kill anyone, but she wasn't opposed to letting an arrow fly to make a statement.

Urion glanced in her direction. "You said this was between you and me. Let it stay that way."

Kaidence bared his teeth and threw himself at Urion, who parried. The swords clattered against one another. Urion was the better swordsman. Moira could see it, and a glance at the men surrounding them told her they saw it, too. The men waited, watching their friend get beat fair and square. It was only a matter of time, but none of them tried to interfere. A few of them winced, and Moira turned back to the fight. Kaidence made a sloppy chop, throwing himself off balance. Urion struck him across his backside with the flat of his sword.

"Stop." Moira took a small step forward. Urion clearly didn't intend to hurt Kaidence, but there was no reason to humiliate him further. No other reason than Urion wanted to. A little smile flashed across Urion's face, and she knew he was enjoying embarrassing Kaidence a little too much.

Kaidence lunged forward to attack. Urion tripped him, sending him sprawling. The way the fight was going, it was more likely Kaidence would land on his sword and slice himself in two.

When he didn't get up, Urion stood over him, contempt clear on his face. "Get up."

Kaidence remained sprawled on the ground. Moira feared he had skewered himself for real. She scanned the crowd. None of Kaidence's friends moved, but she kept a tight grip on her bow.

"Get up!" Urion shouted.

When Kaidence didn't move, Urion lowered his sword and reached down to flip him over by the shoulder.

Kaidence came up holding a knife aimed straight at the center of Urion's chest.

8

Kaidence thrust his arm forward.

Moira recoiled, expecting to hear a shout of pain from Urion and one of triumph from Kaidence. Instead, a small ringing—the sound of metal on metal—split the air.

The knife did not sink into Urion's chest.

They froze. Kaidence's face was a grimace of confusion. Urion displayed a mix of anger and fear. As one, their gazes lowered to the knife. Its point pinned a medallion, suspended from Urion's neck by a thin chain, to his chest, going no farther.

Before Kaidence could try again, Urion punched him, laying him out cold. The knife tumbled from Kaidence's grip and landed in the dirt. Urion scooped up the knife and stood over Kaidence, his chest rising and falling faster than it had during the fight, his breathing harsh. He pointed his sword at the men who stood around him and Kaidence. "Take him and go."

Urion stepped back as two came forward and grabbed Kaidence under his arms. One of them muttered, "This isn't over." Kaidence's boot heels left furrows in the earth as they dragged him away to his horse and hoisted him over it.

Two of the other men watched and followed with nothing more than glares in Urion's direction. The last, a barrel-chested bruiser, older than the others with gray at his temples, inclined his head slightly before he turned to go.

Moira glanced between the two of them, unsure of what to make of the exchange. She lowered her bow, slipping the arrow back into her quiver.

When the last man left their sight, Urion shuddered from head to toe. "We should hurry. Master Zephyr, can you carry your dragoneer?"

"Yes."

"Wait, what are we doing?" she asked.

"We're getting out of here." Urion slipped the knife into the top of his boot and threaded the sword through his belt. The scabbard, Moira realized, was long gone. "Kaidence didn't just lose the fight; he lost a good amount of whatever honor he might have had with that last trick."

Moira slung the bow over her shoulder with her bag. "He tried to stab you when you were in a cage. How much honor could he have had in the first place?"

Urion snorted. "You're right, of course. Not much. But you stopped him earlier when there were only his two comrades watching. Now that he's failed in front of a larger number of men, his pride won't stop him from pursuing me, if only to keep the story of his disgrace from spreading."

"He can't just, I don't know, let it go?" she asked.

"I don't think he can, no."

Moira pointed her thumb in the direction Kaidence's men had dragged him "Those guys saw the same thing I did. You beat him. How's he going to convince them to come along and watch him get killed? That last guy seemed glad you didn't kill him."

"That was his uncle, and I'm sure you're correct. He's probably glad I didn't kill his nephew, if only because his sister, Kaidence's mother, would never forgive him for letting that happen. I don't think they expected to have an audience, or for you and Zephyr to insist on a fair fight. It appears I owe you yet another life debt."

Moira put up her hand before he could bow. "Stop. You can owe Zephyr. Let's get out of here."

"We can move faster if your dragon carries you. Our chances improve if we make it to the city before nightfall."

Zephyr laced his fingers together to form a step. "Moira, climb on my back."

"Are you sure you can carry me?" Moira asked.

He stooped down low. "Of course, but you must hold on tight."

"What about you?" Moira asked Urion.

"I'm a fast runner," he answered.

Moira stepped into Zephyr's hands and, with a boost and a twist, landed on his upper back. "Oof." She hung on with one arm hooked around Zephyr's neck while the other gripped his shoulder.

"All right?" Zephyr asked.

"I think so."

Zephyr straightened to his full height.

He took a hesitant step and stopped. "Are you well, Moira?"

She didn't answer.

"Her eyes are closed," Urion said.

Zephyr rumbled. The sound resonated through her chest where she pressed against his back at the same time as she heard it. "Moira, are you scared?"

Her eyes popped open. "I am not afraid. I just have a... a healthy respect for being this high in the air." She eyed the ground. It appeared to shrink farther away from her. She closed her eyes again. She didn't have a fear of great heights, but this wasn't a great height. It was like being on top of a high ladder that breathed and moved under her. She didn't think Zephyr would let her fall. And if she did, she knew she would survive, mangled but alive.

That was what worried her.

"Let's just go."

Zephyr's head tilted to the side. "Hold tight."

Moira slitted her eyes.

Urion shot forward in a blur. Zephyr followed with a jerk. Moira held back a scream and squeezed her eyes shut, gripping her dragon's neck. With her eyes closed, she could concentrate on finding a toe-hold on Zephyr's back. Through her sneakers, she could feel his scales, the strange combination of overlapping and interlocking plates that covered him. Carefully, she sought the spaces between them, but didn't jam her toes into the tender area. Instead, she set the tip of her toes in slowly, knowing Zephyr would say something if she were hurting him. She relaxed her hold on Zephyr's neck a fraction and heard him grunt, but he didn't stop running.

When she did open her eyes, there wasn't much to see. Trees, mainly. She made the mistake of glancing down. The ground rushed past. She jerked her head upward. The trees were easier to watch. The sun had dipped below the hills and night was falling fast. A flash of lighter green caught her attention. Urion's shirt stood out against the wooded backdrop they fled across. He ran about thirty feet ahead, flowing across the land like water, leaping over fallen branches and downed trees that she would have had to stop and go around.

Moira bent her head close to the scales that covered Zephyr's ear. "Are you seeing this?" She risked loosening her hold around his neck long enough to point at Urion ahead of them.

Zephyr answered with a rumble.

If Urion hadn't pledged to help her find Zephyr, he could have been long gone before those men had returned. Had he stayed, per his words, only because he felt indebted to her? Moira wasn't sure. He still hadn't told them what he was. Even if she hadn't already known, his movements would have given him away as not entirely human. As she watched, he went up and over a hill.

As Zephyr crested the top of the same hill, Moira caught a glimpse at the southern edge of the city they were approaching. Farrago filled the valley below, a dark ribbon of water winding its way through a series of structures. She got a vague impression of some larger buildings near the center, but then trees blocked her view as Zephyr plunged down the next hill.

Urion stopped at the bottom of the hill. "From here we walk," he said. His chest heaved, but beyond that he didn't appear troubled by his run through the woods.

Zephyr slowed to a stop, his sides rising and falling. He stooped. Moira relaxed her hold and slid down his side to the ground, over his scales the whole way. Zephyr jerked as her feet touched the ground.

"What?" Moira asked. "What is it?"

"Tickles," Zephyr said.

Moira sighed, relieved she hadn't hurt him. "Thanks for the ride."

"There's a road up ahead," Urion said. "We'll take it into the city. Stick close to me and we won't have any trouble."

Moira took a step and wobbled. Zephyr's hand under her elbow helped her regain her equilibrium. "Does Farrago have a king?" she asked.

Urion laughed, but there was no humor in it. "No. They have a tyrant... Lord Quintillius. He calls himself a caretaker, but he's not capable of being deposed. Therefore: tyrant. No one can deny he keeps things running, though. Follow me."

They approached a road. In the gathering gloom, no one walked the wide, well-traveled stretch, but Urion waited to be certain it was clear before he stepped onto it with Moira and Zephyr. Outbuildings sprouted, followed by pens for goats, pigs, and other livestock. Then there were stables. Larger homes and more residential-looking places and a few shops followed these. Carts on the road, with people riding or walking alongside them, increased as their path widened to include large walkways on either side, large enough to accommodate a full-sized dragon, Moira realized as she stepped onto one. She walked behind Urion, while Zephyr put himself between the road and her.

Up ahead, two stone towers loomed on either side of the road, marking a checkpoint. Next to each tower, armed guards in brown livery stood watching the crowd. They allowed those on foot to pass, but stopped the carts for inspection.

Moira worried she might draw attention by the way she was dressed. No one else wore jeans, but there were plenty who wore dark trousers. Amongst the small crowd of people approaching the towers, she didn't stand out. She didn't see anyone else wearing colors as bright as the ones in her checked flannel, but her jacket covered the shirt well enough and it didn't hurt that it was getting dark. They passed through the checkpoint without incident.

Horses pulled most of the carts, but on the other side of the towers, they saw a cart tethered to a dragon. Moira and Zephyr slowed to watch as the dragon came to a stop and unhitched himself, entering the building he had stopped in front of through the extra-large opening. Moira couldn't be sure, but the dragon looked male, anyway. He was as tall as Zephyr, but not as slim. There was a row of gray scales protruding down the middle of his back, his scales duller, which suggested to Moira he was older. Was this one of the field dragons? Moira and Zephyr shared a glance before hurrying to catch up to Urion.

The people of Farrago paid them little notice. Torches lit the way the deeper they walked into the city. At one point, Urion turned down a side road that led to an alleyway that narrowed to the point Moira and Zephyr could no longer walk side by side. Zephyr urged Moira ahead of him and fell back to bring up the rear. Urion led them through a warren of walkways with tall walls. Openings in the brick led to small gardens and grottoes.

Urion stopped at one arched opening and passed through it into a courtyard. Candles placed in sconces at regular intervals around the walls lit the yard with a warm glow. Urion marched up to the double doors and pounded on them. One door opened to reveal a young boy. He stared up at Urion, wide-eyed.

"Fetch your mistress, boy. Hurry!" Urion said.

9

The door slammed in Urion's face as the boy presumably fled to do his bidding.

Urion sighed and backed away from the door.

They waited in silence. Large jars of potted plants lined the sides of the rectangular courtyard in the center of which was set a symmetrical mosaic of red and white stone. A sound of rushing water came from the back corner, where a small stream of water splashed down into a stone basin below it. Moira swallowed convulsively at the sound.

Minutes later, the door opened, framing the same boy from before. A woman stood behind him, her bejeweled hands resting on his thin shoulders. She was slender, with a gold chain wrapped around her middle. Without the belt to emphasize her waist, the white pleated gown she wore would have fallen straight from its moorings about her neckline to brush the tops of her bare feet. Billowy dark hair fell in waves around her shoulders, framing a pale face with a pinched expression. The boy glanced up at the woman. She looked down at him and nodded once. The boy shot around Urion, past Moira and Zephyr, and out of the courtyard through the arch they had entered.

Urion didn't stop the boy but watched him go. His eyes closed once longer than a blink, as if he were experiencing some silent pain. Then he turned back to the woman in the doorway.

"How may I be of assistance?" she asked. That was it. No greeting suggesting she knew him. If this was Urion's friend, she had a strange way of showing it.

Urion frowned, drew a deep breath, and pulled himself up straight. "May my friends and I draw from your well and rest for a moment?"

"Please, refresh yourselves." The woman stepped out of the door and raised a hand toward the fountain in the yard's corner.

"Thank you," Moira said. She and Zephyr strode to the stone basin filled by a steady flow of water. An array of cups lined the ledge behind the fountain. Moira snatched a chipped earthenware mug and held it under the stream. There wasn't a cup big enough for Zephyr. She hesitated to drink before her dragon could slake his thirst. Her mouth was dry, but Zephyr had been the one carrying her through the woods.

"The dragon may make use of the basin," the woman said.

Moira thought she was speaking to her, but she kept her eyes on Urion, almost as if she feared he would disappear.

"Who are your friends?" she asked Urion.

Urion chuckled. "Small talk? Really?" He removed the sword from his belt.

The woman didn't look scared.

Urion laid the sword on the ground between them and sat on the edge of one of the large stone pots. "They are of no concern to you, Lavinia."

"Lady Lavinia." She stepped forward to pick up the sword and held it at her side.

Urion's brows rose. "Is that the way of it? Ha. Lady Lavinia, then. You've done very well for yourself." He waited a beat, then added, "My lady."

If his tone sounded mocking to Moira, at least Lady Lavinia didn't run him through with the sword. *Why did he give up the sword?*

Finished lowering the water level in the basin by a good six inches, Zephyr lifted his muzzle out of the water. The basin slowly refilled. Moira snagged another cup and filled it. She took it to Urion, who accepted it with gratitude and drank deep.

He lowered the cup and peered up at Moira from his seat on the planter. "I may have miscalculated. That boy went to fetch the city sentinels, who will arrive shortly. It's me they want. They'll take you into custody, but don't resist. Go peacefully and we'll see each other again."

Moira looked from him to Lady Lavinia and back. "What is going on?"

"Lady— " Urion enunciated the word— "Lavinia has alerted Lord Quintillius to my arrival. His sentinels will be along shortly to collect me." He took another sip of water.

Lady Lavinia arched one brow but otherwise didn't budge.

"What did you do?" Moira asked, staring first at Lady Lavinia and then at Urion, unsure from whom she wanted an answer more.

"I've reported the whereabouts of a person of interest to the city sentinels for a handsome reward," Lady Lavinia said.

"Person of interest? Is that what I am now? Well, at least I'm interesting. How have you been, Lavinia?"

As he spoke, Moira's ears picked up the sound of metal jangling along to a rhythmic thumping, like marching. Her heart pounded, unsure of what was about to happen.

Lady Lavinia *tsk*ed. "Why did you have to come back?"

"You know I don't have a choice," Urion said.

A dozen armed men burst through the entrance to the courtyard dressed in blue and silver livery. They arranged themselves in formation, holding themselves at attention as an older man in a dark brown uniform stepped forward. A helmet shaded his deep-set eyes, his jaw covered in salt and pepper whiskers.

"Did I say sentinels? I meant just one." Urion muttered loudly enough to reach her ears. He finished his water and raised both hands, still holding the cup in one. "I'm unarmed. The dragon and his dragoneer are with me. They'll come peacefully. I wouldn't try to separate them."

Moira edged closer to Zephyr, who rumbled. She was glad Urion had warned her and Zephyr what was about to happen, otherwise she might have done something stupid, like go for her bow. Her hand crept toward it anyway.

The older man frowned, and judging by how deep the lines were around his eyes and mouth, Moira thought that must be his most common facial expression. He nodded over his shoulder and two of the guards stepped forward.

Urion, hands raised, stood as the men approached and flanked him. He lowered his arms. A guard on either side took hold as one of them knocked Urion over the head with a cudgel. His cup tumbled to the paved courtyard and shattered against the stones.

Lady Lavinia gasped. "Was that entirely necessary, Commander?"

The Commander grunted. Then he glanced at Moira and Zephyr and asked Lady Lavinia, "Who are they?" His voice was a gravel bark.

"No idea." She held up the sword with two fingers, as if it were a filthy thing. The commander took it and stuck it in his belt. With that, Lady Lavinia turned on her heel and marched inside, slamming the door behind her.

The Commander studied them but said nothing of Moira's odd attire or the road dust that covered her. He squinted. "You'll come peacefully?"

Moira's gaze shifted from the unconscious Urion who slumped between the two guards to the Commander. "Yes."

He turned to Zephyr. "Your word?"

A clawed hand came to rest on Moira's shoulder, as Zephyr's tail whipped out from behind him to curl around them both. In doing so, it swept one of the blue-and-silver-clad guards' legs out from under him. The guard toppled, his sword clattering against the ground.

No one moved. Another guard coughed.

"My word," Zephyr said.

The Commander grunted again. "We're not equipped to handle a wayward dragon, but we could be." He held out his hand. "Weapons."

Zephyr removed his hand and Moira slipped her bow and quiver over her head to hand to the Commander. He didn't ask her to empty her backpack. The rock hammer and dagger remained inside.

"Lord Quintillius will want a word, I'm certain. Come with me." He left the courtyard, the two guards carried Urion behind him. The rest of the guard waited for Moira and Zephyr and fell in after them.

Outside the courtyard, a rough-cut wooden cart and horse waited. They loaded Urion onto the cart. The wheels squeaked as the transport trundled away.

The commander turned to face them. "We'll have to walk. I didn't know we'd be escorting a dragon." He nodded to a pair of guards behind them. "You two, with us. The rest of you... " he jerked his head in the direction the cart had gone. He squinted at Moira and pointed with his chin in the opposite direction the wagon had departed. "This way." He went first.

Moira and Zephyr followed. The two guards brought up the rear. The grizzled commander took them down narrower and narrower alleyways, many of which were lined with trash and other detritus. Zephyr fell back, putting himself between her and the two guards who kept some distance between them and Zephyr's tail. The sky overhead remained faintly light, but full dark had fallen in the sparsely-lit back alleys they traversed. They passed shadowy figures huddled around fires burning at the end of passageways too narrow for Zephyr to get through. The scrabbling of claws and squeaking came from recessed alcoves Moira didn't look at too closely until the Commander stopped in front of one. He held up a hand.

The sound of stone grinding against stone reached them out of the darkness. Near the ground. two bright red cinders glowed. Moira started, and the noise came again. Zephyr shifted behind her. A low, squat figure made of clay scooched out of the alcove. It was only a few feet tall but wide, and round like a jug with another half-circle dome of clay set on top of its squat body. There was a void where the two shapes met, forming the arc of a mouth. Moira watched a long tail disappear into the black void before the dome lowered, completely closing whatever it had consumed inside. The thing moved along by some means, disappearing into the next alcove.

"What was that?" Moira asked.

"Rat golem," the Commander answered. "Best to let them get along with their business." He turned to peer at Moira, his gaze taking her in again, from the top of her head to the soles of her sneakers. "Not from around here, are you?"

Moira stopped herself from answering, deciding his question was rhetorical.

The Commander's eyes gleamed in the dark. "Farrago attracts all sorts." He started walking again, but not as fast as he had been. "Tell me how you came to associate with that halfling we packed off ahead of you." It wasn't a question.

She had no reason to keep the information to herself, so she told him about finding Urion in the cage at the crossroads and about how he was about to be run through by a young man known as Kaidence.

The Commander grunted. "And you released him." Again, it wasn't a question. He appeared to be one of those people who didn't ask questions he didn't already think he knew the answers to.

Moira would have to correct him. She stopped. "No."

The Commander came to a halt and turned. "You didn't let him out?"

"He got himself out."

He nodded, and they continued walking. "Then what happened?"

Moira explained how Kaidence had returned with more men, fought, and lost poorly, describing how he had tried to stab Urion.

"The halfling killed him?" the Commander asked.

"No," Moira said. "Urion knocked him out. Kaidence's friends dragged him away."

"Lucky," he said, without looking at her.

Moira wasn't sure if he meant Kaidence was lucky for only getting knocked out, or if Urion was lucky for not having killed him.

As they made a few more turns, their path widened into something resembling a well-traveled back road. The Commander didn't ask her any more questions, perhaps assuming he could piece the rest of the story together for himself. Lamps illuminated their way until the road they walked down opened to a wide thoroughfare. People were on either side, and music played in the distance. They turned right and walked down the street. Moira guessed they were somewhere near the center of the city. They stopped and waited for a cart to pass.

Across from them stood a building of polished stone with columns three stories high, the entrance a pair of large ebony doors. A weight settled low in her stomach at the sight of the large stone building lit both inside and out. On either side stood blue and silver liveried guards. Wherever they were going, they had arrived.

10

As soon as they approached, the guards moved to open the towering ebony doors, the large wooden slabs sliding open without a sound. Inside, the ceilings were high enough to accommodate a full-grown wyvern. Thick carpets covered the smooth stone floors of the foyer, muffling their steps. Sconces held lit candles at regular intervals along the curved cream-colored walls, interrupted by paintings of landscapes and hanging tapestries. The two guards who trailed them took up positions on either side of the door. In front of them, a staircase wide enough for two Zephyrs to walk side by side rose to a large landing.

The Commander came to a stop at the bottom of the stairs and waited.

A man dressed in a dark gray jacket and trousers, hair slicked to one side, rushed down the stairs. He hadn't reached the last stair before he spoke. "Commander Rasti?"

"We found these two in the acquaintance of the halfling known as Urion. Treat them as guests of Lord Quintillius… until he speaks with them."

The man stopped on the last step, his head turning from the Commander to Moira and then up to Zephyr. Moira noted that even with the added height of the stair, he wasn't as tall as her. He tugged at the burgundy waistcoat he wore beneath his jacket. "My name is Piperender, Lord Quintillius' secretary. If you follow me, I will show you where you can wait. Thank you, Commander." He gestured to the staircase he had just descended.

"Not so fast, Piperender."

The secretary froze. "Yes, Commander?"

Rasti pulled out a document folded twice over, which he opened. "Sign this receipt showing I delivered unto you one dragon and one dragoneer." He glanced in their direction, squinting. "In reasonably good condition."

Piperender frowned as he took the paper. "Is this necessary?"

"Yes. It is. Sign. " Rasti pulled out a short pen, small feather on one end, a vial of ink connected to a nib on the other. "If there's a problem, I have no trouble interrupting Lord Q for his signature."

Piperender took the pen. "That won't be necessary." He signed the paper and returned it, along with the pen.

With that, Piperender turned away up the stairs. "This way, please."

Rasti said nothing more, but Moira noticed he watched her and Zephyr ascend the stairs, her bow and quiver still slung over his shoulder. He squinted at them until they were out of sight.

The secretary led them down one hallway and then another until he came to a pair of doors and opened them.

He stood back and waited for them to enter. "I'll have food sent up. Please wait here." He closed the doors behind him.

Moira heard a tiny *snick* after the doors shut. She twisted the handle of one. Locked. "Seriously? Couldn't you just knock it down, Zeph?"

"Probably." Zephyr crossed the room to the only window. It was tall but narrow. Decorative bars of wrought iron at least an inch thick ran from top to bottom every six inches. Zephyr wrapped his hands around the bars and flexed. They didn't budge. "We did agree to come peacefully."

"Doesn't mean we have to leave the same way." Moira crossed to the window. It looked out over some kind of interior courtyard, surrounded by high walls. *No way out.*

Opposite a cold fireplace sat a sideboard with a ceramic pitcher filled with water beside an empty basin. A wide chaise sat in the middle of the room; the stone floor between it and the mantel was covered with a patterned rug. Zephyr walked around the room inspecting the paintings and tapestries. Moira went to the chaise and slid off her torn backpack, prepared to settle in and wait, when the door clicked and opened.

The first thing in the room was a trolley, laden with covered dishes of various shapes, but all of a similar size— large—pushed by a young boy who heaved for all he was worth as he turned the corner into the room toward the sideboard. Watching him struggle, Zephyr grabbed the cart by the other end and pulled it across the floor with ease. The boy, suddenly relieved of his burden, lost his footing and fell to his knees. Out of breath, he stood, bowed to Zephyr, then unloaded dishes.

Behind the boy, an older woman watched the proceedings with interest, a small smile curling the corners of her mouth. Her long hair trailed over one shoulder in a single thick plait, her gown a dark blue of the same hue the guards wore. Her expression cleared as the boy finished unloading the cart and pushed the unburdened trolley back to the door with ease.

As Zephyr bent to sniff the dishes, a young girl entered carrying wood and went to the hearth.

"My master bids you welcome," the older woman said. "Please make yourself comfortable." Her brow furrowed as she took in Moira. "What strange raiment— " her brows lifted— "but you are a dragoneer. Perhaps a change of clothes before you meet with Lord Q. Tara?"

"Yes, Miss Vee?" said the girl.

"When you're done with the fire, we'll fetch some clothes for the dragoneer."

Moira frowned. "Thank you?" At least they weren't trying to take her things away from her. *Not yet, anyway.*

"As I said, you are welcome. Please, eat." She raised her hand and gestured to the food steaming on the sideboard.

Zephyr stood by, looking from the food to Moira and back again. Flames licked at the logs in the fireplace. The girl, Tara, stood and went to the older woman's side.

"We shall return," Miss Vee said. They left, closing the door behind them.

The lock did not slide into place. Either they did so in silence or there was no reason to lock the door now. The scent of the food wafted her way, and Moira let the matter of the locked door go. She crossed the room to find plates and flatware left alongside the dishes of food, and casks full of beverage, one of clear water, the other some kind of cloudy fermented ale. Zephyr's nostrils flared.

"What do you think?" she asked.

"No chips. But it smells good."

"Dig in." She got out of the way.

Zephyr plowed through the dishes. Moira dipped in after his first pass. Everything was fine until she sampled some pasta coated in a spicy dressing that lit up her mouth and made her eyes water. Her lips burned where the sauce had touched them and a coughing fit followed, violent enough to make her think she might throw up. Zephyr patted her on the back and advised her which dishes to avoid. He had no trouble with the spicy foods, eating those with relish.

They were slowing down when Miss Vee returned with Tara and another girl, clothing strung across their arms and hands full of boots and belts. Through the open doors, Moira caught sight of a guard in profile, his back to the wall. No need to lock the doors with guards posted outside of the room.

Miss Vee motioned to the girls. They set the clothes on the chaise next to Moira's bag and left again.

"I selected a few things for you. I assumed, as a dragoneer, you would forgo skirts, preferring freedom of movement. Also, boots." There were several pairs to choose from.

Moira didn't have time to say anything before Tara and the other girl came back carrying a folding screen. They set it up in the room's corner near the fire and then left, closing the door behind them.

Miss Vee began sorting through the clothes on the chaise. "Let us find something that will work."

Moira looked at Zephyr, but he just shrugged and kept eating. She set her plate aside and sat on the chaise to remove her sneakers. "Do you see many female dragoneers here?" she asked, stepping behind the screen.

"From time to time. They're not unheard of. It all depends on the region they're from. You must be a long way from home."

Moira said nothing. She took off her jacket and long-sleeved flannel, hanging them over the top of the screen. Miss Vee passed her a pair of canvas trousers and a light blue tunic. All the clothes had ties or button closures and adjusted for a reasonable fit. Moira stepped out from behind the screen. Miss Vee handed her a plain leather belt and then had her try on some boots. The pants were a little short, but Moira tucked the hemmed edges inside the best fitting pair of tall boots.

Miss Vee looked her over, nodding. "Much better. I'm sure Lord Q will send for you shortly. I'll leave this cloak behind for you." She nodded to the yards of dark blue material she left draped over the back of the seat.

"Thank you," Moira said.

Miss Vee bowed to both her and Zephyr, turned, and left the room.

Moira gathered her clothes, rolling them tightly to stuff into her backpack. She included her sneakers after she knocked some of the mud off near the fire.

Zephyr, finished eating, came around the chaise and sat on the rug. He settled and then rocked as a burp escaped him.

"That good, huh?" she asked.

"Mmm." He curled himself into a circle, resting his head on the seat of the chaise next to her.

The food and the heat from the fire warmed her inside and out. Soon, she fought to stay awake. Miss Vee said it wouldn't be long, but with everything that had happened since they'd lost Aaron and Ansel, exhaustion overtook her as she sat before the fire with Zephyr rumbling in his sleep beside her. Her chin brushed her chest, and she lost the fight to stay awake.

She didn't know how much time passed before a hand on her shoulder shook her awake.

11

Miss Vee stood over Moira, her hand on Moira's shoulder. The fire burned low. Zephyr still slept, his head on the cushion next to her.

Miss Vee lifted a finger to her lips and tipped her head toward the door.

Moira stood and stepped around the end of the chaise, careful of Zephyr's tail.

Two guards stood outside. Miss Vee spoke quietly. "Lord Q will see you now. Your dragon may remain here."

Moira glanced back at Zephyr. He rested peacefully, curled into a ball, his head propped on the chaise. She thought about waking him, but didn't want to if she didn't have to. He could sleep while she spoke with this Lord Q. Then they could get down to the business of getting their friends back and going home. She followed Miss Vee down the hall. They turned at the end of the passage. At the end of a shorter hallway stood a large pair of double doors.

Miss Vee pushed open the door on the right and preceded Moira inside. The room was much larger than the one in which she'd left Zephyr. A glance revealed a roaring fire in the hearth with two wingback chairs set in front of it. A revived Urion stood in the middle of the room, as there were no other chairs apart from the pair in front of the fireplace and the one behind a massive wooden desk ornately carved from some caramel-colored wood. The desk chair was large, made of tufted brown leather, and occupied.

Lord Q sat with his elbows propped on the arms of his chair, his fingertips pressed together in front of his weathered features. He wore all black in sharp contrast to the white hair slicked back from his forehead, his pale hands, and even his eyes, a washed-out blue so light they appeared almost gray.

Miss Vee stopped a pace away from the desk and dropped into a curtsy, straightening right away. "The dragoneer, Lord Quintillius."

The man remained seated behind the desk. "Thank you, Miss Viroqua." His voice was deep and modulated.

Miss Vee turned and left, pulling the door closed behind her.

Moira stepped farther into the room. Urion looked better than the last time she'd seen him. He stood on his own two feet anyway, but there was something amiss. His hair fell shorter than it had earlier, the cut ragged, exposing the pointed tips of his ears.

"What happened to your hair?"

Urion blinked, his gaze going from her to Lord Q and back. "It'll grow back."

She nodded and shifted to face the desk. Lord Q observed the two of them over his steepled fingers without a word. The longer he sat there watching them, the more uncomfortable Moira became until she realized that was probably the idea. What had Urion called him? A tyrant. What would a tyrant do? She wasn't sure if sitting in silent reproach was it, but she quickly lost interest. Against the wall, behind the chair, stood a tall pair of matching bookcases filled with books and other, smaller items. A closed door stood next to the bookcases, while another closed door stood across the room near the fireplace.

Sconces lit the room next to more paintings and the largest tapestries she had seen so far. They stretched to the floor. One hung next to the double doors and another across the room, both displaying complicated battle scenes she was glad she couldn't see in more detail. Through a tall window, Moira glimpsed a dark blue sky with a tinge of brightness to it. Morning wasn't far off. How long had she been asleep before Miss Vee woke her?

The door she'd entered through opened. Lord Q's secretary, Piperender, entered with three cups and a cask on a tray. He settled the tray on the corner of Lord Q's desk.

The man himself lowered his hands and rose from his chair in one smooth motion.

Piperender pulled the cork from the bottle and filled the cups. He handed the first to Lord Q, the next to Urion, and the last to Moira.

"That will be all, Piperender," Lord Q said. "Open the doors on your way out."

Piperender bowed deeply from the waist and left both doors open when he left.

Moira stared into the cup, tipping its contents from side to side. The dark brown liquid lapped against the sides. The contents contained alcohol, if the fumes were any sign. Aunt Paige had let her try wine once at a wedding, but that had been clear and fruity-smelling. This was opaque and smelled of spices. It reminded her she wasn't old enough to drink.

Lord Q lifted his cup. "A toast. I bid you welcome to Farrago, Dragoneer Moira."

She glanced at Urion. He stared into his cup. Did she imagine it, or did he grow paler as he stared into its depths? "Um," she said. "I'm fifteen."

Urion lifted his cup in her direction with a smile. "Old enough to drink in Farrago. To your good health." He lifted the cup to his lips and shot back the contents in one swallow.

Lord Q stood watching her, waiting. Disconcerted, Moira thought him unwilling to drink before his guests.

Moira resisted the urge to pinch her nose, but she did squeeze her eyes shut. She raised the cup to her lips and threw back the drink.

It burned like fire going down.

She gagged, coughing.

When she opened her eyes, Lord Q stood across from her, frozen in the same position as he had been before she swallowed the demon alcohol. Urion similarly stood unmoving.

A hush filled the room.

What was going on? The flames in the sconces around the room held still, without a flicker. Over her shoulder, the fire in the grate blazed unmoving, without a pop or a crackle.

The only movement came from the armchair on the left, which she was sure had sat empty, or at least it had until a moment ago. Now a man in long, flowing robes and a pointed hat beckoned her closer. The wingback chair had a tall back, and, with the hat on, put the man's face in shadow. His umber and yellow robes skimmed the stones on the floor.

Moira glanced back at Urion, but he remained fixed in space, a strange statue. She stepped tentatively toward the armchair. As she came closer, the man removed his hat.

Moira recognized his face.

Her knees wobbled.

She plopped into the other chair, unable to stop herself from staring. She'd made a study of the very features that peered back at her. They were similar enough to those in a photo that hung in a place of honor over her desk at home that she would call them the same. The contours of the man's face were striking enough to be startling in that she'd inherited a few of them... the chin, for example, and the nose. However, the eyes were all wrong. There was no recognition, no love in their brown depths, only polite interest.

The backs of her eyes stung. Whoever this man was, he was not her father. "What is going on?"

The man smiled. "It's so nice to officially meet you." He held out his hand.

Moira switched her empty cup to the other hand, then grasped his. When he let go, her hand floated in the space between them a moment before she drew it back. "Who are you? How did you get here?" Had he slipped in through the door near the fireplace? That didn't explain his familiar features or why everything around them stood frozen.

"My name is Copernicus Stumble. You may call me Cal. I've wanted to introduce myself ever since the Librarian paired us together."

"The Librarian?" If the Librarian was involved here, she was more than a little outside her depth. When had he paired her with... She sat back, recognition dawning. "You... *you're* the book?"

He dipped his head. "Indeed. I represent the original manuscript of *The Book of Wyverns.*"

"Okay, then why do you—" she swallowed— "look like *that*?" As she spoke, the stones vibrated under her feet.

"Ah." He ran the brim of his pointed hat between his fingers. "I believe your subconscious has sought an acceptable representation for what I look like and used it to fill in the difference, since we will never meet outside your mind."

"Outside my mind?" Moira glanced from the standing flames back to the other side of the room.

And there she stood. At the same time as she sat enjoying a fireside chat with the book stuck in her head, Moira also stood across the room, eyes shut tight, cup tilted, with her head thrown back.

This is all inside my head? Got it.

"Yes. We have little time," he said.

The stones under her feet vibrated once more. "Why is that?"

"Because we have been poisoned."

12

"Poisoned?" Moira's voice held a sudden edge.

Cal nodded toward the cup she still held. "The poison was no doubt disguised by the alcohol. Don't worry, your dragon's venom is already at work and will neutralize any ill effects."

The stones vibrated again as Moira stood. She looked down at the floor. "What is that?" A quiet roar filled her ears, softly at first, but building.

"Your dragon will be here any moment," Cal said. "You must assure him you are well." He grinned. "Amazing creatures, wyverns."

They were. He would know, having written the book and all.

The stones under her feet shuddered. Her eyes widened.

Cal's expression sobered. "Good luck, Dragoneer."

Moira blinked and was back in front of the desk, rocking forward with the rush of the return to her senses. Her arm still raised, the poison-laced alcohol burned a line down the center of her person to her stomach where it toiled, making her guts churn. Wetness rushed to the corner of her eyes. Her pulse sprinted as her body trembled.

Another roar—this one outside her head—split the air, followed by the thundering of footsteps. There was no need to reach out with her dragon senses. She knew exactly where Zephyr was.

Moira lowered the cup, her glare meeting Lord Q's gaze over the rim. She placed the cup back on the tray and faced the large double doors that Piperender had pulled open on his way out.

Zephyr rushed around the corner so fast he slipped on the stones but didn't go down. Then he stormed forward, teeth bared, his large hands opening and closing on nothing but air. His eyes flashed, pupils slitted. If he'd come across the closed doors in this state, he would have torn them from their hinges. Which meant Lord Q knew what he was doing when he asked his secretary to leave them open. He had expected this reaction, but Moira didn't know what was going to happen next, because Zephyr had a full head of steam and nowhere to go with it.

Moira backed up and raised both hands. "Whoa, slow down! It's okay. I'm okay."

Zephyr growled, scales rippling, fangs bared. His massive shoulders heaved and his nostrils flared with each breath. He saw Urion and snapped his teeth at him.

Urion stepped back, his chin on his chest with a look of what Moira took for guilt. Otherwise, he didn't flee or show any fear. Only remorse.

Zephyr turned toward Lord Q, who still held his cup. Zephyr opened his jaws to emit a terrifying roar. The surface of the liquid in the cup rippled with the reverberations.

Lord Q blinked and eased backward, but otherwise remained unmoved by Zephyr's fierce display.

Zephyr reared back and took to pacing the floor, growling. "Why did you not wake me?"

"Calm down, Zeph."

His tail lashed the air behind him. "Do not tell me to calm down. You leave my side and get poisoned with wyvern venom. Why did you not wake me?"

Dragon venom? Is that what it was?

Lord Q cleared his throat, drawing Zephyr's attention. "My apologies, Master Wyvern. I had to be certain the story I was told was true. I see now that it is. Welcome to Farrago." He drank the contents of his cup after toasting Zephyr.

Zephyr snapped his jaws again. "What did Urion tell you?"

Lord Q settled his cup on his desk. "That you bit your dragoneer. There was no other way to confirm his story. I apologize, but I had to be sure. Now that I am, we can move on." He sat back down in the chair behind his desk.

Zephyr continued stalking back and forth.

Moira had never seen him so agitated. His response exceeded mere irritation or anger. Zephyr was scared. Her eyes narrowed. "Hold on. What would have happened if Zephyr hadn't bitten me?" she asked the room at large.

Urion set his cup on the corner of the desk and answered. "Wyvern venom is incredibly toxic when ingested."

She glanced from them to her still pacing dragon. "So, I would be dead. Great." Her legs itched to take up pacing for herself.

"I'm so sorry," Urion said. "I promised no harm would come to you, but it seems all I've done is lead you into harm's way."

"It had to be done," Lord Q said. "You'll suffer no ill effects. I am convinced you are dragon-bit. There are other matters to discuss."

"Like what?" Moira asked.

Zephyr's pacing slowed.

"Urion tells me you're looking for someone. Perhaps I can be of help."

"Why would I trust you? You just poisoned me."

"As stated, it had to be done. I suggest we move on."

"Why would you help us?"

Zephyr stopped pacing.

"Cooperation could be of mutual benefit," Lord Q said.

Moira huffed. "How so?"

"The man you seek. I know who he is."

Moira's gaze cut to Urion. "What did you tell him?"

"Everything."

Urion had been busy, but she could tell by his haircut that he hadn't had a choice. Had whoever cut his hair used scissors or another sharp instrument?

Moira turned back to Lord Q. "What do you know about the man we're after?"

He leaned forward. "War brews in the land to the west of us. I have a vested interest in keeping it away from the border and out of my city. The man you seek is responsible. His name is Vinton."

"Let's be clear about something." Moira glanced at each of them. "All I want to do is get my friends back and go home."

Lord Q gave her the barest of nods. "Vinton almost certainly has your friends detained at Castle Tern. He took them for a reason. I wonder what he will do when he discovers neither is the one he seeks."

Moira swallowed. He wasn't the only one. Moira had feared for Aaron and Ansel's safety from the start and didn't want to think about what Vinton would do once he discovered his mistake. "How far away is this Castle Tern?"

"Ten days' ride. The journey isn't difficult, just long, at least while relations remain amicable between that nation and ours. You may complete it faster with adequate provisions."

Ten days? How fast could she and Zephyr get there on their own? What provisions did he speak of, and did he mean to provide them? She couldn't have heard that correctly. "I still don't understand. Why do you want to help us?"

Lord Q braced both hands on top of his desk and stood. "Farrago is the largest city closest to the border. We sit at the tip of an unwilling spear. Farrago cannot afford to harbor an individual of interest to the Regent of Castle Tern's High Magician. He has many spies. I don't flatter my abilities to keep them all out of my city. The best thing I can do is to see you quickly and quietly away from here." He relaxed his hands. "In any direction you choose."

"So... if we chose west... ?" Moira asked.

"That decision, made by you, would be beyond my control."

Moira inched closer to Zephyr. "Why let us go at all?"

Lord Q tipped his head to the side, apparently considering her question. When he didn't answer right away, she wished she'd kept her mouth shut and hoped she hadn't given him any ideas. Urion stared, waiting, a crease forming between his brows.

"If Vinton overcomes the resistance scraped together by the true heir to the throne, nothing may stop him. For whatever reason, he's taken an unhealthy interest in dragoneers. I don't understand why yet, but if assisting you thwarts his plans at all, then I will help you in any way I can."

"You're... scared," Urion said. A note of wonder in his tone implied this was an emotion he never thought to attribute to the tyrant of the city.

Lord Q's eyes flashed to Urion. "My interests are entirely self-serving. Farrago cannot bear a war. This is my city, and I intend to keep it out of harm's way."

The scuff of a shoe drew their attention to the corridor leading to the office. Piperender hurried forward, stopping only to close the doors behind him. He rushed to the lord's side and spoke in his ear too softly for any of them to hear.

Lord Q's gaze shot to the doors as he straightened. "How long?"

Piperender stepped back, twitchy and flustered. "Minutes." His wide-eyed gaze went from Urion to Moira to Zephyr. His eyes widened further, and he swallowed.

Lord Q pulled the front of his coat down, smoothing invisible wrinkles in the fabric. He turned to Moira, his mouth set in a grim line. "Hide."

13

"Hide!" Lord Q repeated. "Now. We have guests."

Moira glanced around the room. There were the chairs in front of the fireplace and nothing else. "Where?"

He pointed with his chin across the room, but there was nothing there.

Urion must have understood, because he grabbed her by the arm and pulled her away from the desk.

Zephyr growled but followed.

"Quietly!" the lord said.

Urion went straight to the wall across from the entrance to the office and pulled the tapestry hanging there to the side.

Piperender rushed forward, taking the tapestry from Urion. "Careful." He bent and lifted the tapestry as high as he could. Behind it was a wall of darkness, but not a solid one. The wall hanging covered a void, where the bricks and mortar cut away into the dark to create a space about ten feet deep and shaped like a bowl. The wall curved as if someone had scooped away a section, its entrance covered by the tapestry. "Hurry. And for heaven's sake, don't make a sound."

Moira motioned Zephyr through first. He dropped and crawled forward to avoid the wall hanging. Inside, he could stand without trouble, but he filled over half the space. He wrapped his tail around himself and held it to keep it out of the way. Moira and Urion ducked inside and stood in front of Zephyr, shoulder to shoulder. Piperender lowered the tapestry. Light seeped in around the edges of the fabric and from the movements on the other side, Moira could tell Piperender was smoothing it into place, trying to make it look as if it hadn't recently moved.

Urion nudged Moira. He tilted his head forward. There were two holes at about eye height. From the other side, the holes must have blended in with the warp and weft of the tapestry because she hadn't noticed them before. Urion peered through one while she looked through the other.

Piperender stood in front of the tapestry on the other side, smoothing the fabric. As a series of loud footfalls approached, he rushed back to Lord Q's side, who'd regained his seat, drew out a sheet of paper, and was scratching against it with a feather-tipped pen. Piperender snatched up Urion's cup from the corner of the desk, along with the others on the tray he'd brought earlier, lifting it with both hands. No sooner had he stood with the tray when both doors opened. Two of the blue and silver liveried men she'd taken to be his private security stepped back.

A retinue of six armed soldiers marched through the doors, their leather armor clattering over blood-red uniforms. The last two through the doors mirrored the private guard, except inside the room. The others spread out and filled the space between the fireplace and the heavy desk at regular intervals. They preceded an unarmed man in a tunic and cloak of similar colors, who smiled as he entered. His hands were empty and a short, pointed hat hung from his belt.

A harried Miss Vee rushed in behind him. "My apologies, Lord Quintillius. This gentleman," she spat the word, "refused to wait and did not wish to be announced."

Lord Q didn't look up until he finished writing. He took the note he had written, folded it in half, and held it aloft. Piperender bent from the waist, and as his lord slipped the note onto his tray, he spoke in his secretary's ear, too quietly for anyone to hear. Piperender straightened and left the room in a sedate manner, as if in no rush at all. No telling how fast his feet carried him once he was out of sight, but since no sound of cups hitting the floor reached them, Piperender must have had a good grip on his tray.

Once his secretary was out of sight, Lord Q stood and addressed Miss Vee. "No apologies needed, Miss Viroqua. I'm sure whatever Lord Smew has to say must be very important to seek my counsel before breakfast."

Smew threw his head back and laughed.

Lord Q did not join him.

Smew turned to Miss Vee. "Leave us."

Miss Vee lifted one brow and stayed put until her lord nodded to her. Only then did she curtsy and leave the room.

Smew sighed and turned on the spot. His gaze combed the room; its exits, the furnishings, everything, including the tapestry. "I was expecting—" he spread his hands— "more. Especially from the tyrant of Farrago."

Lord Q remained silent.

Behind the tapestry the temperature rose, though Moira, Urion, and Zephyr remained still and quiet.

Smew stared at the tapestry they hid behind.

A bead of sweat rolled down Moira's temple, but she dared not blink.

Lord Q broke the silence. "To what do I owe the pleasure of your visit?"

Smew turned to face Lord Q. He bent from the waist an inch before he straightened. "My master, the High Magician of Castle Tern, sends his regards. He requires your assistance."

Lord Q sighed. "And how can I possibly be of any help at this hour?"

Smew glanced through the same tall window Moira had. "My apologies. My men and I came straight here as soon as we reached your city, as the matter is of some importance. So glad to have found you awake." Smew paused. "Tell me, how did you know my name?"

Lord Q raised one brow and sat down in his tufted leather chair. His elbows found the arms of his seat as he laced his fingers together. "It was no great leap."

Smew smiled again, apparently amused by Lord Q's deduction.

Moira decided Lord Q knew exactly what he was doing. He'd mentioned Smew by name with no introduction on purpose. Lord Q had said something about not being able to keep all the High Magician's spies out of the city, a fact his own spies probably reported to him.

"The matter concerns a dragoneer."

"There are many dragoneers in this city and its environs. Be more specific."

"This dragoneer is a girl. That should help narrow it down a bit. And she's not just a dragoneer, but dragon-bit as well."

Lord Q squinted. "Truly?"

Behind the tapestry, Moira blinked. Urion shifted beside her.

"It is against the law... "

Lord Q interrupted with a wave of his fingers. "Only so far as the law of Castle Tern may reach. How we deal with dragoneers in Farrago is our business, not Castle Tern's."

Smew dipped his head in acknowledgment. "Indeed. That is why my master requires your assistance. He wishes to evaluate the dragoneer."

Lord Q raised his chin, projecting his voice. "Nothing but wild dragons live beyond your borders. No self-respecting dragon would have anything to do with Castle Tern while it remains a part of the Fells Stronghold."

Lord Smew's eyes narrowed in suspicion as he glanced around the room.

Lord Q gave an airy wave. "But you know that as well as I do."

Moira swallowed, parched from the heat behind the tapestry. If Smew knew that already, he might wonder who Lord Q was informing and while Moira found the information interesting, she didn't want Smew poking around their tapestry.

"Tell me, is that all your master wishes to do? Test the dragoneer?" Lord Q asked.

Smew refocused on Lord Q. "There is no need. She has proven to be most dangerous. She may call herself noble, but she is not. The High Magician would like to see her taken care of before she can harm anyone else."

Behind the tapestry, Moira's mouth fell open in a silent gasp. Urion cast her a concerned glance, but she gave a tiny shake of her head.

Lord Q leaned back. "How does the High Magician know she's dangerous?"

"She attacked my master without cause."

That wasn't the way Moira remembered it. If she hadn't shot the captain of the trolls, this High Magician they spoke of would have killed Bertram without a second thought.

Lord Q coughed, palming his chin. He didn't smile, but Moira got the impression he might have been trying to cover a chuckle with his cough. "If your master had this dragoneer within his reach, why did he allow her to escape?"

"She attacked him. Circumstances were beyond his control."

"What circumstances were those?"

Smew shifted his weight from one foot to the other, perhaps unwilling to admit his master's vulnerabilities. "The girl injured my master, but he is much recovered now. We believe she may make her way through Farrago at some point. Most do for whatever reason." His face didn't show it, but Moira heard the sniff of contempt in his last statement.

"And what of her dragon?" Lord Q asked.

"The dragon is an abomination and should be put to death immediately. It's almost certain the dragoneer has corrupted him."

Moira leaned back, turning her head to peer over her shoulder at Zephyr. She had corrupted him? How did that work? He bit her.

Zephyr blinked and lifted both shoulders.

Moira turned back to the tapestry, sweat slicking her skin now in their cramped hiding spot. The woolen scent of the tapestry invaded her nostrils. At least it wasn't dusty, which made her wonder how often this hiding spot got used.

"What concern is one dragoneer, dragon-bit though she may be, to the High Magician of Tern? I rather thought Vinton would have other concerns at the moment, like the army massing outside his gates."

Smew scoffed. "It is hardly an army. The old king is dead. Unfortunately, his son has decided to take up arms against the current ruler."

"You mean the Regent who refuses to return the throne to Prince Owen, its rightful heir? *That* current ruler?"

Moira knew this information was for her benefit, but hearing it from Lord Q made Smew's cheeks hollow as if he sucked an exceptionally sour lemon.

Lord Q carried on as if he didn't notice. "How fares the Lord Regent? His health, I fear, is not as good as it once was."

Smew acknowledged this with a dip of his chin. "I will send him your regards. His son, Lord Hedrick, refuses to leave his side."

Lord Q got to his feet. "Indeed. I will pass on what you've told me to the city's sentinels."

Smew stayed where he was. "Don't you want a description of the dragoneer?"

Lord Q drew himself up to his full height. "Of course."

Smew smiled. "Perhaps you'd like to write it down?" When Lord Q did nothing more than narrow his eyes, Smew continued, "Or don't you need to? There were three cups on the tray your secretary left with. Perhaps you were celebrating something? A partnership perhaps. One between you and this dragoneer?"

Lord Q's brows arched. "That is preposterous."

"Is it? Then I'm sure you won't mind if my men look around."

"I have nothing to hide. But know that you have reached the maximum extent of my goodwill. Any further and you will be beyond diplomatic protection."

Smew offered him a feral little smile. "Noted." To his men, he said "Check everywhere."

The guard closest to their tapestry made straight for the doorway behind Lord Q's desk. Another headed for the door near the fireplace. Smew didn't move as the guard near the doors roughly shoved the tapestry opposite theirs to the side. There was nothing but a wall behind that one. That left one more guard beside the two at the doors, and he was a few feet away from revealing their hiding place.

Moira and Urion backed away from the tapestry, right into Zephyr, because there was nowhere to go.

As the footsteps came closer to their hiding place, a shout rang out, followed by a splash.

14

The footsteps stopped.

Moira risked a peek through the tapestry.

The door near the fireplace had swung outward. Smew, along with the rest of his guards, faced the open door.

Lord Q didn't budge. "Your men should watch their step."

Smew stalked across the floor. The other guards stayed put.

The distraction bought them a few moments' time. At Zephyr's insistence, Moira and Urion squeezed around him, switching places, which put them at the rear of the alcove. Moira and Urion stood shoulder to shoulder, turned slightly toward each other because of the curved wall at their backs. Zephyr faced them, bending his head down low and curving his tail up and over their huddled forms, the tip landing on Moira's shoulder. She grabbed the end of his tail to keep it from twitching.

"Is that a moat?" Smew asked. His voice was harder to make out than before, muffled by tapestry and dragon.

They heard more splashing.

"Who puts a moat inside?" Smew asked, louder than before.

"It's a very expensive water feature. And very deep," Lord Q said.

"Finish the search," Smew commanded.

Moira imagined the remaining guards resuming their tasks at a subdued pace.

The guard near the door behind Lord Q's desk must have opened it.

"What is it?" Lord Smew asked.

"A corridor." An unfamiliar voice; probably the guard who opened the door.

"See where it leads," said Smew.

"I wouldn't," Lord Q said.

Moira could only imagine what traps might await whoever ventured down the passageway.

"Where does that corridor lead?" Smew demanded.

"I'm not in the habit of having to explain myself. Tyrant, remember?"

There was a pause. Finally, Smew said, "You—come away from there! You—check behind that tapestry!"

This was it. With the wall behind her and Zephyr in front of her, Moira shut her eyes. Beside her, Urion tensed. Zephyr's camouflage could only do so much. Outside was one thing. She didn't expect it to hold up inside the castle. The light shifted beyond her closed lids as she sensed the tapestry being moved to the side.

Moira had read once that every person, every living thing, emitted an I-am-here signal. You could make it as loud as you liked or as small as you wanted. Some people could make theirs very loud and got served first wherever they went. Eyes closed, Moira did the opposite and dialed down her I-am-here signal to a whisper, but she prepared herself for the shout of discovery.

"Anything?" Smew asked.

The light shifted, growing darker, the tapestry falling back into place. Another unknown voice. "An alcove. It's empty."

Urion jerked.

Moira's eyelids snapped open. She gripped his hand to remind him to stay quiet.

Lord Q's voice was icy as steel left outside in winter. "Give your details to my secretary on your way out. He'll see the pertinent information passed on. Good day, Lord Smew."

For a moment, nothing happened. Smew didn't respond, but the clatter of receding footsteps followed in short order.

Zephyr relaxed, standing up straight. Moira edged around him to see through one hole in the tapestry. Smew and his men marched out. After the last passed through the door, Lord Q motioned to his two guards outside the room. They closed the doors behind Smew and his men.

Lord Q turned toward the tapestry. "Come out."

Moira got Urion to help her lift the tapestry. Zephyr crawled out of the alcove.

"That guard did not appear to be blind. Do I want to know what just happened?" Lord Q asked.

Urion spoke before Moira had a chance. "Zephyr and Moira should be in the Light Legion."

Lord Q stood stone still, blinking once. "You need to go." He went to the door behind his desk and pushed it open. On the other side was a dark passage. He stepped back into the office after pulling a lever on the wall. From a distance came a clank and soft rattling. "Take this corridor to the end. Don't get distracted by anything you might see. The stairs will take you down to a room off the kitchens." He turned to Urion. "You know your way to the stables?"

"I do."

Lord Q lifted a brow but nodded.

Urion hurried to the doorway.

"Wait. My bag!" Moira said. She couldn't leave her backpack behind. The hammer and dagger were inside it, not to mention her clothes.

"I'll have your things brought to you at the stables. Smew and his ilk must not catch you in the city or, preferably, anywhere near it." He walked with her to the door. "I do not expect our paths to cross again. Is there anything else I may provide for you for your journey?"

Zephyr trailed behind her, while Urion stood in the doorway, waiting. Moira didn't know where to begin, uncertain of what awaited her beyond Farrago. She glanced toward the fireplace across the room and, as she looked back, caught sight of the wood bookcases. "Do you have a copy of *The Book of Wyverns*?"

Lord Q turned his head to the side, perhaps surprised by her request. "I don't have a copy here, no, but there must be one in the library. I'll have it added to your things. Now, it was almost a pleasure making your acquaintance. Remember, you were never here." He turned to Zephyr and bent forward from the waist—not far, but enough to show his respect for the dragon. "Master Wyvern." He straightened. "Do take care." He raised his arm, showing them the way out.

Moira ducked her head once in response. No need to say thank you. Not after being poisoned.

Urion snagged a candle from the closest wall sconce. He took off down the hall, with Moira right behind him.

Zephyr bringing up the rear. The passage was barely wide enough for the dragon, but he pressed on, following Moira through the gloom. Their feet whispered across the stones as a musty scent filled the air. Along the way they passed two smaller doors, both closed. Urion paused at the first of these, but kept moving when Moira cleared her throat. At the end of the corridor, they took the curved stairs downward. The last step ended at another closed door. Urion tried the handle, but the door didn't budge.

"It's not locked. Here." He handed the candle to Moira. This time, when he tried the handle, he put his shoulder to the door.

The door inched forward in fits and bursts until it was wide enough for her and Urion to squeeze through into some kind of storeroom. A stack of crates sat in front of the door. A clever paint job on the side of the door facing the storeroom blended it with the rest of the wall.

Moira helped Urion shift the crates to make room for the door to open wider. Once Zephyr was out of the stairwell, they closed the door and piled the crates back where they had sat. If she hadn't just passed through the concealed door, she wouldn't have been able to tell it was there.

Urion went to the only other entrance, which looked like a regular door, and pressed his ear to the wood. Straightening, he turned back to them. "The kitchen's through there. It's early, but people are already up and about. Stick close and act as if you have every right to be here." He swung the door open and the three of them slipped out into a large, bustling space.

The room hummed. Every person had a job to do, whether it was carrying a bucket of water, stirring a pot, or plucking a chicken. Everyone was in motion, including them. Their job was to get through the kitchen and out to the stables without drawing attention to themselves. Urion didn't rush, but he didn't dawdle either. He filched an apple from a basket as he passed by and handed it to Moira, dropping two more inside of his shirt. No one paid either Moira or Urion any attention, though Zephyr received a few glances.

They passed out of the kitchen into a small garden enclosed on three sides. Urion led them around a corner into another thoroughfare, reminiscent of the alleys they had traveled the night before, only wider and better kept. Dawn had broken. Long shadows stretched across the ground between buildings. They hurried but were careful not to rush down the cobblestones until Urion turned again, this time into a building redolent of sweet-smelling hay and large, four-legged beasts of burden. They went to the middle, but there was no one else there. The barn's large doors stood open at either end.

"What now?" Moira asked.

Urion looked one way and then the other. "I don't know."

The clip-clop of horses' hooves had them turning to watch two large black horses, each at least sixteen hands high, being driven into the barn. The pair pulled a high-sided, canvas-covered wagon. A figure shrouded in a ragged brown cloak reined the horses to a stop in front of them. "Get in," the figure said.

Urion's head jerked to the side, his eyes narrowing. "You!"

15

The shrouded figure raised his head, and the deep-set eyes of Commander Rasti peered out. "Me."

Urion raised his chin. "I'm driving."

"No. You're not." Rasti turned to Moira and jerked his head toward the rear of the wagon. "Get in. The dragon will have to follow on foot for now." He nodded to Zephyr. "Master Wyvern."

Zephyr rumbled in response.

"We can't leave yet," Moira said.

Rasti grunted and glared at Urion as he climbed up to sit beside him. Through the opening behind where they sat, Rasti pulled out a mass of brown fabric and thrust it into Urion's hands. "Put this on."

Urion shook out the material and put the cloak on, leaving the hood down.

Moira walked down the side of the wagon to the back. It had a tailgate she wasn't sure how to lower. She stretched to see over the top. Latches on either side held the gate up. The wagon's canvas arched overhead, held aloft by a series of curved bows that reminded her of an animal's ribcage. Inside the belly of the beast were crates, parcels, and more canvas lining the sides and most of the middle all the way to the front in a single layer, where they butted up against the seat where Rasti and Urion waited.

The rhythm of rushing feet made her turn. Tara, Miss Vee's young assistant, rushed into the barn, her arms full. "Your things, miss. And a few more besides."

Moira accepted the girl's offering, her things bundled together inside the blue cloak Miss Vee left for her. Through the material, Moira could make out the shape of the backpack she'd left behind. "Thank you. Any luck with the book?" she asked.

"Miss Vee told me to take the copy from the house library." Tare retreated, her gaze straying to the wagon. "Safe journeys, Miss." She left as quickly as she had come.

Moira turned to Zephyr. "Can you put this inside?"

Zephyr set the bundle in the back. Then he wove his fingers together to form a step and gave her a boost over the gate into the wagon.

"Ready?" Rasti called.

Moira slapped the edge of the tailgate and exchanged a look with Zephyr. "Let's go."

The wagon lurched once, and they were on their way. Outside the barn, they kept to a sedate pace and made several turns following the road. Zephyr had no trouble keeping up. Moira set the apple Urion had given her aside and untied the bundle. Inside was her backpack with her regular clothes and sneakers, the rock pick, and dagger. Besides that, Miss Vee had included an additional set of clothes, similar to what Moira was already wearing, and a book. The slim leather-bound volume had a plain brown cover. She picked it up, expecting to experience a jolt, but there was nothing. It was just a book. She fanned through the pages. After what happened in Lord Q's office, she expected to have some connection to the book, but she didn't.

Maybe if she read a few pages...

"We shouldn't go this way," Urion said.

Moira raised her head.

"It's the best route out of the city," Rasti answered.

Through the front of the wagon, she caught a glimpse of two familiar stone towers. They were leaving through the same gate they had entered Farrago.

Urion raised the hood of his cloak. "I've got a bad feeling about this."

Rasti grunted.

They approached the exit, which was guarded by armed sentinels as it had been the night before. One waved their wagon over to the side of the road for inspection. Moira had hoped the commander's presence would get them out of having to stop, but that didn't seem to be the case.

Rasti complied, steering the wagon out of the main road to wait in a line of other wagons with Zephyr close behind. Moira wrapped her things in the cloak once more and took a seat on a crate, attempting to act casual.

Urion sat up straight. "Is that—"

"Yes," Rasti interrupted him.

"—a wyvern sentinel?" Urion finished.

Rasti grunted. "Let me do the talking."

Moira contorted her body, trying to get a look at the unexpected official. Bent double to see out the front, there was indeed a dragon walking amongst the wagons, stopping to peer into the back of conveyances like their own. The dragon sentinel was about the same size as

Zephyr, but heavier around the stomach and the hindquarters with dust-covered muddy brown scales. The brown sentinel livery showed under a large metal breastplate. If pants were a part of the dragon's uniform, he didn't appear to have to wear them. However, a great sword hung from a belt around his waist.

The wagon ahead of them rolled off. Another officer of the guard, this one human, beckoned them forward with a wave of his hand.

"Out for deliveries?" the officer asked in a bored tone, as if it were the thousandth time he'd asked the question.

"Traveling abroad," Rasti said.

The officer frowned, but peering closer at Rasti, his face cleared and brightened. "Commander Rasti? That you, sir? Didn't recognize you out of uniform."

"At ease, Sergeant Levin."

"You've never taken a day, and now you're going away?" He frowned again

"Yes, Sergeant. Will that be all?" Rasti asked.

Levin cleared his throat. "Constable Belcrief will have to take a quick look, and then you can be on your way, sir."

The dragon constable approached the wagon. "Commander." His voice was low, but held less of a rumble than Zephyr's.

"Constable." Rasti dipped his head in acknowledgement.

The dragon started his walk around the wagon.

Sergeant Levin fidgeted. "You are coming back?"

"Of course. After I take my niece and nephew to their grandparents in the east."

"Very wise, sir. The roads aren't safe, even heading east. Is the dragon with you, sir?"

Rasti grunted. "Yes. My nephew's training to be a dragoneer and join the legions."

The constable reached the back of the wagon and nodded to Zephyr, who returned the mute greeting. Belcrief peered into the back of the wagon, his gaze skimming over Moira, who smiled, before continuing to the pile of covered goods. Belcrief's nostrils flared as he inhaled deeply. Then he continued around the other side of the wagon.

Belcrief reached the front of the wagon. "Travel safe, Commander."

"Thank you, Constable." Rasti shook out the reins, and the wagon rolled forward. Zephyr fell in behind them, and in under a minute, they were on the other side of the gate.

"Since when do wyverns join the city sentinels?" asked Urion.

"Since I recommended him. Belcrief used to be in the legions, but lost his dragoneer in a border skirmish just before retirement. Since he didn't have any interest in farming, he came to the city and worked odd jobs doing heavy labor down at the dock. One night we got called down to the riverfront to take care of a load of drunk and disorderly, only when we got there, they'd already dispersed. Those who could stumbled away, while those who couldn't see straight waited for us to arrive. Seems not one of them wanted to tangle with a dragon, which made them a lot smarter than they looked.

"I decided we could use a Sentinel like that and not just on the night shift. It's good for folk to see him out and about, like any other officer of the law. Belcrief does good work. Needs help with the paperwork, but there are plenty of other officers willing to assist him, like Levin. They get along well."

Urion shook his head with a snort of laughter. "A dragon as a city Sentinel. What's next? Trolls? Goblins? Imps?"

Moira got a sinking sensation in the pit of her stomach. She'd gone up against several trolls, each one intent on killing her and Zephyr. Between the two of them, they'd claimed the upper hand so far. No. She couldn't say she would recommend a troll for a position as a Sentinel. Why would Urion suggest trolls? Did he have such low opinions of dragons?

When Rasti didn't respond, Urion scoffed. "You must be joking."

"No trolls. Probably not a goblin. But it would depend on the imp," Rasti said.

"That's ridiculous."

Rasti turned his head toward Urion. "Is it? More people find their way to Farrago every day. Some by choice, some not. Perhaps we should reserve judgment on those who have no choice over the circumstance of their birth and how they come to be in this world. I thought you might understand that better than anyone."

The two stared at each other. Urion turned away first. They rode in silence for a while, the traffic and crowds of people thinning the farther they got from the city.

"Uh-oh," Urion said. "I knew this was a bad idea."

"What?" Rasti asked.

Urion pulled the hood of his cloak lower and wrapped himself tightly in the fabric, hunching his shoulders while stiffening his spine, immediately giving off the impression he was much older than he was.

Rasti didn't ask again, nor did he speed up. The wagon continued at the same pace.

Moira bent forward.

Kaidence, sporting a bruised jaw and black eye, rode toward the southern gate of Farrago with—Moira counted—nine other riders.

"Shh..." Moira straightened, but they had a bigger problem, and he was walking behind the wagon. There was no way to disguise Zephyr or hide him from view. They would just have to hope no one recognized him. Moira held up a finger to her lips, then slid down to the floor of the wagon, hiding from the passersby.

Crouched behind the tailgate, she focused on the clip-clop of horse's hooves striking the dirt road, silently urging them past. For several long seconds, nothing happened, and she thought they had escaped detection.

Then Kaidence's voice rang out. "That's them!"

16

Rasti didn't slow down, and Zephyr didn't turn around at the shout. Moira peeked over the back of the tailgate. Kaidence had stopped in the middle of the road. His mount faced their wagon. The other riders, including his uncle, slowed to a stop but didn't change direction.

Moira ducked. The wagon trundled on.

"Of course I'm certain! That's their dragon!" Kaidence shouted.

Moira risked another peek and caught Zephyr's wince, though he still didn't turn to look over his shoulder... smart dragon. Since Rasti kept the wagon moving, they'd put some distance between them. The sound of pounding hooves broke the tension.

Kaidence shot toward them.

"Time to go," Urion said.

Rasti slapped the reins with a shout. Their two-horse team took off.

Moira sat up. Zephyr ran to keep up with the wagon. Ahead of them on the road, people rushed to get out of the way.

Rasti shouted to be heard over the noise of the wagon. "Bow!" He pointed to a spot near where she sat.

Moira peeled back a corner of the canvas, revealing one of the arched limbs of the bow Rasti had confiscated from her yesterday. As it was, she had the bow, but no arrows.

"No! Don't kill him!" Urion tumbled backward through the opening at the front of the wagon.

Moira suspected Urion might be grossly overestimating her abilities. Besides the fact she didn't know where the arrows were, the boards bucked under her. Sitting up straight was a challenge. *Kill him? I'd be lucky to get a shot off.*

Urion fumbled over the boxes and crates as Rasti urged the horses to go faster.

Then something struck Moira's knuckles. She glanced down. The apple Urion had given to her rolled across the back of the wagon. She snapped it up and grabbed hold of the tailgate to keep from falling over.

Zephyr saw her and ran to the side of the wagon instead of directly behind it.

Kaidence was gaining on them, the rest of his party strung out behind him but getting closer.

Moira took careful aim. She pulled back her arm and threw the apple.

She missed. The fruit sailed over Kaidence's head.

Urion reached the back of the wagon in time to watch her miss. He tore at his tunic, thrusting his hand inside his shirt. "Try again!" He handed her another apple.

Moira took it and squeezed the fruit, willing it to fly true. She pulled back her arm and focused on Kaidence. He rode in a straight line, right at them.

She threw the apple.

It struck Kaidence right in the middle of his already bruised and battered face. The blow knocked him backward halfway out of the saddle. His uncle rode alongside him, getting Kaidence's mount to stop before he fell off. Then he put his horse sideways, blocking the path. The rest of his party slowed behind them and came to a stop. The last sight Moira had of Kaidence... his face bloodied, his nose probably broken, surrounded by his men... he waved his fist in the air, shouting something she couldn't hear. His uncle made calming gestures, while his men stood by, glancing from one to the other. None appeared interested in continuing the chase.

***

Rasti kept the wagon going as fast as he could, hardly slowing to turn west. Urion remained in the back alongside Moira. With the clatter of the wheels too loud to talk over, they both kept an eye on Zephyr instead. Even after Rasti slowed the horses down, they said nothing.

Zephyr kept pace with them, but Moira noticed when he winced.

She shouted to be heard. "Zephyr needs a break!"

Rasti slowed the wagon to a stop in the middle of the road. There was no traffic. They'd passed no one going in either direction for at least ten minutes. Zephyr braced himself against the tailgate, huffing and puffing. His scales glittered with a light sheen.

"All right, Zeph?" Moira asked.

He panted. "Water."

Rasti climbed down from the driver's seat. "There's some in the crate next to you."

Urion lifted the tarp and found a crate full of water skins. He handed a full one to Zephyr, who opened the narrow spout, aimed it at the back of his throat, and squeezed.

Rasti walked around the wagon, adjusting the canvas.

"Brilliant shot back there," Urion said.

"Thanks." Moira pulled her gaze away from Zephyr. "But why did I have to take it? What did you do that was so bad this guy can't let it go? And what are you?"

Rasti reached the back of the wagon. "She doesn't know?"

Zephyr swallowed the last of the water. "Know what?"

Rasti chuckled.

"You tell them," Urion said to Rasti, and turned away.

Rasti passed in front of Zephyr to the other side of the wagon. "Urion's a halfling. Half-human. Half faerie. Fae. Should I tell them who your mother is?"

Urion glowered. "Start with my father."

"I'll leave that story to you," Rasti said. "How did you come to be in the cage they rescued you from?" He continued around the wagon, loosening the canvas as he went.

"We didn't rescue him," Moira said.

"I got myself out, thank you." Urion sighed. "It was a misunderstanding."

Out of sight, from the other side of the wagon, Rasti called, "There usually is with you."

Moira climbed to her feet, suppressing a groan, stiff from riding crouched in the back of the wagon. She climbed over the tailgate and eased herself down to the ground.

Urion followed with ease. "Whatever Kaidence thinks happened is wrong."

Rasti let out a bark of laughter.

Urion glared in his direction.

"Something about a fine lady," Zephyr said.

Moira watched Urion closely. *That* is *what Kaidence said.*

Urion passed a hand over the back of his head. "It started when a pair of brigands robbed me and left me for dead."

Rasti returned to the rear of the wagon. "I didn't think things like that could happen to you."

Urion laughed without mirth. "Well, they can and they do. A farmer's daughter found me on the side of the road in a ditch. She must have recognized I wasn't entirely human... "

"Was it the ears?" Moira asked.

"Probably. She got me into the barn and took care of me." Urion clenched his jaw. "Next thing I know, the girl's father barges into the barn, hauls me up in front of a backcountry magistrate, telling them I took advantage of his daughter. Even though no such thing happened, the judge, rather than ordering my execution, had me caged and strung from a tree. You know the rest."

"Not exactly," Moira said. "Where does Kaidence come into it?"

"The farmer's daughter is his betrothed. Or was."

Moira squinted into the distance. Urion's version of events sounded truthful. "Did the daughter testify at the trial?"

"Yes. She lied through her teeth, but she didn't want to."

"What do you mean?"

"She was kind to me when she didn't have to be. I don't know. I got the sense she didn't want to say what she did, but it didn't stop her from condemning me for something I didn't do."

Rasti grunted. "They coerced her testimony. Not the first time for such a thing. Help me roll up this canvas."

Urion frowned. "What are you talking about, old man?"

"It's obvious," Rasti said.

Moira thought she followed, but said nothing.

Rasti gripped the fabric and rolled it upward. "You said so yourself. The girl's not engaged to this Kaidence fellow anymore. Her father probably matched her with him some time ago, only to discover the man is a worthless twit. So when the farmer found his dear, sweet, soft-hearted daughter had taken in a stray, and a halfling no less, he used you to break his daughter's engagement."

Urion's mouth opened and then closed. "Nothing *happened*."

Rasti paused in rolling up the canvas. "Didn't need to. Just the whiff of impropriety was enough for this Kaidence and his family to back out of the engagement, which is what the girl's father wanted. And probably the girl, too."

Urion stood staring at Rasti, silent.

"I've dealt with this kind of thing before. She probably agreed to testify as long as they didn't put you to death," Rasti added.

"At least in a cage at the crossroads, you had a chance at escape," Moira said. "Which you did. Without our help." Moira nudged Zephyr and went to help Rasti.

Urion stood quietly by trying to absorb what they had surmised but he himself had not.

Moira and Zephyr helped finish uncovering the wagon. They removed the rolled canvas and the curved bows, stowing them away in the wagon's bed.

"Now we can all ride on the wagon. Your dragon's feet need to toughen up, but it won't happen overnight. Let's go," Rasti said.

17

They got back in the wagon. Urion reclaimed his seat up front next to Rasti, where he remained silent.

With the tailgate lowered, Zephyr sat at the back of the wagon, his sore feet hanging over the end, while Moira perched on top of a crate beside him. The extra weight slowed the horses, but the winding road was at least a flat one. She didn't think Rasti was concerned with their speed, only with making steady progress.

Moira tapped Zephyr on the shoulder. "Something happened," she said, glancing back at Rasti and Urion. Moira didn't think they could hear her over the road noise, but she kept her voice low anyway. Zephyr bent his head close to hers while she told him about what had happened when she drank the poison in Lord Q's study and how she'd come face to face, in a manner of speaking, with the book in her head.

Zephyr stiffened as she spoke. "I knew something was wrong."

"I know. I'm sorry. You were resting, and I didn't want to wake you. I gotta say, I didn't expect to be poisoned though."

She unwrapped the cloak bundle and drew out the book. "But at least we've got something to read." She opened the cover. "Listen to this, '*The Book of Wyverns*. Based on original works by Copernicus Stumble.' That's what he said his name was."

Aside from the title page, there was no other front matter, but it told her enough. The book she held in her hands wasn't the original—it had been altered. How many editions could there be?

Zephyr grunted. "What does it say about those who are dragon-bit?"

Moira didn't look up. "I don't know yet. I'll let you know if I run across anything." She turned the pages. What she read was a brief history of the interactions between humans and dragons, followed by a categorical list of the known dragon types. She was momentarily excited when she read a small mention of dragon bites and kept reading further, but there was nothing else.

Zephyr saw her page back to the beginning. "How was it? Anything?"

"Well, it's, uh, interesting. Wyverns are by far superior beings and should never have gotten mixed up with humans, but they did, for whatever reason, and over time the two species appear to have developed a symbiotic relationship or one of mutual benefit. There's not much about dragon bites." Moira flipped through the book. "Here we go. 'Dragon bites are a rare phenomenon, and for good reason. When wyvern relations with humans were in their infancy, two dragons bit two brothers. Each brother gained access to their dragon's natural magic and any special talents, which has been found true in every case since.'" She stopped reading long enough to share a look with Zephyr. "'However, an unbridled rivalry grew between the siblings. The destruction left in the brothers' wake ultimately led to the demise of their dragons and each other. Following these catastrophic events, wyvern elders passed down a blood decree to never again bite members of the same family, weaving the doctrine into their very natures. Since that time, dragon bites have grown increasingly rare. The impetus for such occurrences remains unclear.'"

Moira stopped. "That's it. That's all it says about dragon bites." She held the book up by its cover, spine side up, and shook the pages. Nothing fell out. No answer to all their questions. "Yeah, that's all there is."

She didn't know what to make of the story about the two brothers, but something struck her as odd, beyond the author's assertion that humans ruin everything. Something about the way Copernicus, or Cal, began the story. He might as well have started it with, 'Once upon a time...'.

Zephyr stuck out his hand. "May I?"

She handed the book over. "We can guess why you bit me, though."

"Hmm?"

"I think it's safe to say you never would have bitten me if you hadn't hatched where you did, back on earth, in our reality, in our universe, whatever." She waved a hand. "You know what I mean."

Zephyr raised his eyes. "Go on."

"No one was around when you hatched. Somehow, you found your way to me. I think you bit me, not necessarily because you wanted to, but because you needed to. You knew you weren't where you were supposed to be. What do you remember?"

Zephyr raised his head and looked down the road where they had already traveled. "Very little." He closed his eyes. "There were many emotions. It all happened so quickly, and yet—"he blinked his eyes open— "I never thought those first days would end. Then you came, and they did."

Moira tipped her head toward the book. "Looks like you are a standard brown leatherback," she said. There were other types of dragons, standard greens, blacks, and reds, as well as plate backs like the one they had seen in Farrago, and still others. She pointed to the back of the book. "There's a picture and everything."

Zephyr held the book up, turning it this way and that, his lip curling. "This is a terrible rendering. Ansel could do better."

The name hit Moira like a blow. Ansel *had* done better. He had done so well that Aaron had put it in the school paper. Aaron had said there was something about the piece that made him want to include it. Ansel had let him, though he knew Zephyr's existence was supposed to remain secret.

She didn't know why. They never talked about it.

Moira stared down at the road. "We have to get them back, Zeph."

Zephyr lowered the book and closed it. "We will."

"I'm afraid of what's already happened to them."

"What do you mean? They were just taken last night."

Moira shook her head with a grimace. "I don't think they were. Listen, I know we went to the Librarian as soon as we could, but I don't think time passes the same way here as it does at home. How else could Smew have known to be on the lookout for a female dragoneer? And one who was dragon-bit as well? Ansel must have told them. Aaron didn't know. It would've had to have been Ansel who said something." She closed her eyes. "The man I shot the night of Homecoming, the High Magician—Vinton—he'd recovered by the time he took Ansel and Aaron. Not just fully recovered, but he maybe even looked a little older." She opened her eyes. "And Smew knew my name."

"I did not hear him use it."

"No, but he said something about calling myself noble. He didn't know it was my surname. Urion thought as much when I introduced myself at first before he knew I was a dragoneer."

Her full name was information either of the brothers could have given, but in exchange for what? Her stomach roiled at the thought. How had Vinton gotten those details? What tactics might he have employed?

She didn't want to think about her friends being tortured for knowledge about her. There was no secret of hers worth keeping for them to be hurt over. Moira didn't care if Aaron and Ansel spilled their guts as long as their guts didn't get spilled, not on her account.

They fell into silence, with Zephyr taking a turn to read the book. There wasn't much to it at all. She'd been hoping for a bit more information, or at least a tingle of recognition, but there was nothing. The book in her head was the original version of the manuscript. That was what the Librarian had told her when he transferred the book to her. The version of the book they had with them had changed so much over time the original didn't recognize itself.

Without the canvas cover on the back of the wagon, they sat exposed to the heat of the day. The sway of the wagon took its toll and Moira drifted off, dozing in fits and spurts. Whenever she closed her eyes, images of Ansel and Aaron flitted across her mind. Aaron in Chemistry giving a presentation on fireworks. Ansel sketching in his notepad. Moments from her past that were disjointed and disconnected from her current reality. Every time she jerked awake, the more tired she felt.

They passed a few people on the road and rolled through three small towns, only stopping to let the horses drink from flowing streams. Urion broke his silence to speak with Rasti once or twice, but otherwise kept to himself. Finally, as the sun dipped toward the horizon, Rasti drove the wagon off the road into a dense wood. Off the major thoroughfare, the trees would make it hard to be seen by anyone else traveling by.

Rasti climbed down from the driver's seat. "I'll see to the horses. I have some provisions for the dragon, but not enough for the entire trip. It would help if he could find some of his own food. What do you say, Master Zephyr? Up to a little hunting?"

Zephyr jumped off the back of the wagon, lifting his nose in the air. His nostrils flared, and he stalked off into the woods. After only a few strides, the trees hid him from sight.

"Good. Then maybe you two can gather some firewood. The same goes for us. We have some provisions, but we're going to have to be resourceful and supplement our rations. Take your bow."

"What about me?" asked Urion.

Rasti glared at him. "What about you?"

"Do I get a bow?"

"I thought you could just charm the wee beasties into giving up."

Urion raised one brow, waiting.

Rasti waved a hand. "Fine. There's a sword in the back as well."

Moira shifted canvases aside until she found her bow, then kept looking for her temporarily misplaced quiver. Urion uncovered a sword and scabbard, belting it around his waist. The two set off in the opposite direction of Zephyr, not wanting to spook any of the game he might be hunting.

They collected sticks and twigs in silence for a while until Moira said. "I'm sorry about before. About how you ended up in that cage."

Urion nodded. "I thought... I don't know what I thought. It doesn't matter." He stopped to pick up a stick. "The fact of the matter is, I'm cursed. I just have to learn to accept it."

Moira didn't know what to say to that. They kept collecting wood. Along the way, they stumbled across a small game trail and followed it, collecting more and more sticks until her arms were full.

Ahead of her, Urion turned and hefted his stack. "This is probably enough to get started."

Moira glanced up and froze. Over two dozen grinning faces had slipped forward to block their way without making a sound.

Urion frowned at her and turned to see what she was looking at. His pile of sticks and twigs hit the ground as he reached for his sword.

Moira dropped her load, sliding her bow from behind her back. "What are they?"

Urion backed up to stand beside her, tension clear in every line of his body. "Goblins."

18

The goblins stood three or four feet tall, thin as scarecrows with large round heads and pointed ears. Those in front brandished rusty swords and meat cleavers, while the ones in back held bows, their arrows pointed at her and Urion. Their ill-fitting armor appeared made for humans. Their unpleasant grins suggested what had happened to the armor's former occupants.

Moira drew an arrow in a flash and nocked it.

The goblins hefted their weapons and glanced at one another.

"Well, don't just stand there," a voice growled from the shadows. "Get them!"

The goblins shifted, eyeing one another uneasily.

"But there's two of 'em," said the smallest goblin. "And they're both armed."

Urion tilted his sword, light flashing along the length of the blade. The goblins brandished their weapons while huddling together.

"Stop messing around and kill them!" shouted the voice from the shadows.

"You want 'em dead, you kill 'em," the smallest goblin said, glancing behind him for an escape route. "We should've just done what we always do, jump 'em when they wasn't looking."

"You need battle experience."

"Forget battle experience! Sneak attacks work fine."

The shadows emitted a deep sigh as the goblin issuing the orders stepped into the open. He was by far the tallest at nearly five feet, carrying the largest and cleanest sword of them all. He glared at the goblin horde. "How am I supposed to teach you to fight if you won't fight? I mean, it's only one man and a girl."

"Yeah," the smallest goblin said, "but they look like they know what they're doing."

Moira and Urion exchanged glances. Urion cut the air with a few practice strokes and lunges.

The goblins stared.

"Come on, guys," the goblin leader said. "We can take them."

Moira raised her bow and aimed for a tree well over the heads of all the goblins and fired. With a *thunk*, the arrow sank deep into the bark.

"Great," said the smallest goblin. "Now we made 'em mad."

"Quiet!" roared the goblin leader. "We outnumber them by over a dozen to one. We can't lose. Archers ready!"

Moira and Urion turned toward each other and then kept turning.

"Fire!"

Moira and Urion were already in motion before the goblin leader gave the order. Moira didn't have any faith in the goblins having enough skill to hit them, but there were an awful lot of them. With that many arrows pointed in their direction, one goblin might get lucky. Urion must have come to the same conclusion. They ducked behind two trees a few feet apart as a hail of arrows struck their surroundings, including the trees they hid behind.

Moira drew another arrow. Aiming carefully, she sunk it into the same tree just below her first shot, hoping she might still scare the goblins off, but that hope was dwindling. They might need a little help. She closed her eyes, focused on Zephyr, and thought about goblins, hoping that would be enough to get him headed toward her and Urion's location.

"Not bad, lads, we've got them pinned down. Archers ready?"

Moira drew and nocked another arrow.

Urion watched her from behind a too-narrow tree with a grimace. "You're dragon-bit, right? Why do you even need the bow?"

She paused. Of course, she needed a bow.

Don't I?

Because if she didn't need a bow to fire an arrow…

The thought trailed off.

Moira stepped out from behind the tree.

Urion's eyes widened. "Wait… "

"Fire!"

Moira turned to face the goblin archers as they released their arrows. The slim projectiles flew at her. For a split second, the line of scar tissue at the top of her right arm flared to life. She knew what it was like to get hit with an arrow and wasn't in a hurry to repeat the experience. Her teeth ground together as she drew on her will, mentally noting the trajectory of the pointed shafts hurtling in her direction. She held up a hand, fingers splayed, and the arrows stopped. They stopped and hung in the air long enough for several goblins to gasp. Then they fell to the ground with a patter like heavy rain.

Moira bent over with a grunt, as if she'd taken a punch to the solar plexus. The rush of blood in her ears made a roaring sound. Where was Zephyr? How could he not know they were in trouble?

"What the—!" the goblin leader began. "Never mind all that! When I give the order, charge! Charge!"

The big goblin rushed forward, brandishing his sword, only to be met by Urion, who didn't bother raising his own sword. Instead, he raised a fist and knocked the goblin leader out with a single blow. The tall goblin slumped to the ground and didn't move. The few smaller goblins who had followed him stopped and stood staring at their downed leader before looking at each other.

Moira wrapped an arm around her middle, breathing hard. The goblin horde was so ineffectual she didn't have the heart to bother with them. Neither did Urion.

The goblin leader stirred. Shaking his head, he glared up at Urion, defiant.

Urion held his sword to the goblin leader's neck.

The goblin swallowed.

"Drop your weapons," Urion told the rest of the horde.

Rusty swords and cutlery hit the ground with a metallic jingle.

"Now here's what's going to happen," Urion said. "You're going to give up this life of crime and leave this place, never to return. If you agree to that, I won't put you on a skewer and feed you to my friend's dragon here." He nodded in her direction. "He's hunting for a meal right now, but he'd probably settle for a few goblins."

Heads swiveled her way. Moira put on her sternest expression, which wasn't hard considering what the goblins might have done to them.

"Sounds fair," said the smallest goblin. "Very fair." There was a lot of nodding from the other goblins.

The goblin leader stretched his neck away from Urion's blade. "We need to take our weapons with us. It can be dangerous in the woods at night."

"Do I look like a fool?"

The leader of the goblins scrambled backward and got to his feet. "It never hurts to ask. You've got yourself a deal."

Urion kept his sword up as the goblins quarreled amongst themselves, fading away into the gathering darkness. When the last one disappeared from sight, he came to her side. "Are you all right?"

Moira found it hard to stand up straight. "Not really."

"Can you hold on a moment longer?"

She grunted. "Yes."

It took Urion only a few minutes to work his way through the abandoned weapons, bending or breaking blades and snapping bows. Then he was at her side again, sword sheathed, dragging her arm up and over his shoulder. They headed back to where they'd left the wagon, surprising Moira with how far they had walked in search of firewood.

Zephyr was back. As soon as he saw them, he jumped up from where he sat beside an animal carcass. "What happened?" he asked.

"Goblins," Urion said. "We're going to have to sleep in shifts tonight."

Rasti looked up from the crate he'd been rummaging through. "We were going to do that, anyway."

Moira slid her arm from Urion's shoulder. She sat down hard on the ground, her bow and quiver beside her. "We dropped the firewood."

"What is wrong?" Zephyr asked.

Moira rolled to her side and curled into a ball. "They fired on us."

"She stopped the arrows," Urion said.

Zephyr bent his head close to hers. "Moira, what did you do?"

"Zeph, something's wrong." She should have been able to reach him, but he never came.

Her dragon shook his head, bewildered. "I did not know."

This was not good. "Give me your hand?"

Zephyr's leathery palm slid into hers. No jolt. No shooting pains. Nothing.

What's wrong with our link? It's never failed before.

"Try harder," said Moira. "I'm already on the ground. Can't fall down. Just, you know, nothing too loud." She squeezed her eyes shut tight in anticipation. Unlike previous times when Zephyr had tried to reach out, making her jump, this time she received a mild electric zing equivalent to a small zap of static electricity instead of a lightning bolt. His message: *Sleep.*

Her body took his suggestion as a command. Her eyelids relaxed, but they didn't open. The darkness grew weighted and pulled her down into slumber. As the tension drained from her limbs, though, she couldn't help but worry. She wasn't picking up on Zephyr's missives at their typical strength, and he didn't seem able to receive hers at all.

What's wrong with me?

Voices roused Moira from her sleep sometime later. For a minute, she laid flat on her back, stretched out on the ground, though she could tell someone had covered her with a blanket and found a pillow for her head. The light flickered beyond her eyelids, but she didn't bother to raise them. The smell of roasted meat made her stomach lurch, reminding her of how long it had been since she had eaten anything.

"Will she be all right?" Urion asked.

Zephyr rumbled. "To stop one arrow is no small feat. To stop a whole volley… it took more than she expected. She was not ready."

Rasti grunted. "For being dragon-bit, she has a lot to learn."

There was a pause. "Yes," Zephyr said.

The back of her eyes stung. Why did it hurt to hear Zephyr agree with Rasti when she knew it was true? She did have a lot to learn. Maybe she should be grateful he couldn't pick up on what she was feeling right then. The thought of facing him and the others made her roll away from the fire to embrace the sweet oblivion of sleep.

19

Moira woke to find the embers of last night's fire stirred to life and water heating, her tiredness replaced by grudging alertness and hunger. Urion and Rasti worked to break camp, while Moira ate reheated leftovers from last night's meal: a bowl of roasted meat and some kind of pasta.

"I do not like this. It is too dangerous," Zephyr said.

"I know, but what can we do?" Moira said. She could still interpret Zephyr's feelings when they were intense, but he could no longer pick up on hers.

In the past, she'd tried to erect walls between them with miserable results. Now she'd succeeded where before she had failed, and without even trying. Zephyr insisted his ability to read her emotions was useful in a fight, but he'd had access to her emotions at other times. He'd once used his empathetic knowledge to make her feel better after a fight with her aunt. Moira had noticed something wasn't right and asked him to stop and never do it again. He hadn't done it again and had seemed to realize that just because he might know what she was feeling didn't mean he knew why she felt the way she did. They still had to communicate verbally.

Moira ate with her fingers. "Do you think the poison had something to do with it?"

Zephyr frowned in thought. "Perhaps."

"If you have to bite me again, I'm out, big guy."

He frowned harder.

"Kidding, Zeph. I mean, I hope you don't have to, but..."

"No. It is unnecessary. We will figure it out."

"I know it's not ideal, especially right now, considering where we are, but not every dragoneer gets bitten. They must get along somehow. We'll just have to use our words." Moira poked at a noodle and set the bowl aside.

Zephyr's gaze went from her to the food. "Why do you not eat?"

She mumbled, "My stomach needs a break."

His gaze met hers. "You said you would use your words."

"What?"

"Tell me why you do not eat."

She let out a huff and wrapped her arms around her middle. "I suddenly remembered we're a long way from home, our friends are in mortal danger, and the link we've come to rely on isn't working. But, like you said, we'll figure it out."

Zephyr's head tipped back. "Yes, we will. You do not have to do so alone."

Moira took a breath and held it a moment before letting it go. "Right. Do you want the rest?"

Zephyr finished her food while Rasti hitched the horses to the wagon. Everyone helped replace the curved bows and unfurl the canvas to cover the wagon once more. Everything was ready to go. Rasti met her at the back of the wagon. "Your dragon should walk for now. His feet won't toughen up riding all day. Sit with me. I'd like a word."

Moira made sure Zephyr was okay walking, then climbed up to sit next to Rasti on the driver's seat. Urion sat behind them in the wagon, head tilted back, eyes closed. She couldn't begrudge him the chance to nap. He'd taken two shifts last night while Moira slept straight through.

They set off, finding their way back to the main road.

For someone wanting to talk to her, Rasti didn't act like it. Finally, he asked, "What happened yesterday?"

Moira sat up straighter. "Where should I begin?"

"Tell me what happened with the arrows."

"I don't know."

Rasti watched her from the corner of his eye. "Yes, you do. Now what happened?"

She'd done nothing like it before, stopping the arrows the way she had. If Urion had said nothing, she wouldn't have thought to try what she did. "I blame Urion."

Rasti grunted. "No doubt he is worthy of it. What did he do?"

"He made some crack about me being dragon-bit and suggested I didn't need a bow to fire an arrow. And I thought if I didn't need a bow to fire an arrow, maybe I could do the reverse. So I did. I stopped the arrows."

"How?"

Moira shook her head. "I don't know. I imagined them hitting a wall." She spread the fingers of her hand open in front of her as she had the day before. "They just stopped. Then they fell to the ground."

"All right. Good. How did you feel afterward?"

"Like someone punched me in the stomach with a bowling ball."

"I don't know what a bowling ball is, but I get the idea. Do you know why?"

Moira thought about it. "Um... there were a lot of arrows?" She'd never fired that many arrows at one time, but she'd stopped more than a few yesterday.

"Yes, very good. You stopped a lot of arrows. But being dragon-bit doesn't make you invincible. You overexerted yourself. I've seen it before."

"When?"

Rasti sighed. "A long time ago. I knew another dragon-bit soul. He tried to do too much and ended up being of no use to anyone. We almost lost him. And his dragon. You need to be more careful and consider the source of your magic."

"Right." Her magic failed when she grew tired and yesterday had been a long day. "My strength and my will."

Rasti lowered the reins and twisted around to look at her. "I was talking about your dragon."

Moira frowned. "What about him?"

"He's where your magic comes from."

"Right. The only reason I'm able to do what I can is because Zephyr bit me."

"Yes. And no. You can draw on your dragon's strength when you work your magic, and it can be just as draining for him as it is for you. Imagine relying on him at the wrong moment. He wouldn't be able to defend himself if what happened to you happened to him in the middle of combat."

Moira stared out over the road ahead of them. She didn't know her magic worked that way. There certainly wasn't anything about that in *The Book of Wyverns*. "I would never—" she shook her head— "I've never done that."

"I can see you'd rather take the brunt of it yourself, but if your dragon sees you suffering for it, you might not have a choice." His mouth flattened into a line, and he blinked at the road.

"Is that what happened to the other dragoneer you mentioned?"

Rasti nodded with a grunt. "He nearly sacrificed himself to save our entire legion in one fell blaze of glory." He sniffed. "Damned fool."

"What are the legions? You mentioned them before."

"Legions are comprised of dragons and dragoneers. They're assigned to regiments of soldiers and horses to form brigades."

Moira's eyes narrowed. "Wait, so does that mean *you* were a dragoneer?"

Rasti huffed. "That was a long time ago."

"But that's great!" Behind them, Urion stirred. Moira lowered her voice. "I read *The Book of Wyverns*, but it didn't help. I know I have a lot to learn." His words from the night before echoed in her ears even as she said them.

Rasti sighed. "I'm guessing that's why Lord Q sent me to accompany you."

"Lord Q asked for you?"

"His secretary delivered a note personally. He told me to pick up this wagon full of supplies and head to the stables to prepare for a journey west. But he didn't tell me why." His eyebrows went up with a pointed glance in her direction.

Moira explained how the Regent's High Magician took Aaron and Ansel because he had mistaken one of them for Zephyr's dragoneer and was most likely holding them at Castle Tern. She told him everything that had happened after they lost sight of each other the night before. Rasti grunted when he learned Lord Q poisoned her with dragon venom but he did not comment. She told him about the arrival of Lord Smew, his search for her and Zephyr, and their flight to the stables, where Rasti picked them up. She didn't mention her and Zephyr's broken connection, focusing on the loss of her friends and her desire to get them back and return home.

Rasti listened without interrupting.

When she was done, Moira glanced over her shoulder. Urion slept. Zephyr kept pace with the wagon, his head cocked forward as if to catch what they were saying while keeping a watchful eye on the road ahead and the land on either side of it.

Rasti finally asked, "Where do you come from?"

"That's another story," she said. "Someplace where there aren't many dragons. At least, not like the ones here. Now I want to ask you a question."

He lifted a brow and waited.

"What happened to your dragon?"

20

Rasti slapped the reins lightly against the horse's backs. "Old Horatio? He's alive and well. Retired like me. Helps on a farmstead near the village that sponsored and raised him. I still get a card every midwinter." He didn't look at her.

His answer sounded rehearsed, but on the surface, there was nothing wrong with it. She thought there might be more to the story, but she let it go for now.

"How long were you in the legions?" Moira asked.

"A term is ten years. Started when I was a boy of fifteen and saw enough fighting during my first term to last a lifetime. The general gave me the option to retire or reenlist. I chose retirement. That was a long time ago." He barked out a short laugh.

If she had to guess Rasti's age, she would have put him somewhere in his mid-fifties, which meant he'd doubled in age since he was a dragoneer himself. His knowledge might be out of date—but it was still more than she had. "Urion said something earlier. He told us we should be in the Light Legion."

The reins jerked in Rasti's hands. "Why would he say that?"

Moira explained how they hid behind the tapestry and escaped detection in Lord Q's office.

Rasti listened. "The tapestry across from the doors?"

"Yes." Moira didn't ask how he knew which one she spoke of.

"Your dragon has a gift for stealth," he said.

"You could say that."

Rasti's brows formed an arch. "Well, well, well. Isn't that something?"

"What does it mean?"

"It means your dragon can hide in plain sight, and you, dragon-bit as you are, share a talent for it as well."

"The book said something like that, but it didn't explain how it works."

"Nor would it. It's not a how-to manual. For that kind of training, you'd need to join the ranks of the Light Legion, and you're not even a recognized dragoneer yet, though being dragon-bit helps with that part."

"I'm not joining an army. I'm here to get my friends back and then we're going home. That's all."

Rasti's brows lowered as he flicked the reins. "I'm not sure where the Light Legion operates at the moment, anyway. They're usually near the border. We'll pass that way soon enough." He chuckled to himself. "But they might show you a few things at least. I'll make some inquiries at the next town. May have to send a carrier."

Not certain she wouldn't be press-ganged into joining the military, Moira watched Rasti from the side of her eye.

"The other dragoneer you knew, the one like me, did he retire?"

Rasti kept his eyes forward. "No." He added nothing more.

"What else can you tell me about him?"

He frowned at her, his face a question.

"Where did he come from?" Moira asked. "What was he like? What was his dragon like?"

Rasti's expression cleared even as he shook his head. "I couldn't tell you where Niall and Forboze came from if I ever knew. They were quiet. Kept to themselves. A little jumpy maybe." He stared down the road, his gaze unfocused. "They were always together, never one without the other. A lot of dragoneers get attached to their wyverns, especially if they've been together a long time or seen battle." He paused, lips pursed. "Niall could stop arrows and such, too. Forboze was a big green plate back, good with the spark. We were never in want of a fire on a chill night with Niall and Forboze around, that's for sure. And as quickly as they could light a fire, Niall could put it out with little more than a wave of his hand."

Moira's jaw slid open. "Forboze could breathe fire?"

Rasti turned to her with a frown. "What? No. Forboze had the spark. Niall could make fire with it." Rasti tilted his head. "Breathe fire? I've never heard of such a thing."

Moira frowned with a tiny shake of her head. "That's disappointing."

Rasti guffawed. "That they don't breathe fire? Their insides would get charred."

"Forget I mentioned it."

Rasti didn't speak for a while, but she could tell by the way he would squint and shake his head from time to time that he was still pondering a dragon breathing fire.

The sun was bright overhead in a cloudless sky when the road widened and they approached a little town that included a stable and an inn advertising meals for the weary traveler.

Rasti pulled the wagon over in front of the first building they came to. "We'll stop here, so I can send that message."

A square shingle hung out front. Carved into it was the silhouette of a solitary bird, wings spread, feather tips splayed. "You're going to use a bird to send a letter?"

Rasti climbed down from the driver's seat. "It's the fastest way."

"How will you receive a reply?"

"I'll have it sent ahead to Goodramtown."

"Where's that?"

"It sits this side of the border between the Freelands and the Fells Nation, where Castle Tern lies."

"How long will it take us to get there?"

Rasti sighed. "If we make good time, five to seven days. If not, longer."

Moira glanced into the back of the wagon. Urion didn't stir. "Should we wake him?"

"Leave him. You can head to the town center." Rasti tilted his head toward their horses. "There should be a well. Take the empty water skins and fill them, will you?"

Zephyr helped Moira collect the empties from the back of the wagon. Rasti went inside.

As they started walking, Moira matched her pace to Zephyr's. "Rasti used to be a dragoneer."

"I heard. His experience could be helpful."

Moira glanced down. "How're your feet?"

Zephyr grunted. "Not too bad."

His gait was even, but Moira made a mental note to monitor him for any signs of fatigue.

They passed a couple of wagons stopped in front of other buildings, but didn't see anyone as they continued down the road until they reached the center of town. Scattered around the water source stood a smattering of wagons with items displayed. Townspeople stopped to inspect wares and chat with sellers. She and Zephyr received a few long looks, but no one paid them any more attention than that.

Like the well in Lady Lavinia's courtyard, there was a free-flowing fountain from which to draw water. Moira and Zephyr took turns filling and drinking from the skins. No one approached. They worked in silence. As they filled the skins for the last time, she overheard part of a conversation between a peddler selling earthenware and a local.

"Have you been to the Fells?"

"Aye, I've come straight away from there."

"Is it as bad as they say?"

"Worse, I expect. I didn't travel west beyond the castle. Not much business to be had for wares such as mine in those parts, and you can guess why. Not to mention trolls and soldiers stopping every peddler in and out and again near the border, searching. I had nothing they wanted, but it didn't stop them from getting rough with my merchandise. I was glad to have made it out with as much crockery intact as I did. No, I won't be going back there. Not until they sort out who's in charge."

The two turned away, and Moira lost the thread of their conversation. Finished refilling the skins, she and Zephyr left the well behind and headed back to where they'd left Rasti and Urion with the wagon.

Along the way, they passed an open gate to a stable. Moira paused while Zephyr continued. A boy, not more than ten, struggled to move a manure-filled wheelbarrow stuck in a rut between two flagstones. When the boy leaned into the handles, straining, the wheel shuddered, and the boy tripped, dropping the wheelbarrow on its side. Manure spilled across the stones and the young man snatched off his flat cap, flinging it to the ground.

Moira couldn't help laughing.

The boy went red in the face and shook his fist at her, roaring in fury. He grabbed a rock and hurled it at her.

Moira ducked, though the rock missed by a lot.

A feminine voice broke the silence. "What is the meaning of this?"

Moira peeked around the edge of the gate.

A girl younger than Moira pointed her finger at the boy. "You ungrateful wretch! Look what you've done! Wait until I've told the stable master. You'll be whipped!"

The boy's head and shoulders slumped under the weight of her words. She turned in a flurry of skirts and rushed away.

Zephyr, having noticed Moira was no longer with him, had returned to her side. He set the full water skins on the ground.

Inside the yard, the boy sniffed and ran his sleeve under his nose.

Moira beckoned for Zephyr to follow her and slipped inside. Against one wall leaned a shovel with a broad blade. She grabbed it, and picking up the boy's hat, nudged him in the arm. He jumped in alarm, raising his tear-streaked face. Moira held out his hat. "Here. I don't think we have much time. Let's get this cleaned up."

The boy's eyes went from her to Zephyr, his head tilting back to take in the dragon. He gasped as his jaw slid open. "Uh, uh, I-I... "

Moira snapped her fingers in his face to get him to focus on her. "Stay with me, kid. I know it's a lot, but I think we better get a move on before she comes back."

The boy blinked. "Yes, miss." He grabbed two more shovels with narrower blades. Moira passed the larger one to Zephyr, hurrying to right the wheelbarrow. She and the boy helped, but Zephyr had most of the mess cleaned up in three strokes. Moira took the shovels and put them back while the boy grabbed the wheelbarrow by the handles and, without getting it stuck, rushed it away out the back.

Zephyr went to the corner and found a rain barrel. He picked it up in both hands and brought it over. Zephyr upended the barrel and water sluiced over the stones, running into a gutter where it disappeared down a drain. Zephyr put the barrel back as the boy returned with the empty wheelbarrow, which he set against the wall. Then the boy used a rough sack to mop up the water.

When he finished, the boy faced Zephyr, standing tall, before bending forward from the waist. "Th-thank you, Master Wyvern." He straightened.

Zephyr's face split into a grin, displaying many pointed teeth and fangs. "Call me Zephyr."

The boy's eyes widened as he leaned back.

"Easy there, Zeph," Moira cautioned him. "Sorry about earlier. I shouldn't have laughed."

The boy's expression turned rueful, as if with the mess cleaned up he could see the humor in the situation.

"What's your name?" Moira asked.

The boy swallowed. "Grig, miss." His gaze went from her to Zephyr and back. "Is he yours?"

Moira recalled Rasti's story from when they left Farrago. "He belongs to himself. We travel together."

"Is he a real battle dragon?" Grig's tone held wonder.

Moira squinted. "Yes, my… cousin and Zephyr are on their way to join the legions."

Zephyr hissed, his head whipping around. "Someone comes."

"Let's go," Moira said.

All three rushed to the exit, where they ducked out of sight.

Moira peeked around the gate as she heard footsteps approach. The girl from before returned with a heavyset man, as wide as he was tall.

"Well? What have you brought me here for, girl? There's nothing to see."

"But—but the stable boy..."

"You leave the boy out of this. If you don't have enough work to keep you busy, I'll speak to your mistress. Don't waste my time." The ground shuddered as he stomped off.

The girl stood staring at the cleaned stones where the manure had spilled. She stamped her foot before she, too, turned and left the yard.

Grig let out an audible sigh of relief as he slumped against the gate. "Thank you."

Zephyr straightened, picking up the water skins he'd set aside.

Moira relaxed, one side of her mouth lifting into a smile. "Glad we could help, Grig. You've got a good arm, but maybe don't throw rocks at people just because they make you mad, okay?"

The trundle of a wagon sounded from behind her. Moira glanced over her shoulder. Rasti slowed the horses as he pulled up next to them.

Moira tilted her head toward the wagon. "This is our ride."

Zephyr put the water skins in the back.

Grig stepped forward. "Take me with you."

21

Rasti overheard Grig and gave Moira a sidelong glance. "What's this?"

Grig didn't waste time. "I want to be a dragoneer and join the legions. Take me with you."

Except we're not joining the legions. Consulting them, maybe. How do I put this? Moira's eyes narrowed. "No."

"What? Why? I'm a hard worker. I won't be any trouble... "

Rasti cleared his throat and addressed Moira in a low voice. "Why don't you help with those water skins while I talk to your new friend?"

Moira opened her mouth, then closed it again right away, hoping Rasti would know what to say to Grig, because she didn't. As the retired dragoneer climbed down from the driver's seat, she went to Zephyr's side, casting furtive glances toward the head of the wagon. Grig did a lot of listening and nodding while Rasti did most of the talking. Now and then Grig would say something, but

Moira couldn't hear. She and Zephyr finished their task and stood at the back of the wagon, waiting.

Inside the wagon, Urion stirred. His head swiveled until his gaze landed on Moira and Zephyr. He clambered over the supplies toward them, yawning. "What have I missed?"

***

They left without Grig. Later, as they walked down the road, Moira and Urion kept some space between themselves and the wagon to avoid the dust kicked up by the wheels. Zephyr walked behind them.

Moira kept glancing at Urion. Something was off about his appearance, but she couldn't put her finger on what. Leaving Grig behind distracted her. *Maybe we should have brought him along. He could have helped.* She answered herself with a quiet, derisive snort. *No. We did the right thing. He would have been more hindrance than help.* She pulled her thoughts away from Grig and thought of something Urion might have missed. "Did you know Rasti used to be a dragoneer?"

Urion's brows lifted in surprise. "No, but it makes sense… What happened to his dragon?"

Moira told him about the retired Horatio.

"Odd." Urion bent to scoop up a rock the size of an egg out of the road. "Here." He held the rock out to her.

Moira took it. "What?" She examined the gray lump with a smattering of pink and white minerals.

"You should practice."

Moira knew what he meant, but still. "Could we start with something smaller?"

Urion laughed. "You stopped fifty arrows yesterday. This is nothing compared to that."

She tossed the rock in the air and caught it. "There were a lot fewer than fifty, and they were highly motivating, those arrows."

"Can't hurt to practice. Besides, it occurs to me I've never seen you fight with a sword. I know you're good with a bow. What kind of sword fighter are you?"

Moira lifted one shoulder. "I'm okay. I guess."

"You don't strike me as being falsely modest, so I believe you. When we stop for the evening, you can show me what 'okay' looks like." He squinted at her. "Are you even trying?"

Moira had been focusing on the rock while he talked, but had achieved nothing yet. His critique earned him a glare. After he tucked his brown hair behind one ear, her glare morphed into a stare. "How did your hair grow back so fast? They cut it short in Farrago."

"Oh, that." He bowed his head, refusing to meet her eye. "It's a fae thing. Because of my mother." He waved his hand at the ground. "Would you like a smaller rock?"

Moira shook her head. "I'll take this one for granite. I'm attached to it now."

"Really?" He looked at the rock in her hand.

"No."

Behind them, Zephyr rumbled out a chuckle.

She tossed the rock in the air and caught it again. "So you can just change your appearance whenever you want?"

Urion cleared his throat. "No. Some halflings can, and do, with frightening regularity, but I suspect my ears got cold, so my hair grew out in pure self-defense. It's happened before." He frowned and stared down the road past the wagon, as if thinking of some other time and place.

Moira focused on the felsic intrusive in her hand and held the rock out in front of her as she walked. Concentrating, she released her will and let go. The rock remained motionless. Of course, then she walked into it, knocking it out of the air. She caught it.

Urion's expression cleared. He'd noticed her fixing the rock in place. When she ran into it, he said nothing.

Moira tried and caught the rock again and again until she snatched it out of the air. She had to revise her thinking. She'd done this before a long time ago in her room. Sitting on her bed, she'd nudged a pebble back and forth where she wanted it to go, releasing a bit of her will with each move. Now she wanted to keep her piece of granite aloft and move the rock along with her as she walked. With one hand she held the rock in front of her, the other she opened next to it, her fingers splayed. She figured she couldn't just gather her will and release it in one go. She needed to supply a constant running stream.

This time when she tapped into her will, she visualized doing so literally, as if it were a solid thing. She had to puncture the surface to get at what was inside, which she imagined was more of the same, only less solid.

A small grunt escaped her. The surface tension of her will didn't burst, but keeping it from doing so wasn't comfortable. Like having an itch she couldn't reach, no matter how hard she contorted her limbs to scratch the spot that needed it.

In her mind's eye, she opened the tap enough for a trickle of her will to run free.

She let go of the rock.

It wobbled and jerked, but it stayed in the air. She sucked in a breath and brought both hands down so they were under the rock, keeping it aloft.

And then she tripped. The rock dropped, and Moira fell hard, landing on her knees.

Zephyr was there in an instant to help her to her feet. "All right?"

She stood, brushing at the road dust. "Yeah."

Urion picked up the piece of granite and held it out, saying nothing. He seemed to have used up all his words for the moment, but he offered her a tired half-smile.

Moira took the rock and smiled back, letting him go ahead so she could drop back and walk next to Zephyr. By the time they stopped for the evening, she could keep the tap open and her magic flowing without having to concentrate on it alone. She could focus on the rock, concentrate on not tripping, and hold a brief conversation with Zephyr about his feet. They were tender, but he muscled through and didn't sit in the wagon even when Rasti offered after they stopped to eat strips of dried meat and apples.

The food shored up her physical reserves. Moira continued to practice until Rasti drove the wagon off the road for the night. As soon as she stopped practicing, she swayed on her feet; her gaze unfocused.

Zephyr cupped her elbow in his leathery palm, urging her to sit with her back against a large boulder. With their connection malfunctioning, she noticed he kept a closer eye on her than usual. She drank deeply from the waterskin he brought her and sat in a daze while Urion collected firewood and Rasti took care of the horses. Her eyes blinked close and, when she opened them again, there was a fire in front of her. Urion passed a plate into her hands. More noodles and roasted meat. Two spits over the fire held a pair of rabbits.

Rasti took one, still on the spit, and gave it to Zephyr. Then he filled a pot with a dragon-sized portion of noodles. But before he served it, he picked up a jar sitting next to him and twisted off the lid. Inside was some kind of sauce. Rasti added a little to the pot, giving it a toss to coat the noodles in the concoction before handing it to Zephyr.

"What's that?" Moira asked.

Rasti replaced the lid. "It's hapshulyc. I've not met a dragon yet who didn't have a taste for it."

Zephyr's nostrils flared over the pot before he tipped some noodles into his mouth.

"What's in it?" Moira asked.

"A reduction of onions, garlic, ginger, and the hottest peppers to be found on the continent." Rasti tilted the jar. "Wanna taste?"

"Blech. No thanks."

Zephyr alternated between noodles and bites of rabbit. He seemed to like the hapshulyc. She knew he liked rabbit. She took a bite of her meal. The food hit her hollow stomach with enough force to produce a grumble.

Rasti must have noticed the way she peered longingly into her empty bowl after she finished. "More?" Before she could answer, he gave her another helping. She ate that too.

"Do you have any potatoes?" Moira asked.

Rasti frowned. "A few. Why?"

Moira told him what she wanted to try. Rasti had a pan of hot oil over the fire in no time. Moira took a knife and sliced a potato as thin as she could into the oil. When the slices had crisped up, she dragged them out of the oil into a bowl and asked for more of the spicy hapshulyc to coat them. She handed her campfire-made spicy potato chips to Zephyr, who grinned.

"Almost like the real thing," he said, which Moira took to mean they weren't quite the same, but he wouldn't complain.

The food, as it had in the middle of the day, revived her to a point where she could muster up the energy for what came next.

Moira caught Urion's eye. "Still want to see what I can do with a sword?"

22

Urion selected the blade he'd used against the goblins, while Rasti poked around in the back of the wagon until he came up with another sword for Moira. Despite the new scabbard, upon drawing it she recognized it as the sword she and Zephyr had brought with them. They hadn't seen it since Urion used it against Kaidence, and the Farrago guards had confiscated it. A small smile touched her lips. The grip, familiar in her hand, reminded her of sparring with Ansel. Her smile faded. The weight of the sword pulled not just at her arm but at the pit of her stomach.

Rasti continued his search through the back of the wagon.

Zephyr licked the last of the hapshulyc from the pot.

The day edged toward twilight. Moira ran through some practice drills, watching as Urion did the same. "We both know I'm not going to win any skirmishes, right?"

Urion's brows arched. "Of course. We'll just see what you can do."

It wasn't long until Moira stepped back to rest, gasping for breath. "I'm better with a bow."

Sparring had not winded Urion, but she was glad to see he'd broken a sweat. "Your defense is decent, but it won't win you any fights. It's a good thing you have a dragon at your beck and call."

She huffed. "He's not at my beck and call." *Especially now*, she added silently to herself.

Urion stood tall. "Do you know how to tell you've won a fight?" He didn't wait for her to answer. "You walk away from it. Do everything to ensure you're the one walking away."

Rasti grunted from where he leaned against the back of the wagon. "He means there's no such thing as a fair fight."

Zephyr, finished eating, watched from close by. "Like this?" He whipped his tail forward and swept Urion's feet out from underneath him.

Moira's eyes widened.

Rasti laughed.

Urion scowled at Rasti, but couldn't sustain it for long. "Yes. Master Wyvern. Just like that." He climbed back to his feet, exchanging a grin with Zephyr.

"Put those away. It's getting dark," Rasti said. "Master Zephyr, I have something for you."

Moira slid her sword away and went to the back of the wagon with Zephyr. Rasti pulled a long bundle forward and flipped the wrappings back to reveal a sheathed sword; the scabbard the largest she'd ever laid eyes on, intricately inlaid with two different colored metals. Rasti took out the weapon, scabbard and all, and held it with both hands, offering Zephyr the hilt. The blade, when Zephyr finally drew it out—it took a while, it was a long sword—flared and curved, giving the tip of the sword a nearly triangular shape. The woven pattern stamped into the metal above the guard writhed in the firelight.

Zephyr's gaze traced the edge of the blade as he held it aloft.

Urion came to the back of the wagon. He shot Rasti a frown. "Where did you get a dragon sword?"

Rasti watched Zephyr turn the sword this way and that, admiring it in the light. "I had one lying around."

Urion's chin dipped. "Your dragon retired."

"That he did." Rasti set the scabbard aside in the wagon. "It probably needs sharpening. I've got a stone around here somewhere. It will give you something to do on watch."

Later they sat around the fire, the crackling of the flames mixed with the sound of Zephyr running the stone along the edge of the sword.

Zephyr broke the silence. "This is a fine blade."

Urion, wrapped in his cloak, pulled it tighter around himself. "It is, but I wonder what happened to its previous owner, since dragons hold on to their swords when they retire."

Zephyr continued sharpening the blade, though he glanced up.

Moira peered through the flames at Rasti, who watched the wood burn. "I thought you said he retired."

Rasti crossed his arms. "My last dragon retired, yes."

"Last dragon? How many have you had?" Moira couldn't imagine working so closely with more than one. *One's enough.*

Rasti sighed. "Two." He sniffed. "That's life in the legion. Battle dragons get sick, injured, or even die. Dragoneers, too."

"What happened?" Zephyr asked, still working the stone down the blade.

Moira was glad he did. It would be harder for Rasti to ignore him. Her dragon had a way of making himself heard, even if he wasn't being loud.

Rasti glanced at the dragon sword in Zephyr's hands and then stared into the fire. "He died."

Zephyr stopped sharpening the sword and waited.

Rasti cleared his throat. "Ibsen and I were together for eight years. We fought back-to-back at the border and all over the Freelands. One summer we had to go to the outer isles. A fleet of fifteen got us there, two dragons to a boat." One corner of his mouth quirked upward, there and gone. "Anyway. We were a long way from home when it happened. Ibsen and two other dragons came down with a fever, lost their appetites, couldn't keep anything down. They were just the start. The sickness ran through the rest of the wyverns. One night, Ibsen went to sleep and didn't wake up. He slipped into a coma and died a few days later. He would have gladly fought a thousand trolls and died in battle happily as opposed to going in his sleep like that. We lost him and five more besides." Rasti picked up a twig and tossed it into the flames. "Nothing anyone could do."

He spoke the last part firmly, as if he'd told himself this many times. Whether he believed it, Moira questioned. The sense of fresh loss in his voice suggested otherwise.

"In the legion, you make adjustments and keep fighting. We lost dragoneers too. Back at our garrison, they paired me up with old Horatio. His dragoneer died of a lung infection." Rasti stared into the fire. "Thankfully, our time together was brief. He retired within a year, and I couldn't see staying on when my term ended." He paused with a glance at Zephyr.

He didn't have to say it, but Moira knew. Rasti couldn't see himself staying on in the legions without Ibsen.

Rasti crossed his legs at the ankle. "I didn't want to buy a farm. So I went to Farrago to join the city's sentinels. Horatio returned to the village that helped raise him and his dragoneer. That's where he's been ever since. He's content there, happy to sow seeds and bring in the harvest when the time comes."

"The village raised a dragon?" Moira asked.

Rasti crossed his arms. "You don't have that where you're from? It's a lengthy process to receive approval. Not many do it."

"Why not?" Moira asked.

"You need space for a growing dragon and the means of feeding one. The wyverns need training and a properly trained dragoneer to match. They have to attend the tournaments at the capital for assignment to an appropriate legion."

"That sounds like a lot," Moira said.

"It's a bit of an investment, but it's worth it to the village."

Urion stretched his legs out in front of him with a yawn. "He's talking about taxes."

Moira glanced from Rasti to Urion and back. "There are tax breaks for raising a dragon?"

Rasti tipped his head forward. "Tax breaks?" He raised his brows. "That's an interesting way of putting it, but yes. Raising a battle dragon exempts the village from the legion tax. If the harvest is good for several years then it makes sense."

Moira took a moment to consider the vast infrastructure needed to raise a dragon from an egg to adulthood. "You said Horatio returned to the village that raised him *and* his dragoneer."

Rasti uncrossed his legs to prop his elbows on his knees. "His dragoneer was an orphan, as most of us were in my day." He shrugged as if his being an orphan was simply a fact of life. "Now and then, you'd get a boy who showed up wanting to be a dragoneer, but his family would get to him, talk him out of it. Nowadays a few more families allow their younger children to train. Even if they don't join the legions, it's good to have someone around who knows wyverns. They can help with the retirees, like Horatio." His gaze returned to the fire. "Truth is, Belcrief could use one back in Farrago. I've been doing what I can, but he needs someone dedicated to his health and well-being."

"And anyone can be a dragoneer, even girls?"

Urion snorted. "Obviously."

Rasti lifted a brow at Urion. "There were a few in my legion, and their numbers have only increased with time."

Moira remembered how Lord Smew had come to Farrago looking for a girl and her dragon. She was glad her situation was not unique, and he would have to do some searching to determine she wasn't among those in or around the city. "What about female dragons? Are there any of them in the legions?" she asked.

"The only female dragons I know of who serve the legions are freemartins, unable to produce viable eggs."

Urion yawned again, louder this time. "Right. Are you two going to talk all night?"

"One more thing," Moira said.

Urion groaned, which made Rasti smile. Zephyr picked up the stone and went back to sharpening his sword.

"What did you say to Grig to get him to stay behind? He looked ready to jump in the wagon with us."

"Aye, I think he was, but he's a little young yet," Rasti said. "I told him the truth. If he wants to be a dragoneer, there's no reason he can't be. If he feels the same in a few years, I told him to present himself to the sentinels in Farrago and ask for me. I have connections." He unfolded his arms and raised a fist to his mouth, capturing a yawn. "Time to turn in. You and the dragon are up first. Wake Urion in a couple of hours to take over." He pulled his cloak around himself and settled on the pallet he'd made near the fire earlier.

"Good night," Moira said.

Rasti grunted. Urion was already snoring lightly.

Zephyr ran the stone down the blade one last time and set it aside. He checked the edge with the edge of his thumb and nodded to himself in a satisfied way. Then he set the sword down within easy reach.

Moira was glad they had the first shift. Her mind turned over what she'd heard. She threw more wood on the fire. Sparks floated upward, then disappeared.

Her thoughts kept circling back to the fact that Rasti was an orphan. It wasn't something she expected them to have in common. Moira didn't usually think of herself in those terms, but the word applied. Her parents were gone. Fortunately, she'd never been without her Aunt Paige's guardianship. But aside from Aaron and Ansel, Zephyr was her only reminder of home, and he wasn't even from there.

Zephyr shifted beside her, and she caught him glancing at the sword. "It is a fine weapon." His voice purred so low she wondered if he had spoken at all, but their link still malfunctioned. "I hope I am worthy of it."

Moira kept her voice low in reply. "I don't think Rasti would have given it to you if he didn't think so."

Those were the last words they spoke until it was time to rouse Urion, who grumbled but awoke without trouble. When Moira curled up next to Zephyr, her head pillowed on her arm, she had no problem falling asleep. The trouble was staying that way.

23

It must have been the fire. The light flared and flickered against her eyelids. Moira blinked her eyes open, expecting to find Urion adding more wood to the fire, while Zephyr snored next to her.

Instead, she gripped the arms of the chair where she sat in front of a roaring fire. Her gaze darted to and away from the fire in the grate, but the light it shed flared, affecting her vision. Her heart pounded. Where was she? The chairs, the fireplace, there was something about them. She focused on their familiarity and found herself back in Lord Q's office. But she'd never physically sat in the chairs, which meant…

Copernicus 'You can call me Cal' Stumble sat in the chair across from her. He wore the same robes as before, along with the visage that didn't belong to him. "Hello again," he said.

Moira glanced around, but there was nothing to see. "Hi." It was just the chairs, the fire, and them. The fireplace wasn't even in a wall, but freestanding; everything else was cloaked in darkness. "What's going on?"

"You have questions."

Her gaze snapped to his. "I'm doing this?"

He shrugged, his hands raised, palms up.

"I'm doing this," she repeated. Her muscles tensed. "I read your book."

He lowered his hands. "No, you have not. You read a version of my book. The original is quite different. A plethora of additions, deletions, and other alterations have resulted in a work that no longer reflects my initial prose."

"Um. Okay. I get that now. Do you know what's wrong with the connection between me and Zephyr?"

Cal paused. "When a dragon bites a human, we have learned it connects them in such a way as to allow the human access to the wyvern's intrinsic natural magic and abilities. Little is known about this phenomenon, as dragon bites are a rare occurrence."

Moira jammed her head back against the chair to stare up into the darkness. "Tell me something I don't know."

"The naming of the dragon appears to be an important ritual. Similarly, the acceptance of the name by the wyvern helps cement the relationship. There may exist other aspects related to the dragon's ultimate choice of dragoneer, but these are also as yet unknown."

She made a disgusted sound. "This is not helping. I need to know how to fix the connection between me and my dragon."

"You suffer from a block."

Her head came off the back of the chair. "How do I get rid of it?"

Cal steepled his fingertips over his lap. "Discover the root of the block. Come to terms with it. This will restore your connection."

"Oh, is that all?" He seemed to know she didn't expect an answer to that one. He was in her head, after all. She sat forward. "Tell me about the two brothers bitten by the two dragons."

Cal smiled. "They were twins."

Moira frowned. "The brothers? Or the dragons?"

"The brothers."

Once upon a time, two dragons bit twin brothers. Something still didn't sit right, but she couldn't put her finger on what was bothering her.

"What happened to them?" she asked.

A log shifted in the fire, throwing up a shower of sparks. She glanced that way to find the fireplace gone. She lay on her back, hands folded across her torso. Zephyr was curled up beside her, creating a tall hummock. The sky was dark overhead, and Urion, still on watch, stood at the edge of the firelight. She couldn't have been asleep long. She rolled to her side and closed her eyes, thinking about her dream. Or was it a vision? She wasn't sure.

Whatever part of her subconscious that interfaced with the book in her mind was trying to tell her something. Her connection with Zephyr suffered from a block on her end. If she knew what kind of block it was, she could get rid of it, but the book couldn't tell her that. *There has to be a way.* She thought of Cal as she struggled to get back to sleep, hoping to have more of her questions answered, but when she drifted off, she slept straight through the rest of the night.

***

The next morning Rasti fit Zephyr with a long, wide leather belt for the dragon sword. Zephyr put both aside before they set off; he rode in the back of the wagon to give his feet a break. Urion alternated between walking and jumping up in the back next to Zephyr.

Moira rode next to Rasti, working to keep a larger rock than the one she'd used the day before in the air in front of her as they traveled down the road. The rock tumbled and jerked, but she could glance away from it and it wouldn't fall. Her skills were improving, as the mental muscle needed to keep the rock in the air and do other things grew stronger.

Rasti said nothing at first, as was his way, she was discovering. Then he asked, "What would you do if your dragon got sick?"

Moira glanced away from the rock. "How sick?"

"What if someone poisoned him? Would you know what to do?"

She caught the rock as it fell out of the air. "No. And who would want to poison Zephyr?"

Rasti cast her a look from the side of his eye. "Who would want to poison you?"

"Hmm. Good point."

"Much easier to poison him than kill him in a fight, that's for sure. The good news is dragons typically have a hardy constitution, but some stronger poisons could bring him down. What you would do is check his gums." He told her what color they were supposed to be and what color they would become if someone poisoned her dragon.

Moira stared at him. "Should I be writing this down? I feel like I should write this down."

"Probably." Rasti transferred the reins to one hand and twisted on the seat. "Hand me that bag there." Moira lifted an oilskin bag free from behind the seat. Rasti passed her the reins and opened the bag, searching. He came up with a small bound book and a feathered pen connected to a vial of ink. "You can use these." He handed them over and took back the reins.

Moira yearned for a ballpoint pen. It took her a while to learn how to adjust the flow on the vial of ink to stop leaving splotches as she wrote, but she figured it out, which was good because there were a lot of notes. They moved on from poisoning, and Moira learned the best place to check Zephyr's temperature was the skin between his shoulder blades. A dragon always showed signs of a fever there first. She could check his pulse by pressing two fingers to the large artery behind his scaled ear that sat flush against his head. His resting heart rate should be anywhere between 40 and 50 beats per minute. Rasti didn't stop at physical ailments but offered her important information on the mental health of dragons, such as the five signs of a sulky dragon and how she might bring Zephyr out of it.

"My secret weapon with Ibsen was always hapshulyc, the spicier the better. Spreading some of that on a fat loaf of bread would always bring him around."

"Ah, the way to a dragon's heart is through his stomach?"

"Ha. I like that." Rasti blinked, his expression sobering. "You don't want to be around a starving dragon. It may be different for you being dragon-bit, but it's a dangerous position for anyone, including dragoneers." He stared at the backs of the horses working to pull the wagon down the road. "Ibsen and I spent one winter stationed on the northern border. The enemy attacked our supply routes. We ran out of everything, including hapshulyc. There was hardly a noodle to be found. Halfway through winter and game scarce, they ordered all of the dragons into the hills so they wouldn't eat the horses. That's when a horde of imps attacked. Ibsen took a mace to the side before we could drive them back. Nothing life-threatening,

but his wounds needed tending before they got infected."
He paused.

"What happened?"

Rasti pursed his lips and exhaled. "There was a lot of hissing. And the occasional snap, but I didn't get eaten. Afterward, a few of us hiked to the next valley. They thought we'd deserted, but we only went hunting. When we came back with a handful of rabbits, the commander looked the other way. It was enough to tide our dragons over until the resupply came through. But if that had been me and Horatio? Not sure I would have all my limbs."

Moira glanced into the back of the wagon. "What you're saying is we have plenty of food."

"Yes, plenty. We'll resupply in Goodramtown. There's not much beyond that. Once we ford the river to cross the border from the Freelands to the Fells, it's on to Castle Tern."

Moira frowned. "About that." She told him about the peddler she'd overheard at the town well. "How are we going to get to the castle if they're stopping and searching wagons? It doesn't sound like there are a lot of dragons to blend in with."

"We know they've cast a wide net for you. Searching wagons as they come in isn't new, but it sounds like they're looking for something specific a peddler might have. You're right, there aren't many dragons in the Fells. Castle Tern is as far as they travel, and they do not linger. We're fortunate Zephyr is so stealthy. I'll think about it. What do you know about talons?"

"Not much," she said, struck off balance by the *non sequitur*. She told Rasti about fixing a smaller split talon for Zephyr with duct tape, which required an in-depth description. Afterward, she filled several more pages with notes about dragon-talon care before they stopped for a quick meal. Zephyr got down from the wagon and Moira followed, happy to take a break from note-taking.

Urion stood at ease, staring at the side of the road.

Rasti offered him an apple.

Urion waved it away. "I want some berries. Do you want some berries?" Without waiting for an answer, he plunged into the overgrowth alongside the road, sinking up to his knees in vines and brush. He pushed through, using his sword to clear his way to a taller bush set back from the roadside. Once there, he sheathed his sword and began picking at it, loading whatever he gathered into the reservoir he made of the front of his shirt.

They all watched him while they ate, Rasti chuckling. When Urion returned, his shirt full of mulberries, Rasti's chuckle turned into an outright laugh.

Moira didn't get it. "What's so funny?"

Urion offered her some. "Ignore him."

Moira accepted a few berries and popped them in her mouth. They were delicious and a welcome change from what they'd been eating. "Mmm, good!"

Rasti laughed harder.

Moira shook her head at his amusement and smiled to herself. "What is going on?"

Rasti's laughter trailed off. "This one decides he wants berries, and, of course, there are sweet berries, ripe for the plucking in the exact place we randomly decide to stop along the way. He's just so damn—"

Urion shot him a glare. "Don't say it."

"—lucky," Rasti said, huffing a last laugh as he shook his head.

24

Urion pulled out his sword for a sparring match after they made camp. The practice brought to mind past training sessions with Bertram. And that brought Ansel to mind. From there, it was a quick leap to Aaron and what had happened, along with a staggering sense of helplessness. Her chest heaving in panic, she had to stop, overwhelmed by the prospect of where she was, why she was there, and what she was supposed to do. Urion stared. Zephyr put his own practice aside to help her with her breathing until she could regain some composure.

Moira pulled herself together. "Sorry." They resumed sparring.

With the past fresh in her mind, she was glad Bertram had trained her to use her magic when firing arrows, because her sword skills needed work. She struggled to move beyond the basics. The only way she would know if she was good enough was if she lived. Urion was patient, but he wasn't a natural at teaching the way Bertram had been. Still, she kept at it until it was time to eat the deer Zephyr had hunted and Rasti prepared, along with the ubiquitous noodles.

As they sat around the fire. Moira's thoughts turned to her aunt's desserts. "You don't have any more of those berries left, do you?"

Urion glared. "You know I don't."

A low chuckle escaped Rasti. Urion turned his glare on him, making Rasti laugh harder.

What am I missing? Moira shared a glance with a frowning Zephyr. "Please tell us what's so funny."

Urion sneered. "Do you want to tell them, old man?"

Rasti rocked backward and forward. "No, I'm sorry. I'll stop. Please." His laughter died, though he still smiled. He waved his hand at Urion to speak.

Urion heaved a sigh. He stared into the fire. "My father was a powerful magician. Some would say the most powerful magician in the Freelands and the Fells. He carried the pointy hat with pride. Not like that Lord Smew in Farrago." He glanced in her direction. "Remember? He couldn't quite pull it off."

"I remember." Moira recalled seeing the pointed hat hanging from Smew's belt. She also recalled Cal wearing one.

Urion resumed staring into the flames. "My father did many great things in the name of the Freelands before he retired. Very smart man, my father. Most magicians die horrible deaths. Anyway. One of his escapades landed him in Faerie, where he encountered the queen. He was powerless to resist her. They had a... I wouldn't call it a relationship. Let's say... an interlude. That resulted in me. For whatever reason, she saw the pregnancy through. I believe my coming into being was a novel experience for her. Once she had me, she didn't know what to do with me." He stopped and blinked into the firelight.

"What did she do with you?" asked Moira.

Urion sighed. "Please understand, my mother isn't evil. She's simply not human." He gave his head a tiny shake, as if to clear his thoughts. "Somehow my father convinced her to let him have me. He escaped and raised me away from my mother and Faerie. Of course, then he had to curse me."

Moira's brow puckered. "You just said your father rescued you. Why would he curse you?"

"He didn't mean to. What he did was bless me. With luck."

Moira still didn't follow. "He blessed you by making you lucky?"

"He cursed me with good fortune."

Moira glanced around the fire. Rasti smirked, but maintained his silence. Zephyr stroked his scaled chin.

Moira shook her head. "Being lucky doesn't sound like a curse."

Urion turned to her, his brows arched. "Doesn't it? Shall I remind you of how we met? Do you think I wanted to be thrown into a cage at a crossroads?"

She pondered his question. *Attacked and left for dead. Used to break an unwanted engagement. Imprisoned. Right. Not such good luck after all.* Her brows went up at the implications of what he was saying.

"So, you see," Urion nodded at her, "I can act at my discretion, but only insofar as my luck will let me."

Moira frowned. "Then how are you even here right now?"

Urion lifted a single brow. "I think you mean why."

"Okay. Why then?"

Urion raised both shoulders. "Perhaps because I owe you a life debt? I don't know." He relaxed. "Was it my luck that brought you to my aid? I can't say. Nor can I say what will happen when it runs its course." He made a slashing motion with one hand. "But try not to think about it too hard. You'll give yourself a headache. I know I do." The way his jaw clenched told her he'd thought about it far too much already and, Moira figured, countless other scenarios besides. Urion had reason to question everything that had ever happened to him. She imagined it would indeed cause his head to ache.

She considered this new information. "Your father's a retired magician, and your mother is the queen of the fae. Does that make you, like, royalty?"

Rasti snorted.

Urion answered, his voice flat, "I'm a halfling. Nothing more."

"Are there others like you?"

"Some. It's not unheard of for the female fae to bring a birth to term."

Rasti crossed his arms. "Imps are far more likely."

Zephyr lowered his hand from his chin. "You are an imp?"

Urion leaned forward, elbows on his knees, his fingers interlaced. "No. My mother was fae. Imps come from a male fae and a female human."

"Like the imp general?" Moira asked.

Rasti sat up straight, his expression fierce. "Imp general? What are you talking about?"

Moira shared the overheard words of Vinton, the High Magician, from what seemed so long ago.

Rasti looked from her to Urion. "Lord Quintillius knows of this?"

"I told him," Urion said.

Rasti uncrossed his arms and pushed himself off the log. He paced, irritation clear in every step. "This is worse than I thought. Possibly worse than anyone knows."

"Agreed," said Urion.

"What?" She looked from Urion to Rasti. "What is it?"

Rasti stopped and swung around to face her. "It could be nothing, but if the High Magician of Castle Tern has an imp general..."

"That would be bad." Urion's deadpan delivery matched his slumped posture. "For several reasons."

Zephyr shifted beside her. "What does an imp look like? We have not seen one."

"They're brutes," Rasti said. "Roughly man-sized, they can be aggressive, fearsome warriors. Typically they organize themselves into small raiding parties, but nothing larger than ten or a dozen fighters at most. Anything larger than that is rare, but if they have an imp general, they could have an imp army."

Rasti's chin jerked to the side. "I'll make more inquiries in Goodramtown. Won't be long. We've kept the wheels turning." But Rasti still looked worried. "How is it a full-grown dragon and his dragoneer know so little?"

Moira and Zephyr exchanged a quick glance. "We're not from anywhere near here. We're very far from home."

Rasti raised his gaze to hers. "Where is that?"

Moira considered how much to say. "Another place. More like another... world."

Rasti blinked as if trying to come to terms with what she was telling them.

"Like Faerie?" Urion asked.

Moira squinted, her head tipped to the side. "Not really. There's little magic and few dragoneers." *One dragoneer, to be exact.* "And what dragons exist are small. Zephyr only grew when we got here."

Rasti's gaze swept over Zephyr. "And why are you here?"

"The captain of the trolls, this Vinton, kidnapped my friends because he thought one of them was Zephyr's dragoneer. We're going to get them back."

Rasti said nothing more, nor did he run screaming into the night. Either way, maybe it was Urion's luck rubbing off on them.

They slept in shifts again and for the next three nights as they continued their journey west to Goodramtown.

At some point most days, Moira wound up sitting next to Rasti, taking notes about dragons. She asked questions and filled page after page in the notebook he'd given her. Then she reviewed the notes she'd taken when she wasn't walking with Zephyr, whose feet were toughening up nicely, or practicing with Urion, studying the material as if she expected to be tested.

At night, after dinner, Zephyr and Moira would stay up to take the first shift together while the other two turned in. They never talked much, not wanting to keep Rasti or Urion from their rest.

These were the times Moira focused on the connection between her and Zephyr, trying to figure out how to repair it. She would quiet her mind and reach out to Zephyr, but when she looked at him for confirmation, he would meet her eyes with a shake of his head. Moira would fall asleep each night expecting to meet Cal again in her dreams, but the book in her head remained silent. Not even her subconscious could make a connection.

And it was getting worse. She encouraged Zephyr to reach out to her with everything he had, but nothing came through unless they were in direct physical contact. Even then, his missives were like trying to tune into a radio station whose signal was mostly static.

She could tell Zephyr didn't appreciate being cut off from her, but she tried not to let her worry about their connection show. Aside from when he hunted, he rarely left her side or her sight. Often, she caught him watching her. She would smile when she caught his eye, but sometimes she couldn't. Inevitably, he would bump her with his shoulder.

The first time sent her sprawling. After that he was gentler, the action always followed by a mention of the weather or the food, his attempt to draw her out and gauge her mood. She knew what he was trying to do and always responded, reassuring him she was as fine as she could be, given their circumstances. She couldn't forget how far they were from home and what they were after, but those thoughts often got pushed aside to deal with problems they had at the moment. Still, their lack of connection provided proof that getting their friends back was going to take more than the two of them.

The morning of the day they were due to reach Goodramtown, Moira asked Rasti what to expect when they got there. He told her he wanted her and Zephyr to help him load supplies while Urion refilled the water. Then he would retrieve any replies to the letter he'd sent.

Goodramtown turned out to be the biggest town they had seen since Farrago. No gate or sentinels surrounded the busy place, but people filled the streets going about their business. Urion left to find water while Moira and Zephyr helped load Rasti's purchases onto the wagon. Urion still hadn't returned by the time they were done. Rasti drove them to a building that bore the familiar shingle of a bird carved into it. While he crossed the road to go inside and check for a reply to his message about the location of the Light Legion, Moira sat up front, holding the reins. Zephyr came to stand beside her. The two of them people-watched and dragon-watched. There were a lot of the former but few of the latter.

Across the street, a man strolled past. He caught sight of them, his head twisting. He stopped and stared.

Moira frowned and shifted in her seat. "Zephyr..."

The man turned and entered the door Rasti had gone through. Moments later, Rasti emerged with a small envelope, and Urion appeared ahead of them carrying the water skins.

Urion hurried to her side of the wagon. "Pull up your hood. We've got trouble."

25

Moira raised the hood of her cloak as Urion rushed around Zephyr to the back of the wagon, where he flung the full water skins inside.

Rasti climbed up next to her and took the reins.

Urion jumped in and scrambled over the crates to the front seat. "We've got to get out of here," Urion said. "I'll explain once we're out of town. Keep your hood up and your face covered."

There was enough room in the streets for Zephyr to walk beside them, but at Urion's words, he fell in behind the wagon. His sword was in the back. Rasti hadn't thought it a good idea for him to carry the weapon through the streets of town. A dragon with a sword could attract unwanted attention. People might question where the rest of his legion was located. Zephyr had laid the weapon in the back with reluctance and hadn't been far from it since.

Urion glanced at everyone they passed in the street while Rasti drove with purpose. They made it through town, subjected to more than a few long stares, but nothing more. Outside of town, they stopped in a secluded grove off the main road.

Zephyr took his sword from the back and belted it around his waist.

Urion handed Moira her bow from the back. She took it without comment.

Rasti watched. "What's happened?"

Urion didn't answer right away, handing Moira her quiver of arrows along with her backpack with all her clothes (old and new), the rock pick, and Vinton's dagger. Urion set on his lap the sword Rasti had given him. "Wanted posters. When I went to fetch the water, Moira's likeness was on display at every turn. She and a young dragon who might be Master Zephyr."

Moira's mouth fell open. *What has Ansel done?*

"No telling how long the posters have been up, but they didn't look old. They asked for written word of any sightings to be sent to Castle Tern. Best to be prepared from here on out." Urion passed her her sword and jumped down to buckle on his own.

"We might be too late." Moira told them about the man outside the building where Rasti had stopped to check for messages. She pointed to Rasti's chest. "What's in the envelope?"

Rasti pulled it from inside his cloak. "Good news, perhaps. My contact suggests we'll find the Light Legion after we cross the border into the Fells."

Urion's head jerked back. A look passed between him and Rasti.

"What are we walking into over there?" Moira asked. She put on her sword and slipped the one remaining strap from her backpack over her head alongside her quiver. Her bow she carried.

Urion turned to her. "You know a little of it already. When the prince was eight years old, the true king of Castle Tern died. The queen died not long after, leaving the prince and his younger sister on their own. The High Magician proposed the king's advisor as Regent until Prince Owen would come of age at eighteen and assume the throne."

Rasti harrumphed. "Everyone agreed to it. They knew what they were doing, and they did it anyway."

Urion's chin dipped. "The King's advisor also has a son, Lord Hedrick, a little younger than the prince."

Rasti glowered. "When the Regent dies, and he will, it's only a matter of time, the High Magician will install Lord Hedrick on the throne... until he can find a way to dispose of him and take it for himself."

Urion's expression turned grim. "Many fear it is as he says."

Rasti held the envelope aloft. "Prince Owen is gathering an army to take back the crown. Few have rallied to his call, but more arrive each day. If the High Magician has grown an army of imps, he has good reason." He took the envelope in both hands and tore it down the middle. "But if the Light Legion is in the Fells, then Owen may have more help than he knows." Rasti tore it again and again into tinier and tinier pieces of unreadable confetti.

It sounded as if they were walking into a decade-long struggle for power. *Just add one dragon and dragoneer, then stir.* A messy predicament, for sure. "As far as we know, Ansel and Aaron are at Castle Tern." She looked at Zephyr. "We just want to get our friends and go home."

Zephyr dipped his head once to show he agreed. She didn't miss the way he palmed the handle of his sword, however.

"I will help in any way I can." Urion fingered the chain around his neck.

Rasti peered at all three of them.

"Zephyr has a gift for stealth," Moira said. "We'll find a way into Castle Tern, get our friends, and go home." The plan sounded oversimplified even to her ears, but they had to start somewhere.

Rasti looked as if he'd just had to swallow something that didn't want to go down. "Yes, but Imagine what you could learn from the dragons and dragoneers of the Light Legion."

"We don't have time," Moira replied.

"Plans might have to change."

Moira exhaled in a rush. "I understand, but our friends are in danger. We have to keep moving."

"Aye, we do. Good thing I've figured out a way to get you into the castle, but you won't like it."

His words made her stomach take a dip. "Why is that?"

"It'll depend heavily on Zephyr's abilities to get you out again. We can discuss it later. As you say, we need to keep moving." Rasti flicked the reins. The horses began walking again.

Moira and Urion walked behind the wagon, alongside Zephyr. Moira's thoughts turned to what could go wrong. There were too many scenarios to count. The ones where they couldn't find Aaron or Ansel or didn't get to them in time made her breath catch and her chest ache. Those were too awful to contemplate. She pushed her thoughts aside and put one foot in front of the other, trying not to borrow trouble. There was no way of knowing what would happen until they reached the castle.

No one traveled in the same direction as them. They passed people with carts full of home goods headed away from the Fells who murmured amongst themselves. Their tone was worried, agitated. Moira kept her hood raised and her head down.

When they had passed no one for some time, Moira thought she might be able to lower her hood.

Urion's head snapped up. He peered down the road behind them, and then forward. "We should be close. I thought we would hear the river by now." No birds sang from the trees on either side of the road. The creak of the wagon trundling ahead of them and their footsteps were all that filled the silence.

A troll stepped out from beneath the canopy of trees onto the road in front of the wagon. At least seven feet tall, with shoulders a meter wide, heavy leather armor covered most of its orange-tinted skin.

Rasti brought the horses to a stop with a soft, "Whoa." One squealed and stomped while the other snorted, shifting, dragging the cart sideways.

Moira and Urion stopped behind the wagon. Zephyr stood close to them. Moira scanned the trees. Two. Three. Four. The more she looked, the more trolls stepped out of the forest, sporting a wide variety of unnatural coloring, from yellow to grayish-blue to purple. Two more trolls of equal height joined the first to block the road. Of the others, some were taller than Moira, but she didn't consider any of them short. These trolls differed from any she'd ever come across before. Never had she seen so many, nor so organized. If Moira and the rest of them hadn't been upwind, she was sure they would have smelled them first. Now it was too late to run or hide or have Zephyr use his camouflage.

An ache radiated down her right arm. She'd taken an arrow to it the night they confronted Vinton, the captain of the trolls. Zephyr had helped heal her wound when he returned to her side. Moira tightened her grip on her bow in her left hand but kept it at her side. Her right hand curled into a fist as she peered into the woods on either side of the road, searching the shadows and the trees. Beads of sweat sprang out across her forehead.

The troll who stepped in front of the wagon spoke. "What business?"

"I'm away to the Fells to sell my wares." Rasti gestured at the back of the wagon. "Along the southern route."

The troll's lip lifted in a sneer, displaying a mouth full of sharp broken teeth. "No peddler I know of travels with a dragon."

They don't recognize Zephyr. They wouldn't. He had grown since the last time Ansel or Vinton had seen him. Moira pursed her lips.

"The dragon is my nephew's. They travel with me for protection before they join the Legions."

Did Rasti really think they were going to talk their way past this little roadblock?

"Protection?" the troll asked. "What good is one worm?" Laughter rolled through their ranks. Finished expressing their mirth, their leader focused on her. "Who else travels with you?"

"My other nephew," Rasti said.

Beside her, Moira sensed rather than saw Urion tense.

"Tell him to lower his hood."

Moira had not changed nearly as much as Zephyr. As soon as she lowered her hood, they would know she was the dragoneer they sought. Maybe she should have considered straightening her curls. Or cutting her hair.

Nah.

"Nephew," Rasti called. "Show yourself."

Moira raised her free hand to reach for her hood, slowly at first, but kept on reaching until her fingertips grazed the feather of an arrow in her quiver.

Several trolls hissed.

This was all the signal Rasti needed. He slapped the reins against the horse's backs with a shout. One horse reared. The troll who'd done the talking jumped clear and went sprawling out of the way as opposed to getting trampled when the wagon shot forward. As she watched the wagon recede from view, an arrow sank into the tailgate, sending an icy cold spear of dread down her back.

Moira finished pulling her arrow free and ducked.

Another arrow flew over her head and bounced harmlessly off of Zephyr's scales. His hand landed on her shoulder. "Go!"

Moira didn't have to be told twice. She dodged in the direction the arrows had come from. Around them, too many trolls to count drew their swords. So did Urion, just in time to stop a troll from slicing him in two. Zephyr took out a spray of trolls with a sweep of his tail, sending at least one hard into a tree. The others crashed to the ground. More trolls rushed forward to take their places.

That is, until Zephyr pulled his dragon sword free of the scabbard. The trolls in front stopped so abruptly the ones behind ran into them. Moira wondered if they might be reevaluating how dangerous they thought one dragon could be plus any other poor life decisions that had led them to this point.

Under the trees, the sound of Moira's breathing filled her ears, but it didn't drown out the fight taking place on the road. Zephyr roared. She recognized it for the battle cry it was and kept moving. Moira positioned herself behind a tree, and peeked around it with caution. The fight raged on. The wagon was nowhere in sight.

If I were a troll, where would I be? Seeing nothing on the ground, she lifted her gaze. There. In the split of a tree stood an archer, bow raised, ready to fire. Moira didn't hesitate. She stepped out and released her arrow with a pinch of her will. The troll tumbled to the ground and didn't move.

Edging through the trees, Moira monitored the fight. Zephyr cut swaths through the troll's ranks with sweep after sweep of his dragon sword. The trolls that survived scattered long enough to regroup and try again. Zephyr met them each time, decimating their numbers. Across the road from him, Urion took on a much larger opponent, deftly insinuating himself inside his attacker's reach and dealing wound after wound until the troll fell. As soon as it did, another moved to take its place. Urion took on that one too, but didn't see the troll behind him.

Moira fired from amongst the trees. The troll sank out of sight. The rest surged forward, crowding Zephyr and Urion together, forcing them to fight back-to-back. This wouldn't have been so bad, except for Zephyr's tail. Urion avoided it as best he could, but it was only a matter of time. Moira watched as Zephyr's tail swept the halfling's feet out from beneath him, which was when she saw the arrow fly through where Urion had been standing a moment before. Crouching low, Moira turned back to the trees in search of the other archer. This one stood next to a tree. She fired. The troll fell to the ground with a clatter.

On the road, the three largest trolls unsheathed their swords. They had hung back, waiting for this moment. Their fellows had taken the brunt of Zephyr and Urion's initial attack to wear them down. It had worked. Zephyr took a halting step forward, limping slightly. Urion's nose bled. The troll that had done all the talking stood back and let the other two stride ahead of him, leading from the rear.

As the two trolls went for Zephyr, Moira fired at their leader. Her arrow found its mark in his chest. She didn't think that would be enough to stop it, and it wasn't. But as the troll turned, another arrow protruded from between its shoulder blades. Up the road, Rasti lowered his bow. The troll fell to the dirt, and Rasti hurried forward, drawing another arrow as he did.

Moira did the same.

A shout sounded at the lead troll's demise. "Archers!"

Zephyr continued to fight, arrows having little effect on his scaled hide. The rest of them did not have the same advantage. Urion took what cover he could, while Rasti continued to run toward the fray. Moira slipped behind a tree and kept her eyes on the fight. An arrow sprang from the dirt next to Urion, making him curl into a ball. Another sprouted from the ground near Rasti's running heels. They came from the other side of the road. She'd taken care of the pair of archers on her side. Rasti shouted for Urion and ran for the trees where the shots come from. The halfling sprang to his feet and sprinted into the trees.

Moira fired at one of the several trolls harrying her dragon, hitting it in its sword arm. It roared in either pain or frustration, but did not let up. Though Zephyr had three feet of height and a longer reach, the trolls still outnumbered him. Moira kept firing. She didn't stop. Not until, between the two of them, the last trolls fell to the ground.

When nothing else attacked, Moira turned to the trees where Urion and Rasti had disappeared, her bow raised. Urion limped into view. He went to wipe his bloodied nose on his sleeve, seemed to think better of it, and wiped his sweaty forehead instead.

"Where's Rasti?" Moira asked.

"Here." The old dragoneer stepped out of the trees, his bow at his side.

Moira relaxed enough to lower her hood.

Zephyr peered into the gloom under the trees. "Any more?"

Rasti shook his head. "No. Best not to linger. The wagon's just down the road."

The four of them set off with Moira next to Zephyr inspecting his scales, confirming he was unhurt for herself.

"Interesting strategy back there," Rasti commented when they reached the wagon.

"What's that?" Moira asked.

"Dragoneers rarely leave their dragon's side in the middle of a fight."

Moira didn't know what to say. Zephyr had been the one to tell her to go, so she went. She had thought nothing of it.

"You still had your hood up," Rasti said. "They must not have recognized you, otherwise things could have gone very differently. Instead, they thought Zephyr the greater threat."

Urion coughed. "From what I saw, Master Zephyr was the superior threat."

Moira thought so, too.

"It worked out that way," Rasti said. "Had Moira stayed, they would have known she was the one they sought and done everything to capture her." He turned to Zephyr. "If that had happened, how much of a threat would you have been then?"

Zephyr, trying to clean the blood from his blade, said nothing, but Moira saw the way his tail drooped. His only comment was a slight hum under his breath.

"You confused them," Rasti told Zephyr. "Well done. Let's get going."

Urion sighed. "Yes. Let us continue toward even more certain danger."

Rasti drove the wagon while the rest of them remained on foot. Wary of further attacks, they kept silent and remained alert. A few minutes later, they came to a river.

Or where a river should have been.

Rasti stopped the wagon. Moira, Zephyr, and Urion came forward to stand beside it. They stared out over a mostly dry riverbed.

Moira could make out where the water should have flowed from right to left. Upstream, the riverbed curved away to the west, and she lost sight of it. Downstream, she could see farther to where the water had deposited large boulders, scouring them smooth. Travelers had worn down the bank in front of them from a sharp bank to a gentler slope. A similarly worn back waited for them on the opposite side, about fifty yards away, making this the widest spot for some distance in either direction. Fording the river here made sense.

If there had been any water in the river.

Instead, there was a silvery stream in the center, a few feet wide.

Urion walked into the riverbed. "Must have been a dry year."

Rasti slapped the reins, urging the horses forward. Their hooves skidded as the wagon bumped its way into the channel. Moira and Zephyr followed. She kept her gaze on the opposite bank. Once they were on the other side, they would be in the Fells. Having seen more trolls than she wanted to already, she didn't know what to expect once they reached the other side. However, nothing moved on the opposite bank.

Urion reached the stream and bent down to submerge his hand in the water. He stood again, using the water to wash the blood from his face. Then he flicked his hand dry and stepped through the stream.

As Urion crossed the water, a ruckus kicked off behind them. Moira stopped and turned. A large flock of birds rose, as one, into the air from the branches of a tree behind them and flew straight over her head toward the wagon.

Rasti brought the horses to a stop at the raucous sound, seeking its source. He doubled over, throwing his hands over his head as the birds rushed the wagon, flapping and squawking, before turning sharply to disappear upriver in a flurry of wings.

The ground beneath Moira's feet trembled.

Rasti sat up straight, arms swinging, to bat away any remaining birds.

On the other side of the stream, Urion braced himself, bending his knees, his focus on the riverbed under his feet.

Zephyr stared at the ground as well. Then his head snapped up and his head turned to the right, the same direction the birds had disappeared.

Moira followed his gaze. She heard it too. A quiet roar grew steadily louder.

The horses reared. Unprepared for the sudden jolt, Rasti lost his hold on the reins. He tumbled out of the seat and hit the ground, rolling clear of the wagon's wheels. The horses raced toward the opposite bank. Urion jumped out of the way as they passed him.

Rasti scrabbled upright, holding his shoulder.

Zephyr went to him.

The deafening roar turned Moira's focus upstream. Dumbstruck at the sight, Moira stood entranced as a wave of water crashed into the bend, spraying high into the air, a glittering mist of droplets above the flood rushing straight for them.

26

There was no time.

A frigid rush of air displaced by the oncoming water blew Moira's hair back. In the instant before impact, she turned toward the far side of the river.

Urion was nowhere to be seen.

The horses and wagon crashed onto the opposite bank.

Rasti lay on the ground, holding his shoulder.

Zephyr had one hand on his sword, the other stretched out toward her. However, she was much too far away for him to reach.

A movement out of the corner of her eye.

She blinked and the wave hit.

The weight of the water smacked her down, but it didn't keep her there. It scooped her up and carried her along, tumbling end over end. Then the shock of the cold paralyzed her. Freezing water filled her eyes and ears and nose. It stung. She couldn't see anything and didn't know if her eyes were open or shut. The water tossed her every which way, but she held her breath. For a moment, she relaxed. It was easy to stop fighting and let the water carry her, going with the flow.

Until her shoulder struck a solid object. Her lips parted. Icy fluid filled her mouth. Panic seized her. She didn't want to drown. In desperation, she kicked, trying to swim, unsure which way was up.

How long had she been under? Fifteen seconds maybe? She thought she could hold her breath for a minute.

The water dragged at her clothes. Her lungs swelled. Her chest burned. She trickled water and air out from between pursed lips. Her teeth clenched. She clawed at the water.

Thirty seconds. She couldn't find the surface. She was drowning and knew it. Her ears roared. Her shoulder hurt. She kicked her legs harder.

Forty-five seconds. She flailed and lashed out, suddenly angry. *I can't die—Zephyr needs me—come on—fight!*

Moira punched at the water. It hissed in her ears. Her head was bursting, her eyes scoured by the water. She couldn't breathe.

A whole minute. She kicked and kicked, but it was no use. Her leg muscles cramped. Everything hurt. Something rough brushed her hand. A branch? A root? She tried to grab it, but it slipped through her numb fingers.

She struggled. She opened her mouth and sucked in water. Her chest spasmed. She tried to cough it out, instead taking in more water. This was it. She kicked once more, giving it everything she had.

It wasn't enough.

Her eyes closed, and the water took her.

Something clamped down hard on her wrist. It yanked on her arm, pulling her into the air. Free of the water, she lost the fight to stay conscious.

Moira rested on the ground. A fire crackled nearby. Her eyelids weighed a ton. With effort she raised one, but closed it again right away to shield it from the flickering campfire light. Her hands rested on her stomach, the fabric under her palms dry. She turned her head away from the firelight and opened her eyes. *Who saved me?*

Night had fallen. Her chest ached from coughing, her stomach hollow from retching. The river's rushing waters gurgled close by. *Where is Zephyr? Urion? Rasti?*

She squinted and turned back. Her eyes widened in recognition. "What are you doing here?" Her voice was little more than a rasp.

The Librarian, sitting by the fire, turned his head toward her. "You should be happy I was available. If you recall, you have something that belongs to me."

"The book," she whispered.

"Yes. The book."

The exchange sapped what little strength she had. Moira closed her eyes again. Dressed in a black tunic, trousers, and cloak instead of a suit, with longer hair and a hint of a beard, the Librarian seemed almost human. Something had ruffled his flawless exterior, breaking his omniscient demeanor.

She may have drifted off, because the next time she opened her eyes, the fire had died back a little, and the light didn't bother her eyes so much. The Librarian still sat across the fire from her, but Cal had joined him.

Cal, wearing the same clothes and face he always did, returned her gaze with a smile.

Moira's chest tightened. His smile reached his eyes, the way it reached her father's in the photo of him at home. "Am I... am I dead?" she asked. Her voice had returned.

An irritated grumble escaped the Librarian. "Not for lack of trying."

Her father—her *father*—shook his head. The firelight wasn't the only thing that shone in his eyes. There was recognition. There was pride. And there was love.

Her eyes welled.

Her father's brows lifted. "I'm never very far away. You have a problem. Tell me."

Moira sucked in a breath, her lungs stinging. *I've got a lot of problems, Dad.* Her broken connection with Zephyr loomed to the forefront of her thoughts. "I'm afraid..."

"Fear is not a bad thing. Sometimes it can be useful. What are you afraid of?"

The breath shuddered out of her. "I've lost Zephyr. He's gone. I can't reach him."

"You're afraid of being alone?"

Is that it?

She could do amazing things because of Zephyr's bite, but could she do anything without him? Did she want to? Her breath came faster and faster and she closed her eyes.

"Listen to me, daughter." Her father's voice soothed her. "You are not alone. It is normal to feel alone or lonely, but you are not actually alone."

Moira blinked her eyes open. She stared up into the night sky, tears rolling past her temples into her hair.

"There's more," he said.

How does he know? Moira didn't want to answer. Words, once said, couldn't be taken back. Yet there was no reason to be anything but truthful. "I don't want to die alone, not like y—" She stopped herself and swallowed back the words, sniffing hard.

"I've got news for you, kiddo," he said. Even by the dim light of the fire, she sensed the smile in his voice. "Everyone dies alone. It's a threshold only one person can cross in their own time, in their own way. When you cross, you do it yourself. No one else can do it for you. But you're not alone now. You don't have to be alone. Not before and not after."

She stared, considering his words. She and Zephyr were connected, but Moira was her own person. There were things she had to do for herself that Zephyr couldn't. Likewise, there were things only Zephyr could do. They were individuals apart, though their link drew them together. Their connection meant they didn't have to be alone. They could exist together, but separate. And though apart, they would always be connected by the link they shared. She sucked in a breath. They would always be together because they chose to be.

"You've got a lot to think about, but you need your rest." Her father smiled again and faced the flames. "We'll keep the fire going until morning. Sleep now. I'll keep watch."

Moira's eyelids drifted shut. The darkness drew itself up, blanketing her in peace and dreamless sleep.

27

Her father kept his word. Moira woke to find the fire's ashes smoldering the next morning as if someone had indeed kept the fire going all night. Grayish light filtered through the leaves of the trees above her.

She was alone.

No Librarian.

No Cal.

No father.

What had happened? She knew the Librarian would likely never explain.

Moira closed her eyes again and concentrated. She started at her toes and moved upward, tensing and relaxing muscles to see what hurt until she was satisfied her body was bruised but not broken. Meanwhile, the skies overhead had brightened, and, with a groan, she pushed herself up to a sitting position.

Her head swam, making her lightheaded. When the blood no longer rushed in her ears, she took in her situation. There wasn't much to see but trees.

Somewhere in the ordeal, Moira had lost her boots, but not her socks. Her backpack and quiver were gone, as well as her bow. The scabbard belted around her waist was empty. She had only the clothes on her back and the socks on her feet.

But I'm alive.

Could she stand?

She could. But she had to crawl to a tree to do it. Wrapping her arms around the trunk, she pulled herself upright. Then she pressed her back to the bark. From there, she could make out the silvery ribbon of the river, closer than she thought. The water rushed past less than fifteen feet away.

Walking was another matter. She ping-ponged from tree to tree, her legs trembling with the effort as she picked her way to the river's edge.

The water flowed from right to left, which meant she was still in the Freelands and would have to cross. She did not ponder how she might rescue Aaron and Ansel on her own. One thing at a time.

With no way of knowing how far she'd been washed away, following the river upstream appeared the best course of action. Without shoes, she made slow progress. She tired quickly, but pushed onward. Ahead, the river narrowed to about fifteen feet. The water spurted between a pile of boulders. She would have to go around. Away from the water, the terrain steepened. Moira scaled a rock face as tall as her, climbing a vertical fissure like a ladder to the top.

Trees and more trees. No people. No dragons.

Her legs folded. There was nothing and no one to help her. She closed her eyes and took a steadying breath before reaching out with her dragon-o-meter, wishing against hope that it would work this time, that she would know which way to turn to find Zephyr.

Nothing.

A sharp pain in her chest made her gasp. A sob tore at her throat. Before the rush of hot, salty tears could race down her cheeks, she threw back her head and yowled. The release eased her pain, so she did it again. And again, until her throat was raw. She was alone.

She sniffed.

Her father had said she would never be alone. Not really. She had believed him. She believed him because she knew she would find Zephyr. That was what she was going to do. Because she chose to, and if she had to find Zephyr on her own, then she would. He would do the same for her.

Moira closed her eyes. "Zephyr." His name passed her lips like an invocation.

MOIRA.

A jolt moved through her.

Her eyes snapped open.

MOIRA.

Her heart pounded as she reached out with her dragon senses again. Zephyr was on the move. Her internal compass shifted by degrees as she probed their connection. She stared out over the river from her perch atop the rock, fixing the image in her head. She closed her eyes, trying to show Zephyr where she was.

Light flickered in the corner of her eye. Something blurry? No, something moving. She squeezed her eyes shut tight. In her vision, trees rushed past, scanning back and forth. Her head swiveled to the side and, with her eyes still closed, she saw the river.

Moira sucked in a breath. She saw what Zephyr saw. He was running through the trees.

Eyes open, a huff of laughter escaped her. The least she could do was attempt to meet him. *Keep going, Zeph. Don't stop now.* She climbed down from the boulder and used their connection to move in Zephyr's direction, sticking close to the river.

She shut her eyes tight again. The trees still flew by as Zephyr followed the river, the water flowing from his left to right.

He's across the river.

Moira moved as fast as her unshod feet and tired body could carry her. She was getting close. She knew it. The banks of the river were widening again, the water moving not as swiftly, but not by any means slow.

Across the river, something moved.

Moira froze, her chest heaving.

A flash of white moved between the trees. Urion's shirt bright in the sunshine, and a little way behind him, a dark brown and green-scaled hide emerged from the trees.

Moira raised both arms and waved them over her head. "Zephyr!" Though yelling, she didn't expect to be heard over the roar of the water.

Her dragon ran up to the opposite bank.

She wanted to jump up and down at the sight of him, whole and upright, but she didn't have the energy. She settled for laughing, suddenly giddy at the sight of him. Zephyr's teeth flashed in the light as he mimicked her motion from earlier and waved back at her.

A few seconds later, Urion rushed up next to him. His posture sagged in visible relief, and his hands went to the tops of his knees.

Her side of the river had a steep bank. It would be hard to cross there and the thought of stepping into the water made her stomach clench with dread.

Zephyr waved to get her attention and pointed back upstream.

Moira nodded and headed that way, picking her way carefully along the edge, unwilling to let Zephyr out of her sight. He and Urion kept pace with her.

After several hundred feet, the river widened, both banks rocky but not steep.

Zephyr motioned for her to stop.

Moira stepped out onto the rocks, slippery from the spray. The water was clear near the edge but grew murkier farther out.

Zephyr held up his hand, fingers splayed, patting the air in front of him. He took off his dragon sword and handed it to Urion. Zephyr stepped into the water.

Moira watched, waiting.

Zephyr made slow progress. He focused on the water and tested every foothold. Halfway across, Zephyr sank eight feet into the water. He kept his feet under him and his head and shoulders above the surface of the water. In a moment, he was past the middle, and with each step emerging more and more from the water until he was right in front of her. breathing hard.

They stared at each other. A chasm stretched between them, though they stood but a few feet apart. Emotions filled the space between them that couldn't be put into words.

Moira swallowed. "I'm not dead."

Zephyr's massive head nodded.

She cleared her throat. "I knew you would come looking for me if you could. Did you doubt I would do the same for you?"

Zephyr's slate gray lips turned down at the edges as his head moved from side to side. "Never."

Her chin wobbled.

Zephyr's arms opened, and Moira flew into them. His huge wyvern hug drove the air from her lungs.

Moira croaked out the words. "Can't... breathe..."

Zephyr let loose a rumble of laughter. He wove his fingers together to form a step, stooping down. "Hop on."

28

Moira clung to Zephyr's neck as they crossed the river. Her heart squeezed hard at the deepest point, but Zephyr hummed and gripped the hands she had clasped around his neck in one of his much larger ones. The vibrations distracted her, and she remembered to breathe. She couldn't blame the water. It was only doing what water did.

As soon as her feet touched the ground, Urion wrapped his arms around her, tight.

Moira gripped him back, too tired to do much else than stand there.

Urion released her and stepped back. "Zephyr said we had to find you. I didn't think you would make it."

A shaky laugh escaped her. "Neither did I." She glanced between the two of them, searching. "Rasti?"

Zephyr met her gaze. "He did not."

Moira sucked in a breath.

"The water tore him from me." Zephyr flexed his hands. "When I found him, he was gone. I buried him… deep, to keep the animals away. I marked it with a large stone."

The backs of Moira's eyes prickled as she pressed her lips together. She had no words, so she simply dipped her head.

Zephyr's hand landed on her shoulder. "Let us rest."

They camped under the trees next to the river. Conversation halted while they collected wood for a fire. After everything, the simple act of gathering wood was both exciting and yet mundane enough to let Moira's mind wander. How Urion summoned a spark for a flame, she wasn't sure, but they had nothing else to comfort themselves with but the fire and each other's company.

As they warmed themselves, they spoke little. From what they did say, Moira pieced together how they survived the flood, found one another, and started searching for her.

Moira inhaled deeply. "I would have died if someone hadn't dragged me out of the water."

Zephyr jerked. "Who?"

She couldn't suppress a shiver. "The Librarian."

Urion squinted. "A librarian saved your life?" He cast a confused glance in the river's direction.

"Not a librarian. *The* Librarian."

"There are no libraries here."

Moira sighed. "I know. He's… something else." She shared a glance with Zephyr, thinking of the book in her head, the only reason the Librarian had for being concerned about her well-being.

Zephyr rumbled beside her in understanding. He knew.

Urion added some more wood to the fire. Before sunset, the three of them were asleep. With Urion on one side of Zephyr, Moira huddled close on the other, unwilling to be separated from her companions any farther than their dreams.

The next morning, they followed the river upstream, unsure of how far the river had taken them from their intended path. Moira worried whether they should try to find the road again. Whoever had released the waters likely believed they were dead. "Is it safe to take the road?" she asked. "Will they still be looking for us?"

Urion, picking his way along the water's edge, called out to them and lifted something wet.

Zephyr rolled his eyes and spoke so low only Moira could hear him. "Of course he would find something."

"I'm just happy his luck is on our side."

At the water's edge, Urion held her backpack aloft by the strap.

"What?!" Moira made her way to him and took the bag. It was heavy, but that could just be because it was soaking wet. The largest compartment had come open. "No shoes." Her clothes were missing as well. The rock pick and dagger were still there. She zipped them away. The smallest zippered pocket remained closed. All the items she's stowed there were safe, if wet, like the cell phone she'd turned off, put away, and not thought of since, just like she was going to do again now. It reminded her of just how far she was from home at that moment.

Moira zipped everything closed and slipped the strap over her head.

They kept walking. The river narrowed, the land around it growing steep. They headed inland, where the terrain wasn't as rough. Away from the water, the dense growth of trees made it hard to maneuver. Without shoes, Moira slowed them even further.

Zephyr stopped and offered her a ride.

She slipped onto his back to the sound of a gasp.

Both of their heads whipped around to see someone short in stature bounding away through the trees.

Moira turned to Urion from her perch. "Did you see that?"

"Yes," he said and took off after them.

They were fast, whoever they were, and they must have known the terrain. Urion wasn't able to catch up. Zephyr had his own troubles with her on his back and finding a path through the densely packed trees to accommodate his size. Urion and his quarry disappeared.

Zephyr paused for a fraction of a second. The twitching of his head told her he was picking a path. Then he sidestepped several times around different trees toward the spot she'd last seen Urion.

Without warning, they stepped from the woods onto a road. It wasn't much of a thoroughfare. More of an overgrown track with two strips of mud.

"Which way?" Moira asked.

"There." Zephyr pointed to the ground and what she presumed was a fresh mark. Zephyr headed that way. Over a rise stood a small hamlet. Far from picturesque, the weathered buildings were close to falling over, more leaning than standing, in a rough semicircle. This close, she could hear the peal of a hammer against metal at regular intervals.

Urion stopped.

A high-pitched shout pierced the air. Shorty ran into a low-ceilinged shack with three sides. The ringing stopped.

Zephyr came to stand next to Urion. Moira slid from Zephyr's back.

People poured out of the buildings. Most were men, but Moira saw plenty of children spill out of one of the larger structures. The children squealed with excitement, and perhaps a little fear at the sight of Zephyr, but didn't freeze up. A few of the men did, but others appeared to know what to do and dragged those suffering from dragon freeze around by the arm so Zephyr was no longer in their direct line of sight. The rest stood by staring at Zephyr and their small party or glancing from one to the other, as if waiting for something. The standoff reminded Moira of when she and Urion had come across the gang of goblins in the woods.

A tall man wearing a leather apron stepped out of the shack with three sides, which Moira took to house some kind of forge, from the smoke that followed him out. All eyes turned toward him. One of the man's hands rested against Shorty's back. The other held the handle of a large hammer. His hair was mostly silver, but he stood straight and tall, a grim expression deepening the lines around his mouth. Shorty had her arms wrapped tight around his waist. Shorty was a girl, her face dirt-streaked, eyes wide with fear, long brown hair tangled with twigs and leaves. Her pants hung in tatters below her knees. She looked older than the rest of the children, but far from adulthood.

Moira glanced around at the assembled villagers, frowning. Where was everyone else?

Zephyr grunted in agreement. As soon as she had the thought he had picked up on it.

Urion spoke softly. "There is something very wrong here." He lifted one hand in greeting and said, louder, "We're just passing through. No need to trouble yourselves. We'll be on our way."

Moira didn't think it would be that easy. These people didn't seem to be in a hurry to turn them into whatever authorities might be nearby, but neither did they appear ready to let them be on their way.

Though it was Urion who spoke, the blacksmith's gaze hadn't left Moira and Zephyr. "We don't see many dragoneers out this way."

It wasn't a question.

Moira didn't say anything. He was assuming she was a dragoneer. There was no reason for her to speak and confirm his suspicion. Then again, not denying it was all the confirmation these people needed. It wasn't just the blacksmith's attention she and Zephyr held, but much of the rest of the village's focus as well.

The blacksmith patted the girl on the back. She released him but didn't leave his side. "You look as if you've had some trouble." He stared at Moira's unshod feet.

Moira peered at the hammer he still held, albeit loosely. "Nothing we couldn't handle."

The blacksmith raised the hammer and gripped the head in his free hand. Then he let go of the handle and held it out to the girl for her to take. She accepted it, letting her arm fall at her side. "Maybe we can be of help to one another. My name is Brixton. We could use a dragon for some of the work we have around here. If the wyvern doesn't object, that is."

Moira glanced around at the assembled villagers. "We're kind of in a hurry."

"We don't mean to keep you, and we won't tell anyone we've seen you if that's what you're worried about." He glanced at the surrounding men. Each one who met his gaze nodded before he turned to face Moira again. "But we could use your help," he said. His tone was matter-of-fact, but something in the man's eyes pleaded with them to stay.

Zephyr rested his hand on the hilt of his sword, not because he thought there would be trouble, she knew, but because he found the stance comfortable. Beside them, Urion shifted his weight from one foot to the other. When she caught his eye, he tipped his head. The decision was hers.

"We might be able to," Moira said. "But first, tell me where the women are."

29

Brixton lowered his head and patted the girl on the shoulder. Moira couldn't tell if the touch reassured the child or himself. The blacksmith motioned to the shed. Shorty shuffled away, but not before shooting the three of them a worried glance. Brixton approached them while a murmur moved through the rest of the men gathered. A few of the older boys and an adult tried to shuffle the children back inside the larger building.

At a respectable distance, Brixton stopped and spoke in a low voice. "They're gone." His hand rubbed the back of his neck. "Please stay." He lowered his hand. "I'll explain later, but we truly need your dragon's help. We need all the help we can get." He issued instructions to several of the men.

Moira, Zephyr, and Urion huddled together. "What do you think is going on?" Moira asked.

Urion stared at the men and the children being ushered away, his jaw tight. "I can hazard a guess, but I'd rather hear it from them."

Brixton faced them. "We have some land that needs clearing. Hackett and Reems will show you." He pointed to the two men behind him, one older and white-haired, the other one young enough to be a little older than Moira. "If you want to wait here, we can find you some boots," he said to Moira.

"No." Moira gestured to Zephyr. "Where he goes, I go."

Brixton blinked. "Of course." He turned to Urion.

The halfling didn't wait to be asked. "I'm with them."

Averting his eyes, Brixton faced Zephyr, and bent forward at the waist. "Thank you, Master Wyvern."

Zephyr's hand lifted away from the grip of his sword. In Moira's head, it was as if a brick dropped into place, solid and unyielding. "Zephyr." With nods, he introduced Moira and Urion as well.

Brixton straightened, still avoiding direct eye contact with the dragon. "I am well met, Master Zephyr." He raised a hand. "Please, follow my men. They'll take you to the worksite. In a couple of hours, we'll be happy to have you join us for supper."

The older man, Hackett, led them into the woods. The younger one, Reems, trailed behind. The men had thinned the area, but there were stacks of logs to chop, more trees to bring down, and many logs to be hauled away. Beneath waxed tarpaulins were several axes and a two-man saw.

Zephyr pressed Moira into sitting against a felled log. He took off his dragon sword and passed it to her. "Keep watch."

"I—I can help!" she sputtered.

Zephyr harrumphed. "You can help by staying out of the way. Have you ever cut down a tree?"

"Have you?" she asked.

"You can watch. You are still weak."

Zephyr twisted his torso first one way and then the other, limbering up. "This work comes naturally to wyverns. It will be fun."

Urion saw this and took off his sword as well. "Watch mine, too?" He set the sword beside her and rolled up the sleeves of his tunic.

"Sure." Moira made herself comfortable. She tipped her head back. What she could see of the sun through the canopy of leaves warmed her, and she closed her eyes. Not even the sounds of multiple axes striking wood could keep her from dozing off.

It was the sustained silence that caused Moira to stir. She wiped the drool from the side of her mouth with the back of her hand. The site had transformed while she slept. Several trees had been felled and stacked to the side, while the older logs had been split into firewood.

Urion stood beside her, holding out a water skin.

Moira thanked him and settled back to watch as the woodcutting resumed. Zephyr had been hard at work while she slept. He could take down a tree in fewer strokes than the rest of them, and he could work a two-man saw all on his own. He didn't have to be careful with the trees, and Moira noticed his talons score the wood he handled. Zephyr and Urion took turns checking on her, but what Moira didn't expect was the attention she received from Hackett and Reems. When Hackett's eye caught hers, she smiled. The older man's mouth twitched, and he glanced away. Reems' gaze met hers once, and he blushed.

Immediately after, his ax struck a glancing blow against a piece of wood that should have been easy to split. The error restored his concentration, however, the snuck glances continued. Moira wasn't sure if he was flirting with her, but then Zephyr stood in the way for several minutes, which meant the boy couldn't glance her way without also seeing Zephyr.

By the time they headed to supper, Moira felt, if not refreshed, at least rested. Back in the tiny hamlet, Hackett and Reems led them back to the larger building. Zephyr had to duck to get inside, but otherwise was fine. Candles and lamps lined the wall and sat on long tables with people seated on benches. Moira was surprised to find more people inside than had been there earlier. Aside from a few older women with gray hair who served food and girls the age of Shorty or younger, the room contained all men and boys.

Heads turned as Brixton invited them to sit. Zephyr sat on the ground at the head of one long table. Moira and Urion on either side of him. The older women brought bowls of stew and thick slices of bread. Zephyr got a bowl the size of a soup pot and a whole loaf of bread to himself.

Moira caught the attention of a boy passing by who seemed to be seven or eight. "Have you got any hapshulyc?"

The boy's eyes widened, and he was gone. In less than a minute, he returned bearing a full jar. The aromatic scent came off the sauce in waves, threatening to singe Moira's nose hairs. She tried not to inhale as she tipped some of the stuff into Zephyr's bowl. Her dragon split his loaf of bread, and she poured a bit on that as well. Moira shuddered and handed the jar back to the boy. "Thank you. Please take that away." The boy left, but came right back with three pairs of boots. Two fit, but she kept the pair came up to her knees because it reminded her of the ones she'd lost. She thanked him.

After their first couple of bites, Brixton brought over a pitcher and three cups to the end of their table. "May I join you?" He filled the cups with a weak ale and gave the pitcher to Zephyr.

Moira eyed the beverage suspiciously. Taking a sip, she found it truly was weak and reminded her of unsweetened tea. Conversations flowed around them and Moira relaxed. At the far end of the table, Shorty drew in an oversized book.

Brixton noticed her staring. "My daughter, Heather Ann."

Moira blinked and, for a second, Ansel, his head bent over the paper, replaced the image of Heather Ann. She blinked, and the image fled. Zephyr's arm nudged hers. She nudged him back.

"You asked where all the women are," Brixton said, his eyes on his cup.

Moira didn't think she imagined the room growing quieter. "Are they... dead?"

At the word 'dead' Brixton winced. "We don't know. By now, they could be." His shoulders hunched, as if what he had to say was physically painful to him. "They took them from us a little over a year ago."

Brixton's eyes grew bright as he spoke. "They came for the children first. Threatened to kill them all unless the women went with them." He stared without focus. "We agreed. Don't fight. Go quietly. But as soon as the children were safe, my eldest daughter, Jeanette..." He stopped.

"What happened to her?" asked Moira.

"She took the finest sword I ever made, a soul sapphire set in the hilt, and killed half of them before they brought her down and hauled her away." His chin quivered. "And I watched it happen. We all did. To protect the children." His chin dropped to his chest.

Moira glanced around the room. Several men hung their heads while a few openly wept into their cups. The elders held tight to the younger children as conversation slowly resumed. The stew she'd eaten sat like a lump in her stomach. "Who took them?"

Brixton's spine straightened. "Soldiers. And trolls. By order of the crown, our duty was to turn over the women." He scoffed. "The Crown. Only the true heir isn't on the throne, is he? And now even the Regent is dead."

Urion's cup hit the table with a thud. "When?"

"Yesterday. Bad news travels faster than good. Prince Owen isn't eighteen for days yet. Seems likely Lord Hedrick will seize the throne for himself before then. If he does, it'll be war.

"The Regent ordered the women taken?" Moira asked.

"So they said, but he's been sick for years. This has the stink of the High Magician all over it." Brixton's lip curled. "He's the only one who would work with trolls."

"Where did they take them?" Moira asked.

"We tracked them to the gates of Castle Tern."

Moira glanced from Urion to Zephyr. "We're headed that way ourselves."

"We figured," Brixton said. "Any able-bodied dragon would be headed in that direction to join Prince Owen." His gaze tangled with Moira's as he leaned forward. "That's why we want you to bring our women back."

30

Moira experienced a full-body spasm that brought her to her feet with a wince. "Please excuse us."

Brixton's mouth dropped open, but he didn't stop her.

Moira signaled to Urion with a tilt of her head. "Outside." She knew Zephyr would follow. Judging by the murmurs behind her, the townsfolk got out of his way.

Once outside, Moira drew a deep breath. She led Urion and Zephyr back in the direction of the work site, wanting to gain some privacy. When she thought they were far enough away, Moira spun to face her companions. "Why would the High Magician take the women?"

"Well, he doesn't need them to work the fields or clean the castle," Urion said.

Moira pointed at the ground. "This is not the time for jokes."

Urion straightened. "It is as Rasti and I feared. Vinton is building an army of imps. He's using the women to do it. He almost certainly plans to put Lord Hedrick on the throne. Prince Owen won't stand a chance without an army of his own."

Moira scrubbed at her face with both hands before she lowered them. "How is this even possible?"

"Well, he's probably captured some male fae and..."

"Stop!"

"Was that a rhetorical question?" Urion asked.

Moira made a slashing motion. "Tell me about the imps."

Urion lowered his head, but looked up to meet her gaze. "Imp gestation is much shorter than human." When Moira didn't interrupt, he raised his chin. "It takes about three months. Growth and development are accelerated as well. From the time of conception, you can have a full-grown imp in less than six months."

Moira paced. "Are they anything like trolls?"

"No. Trolls are disgusting creatures. Imps are neither good nor evil, just easily impressed upon. They're similar enough to humans but cast out of society because they're different, and the fae don't care enough to bother with them, halflings that they are." Urion's mouth twisted. "They form small bands and rustle livestock to stop themselves from starving, but otherwise, they keep to themselves. Their lifespans are shortened because of the sped-up growth, and they aren't able to reproduce."

Moira stopped to run a hand down her face. *How many women like Aunt Paige—how many girls my age—have been kidnapped, used, and discarded like they were nothing?*

She faced Zephyr. "What do you think?"

Zephyr rolled his massive shoulders, one hand on the hilt of his dragon sword. "Our path leads to them."

Moira stared at him, chewing the inside of her lip as she decided. "Right." She shook out her hands and marched back toward the group of buildings. Urion eyed her as she passed him, but she noticed he fell in behind her, next to Zephyr.

Back inside, Brixton now stood near the front of the room. As Moira approached, he turned to her, his expression wary. Conversation stopped, but the scraping of benches and whispers told her Zephyr had followed her inside.

"You want me to bring your daughter back," Moira said.

Brixton shook his head. "No. Not just my daughter. All the women."

Moira glanced around the room, meeting no one's eyes. "All of them?"

"As many as you can," Brixton said. "We want our women back."

Moira continued to look out over the people. "And, again, I ask, all of them? The ones who have been abused? The ones who might carry imps? What happens if I bring them back?"

Would they cast glances from the side of their eyes at their friends, neighbors, wives, and daughters? Would they whisper about them, not caring if the women overheard? A few heads lifted at her question while others shifted to avoid her gaze, obviously uncomfortable with her questions.

Brixton, however, was not. "We take care of our own." His voice was firm.

Moira stared out over the sea of faces watching her. *That's what I'm afraid of.*

The blacksmith inhaled sharply as he picked up on her meaning. "No more harm will come to any of our women. Or their offspring."

"Are you sure?" She turned and stared out over those assembled before her, her words carrying to the far corners and out the open doors. "Any woman who returns is a victim of the High Magician. Don't make them your victims as well."

Listen to me, I sound like I might not only throw over a royal imposter and liberate the imprisoned women, but somehow see them home. This hiccup in Moira's thinking made her flinch. No one seemed to notice, but beside her Zephyr cleared his throat.

"I swear they will come to no more harm," Brixton said. "Not at our hands." His voice was firm. "We want all of them back. As many as you can." He held out his hand, his fingers splayed.

Moira stared at the proffered limb and decided he meant to grasp forearms instead of hands. She reached out and gripped the lower part of his arm with hers. "I'm glad to hear it, but I won't make any woman return against her will." Her stomach roiled as her cheeks heated. "If we even get the chance."

Brixton released her arm. "I understand better than you know, but we had to ask. If you're going to Castle Tern, we want someone there to remember we're here. We'll help you in any way we can."

Minutes later, they gathered around a map of The Fells laid across the table. Heather Ann sat at the other end.

The river had washed them a great distance downstream. As a result, even after all the walking they had done, they were much farther south and west than Moira could have imagined. They still had a long way to go to get from Councy Forest, where they were now, to the clearly marked Castle Tern.

"This'll be the fastest way to the castle." Brixton ran his finger along the road. It followed the river for a short distance eastward, then diverged from the waterway and ran more or less north to the castle.

"We're not going to Castle Tern," Moira said.

Urion's head lifted. "We're not?"

"We're going to find Prince Owen."

Zephyr's massive head hovered over the map. "Where does he build his army?"

"The Regent may be dead, but he made it clear what would happen to anyone assisting the prince." Brixton paused. "Of course, everyone knows where Prince Owen's camp is." He pointed to an area to the north and east of Castle Tern, close to the Freelands, but still in the Fells. "This same route is still the closest to being the most direct."

"We're not going that way," Moira said. "It's too exposed. We need to avoid the road. Whoever tried to wash us away with the river probably thinks we're dead, but any girl traveling with a dragon is going to be suspicious. I don't want them to see us coming."

"The river? That was you?"

Moira nodded. "That's kind of how we got here."

Urion pointed at the map. "Vinton held back the waters until we tried to cross. If you remember the birds, they were probably bespelled."

Moira's mouth went dry. *He held back the river with his magic?*

Brixton stroked his chin. "You'll want plenty of cover then. Go this way." He traced a route that would take them around Castle Tern to the west and dropped them into Prince Owen's camp from the north. "It adds a day or more to your journey, and time isn't a luxury you can afford since the death of the Regent."

"We'll leave first thing," Moira said.

"That would be best. Excuse me." Brixton got up and called to a few of the men around the room, including Hackett. When he finished speaking to each one, that man would then head out into the night.

Moira left Urion and Zephyr looking over the map and slid down the bench. Heather Ann raised her head when Moira stopped across from her.

"You really a dragoneer?" Heather Ann's voice held equal parts wonder and disbelief mixed with general inquisitiveness.

The corners of Moira's lips curled up. She scratched an imaginary itch on her nose to cover it and tried to frown. "It's Zephyr, isn't it? He gives me away every time."

Heather Ann turned toward the dragon. She shrugged and went back to drawing.

"You must have known that, though. Isn't that why you ran?"

She shrugged again, but didn't look up.

"What made you think I was Zephyr's dragoneer? Someone not as smart as you might have thought it was my companion." Moira lifted a finger to point toward Urion.

Heather Ann stopped drawing. Her head tilted to the side as she considered Moira's question. "You were on his back. Only a dragoneer rides on a dragon."

"Zeph really did give me away, then. What are you working on?"

Heather Ann spun the book around. Her current sketch was of Zephyr. Moira smiled. He was a popular subject. It was less of a portrait than a snapshot of him in action. The young artist had captured his strength and power in a few strokes, but Moira couldn't help but think of Ansel. The wanted posters Urion had seen gave her hope that he was still alive. Who else could draw her and

Zephyr's likeness in such detail? And if Ansel was still alive, then maybe that meant Aaron was, too.

"You don't like it?" Heather Ann asked.

Moira cleared her expression. "I do like it. It's very good."

Heather Ann didn't look as if she believed her.

"I have two friends I'm here to find. One of them is an artist like you. Can I see what else you've drawn?"

Heather Ann showed her, flipping through the large flat book that had seen better days, its pages yellowed and some water stained. Heather Ann hadn't let that stop her. She'd started with still life, lots of swords and tools—but she was a blacksmith's daughter—and moved on to people.

There was a picture of a boy kicking a ball, and another of a girl with her skirts billowing as she spun. Moira pointed. "Who's that?" The subject's long hair covered her face, but the drawing beautifully captured the movement.

"My sister." Heather Ann said it in such a way that told Moira this was the missing Jeanette. "She's not here anymore."

The pictures changed to landscapes, flowers and more Zephyr. Moira strongly suspected the figure on his back might be herself. She wasn't sure if the strong, confident lines could really be her, but the curly hair was kind of a clue.

The book was almost full. "These are wonderful, but don't draw too many pictures of Zephyr. It will go right to his head."

Heather Ann took the book back. "Are you going to find my sister?" Her eyes searched Moira's face.

Was she? All she had originally planned to do was find her friends and go home, but that wasn't all, not really, not if she was being honest with herself. She'd also planned to stop Vinton from coming after them ever again. How she was supposed to do that had never been entirely clear, but it had to be done. She didn't want Zephyr living with the threat of the High Magician looming over his shoulder for the rest of his days. Neither did she. Now these people were asking for her help. They were counting on her, too.

As Zephyr said, their path led to the women. However they chose to get to Castle Tern, the women would be there. *But will we be able to find Jeanette and help her or any of the women?* Moira didn't know, but she had to tell Heather Ann something. Kids knew whether they were being talked down to or leveled with. How many people had told Heather Ann everything would be okay only to have everything not be okay?

Moira's eyes met hers. "I don't know. But I will try." It was as close to a promise as she could make.

Heather Ann seemed to accept the words for what they were: just words. She went back to her drawing.

Moira rejoined Brixton at the other end of the table. He'd seen her speaking with Heather Ann and had not interrupted. "Drawing helps her..." His voice trailed off before he cleared his throat. "Meet back here in the morning, and we'll have supplies to help you on your way."

In the corner of the room someone brushed the strings of an instrument. Conversation didn't stop as a voice joined the player in a not-quite-happy song. Brixton excused himself and stepped away to talk to someone.

After the first song was sung, another started. Urion borrowed a deck of cards from someone and shuffled them.

Moira raised a skeptical brow and spoke low enough so only he and Zephyr could hear her. "If you think I'm playing a card game with you, it's not happening."

Urion tilted his head to the side with a small smile. "That's fair. This, however, is not a playing deck." He spread the cards in front of him with a swipe of his hand. "Master Zephyr, pick a card."

Zephyr's eyes shone like yellow beacons. He reached out and tapped one talon-tipped digit against the back of a card near the middle of the spread.

Moira knew he could skewer the card without trouble, so he had to have been trying to be gentle.

Urion removed the card Zephyr chose from the rest and set it in front of the spread, face down. He looked at Moira. "Pick a card."

She plucked a card from near the bottom of the deck.

Urion took her card and set it next to Zephyr's. He seemed to choose one for himself with very little thought and lined it up with the others. "I asked the deck a simple question and had us each draw a card to see what our futures hold. Let's start with the biggest future." He flipped over Zephyr's card, and she saw there were no numbers or any shapes she associated with a pack of playing cards, but pictures instead. It reminded her of a deck of tarot cards, which she had no experience with, but Urion appeared familiar enough with them.

Urion kept his finger on the card. "Well, well, well. Swords. Lots of them. Can't say I'm surprised. Looks like you're in for a fight, Zephyr. No doubt you'll be prepared for it."

Zephyr rumbled, but didn't comment.

Urion lifted his hand from the card and moved to the one Moira had chosen. He glanced up to meet her eyes as he turned the card over. He kept his hand on the card as he had before and looked down at it. His eyebrows flew up. "Huh. I expected more swords, but what we have here is the staff, which alludes to power. Just one, though. But it's a big one. The queen of the staff." Moira didn't miss the small frown that pinched his brows together, as if he wasn't sure what to make of the card concerning her future.

His expression cleared as he moved to the last and final card without reverence. He flipped the card over. "Moons. What a surprise." He glanced at the card and did a double-take. He picked it up, frowning as he tilted it this way and that, holding it close to his face. "Those shouldn't be there," he mumbled.

"What is it?" Moira asked.

Urion shook his head and tried to laugh off his reaction. "Something I've never noticed before. Those trees in the back—in the branches—there's a sword, and a staff, and the outline of a chalice as well. It must just be this deck." He pushed the cards together and set them aside.

Moira glanced at Zephyr from the side of her eye to find him giving her the same look. The last card had rattled their friend. "What does the chalice mean?"

"They correspond to matters of the heart."

"And the moons?"

"They're meant to suggest fortune. It's all open to interpretation, of course."

If it wasn't the moons that were bothering him, it had to have been what he saw in the background. Urion cleared his throat and Moira got the impression he didn't want to talk about it.

Moira turned away from the cards. "Speaking of fortune, I really thought we could get in and out of the Fells and Castle Tern without trouble. We'd sneak in, find Aaron and Ansel, get out, and figure out how to get home from there." She shook her head at how ridiculous it sounded when she said it out loud. "That's not going to work anymore."

Zephyr drank from his pitcher. "What changed your mind?"

Urion shifted in his seat. "Was it the women?"

Moira pursed her lips for a moment. "I rather think it was the High Magician trying to flush us down the river like garbage that did it, but I should have realized it wouldn't be that simple." Her gaze skipped across the backpack she'd thought lost and gone forever until Urion found it that morning. Inside was her rock pick and the dagger Vinton had thrown at Zephyr. Ever since Zephyr pulled the blade from his wound, she'd wanted to return it personally. With force. That was long before the river knocked their party asunder. "Rasti had an idea for getting us inside the castle, but he didn't tell me what it was." Just saying the old sentinel's name made her heart squeeze.

Urion huffed once. "Rasti had an idea and didn't share it? Imagine that." He made the statement with no heat, his face downcast.

If she dwelled on the loss of Rasti, she knew it would be too easy to make her desire to see the dagger returned about revenge and nothing else. But it wasn't about revenge anymore. Learning about the stolen women changed things. Whatever Vinton was doing, he needed to be stopped. They couldn't go in, grab their friends, turn around, and just leave. Not without helping the people Vinton was hurting. If their best chance of helping them meant aligning themselves with the rightful heir to the throne, then that's what they would do.

Brixton rejoined them. "I've found you a place to stay for the night. As soon as they put the cows out to pasture."

31

The next morning, Moira was surprised that Cal and the Librarian had left her alone for the night, with neither one lurking in her dreams. Reunited with Zephyr, their connection restored, Moira wondered if part of her mind, at least, was more at ease.

Morning fog filled the space between trees in thick, soft layers, leaving the treetops to rise above like spires. Brixton, Hackett and a few other men from the night before greeted them at the meeting house doors. They'd brought together everything they could think of that might help her, Zephyr, and Urion on their journey.

Moira went straight to a slightly used sturdy, dark brown leather pack. It had plenty of room for food, water, her rock pick, and the dagger. It also had room for her old torn backpack, which she folded as best she could, shoving it to the bottom. The strap had broken, her clothes were gone, but she wouldn't leave one of her last reminders of home behind.

Besides provisions, the townsfolk gave Moira and Urion new cloaks and an extra set of clothing. She yearned to change into clean clothes, but it made more sense to keep them in reserve. What she really yearned for, and what she would never take for granted again, was a washing machine.

There were also weapons to consider. The raging waters of the river had taken her quiver, bow, and sword. Moira wore the empty scabbard at her waist out of habit, used to the feel against her hip. Brixton offered her a new sword, holding onto the blade so she could take the hilt. It weighed less than the one she'd lost.

Brixton motioned to the sword. "It's nothing fancy."

"It's not?" Moira tilted the sword. The sharpened edge reflected the early light, gleaming, the grip and hilt made of metal strands, first twisted, then woven together into an intricate pattern.

"It'll get the job done, but you'll need this." Brixton lifted the scabbard that belonged to the new sword.

Right. She would have to get rid of the one Rasti had given her. It wasn't doing her any good. The sword was long gone and this new sword wouldn't fit. Still, she was reluctant to part with the empty scabbard.

Brixton must have sensed her hesitancy. "That belong to another sword?"

"Yes." Moira tentatively unbuckled the empty scabbard.

"I'll take care of it."

Moira let go of the old scabbard with a long look. Then she belted on the new one and thanked him.

Besides the sword, there was a bow and a quiver full of arrows. She accepted these readily, sliding both over her head. Their combined weight was a comfort she hadn't realized she'd been missing.

Zephyr admired a selection of knives, but didn't take any.

Brixton gave Urion a sword and scabbard, too.

With everything packed, strapped, or slung in one place or another, the three of them faced the old blacksmith, who eyed them one last time for any missing item. "Ready?"

They were.

Brixton stepped forward and offered Moira his hand. "Remember us. And good luck."

He couldn't know about Urion's curse. *I'll take all the luck I can get.* She accepted his hand. "Thank you. For everything."

Brixton let go. "Safe travels."

Moira nodded and turned away to walk beside Zephyr out of the hamlet of Councy Forest, wondering if she would ever see it again.

Urion had the map they'd studied the night before. He took the lead, heading east out of town.

***

When it came time to leave the road and turn north, they paused, each meeting the other's eye with grim determination all around.

They didn't speak, keeping their thoughts to themselves.

Moira tried not to dwell on her naiveté. It was laughable to think they could traipse into the Fells, regain her friends, and get away again without someone noticing.

Some small part of her remained hopeful for a quick resolution, but the rest of her thought differently. As the day passed and her feet grew weary, she decided there was nothing wrong with being optimistic. She shouldn't disparage hope in whatever form it came in, because sometimes that was all people had. And the people of Councy Forest had placed theirs in her.

No pressure.

They stopped long enough to pull food from their packs, continuing to walk as they ate. Zephyr veered off to supplement his lunch and rejoined them later.

Moira's thoughts turned to Aaron and Ansel. She wanted them back, whole and unhurt, but that wouldn't be enough now. The twins' plight had intertwined with the women of Councy Forest. The solution included Castle Tern and the High Magician. They were all related somehow. Moira needed a plan.

Not for the first time, she wondered what Rasti had had in mind to get them into the Castle and out again. He'd said she wouldn't like it. His plan had probably been to sneak them in through the garbage dump. Or maybe not. She had no way of knowing, but they had to think of something.

They didn't stop until it grew too dark to continue safely. By then, they were exhausted and ate a cold meal of the same dried meat they'd eaten in the middle of the day. Zephyr, content from his previous meal, didn't go hunting, but swept the ground clear as best he could with his tail and collected boughs for Moira and Urion to sleep on.

Moira's new boots chafed. She sat and removed them, exposing her blisters to the air with a sigh. The wounds would heal overnight, she was sure of it. The state of her feet reminded her to check Zephyr's. He hadn't complained, and she was happy to see the bottoms of his feet had toughened up nicely. They were a little swollen, but he would be fine. Moira and Urion wrapped themselves in their cloaks, said goodnight, and fell asleep on either side of Zephyr.

They were up as soon as the sun lightened the sky from inky black to a less intense indigo the next morning. Zephyr hunted again as they set out and caught up with Moira and Urion as the sun raced a line of clouds overhead.

Urion continued to lead, and whether blessing or curse, they met no one along their path, even though they passed farms close enough to hear the lowing of stabled livestock.

Late into the second day, the roiling clouds above finally made good on their threat of rain. As the first fat drops hit the ground, Moira suggested they seek shelter.

Within minutes, Urion had found an overhang of rock large enough for all of them to squeeze under as long as Zephyr sat.

Tucked away out of the wet, Moira and Zephyr shared a look, but made sure not to let Urion see. His good fortune was their good fortune. Urion might not wish to acknowledge his blessing/curse, but she and Zephyr were thankful for it.

With nothing to do but wait for the rain to stop, Moira slid her pack to the ground and asked, "What do we do when we find this Prince Owen?"

Urion stared into the rain. "We get him to listen to us."

"How hard is that going to be?"

Urion shrugged. "Under normal circumstances, very, but with the death of the Regent and Prince Owen turning eighteen, he might be interested in talking to the dragon-bit dragoneer that Castle Tern is so interested in."

Zephyr ducked down to peer out at the sky. "How much farther?"

Urion crossed his arms, tucking his hands into his armpits. The rain had brought a dip in temperatures with it. "We've made good time. I'd estimate we're already past

Castle Tern. If we maintain our pace, we should reach Prince Owen's encampment late tomorrow."

Moira mirrored Urion's crossed arms and pressed her back against the uneven rock wall. "So, what do we tell this Prince Owen if we get the chance?"

"We tell him Vinton has an unhealthy obsession with female dragon-bit dragoneers in general, and you in particular. We tell him the High Magician kidnapped not only your friends but women from across the Fells to breed an imp army."

Moira gazed out at the rain. "How could he not know about the women?"

Urion heaved a heavy sigh. "I don't know. But he's only a prince, and he's not in charge. My understanding is that Owen and his sister were raised away from Castle Tern by General Hill. He was once Commander of the King's Guard."

Moira glanced at Urion. What she saw made her turn to stare at him. She wasn't sure when it happened, but he appeared beyond frustrated and well into exasperation.

"What's up?" Moira asked him.

Urion's brows pinched together as he peered up at the cloudy sky, much like Zephyr had. "I *want* to believe the prince doesn't know his future subjects are being stolen and abused, but it's hard to believe that no one at all knows." He drove both hands through his hair, exposing the points of his ears. "How could it have come this far? And how are we supposed to do anything about it? We are but one dragoneer, one dragon, and one... halfling."

Moira heard a note in Urion's voice she didn't care for when he referred to himself that way.

Neither did Zephyr. "What is it?"

Urion lifted the chain around his neck and pulled out the medallion he always wore, the one that had stopped Kaidence's knife. "My luck is running out."

Two inches in diameter and made of gold metal that shone in the rain-dampened light, the medallion hung by a chain strung around his neck of the same material which pierced the flat circle through a hole near its uneven edge. A series of symbols pressed into the metal brought to mind doubloons and pirate treasure.

Zephyr lowered his head for a closer look.

Urion didn't flinch. "My father gave this to me. He said it would save my life three times. Over the years, I've tried to get rid of it, thrown it off cliffs, hurled it into oceans, given it away to strangers, but it always comes back to me. I've thought it gone a thousand times, only to look down and find it strung around my neck like a noose."

Urion lowered the medallion. "Ever since Kaidence tried to kill me, I've felt different. As if something's changed." He tucked the disc back into his shirt. "There were the goblins that slunk up on us. Your picture is posted everywhere in Goodramtown. Then we lost Rasti." Here he stopped and his shoulders hunched under their eyes. "I thought I'd lost you all."

Moira leaned forward. "But you didn't. Even if you had, it wouldn't have been your fault." She fumbled with what to say next, settling for an incredulous tone. "You need to give yourself a little less credit. Your luck's not that good. Or bad."

Zephyr clasped Urion on the shoulder with his large scaled hand. "You will know when your luck has run out. You will be dead."

Moira's eyes widened, but Urion laughed.

Zephyr's attempt at consolation, clumsy in Moira's eyes, appeared to have done the job. He released Urion's shoulder.

Urion shook his head, his smile fading. "There's still only three of us."

Moira tipped her head forward. "Zephyr should count as more than one."

The corners of Urion's mouth turned up. "Fine. We are one dragoneer, one halfling, and one dragon who… "

"He's at least, like, three people," Moira said.

Zephyr grunted. "More like six."

They all laughed.

Once the rain tapered to a drizzle, they emerged from their shelter. They pushed on until it grew dark, and then even farther. Exhausted, they didn't bother with a fire, not having the energy to hunt for wood or anything to cook over it. Zephyr barely cleared a place for them to rest. The space he swept was flat. That was good enough for Moira. She wrapped herself in her cloak and laid down, asleep as soon as she closed her eyes.

She wasn't sure how much time had passed before an explosion woke her.

32

Urion sprang to his feet. "What is that?"

In the predawn darkness, the far-off explosion echoed in the low hills that surrounded them. Moira sat up.

A fresh series of booms like distant thunderclaps without a storm, rolled across them. Distant flashes of light briefly illuminated the clouds along their path.

She found the boots she'd pushed from her feet the night before and pulled them on in a hurry

Zephyr raised his head and sniffed the air. "Something burns."

Within minutes, each of them had their swords buckled into place and they were on their way. The explosions tapered to a stop, but left a newfound urgency in their wake. In the darkness, Moira tripped twice. Each time Zephyr, trailing behind, helped her to her feet.

A little later, around the curve of a hill, there was a break in the trees.

Ahead of her, Urion stopped and pointed.

The early morning sky had lightened enough to make out a dark smudge of smoke smeared in a column from the ground upward.

Moira stared at the streak of darkness. If she had to guess, she would have estimated it to be a couple of miles away from where they stood. "Is that Prince Owen's camp?"

"Wrong direction." Urion gestured straight ahead of them. "The camp is this way. That is headed back toward Castle Tern, but much closer."

"Do we check it out?" Moira asked.

"That's up to you, but we should hurry." Urion said.

Moira knew they should probably continue on to the prince's camp, but there was something very odd at work. It seemed too much of a coincidence not to be important. She shivered despite the sweat running down her back. "Let's do it."

They took up a slow jog towards the column of smoke, approaching it faster than Moira expected. She struggled to keep up, but knowing how every minute counted, she pushed herself.

They neither stopped nor rested until they hit a wide path showing heavy, recent usage. The path was wider than any they'd passed in the last couple of days. Urion stopped jogging and stepped onto the path.

A large bird let out a squawk and took off, wings flapping.

Moira flinched and hurried to catch up. They all walked together in silence for about ten minutes. Moira moved as quietly as she could, but she still made more noise than Urion or Zephyr. She couldn't help it. The surrounding woods were silent and eerie. Smoke rose ahead, obscured by trees and the rolling topography.

As the breeze shifted, the acrid scent of burnt wood and flesh assaulted her senses. Her eyes teared, and she gagged at the fumes. Further along, they found a dead and burned horse, its head pointed away from the direction they traveled. It wore a saddle, but Moira saw no sign of its rider.

Urion stopped and turned to face them. "Stay here."

"Why?" Moira made to take a step around him.

Urion took the same step, planting himself in her way. "If this is a trap, we don't want to walk into it. Let me investigate." His focus shifted to Zephyr. "Master Zephyr, please wait with your dragoneer under the trees and out of sight."

Moira bristled, but before she could come up with a counter-argument, Urion had run ahead, ducked into the trees and disappeared.

Zephyr stepped toward the nearby trees, but Moira went over to inspect the dead horse. Insects buzzed over the remains. The parts of the horse not scorched had been gray, which made it easy to see the damage. Multiple puncture wounds on its side, chest, and neck suggested a painful death.

Her stomach clenched. What could have caused such damage? A grenade? Something similar? She shoved the thought away, afraid for it to take root. She looked up the road to where Urion had gone and wondered what more he would find.

Zephyr tapped her shoulder and motioned to the trees. Grudgingly she joined him, and they waited.

The sun continued its upward trajectory, shrinking the tallest shadows. Moira had concluded it was about time to go after Urion when the halfling strode out from under the trees, his face a blank mask. He leaned against a tree and breathed deeply.

Moira frowned. "What is it?"

Urion had to clear his throat twice, as if he were fighting for air, before he could speak. Whatever he had to tell them, she knew it wasn't good. He swallowed. "The Light Legion." His next breath escaped him with a shudder.

"We found the Light Legion?" Moira asked.

"The Light Legion... is dead." His shoulders slumped, his agitation turning to a stolid form of physical torpor as if he'd said what he'd had to say and now his body demanded respite. He slid to a seated position at the foot of the tree.

Moira fell back a step, physically knocked off balance by the news. "All of them?"

"Dragons. Dragoneers..."

Urion described the carnage, which sounded like the mutilated horse multiplied by thousands.

The Light Legion was gone. All those people. All those dragons.

Gone.

Rasti had thought the Light Legion could help them. *If the Light Legion couldn't win, then how can we? Ansel, Aaron, Zephyr... we're all going to die here.*

Her breathing sped up and a dull ache spread through the middle of her chest. She backed up another step and ran into something solid, a wall covered in scales.

Moira gasped. Her throat tightened. If she couldn't stop, she was going to pass out. When this happened at home, Aunt Paige would use a weighted blanket, folded up and placed on her chest, to help slow her breathing.

Zephyr's massive arm slipped lightly across her shoulders, pulling her to face him. His hand covered hers and gently pressed her palm into the scales on his side. They vibrated. He was speaking. She was sure of it, but she heard the words through their connection. *Breathe, Moira. In. Out.*

Her palm rose and fell as he inhaled and exhaled. She matched her breathing to his as she leaned into Zephyr. Her heart rate slowed, and she no longer imagined she was underwater. Her ears cleared, but there was nothing to hear. Silence reigned; her cheeks were wet with tears she wasn't aware of having shed.

Moira stepped back from her dragon, wiped her eyes, and took another deep breath.

Urion appeared pale and shaken. He peered at her with questioning eyes.

Moira met Zephyr's calm and steady gaze. "We have to find Prince Owen."

33

They retraced their steps, saying little. Eventually they happened across a road, which they followed. It led them to a large encampment in a meadow. Stretched wide for a hundred yards to either side stood tents of every color and size. Cook fires burned in front of some, with pots or spitted meat roasting over the flames. Men, women, and children tended to their fires and each other.

"I think we found him," Urion said. He continued down the road with a purpose.

The people would have ignored them if it weren't for Zephyr. Heads turned as her dragon passed, and a few cheers went up. A group of children ran beside him on the road. A few made a game of tagging the tip of his tail, but Zephyr held it aloft and out of the children's grasp. They gave up when Zephyr reached the tree line.

Under the canopy of trees, the road continued, but the tents were smaller, there were no children, and the adults dressed better. Nearly everyone carried a sword or a bow, noting their passing with salutes or quiet hails. *Zephyr seems popular.* In Moira's estimation, she and Urion were only welcome by association.

They reached a point where the tents took on a standard shape and color, and the men and women wore armor. They emerged from the trees into another wide meadow, filled with the largest tents yet, which flew purple pennants from the highest poles. A squad of soldiers stepped in their path.

The men wore the same blood-red uniforms as the soldiers who had arrived with Lord Smew in Farrago. Did that mean they'd deserted the Regent? Moira didn't have time to wonder long, as she became distracted by the sight of another dragon.

Behind the soldiers was an unarmored dragon, a dragon sword fastened around its middle. Its scales varied in hue from the shade of just-pressed olive oil to the deepest of evergreen, which probably made it some kind of common green. She wasn't sure. She couldn't remember all the classifications from *The Book of Wyverns* off the top of her head. The dragon wasn't a plate back, though. She knew that. It stood a smidge taller than Zephyr, perhaps ten and a half feet total, and was wider in the shoulders. Its narrow face made its snout appear pointed. Virulent green eyes blinked at them, but the dragon stood at ease, one hand propped loosely on the hilt of his sword.

The tallest soldier raised a gauntleted hand. "Hold." His tone was bored, his expression tired.

Urion addressed the soldier. "We seek an audience with the rightful heir to the throne of Castle Tern."

"You and everyone else in the Fells. Move along. Back the way you came." The soldier made a shooing motion and took a step forward.

Moira tore her gaze away from the dragon to look at the entrance of the largest tent. Several people passed the guards outside and entered. If the prince was inside, they had to see him.

Urion didn't budge. "We have important information for the prince."

The soldier sighed. "Give me the important information. I'll make sure he gets it." He pasted a false smile on his face. No telling how many times he had heard stories similar to theirs. The soldiers behind him shifted their collective weight. The other dragon squinted as he took in Zephyr but remained at ease.

Zephyr drew himself up straight at the other dragon's appraisal, before his acid green eyes turned on Moira, the vertical pupils slimming. She blinked but otherwise didn't react.

Urion smiled. "This information we have is for the prince's ears only. It concerns my friends here." He motioned to Zephyr and Moira.

The green dragon's eyes flashed. The soldier's mouth turned down at the corners. He opened his mouth to speak but didn't get the chance.

The green dragon hissed. "Let them pass, Cale."

The soldier turned. "We can't just let them by, Sorrence. We have orders."

Sorrence crossed his arms. "Let them pass."

Cale shook his head. "Why?"

Sorrence's green eyes focused on Moira. "Show them, dragoneer."

Moira's forehead bunched while her lips pursed. *What am I supposed to do?*

Urion bent down. He grabbed a rock from the road and handed it to her.

"What are you going to do with that?" Cale asked.

Moira showed him.

Cale stepped back. "You'd better see the prince." He and the other soldiers stepped aside.

Moira let the rock fall back into her hand and tossed it to Cale.

He jumped, startled, but caught it.

Sorrence escorted them to the main tent in silence and offered a wary nod to Zephyr before he rejoined his patrol.

At the entrance, the guards made them leave their bags outside, but didn't confiscate their swords. Moira and Urion caught a few glances upon entering, but heads turned when Zephyr came in, bending down to squeeze through the tent door. Once inside, the ceiling was high enough for him to stand without trouble.

Several small groups of people leaned in to hushed conversations. The atmosphere inside the tent was subdued but charged. Urion ushered them away from the door to the side near a long table laid with plates of meats and cheeses and pitchers of ale and water.

Zephyr inhaled deeply through his nose over the food, but shook his head, dejected. "No chips."

Moira eyed the room. A few people cast furtive glances in their direction. Others kept looking at the door, as if waiting for someone specific to come through it.

At the far end of the tent was a dais with a wide, low-slung wood chair at its center. Other chairs circled the dais, but only one sat on it. All were empty.

Under the guise of pushing the hair back from her face, Moira spoke to Urion under her breath without moving her lips. "Which one is he?"

Urion shook his head, his eyes scanning the crowd.

Near the dais, a man who'd kept glancing at them since they entered broke away from the group he conversed with and headed straight for them. His armor reminded Moira of Cale's out front, but different. Older maybe. His tanned head bore no hair except for a gray goatee, the sides of which accentuated the deep creases in his cheeks. His eyes, deep set with lines at the corners, shone with alertness.

He stopped within a few feet of them. "State your business." He spoke with quiet curiosity rather than the harsh tones she might have expected, seeing as how they were crashing the party. Moira thought Zephyr might have had something to do with that.

Urion spoke first. "We need to speak with Prince Owen."

"Or, perhaps, General Hill," Moira said.

The man's chin jerked upward. "I am General Mattias Hill. Should I know you?"

Moira opened her mouth to answer, but there was a shout from outside. "Rider coming in!"

The sound of pounding hooves reached them from outside. Everyone turned toward the door as the drumming of hoofbeats ceased. Moments later, a well-dressed man burst through the door covered in dirt and road dust, eyes searching. He crossed the tent to speak with the group of people the General had left.

Without a word, General Hill fell in behind the horseman.

The rider came to a stop and dropped to one knee. "Prince Owen, I have news of Lord Hedrick."

The young man he knelt in front of had dark hair and a swarthy complexion, beyond the normal tan he might have gained from spending time outdoors. From across the tent, Moira could see his eyes were a pale, watery blue.

Prince Owen's chin lifted at the mention of the name. "What is it?"

"Lord Hedrick has been bitten by a dragon, sire. He is now the dragoneer to a standard black leatherback." The messenger stopped to swallow. "Named Kingkiller."

34

Zephyr's tail whipped through the air behind him, threatening to take out a tent pole.

Another dragon? And another dragoneer?

At first, no one said anything. Then everyone talked at once. Hill had to yell to be heard. "Clear the room!"

The guards came alive when called to action, urging people from the tent. One approached the three of them from the side, hands raised to push them out the door.

"Not them!" Hill shouted, pointing in their direction. "They stay!"

While the guards herded everyone else out of the tent, Moira found a pitcher of water at the back of the long table of foodstuffs. She took two empty cups and poured one for herself and one for Urion before handing the pitcher to Zephyr.

"How much trouble are we in?" she asked.

"Enough," Zephyr said.

Urion sipped his water. "We'll find out soon."

The guards left two of their own to stand on either side of the door until Hill waved them away as well. Then it was just Hill, Prince Owen, the messenger, Urion, Zephyr, and her.

Prince Owen motioned for his messenger to rise. "What happened, Elias?"

The messenger stood. "I went to the castle to deliver your message to the High Magician. He seemed pleased to receive me." The messenger shuddered with the retelling. "He brought me into the throne room. Lord Hedrick was there with a fully-grown dragon, and Lord Vinton said I should offer Hedrick my congratulations, for he is not only a dragoneer, but dragon-bit as well."

Prince Owen and Hill listened without comment, but it was the prince who spoke first. "Did he reply to my message?"

Elias shook his head. "He said only to tell you of Lord Hedrick's good fortune and give you the blessed dragon's name."

Prince Owen gazed at the ground. His brows drew together. "Your courage is noted, Elias. Thank you. Go, now. Rest."

Elias tapped his left shoulder with his right fist and left the tent. Prince Owen kept his gaze averted. His shoulders slumped. "How could this have happened?"

Hill kept his gaze on the prince, but shook his head. For the moment, they seemed to have forgotten they had company.

Moira cleared her throat.

Prince Owen raised his head, blinking as if the sun had just come out and the light was too bright. Moira knew he was only three years older than she was, but his hooded gaze made him seem older.

Moira understood why she had not noticed him at first. The prince wore a plain white tunic, dark trousers, and tall boots. Without a crown or anything else to distinguish him, he looked ordinary.

Hill turned to them. "Our visitors. Who exactly are you? What is your business here?"

Moira set her cup on the table and came forward. "My name is Moira Noble." She bowed her head because it seemed like the thing to do. "This is my dragon, Zephyr, and our friend, Urion."

"Your dragon?" Prince Owen asked. The way he emphasized the first word told her what he was thinking.

Moira answered with a solemn nod. "Vinton took two of my friends. I've traveled here to get them back."

Hill stepped forward, anger in the line of his shoulders. "They're as good as dead."

Moira didn't see Zephyr move, but from the way Hill's eyes widened, he must have stepped forward. She pressed her lips together, taking a moment before she spoke. "I don't think so. Vinton's been looking for us... me, actually." She stopped, thinking it over. "Could Vinton have gotten his hands on a dragon egg?"

Hill answered. "It's possible, but dragons in the Fells are rare. They're more plentiful in the Freelands. That's part of the reason this is such a mess."

"What do you mean?"

The prince motioned to Zephyr. "Dragons like yours are honorable and upstanding. I had thought no dragon would align itself with the likes of Vinton. But by having a dragon on his side, the people will think he is in the right and that Lord Hedrick should become the next king of Castle Tern."

A huff of disbelief left Urion, still behind her. "With due respect, that's ridiculous."

The prince raised a brow and nodded. "As much as I agree, I'm afraid that's how the remaining nobility inside the castle walls will see it. Urion, is it?"

Moira heard Urion set his cup down before he stepped up beside her. He extended one leg and bent forward from the waist.

"It is," Urion said, his eyes on the ground.

Hill stepped in close to the prince. He whispered in his ear and stepped back again.

The prince showed no reaction. His tone, when he spoke, went unchanged. "A halfling fighter from the Freelands."

Urion straightened. "My reputation precedes me."

"Not by much." Prince Owen returned his focus to Moira.

"Where I'm from, there aren't any dragons like Zephyr," Moira said. "With none of his own kind nearby after he hatched, his instincts took over. He found me and bit me because he had to."

The prince drew his head back to reappraise her. "You are dragon-bit?"

"Zephyr had to do it, and if Vinton got his hands on a dragon's egg, then all he had to do was wait. Once it hatched, he kept Lord Hedrick close. The dragon would have felt compelled to bite Hedrick out of instinct."

Hill shook his head. "This dragon is already fully grown."

"Fire rocks," Zephyr said.

Moira looked around at Zephyr and then back. "Dragons eat igneous and volcanic rocks to speed their growth."

"The Outer Isles are volcanic," Urion said.

Moira thought back to the overheard conversation between two merchants on the journey. "Peddlers have been having their carts searched at Castle Tern and the borders. Maybe they've been looking for rocks?" She drew herself up tall. "That has to be it. Vinton hatched a dragon, got it to bite Hedrick, and fed the dragon fire rocks to make it grow. Now he's got a full-size dragon, dragoneer, trolls, and an army of imps."

Prince Owen blinked. "An army of imps?"

Moira searched his features and noted his reaction. The prince appeared genuinely surprised. "Vinton's kidnapped dozens of women from across the Fells and is using them to breed an army of imps."

"Impossible." Prince Owen whipped his head around to stare at Hill. "What is she talking about?"

Hill hung his head and did not raise it.

The prince noticed and faced him.

As the silence lengthened, Hill's cheeks grew ruddy. He cleared his throat. "I am sorry, Owen. It is as she says. I only learned of it recently. All small, remote towns. It's not clear how long this has been going on."

"At least a year," Urion said. "A marauding band of trolls and soldiers took the women from Councy Forest that long ago."

"I'm sorry, Your Highness. I wanted to have the full picture before I told you."

Prince Owen recoiled from the man Moira knew he had to consider not only his most trusted advisor, but his surrogate father. He set his hand upon Hill's shoulder. "Don't shield me from the truth. Not even the partial truth." He released the general. "Imps are not naturally aggressive, but they will fight when they need to. We will need all the help we can muster."

Moira took a cautious step forward. "We have more bad news, Your Highness."

Owen set his chin. "Go on."

"On our way here, we came across the scene of a bloody battlefield. If you planned for the Light Legion to join you, that won't be possible. They've been destroyed."

35

The prince closed his eyes as Moira's news reached his ears.

Hill stared in disbelief. "The entire legion?"

Urion answered him. "No survivors."

The prince covered his mouth for a moment. "Do you know what happened?"

The image of the dead horse flickered through Moira's head. "We don't know for sure. There were a series of explosions."

"I've never seen such widespread damage." Urion went on to describe how the bodies had burned where they stood, riddled with holes as if hit with thousands of arrows at once.

The prince looked to his general. "How could it be anything but magic?"

Hill made a noise of disgust. "Agreed. It has the stink of Vinton all over it."

Across the tent, behind the dais, another set of tent flaps parted and a girl entered. She strode with purposeful steps toward the prince over the dais. "Greetings, brother. What news from Elias?" She came to a stop at Owen's side.

So this is the princess.

Her head turned toward Moira, Zephyr, and Urion. "And who are these?"

"Day." Prince Owen greeted his sister. "This is Master Zephyr. Moira is his dragoneer, and Urion is their friend. They've brought terrible news. The Light Legion is no more."

Princess Day gasped, the revelation rendering her mute for a few moments before her good breeding must have kicked in. She appeared to gather herself and then nodded to Zephyr, Moira, and Urion, meeting each of their eyes in turn. "I am well met."

"You should be resting, Princess," Hill said.

Prince Owen pressed the backs of his fingers to her forehead. "Did the doctor say you could get out of bed?" He ducked his head to look into her face, which was softer and rounder than his but held the same blue eyes. The tunic, trousers, and boots the princess wore were similar to her brother's, but her shirt was blue and embroidered across the front. The handle of a dagger stuck out above the blood-colored sash she wore wound about her waist. Her dark hair brushed her shoulders, displaying a wave her brother's locks lacked.

"Yes." The princess leaned away from her brother's hand. "I was better yesterday. The doctor was being overly cautious. I'm fine. Fully recovered."

The prince picked up her hand. "What's this then?"

The sleeves of the princess' tunic weren't long enough to disguise a white bandage wrapped around her wrist, over her palm.

The Princess pulled her hand free. "It's nothing. I punctured it on something sharp in my tent. Stop trying to distract me. Is it true? Has Hedrick been bitten?"

"Where did you hear that?" Prince Owen asked.

Princess Day leveled her brother with a look. "Elias delivered the news to a room full of people. How many of them do you think rushed to tell me?"

Prince Owen stepped around his sister onto the elevated platform, and sat in the single chair on top of it. His sigh seemed to confirm everything.

Perhaps seeing she was unlikely to get anything out of her brother, the Princess turned to Moira, at the same time taking in Zephyr and Urion before focusing on her. "Did you three belong to the Light Legion?"

Moira blinked. "No, Zephyr and I have come a long way to get here." She stopped. "However, I am dragon-bit as well." It was the first time she'd ever said so, but she relished the chance to say it out loud.

Princess Day's eyes narrowed. "How strange you arrive the same day we learn of Lord Hedrick."

Moira told her about Aaron and Ansel and how she suspected Vinton orchestrated the dragon's biting of Lord Hedrick. When she got to the part about the imp army, the Princess paled, her expression horror-struck.

Prince Owen didn't interrupt, but slumped forward and buried his face in his hands.

When Moira finished, Princess Day turned to her brother. "We cannot forsake any more of our people to the whims of the High Magician. The Regent is dead. It is time to take back Castle Tern."

Prince Owen raised his head. "My birthday is not for another two days. The law dictates—"

"The Law?" The princess rounded on her brother. "Vinton is a traitor to our father's kingdom. What of that law?"

A smile pushed at the corners of Moira's mouth. *Princess Day, you are officially one of my new favorite people.*

"Mattias?" Prince Owen asked.

Hill shook his head, not meeting anyone's eyes. "I would counsel caution in all instances."

Princess Day sighed loudly. "Of course, you would. You've been a father to us since the day ours died. If we do nothing, harm will still find us. I would rather meet it than wait for it to find us. The time has come. Why did you bother training us all these years if not for this moment?"

Prince Owen's expression wavered on the edge of indecision. "Are two days going to matter?"

Moira cleared her throat. "What did your message say? The one you sent to Vinton that your messenger was so brave to deliver."

Prince Owen paled at the same time as two bright spots of color bloomed high on his cheekbones. "I asked when I could expect to take my rightful place as heir and be made king."

Princess Day turned to her brother. "You didn't."

"I did."

A small sound escaped the princess as she smiled. "How impertinent of you, brother. There may be hope for you yet."

"Don't think too highly of me. I sent that message before I knew what had become of the Light Legion."

"Then I'm happy Vinton didn't kill Elias and send him back to you in pieces. At least now you have your answer. You cannot wait." She scoffed. "Kingkiller. What a ridiculous name. Do you think Vinton suggested it?"

Again, Moira cleared her throat. "He might have suggested it, but Lord Hedrick would have had to do the actual naming." She turned to Zephyr for confirmation.

Zephyr lifted one shoulder and nodded.

Princess Day gestured to her. "Dragoneer Moira, you're the expert. Is time of the essence?"

Moira stepped closer to the prince and princess. "Lord Hedrick's dragon-bit abilities will grow stronger each day. If he thinks you're waiting, then your only advantage is surprise." She paused. "For myself, I'm going to Castle Tern to free my friends and as many people as I can. I'd appreciate your help."

"What do you suggest?" the princess asked.

Moira sucked in a breath, steeling herself. "We knock on his front door."

Prince Owen sat forward. "And then what? He invites you in?"

"Yes. Because he's been looking for us. Urion will deliver us to the castle and collect the reward." She glanced over her shoulder to see Urion start, though he was quick to cover his reaction with a nod of agreement.

The princess frowned. "You'll almost certainly be thrown in a cell. You must realize that."

"I'm counting on it. Once Urion has his reward, he'll find the nearest inn and settle down for the night. It should give him plenty of time to track down where they've put Zephyr and release him. Together they'll work to open the main gate, which will allow your forces entry. In the meantime, I'll escape, track down my friends and free them. After they're out of harm's way, Zephyr and I will join the fight. We'll take down Vinton and get rid of the pretender any way we can."

The prince, princess, Hill, and even Urion stared at her with a mixture of wonder and disbelief. Zephyr alone kept his feelings off of his face, though Moira could tell by the set of his wyvern's jaw he was not happy with her plan. At least he didn't let it show. Thankfully, he didn't use their connection to let her know what he thought of her plan either.

Prince Owen recovered first. "That is madness."

"With all due respect, I don't think it is. Zephyr and I should have been a part of the Light Legion. That's not possible now, so we'll have to do it on our own." When no one said anything, she added, "I'm open to suggestions."

"Mattias?" the prince asked.

Hill blinked, frowning. "The odds are astronomically against you."

When are they not? Moira couldn't suppress the shudder that ran through her, but her breathing remained even and her voice steady. "I know."

The prince stood. "Then we have much to do. When do you leave?"

"How far is the castle?" she asked.

"It'll take you a few hours to get there by wagon."

"We'll leave this evening."

"Come with me until then," the princess said. She turned to her brother. "We'll be in my rooms."

36

With their backpacks returned by the guards, Moira, Zephyr, and Urion followed the princess out through the rear of the tent. They wound through a series of smaller pavilions until the princess stopped at the entrance to one. "Please come in." She pulled the flap aside and entered.

Zephyr, as usual, had to duck through the door. Though he could stand up straight inside, the ceiling wasn't as high as the previous tent. His head brushed the canvas.

To one side of the tent, a chair sat in front of a desk, doubling as a vanity. The surface contained a curious mix of jars, brushes, paper, and feathered ink pens with a large oval mirror standing behind it. A single bed covered in furs and blankets sat in the middle with a closed trunk at one end. On the other side of the tent was a rail from which clothes either fell neatly from hangers or had been tossed over the top without bother. Under the rail, another trunk spewed more clothes and shoes.

Princess Day lifted a bell from the top of the desk and rang it. It emitted a distinct tinkling sound. She set the bell down on a stack of papers, and immediately lifted it again to straighten the stack of writings. "Shouldn't be a minute."

Moira glanced at her companions. *Minute for what?*

Two women came bustling into the tent. One had fair skin with long blonde hair, while the other's skin tone was closer to Moira's in terms of its melanin content, her dark hair braided and rolled into a coil. The blonde wore a long dress and apron, while the other wore a deep red embroidered tunic and pants. Both women stopped when they saw the princess had company.

"Joanna and Lyla are my ladies-in-waiting." The princess frowned as she glanced around the tent. "Ladies, I think we shall require baths and food. In fact, quite a lot of food. And an extra chair."

The dark-haired one, Lyla, started to do the princess' bidding but stopped when she saw the other didn't move. She laid a hand on the blonde's arm. "Joanna?"

The other lady-in-waiting remained frozen.

"What's the matter?" asked the princess.

"Allow me, Princess," Urion said. With a pointed look at Moira, he went to stand in front of Joanna.

Moira nudged Zephyr to get his attention, then tilted her head to the back of the tent. They strolled around the bed until they were on the far side of it near another set of tent flaps.

Urion grasped the woman by the arms and turned her away from where she had come face to face with a one-ton, yellow-eyed dragon. "Joanna," he called several times, gently but firmly.

Joanna came back to herself with a little jump. This propelled a short scream from her throat which Moira imagined had gotten stuck there like a cork in a bottle when she first laid eyes on Zephyr.

"It's all right. Is Zephyr the first dragon you've met?" Urion asked.

Joanna nodded. She turned her head toward her mistress. "I'm so sorry, Your Highness."

The princess waved away her apology. "Don't be silly. I completely forgot. Are you well now?"

Joanna stiffened her spine. "Yes."

Assured she was well, Urion released her and the ladies left the tent.

Moira spoke up. "We don't need to bathe… "

"Yes, you do," Zephyr said.

Urion plucked the front of his tunic. "Speak for yourself."

Day leaned back against her desk, arms crossed. "I appreciate the fact that you don't want to put me or my people through any trouble, but it's the absolute least we can do. You need to prepare yourselves." She uncrossed her arms and stood. "Come. Put your things down. Make yourselves at home." She nodded to the set of tent flaps Moira and Zephyr stood beside. "The bath is through there, but it will take some time to heat the water. I'm sorry, I don't think we have a bath large enough for a dragon."

Zephyr made a rumbling sound. "I have had quite enough of water lately, but thank you."

"I'll see about something to drink then." Day left the tent.

They removed their backpacks and weapons. Joanna and Lyla returned with platters of food and two guards carrying a trestle table to set the food on. Joanna sneaked peeks at Zephyr but didn't freeze up again.

Left alone, the three of them picked at a selection of cold meats and cheeses until Urion pulled a deck of playing cards from somewhere and tried to teach Zephyr a game. Watching Urion and Zephyr play, she wondered if they shouldn't all be doing something more to get ready, but then let the thought go, deciding to take advantage of the opportunity to eat and rest while they could. No telling when they would have the chance to do so again.

Day returned with a servant carrying two jugs, one of water and one of wine. She dismissed the servant and poured cups for them herself. "I have something else for you as well." She held out a small leather case. "It occurred to me that you never said *how* you planned to escape the cell you are so set on being thrown into, and I thought these would help."

Moira opened the tiny bundle to find a set of lock picking tools.

Moira thanked her and the two lapsed into an awkward silence as they watched Urion and Zephyr play cards.

The princess, however, must have trained for this sort of thing. "Do you like being a dragoneer?"

"I…don't really have a choice."

Day smoothed the bandage on the back of her hand holding the cup. "How silly of me. Of course you don't."

Moira rushed to reassure her. "It's okay. It's just no one's ever asked me that before. It's, um, yeah, it's…different."

Day chuckled. "I would think so."

"Have you been around many dragons?"

Day sipped from her cup. "Yes. Mattias hired retired battle dragons and their dragoneers to help bring in the harvest every year." She turned to look at Zephyr. "You must be close."

"We are, but I don't think it's just because of the bite." Moira remembered the way Rasti had spoken of his dragon Ibsen, who hadn't died in battle but from some horrible disease. Even speaking of it years later still affected him. "I think other dragoneers grow just as close with their charges over time, even if they're not bitten."

"From what I saw of the pairs that came to the farm, that seems to be the case." Day's lips curled. "I can only imagine what I would—" She cut herself off as Joanna and Lyla, along with a procession of others, filed through the tent hauling buckets of water.

They returned in the same order.

Joanna stopped beside Day. "The bath is ready, Your Highness. It's also time to change your dressing."

Day held her arm out for Joanna to begin unwinding the bandage.

Dressing removed, Moira saw that the princess had indeed punctured the base of her palm on something sharp. More than once. Bruising made it difficult to see the wounds clearly, though they appeared to be on the mend.

Must be all the dressing changes.

Moira gestured to the injury. "How did you do that?"

"I'm not sure, really. Maybe in my sleep?" Day indicated the rail of clothes with a tilt of her head. "Help yourself to anything you need."

Moira glanced at the rail. "I have clothes, but I was wondering... "

What followed was a brief conversation about clean underwear. Day gave her a set of never before worn underthings that weren't quite her size. Moira crossed her fingers and hoped they would fit as she was about half a foot taller than the princess.

Urion didn't get up, which Moira took to mean she could go first. She pulled the clean set of clothes from her backpack and headed to the bath. Milky water scented with flowers and spices steamed inside the tub, but she wasn't about to complain.

A hint of trepidation raced up her spine at the thought of getting into the standing water, but she shook it off. Her toes curled with the heat as she sank below the surface. Every muscle tensed on contact with the fragrant water. Moira sighed and just sat there for a moment. Once her muscles relaxed, she used the cloth left on the side of the tub to wash away the dirt and sweat from their journey. At the end, she shut her eyes tight and dunked her head, unconcerned with what she was going to do with her hair afterward, focusing on how good it felt to be clean again.

Refreshed, she got out and used one of the towels on a stand nearby. Clad in clean clothes, she returned to the other room. Urion shuffled the deck of cards by himself while Zephyr stood over the table of food. Day spoke quietly with Lyla in front of her desk.

When Day saw Moira, she rang the bell. Joanna reappeared with her retinue to empty and refill the bath.

Moira got out of the way and went to Zephyr's side.

He looked up as she approached. "You smell better."

"Gee, thanks. Who won?" she tipped her head toward Urion.

"He cheats."

She laughed. "He doesn't have to."

Day called out to Moira, "Come and have a seat." She indicated the chair in front of the vanity.

Moira smiled. "What's going on?"

"Lyla's going to do your hair." She paused. "If that's all right?"

Moira sat down as requested. "My schedule is wide open."

Urion took his turn in the bath while Lyla got started with a heated comb, pulling and twisting Moira's curls into submission. Zephyr settled down on the other side of the tent and closed his eyes to take a nap.

Lyla tucked and tamed Moira's locks into two rows that met at the back of her neck where they were plaited together. Moira admired her work in the mirror, content that her hair would be out of the way.

"Perfect," Day said. "Now I want you to have something." She went to the trunk at the end of the bed. Throwing back the lid she woke Zephyr, who lifted one spiny brow at the interruption. He sat up with a dragon-sized stretch that threatened to bring the tent down.

Day rifled through the trunk and returned with a fancy silver comb. But it wasn't just a comb. The center of it pulled away to reveal a very sharp fixed blade about three inches long. "I never leave home without a blade about my person. In the event you need to use this one, try not to cut off all your hair."

37

The driver's seat of the uncovered wagon rocked under Moira as they lumbered over uneven packed earth toward Castle Tern's main gate. Urion drove. Zephyr sat in the back. Ropes bound both Moira and Zephyr's outstretched wrists, tight enough to be believable, but not enough to be uncomfortable. They'd departed the prince's camp in the early evening and dusk had fallen along the way. Before they reached the sight of the guards at the south gate, Urion brought the wagon to a stop.

Moira peered at Urion through the gloom. "Why are we stopping?"

"Are you absolutely sure about this?"

The time for bravado had passed, not that she'd had much to start with. Moira swallowed, choked, and tried again. "No. I'm not sure of anything." She had no idea what was about to happen. It could all go sideways at any moment.

Urion sighed. "Well, thanks for being honest."

Moira lifted her bound hands. "Just stick to the plan. Take the reward money and go. Find a way back in and get Zephyr out."

"And you really don't think Vinton will kill you both on sight?"

Moira raised her shoulders. "I don't know. Call it a hunch. I don't think he will." She relaxed. "Not now." She spoke the last words more to herself. She imagined Vinton must have plotted and schemed to arrange their demise at the river. Since then, the Regent had died, and a dragon had bitten Lord Hedrick. How much did Vinton know about dragoneers?

Urion twisted around in his seat. "And you're okay with this?"

"I am not okay with any of this," Zephyr said. "I will not be okay until this is over and we have what we came for. But I have faith in Moira and my sword."

"Your sword is back in Princess Day's tent," Urion reminded him.

Zephyr offered a low grumble in response.

Urion had his sword and Moira's dagger, the same blade Vinton had thrown at Zephyr back home. The handle of it stuck out of Urion's belt. Zephyr would have to find another sword. *Or two.*

Urion set the reins down. "You'd better take this." He tugged at the neck of his shirt and pulled the chain with the gold coin his father had given him over his head.

Moira stared, skeptical. "I thought you couldn't get rid of it if you tried."

Urion slipped the chain over her head. "I can't and I'm not. You're borrowing it." He picked up the reins again, muttering under his breath.

Moira lifted her bound hands to tuck the gold piece inside her shirt. The medallion was still warm from Urion's chest. *He must think we're in real trouble.* She swallowed, unable to find the words to reassure him.

Urion grabbed the dagger out of his belt and aimed the point at her side. "Time to put on a show." He flicked the reins with his other hand.

The horses walked on. Around a bend, the castle gate stood shut tight against intruders and everyone else. Soldiers in matching red tunics and trousers with leather boots and helmets stood watch. Swords sheathed alongside javelins and shields resting against the castle wall suggested the soldiers did not view the new arrivals with alarm.

A single metal-encrusted figure, presumably an officer, stepped forward. Once Urion disclosed the identity of the captives he would escort to the High Magician, the doors opened.

An armed escort met them on the other side of the castle gates and ordered Urion to follow. Torches lit the way. The white stone walls of the keep rose forty feet over their heads with spires and towers taller than that, but before they could reach it they had to travel a road lined with buildings on either side. Moira made out a forge, stables, workshops, and stores. There weren't many people on the roadway, but every doorway filled to watch them pass.

As they drew closer, Moira didn't hide her fear, in part because she didn't think she could. From behind, Zephyr reminded her to breathe with a quiet word. A large part of the plan hinged on her keeping it together. She couldn't afford to go to pieces now.

More guards stopped them at the bottom of the keep's entrance and Moira saw the first trolls she'd seen since their fight in the woods. An armed pair stood at the top of the stone steps on either side of a set of double doors. The human guards escorting her, Zephyr, and Urion kept their distance from the trolls.

Urion gripped Moira by the neck and kept the dagger pointed at her side. Zephyr growled, she knew, at this treatment of her, but said nothing. At the top of the stairs, the trolls admitted them into a large foyer.

And, here, inside the main entrance to the keep, Moira caught sight of imps for the first time. They stood guard around the foyer holding tall steel pikes pointed at Zephyr, each dressed in the same uniform as the human guards at the gate. The one closest to her stood a half-foot shorter than herself, which, judging by the others, seemed to be the going size of imp. At first glance, they could have passed for average-sized humans. Upon closer inspection, though, she saw the imp's features were oddly smooth, their noses flat with deep-set dark eyes and thin lips. Their dark hair was fine and straight, trimmed high over pointed ears. Also, she thought, the pale flesh of the imp next to her had a greenish tint to it.

A large purple-gray troll with greasy hair came through a pair of doors. "This way," it said in a deep, guttural tone.

Urion tugged her by the neck to follow. She knew it was an act, but it annoyed her. She let her irritation show. It was better than looking as scared as she felt.

By the sound of it, the pike-wielding imps fell in behind them.

They entered a long hall with a balcony running around it about halfway up. This had to be the throne room. The large gilt chair on top of the stepped platform at the end kind of gave it away. What surprised her was the young man sitting in it, one leg thrown over the arm, like he owned it. His dark clothing made his already pale features appear washed out and colorless. HIs nearly white blonde hair didn't help either. Only his eyes held a spot of color: they were brown.

"Stop." The troll faced them. They were several yards short of the first step that led to the throne.

The figure in the chair spoke. "I am King Hedrick. Welcome to Castle Tern." He gave an airy wave.

Moira was more certain than ever they'd made the right choice by coming and meeting Vinton and Hedrick head-on if the latter was already calling himself king.

"What a wonderful specimen of wyvern." Hedrick lowered his leg from the arm of the throne and stood. "I have my own." He raised his right hand.

To that side of the throne, the deepest shadows stirred. A solid black wyvern unfurled itself from where it had been lying curled with its back against the steps in a slow unwinding of scales. The dragon was as tall as Zephyr. His electric blue eyes were half closed and took them in with a dispassion that seemed to teeter on boredom.

"This is Kingkiller," Hedrick said.

Kingkiller's eyes rolled at the introduction. His slate-black lips lifted in a sneer, displaying one large white fang, before he turned his back on the throne and King Hedrick in what Moira could only describe as a huff. From the lack of a reaction, no one thought this behavior strange.

Moira glanced at Urion from the corner of her eye. His brow puckered. She badly wanted to see what Zephyr made of Kingkiller, but her dragon stood behind her and the weight of Urion's hand on her neck kept her from turning her head to see.

"Kingkiller, huh?" Moira said, not hiding her irritation or amusement. "I don't think you thought that one through."

Hedrick—she couldn't think of him as a king or even a lord after having met him— glowered.

Urion increased the pressure on her neck by an infinitesimal amount, but Moira grunted and bent lower as if he had caused her pain.

"I've brought you the dragoneer and her dragon. I want my money."

Hedrick's expression cleared. "My High Magician, Lord Vinton, will see to your reward." He focused on the dagger Urion pointed at her side. "How did you capture them?"

An oily smile slid over Urion's features. "I used my considerable charm."

Hedrick's eyes took Urion in from head to toe and back again. He lifted a single brow. "And how do you keep the dragon in check? You don't expect me to believe tying his hands keeps him in line, do you?"

Urion tipped his head toward Moira. "I've got her. He won't do a thing as long as she might come to harm." He brought the dagger forward, pressed the flat of the blade across her abdomen, and grinned for Hedrick's benefit.

Hedrick laughed. "I can almost believe your charm was enough."

Moira turned her head away from Urion, her gaze to the side. Let him and everyone else think Urion had wooed her out of her good sense.

Hedrick came down the steps, stopping at the bottom. "We can do away with the ropes. The dragon will remain bound, but I want the dragoneer free."

Urion released her neck and pulled her around to face him, by her bound wrists. He used the dagger to cut her free. The ropes fell at her feet. She stole a peek at Zephyr. His tail lashed the air in irritation, but he otherwise didn't move.

"Remind me of your name again?" Hedrick asked her.

Moira rubbed at the marks left behind by the ropes. Hedrick knew perfectly well what her name was, he just didn't want her to know he knew it.

"Moira."

"Ah, but it's not just Moira, is it?" Hedrick said.

"Moira Noble."

Hedrick chuckled. "That's right. You call yourself noble, as if it will make you so."

Moira lowered her hands and faced him. "It's my name. Call me an onion, I'll smell as sweet. Or something like that."

"That's not what Lord Vinton thinks."

Moira didn't suppose that Vinton thought she smelled, but she also didn't know what his obsession with her name was. Bertram hadn't wanted her to call the Librarian by the name she did because words had power. For whatever reason, it sounded as if Vinton thought her name had some special power to it. If that was the case, she would take any advantage she could get.

Hedrick gave her the same once-over he had given Urion. "Let's see what you can do." He drew a dagger from behind his back, similar to the one Urion kept trained on her middle. Hedrick stood the dagger point down over his open palm. He let go. For a second, the blade balanced on its point in the middle of his hand. She spotted the moment his magic took over and kept the dagger upright. He lowered his palm away from the point and backed up a step. The dagger remained fixed in space.

She'd done the same thing with a pebble in her bedroom the first time she experimented with using her magic and her will. She'd progressed since then.

Hedrick's dark eyes flashed. "Take it."

Moira assumed he meant with her magic. She focused on the blade, holding it aloft easily. Visualizing it moving toward her, she drew on her will to make it happen. The blade shuddered in her direction a couple of inches and stopped when she met resistance. It had to be her magic in competition with Hedrick's.

His will kept the dagger from getting any closer to her.

It can't be this easy, can it? Moira willed the dagger to turn, the end lifting to point at Hedrick. Then the blade stopped as it encountered the same resistance. What would happen if she could raise the tip of the dagger until it was pointed at Hedrick's center, then stopped trying to hold it? They struggled over the turning of the blade, each trying to find the seams of the other's magic where they could get a finger hold and push the other's will aside.

Hedrick's face was a picture of concentration to match her own. Beads of sweat gathered across his brow.

Behind her, Zephyr shifted his bulk, careful not to distract her.

To her amazement Kingkiller did nothing. In her peripheral vision, the dragon sat, unconcerned that Hedrick was under duress and might come to harm in any way. Moira couldn't be sure, but she didn't think it was because of his overwhelming confidence in Hedrick's abilities. Kingkiller appeared to not care one way or another what happened to his dragoneer.

Hedrick might not know it, but he had a very, very sulky dragon on his hands.

Moira redoubled her efforts. The dagger's point inched toward Hedrick.

A voice barked from the back of the room. "What is going on?"

38

Vinton had joined them at last.

Moira hadn't heard that voice since the night he kidnapped Aaron and Ansel. She relaxed her will.

Hedrick stepped forward and snatched the dagger out of the air, slipping it out of sight. "We have visitors."

Vinton was clad in shiny armor, with a sword at his hip and a red cloak trailing from his shoulders. His hair was cropped close to his skull and his eyes glinted over a crooked nose and slash of a mouth. Moira smirked at the thought he'd recently had an unpleasant encounter with a barber.

Beside him, six heavily-armed imps kept close. Another waited nearby, also wearing armor. On the balcony overlooking the hall, ten more imps took up positions with bows drawn and arrows directed at Moira and Zephyr.

"Where are her restraints? Tie her hands!" Vinton ordered.

The purple-gray troll who had shown them into the hall grabbed a length of rope from an imp.

Moira didn't move. *Well, I'm not going to help.* The troll had to lift her wrist to tie the rope to it.

As the troll lifted her other wrist in front of her, Vinton shouted at the creature. "Not like that. Behind her back."

Hedrick scoffed. "She is only one girl."

Vinton glared. "One I've underestimated. I won't do so again. Search her."

Uh-oh. The troll finished restraining her and began to pat her down. Moira stood there as the troll pulled the case of lock picking tools from the top of her boot. Finished, the troll backed away, taking her tools with him.

Vinton approached the front of the room, the imps trailing behind him. He stopped next to Hedrick, his watchful gaze going from her to Zephyr, to Urion, and back. "I see it now. Strange that I missed it." He met Moira's gaze. "I've learned so much about you from your friends."

"Where are they?" Moira spoke in a heated rush of words she almost wished she could take back.

Vinton's eyes glinted as he spoke to the metal-encased imp beside him. "Collect our other guests."

The imp turned to do Vinton's bidding, leaving the throne room through a side door.

Her heart leaped as she watched him go. Aaron and Ansel were alive and they were coming. Her muscles tensed.

"As I said, I've learned so much about you from your friends. I feel as if I know you."

"Then you know what I'll do to you if you've hurt them."

Vinton dismissed her words with a wave. "Oh, they're not half bad. They've been very helpful. You shouldn't worry for them. You should worry for yourself."

The imp returned through the door he'd left through.

Vinton raised an eyebrow, but kept his gaze trained on her. "And here they are."

Behind the imp, Aaron and Ansel walked into the hall.

Moira resisted the urge to shout and run to them, acutely aware of the arrows pointed at her, the troll at her elbow, and Vinton's gaze on her like a physical weight. Her knees wobbled, but she covered it by turning to watch the imp bringing her friends forward.

They appeared unhurt, clean, and well fed. Vinton had dressed the twin brothers in matching outfits, which she knew they must have hated, because as long as she'd known them they'd avoided it at all costs.

They walked under their own power without restraints, but Moira sensed something odd about their circumstances. Ansel clung to Aaron. The last time she had seen them, Aaron had barely been conscious, but now Ansel kept twitching and looking over his shoulder. His lips moving, as if he was talking to himself, yet he made no noise, seemingly unaware of his surroundings. Beside him, though, Aaron, silent, his face pale, stood glaring. His clenched fist rested atop his brother's shoulder.

"Ansel? Aaron?" She called their names, her voice filled with questions.

Ansel jerked upon hearing his name, but didn't look around at her. Aaron's gaze slid away from hers with a shake of his head. His jaw clenched.

Heat flushed through her. "What did you do to them?" she asked.

"They're alive. For now," Vinton said.

"Let them go. You have me. You don't need them anymore."

"Oh, I think I do. If, for nothing else, to ensure your cooperation." Vinton smiled. "But truly, they've been amusing. I can't wait to see if you're half as entertaining."

He turned his focus to Urion. "And who do we have to thank for delivering another dragon and dragoneer to our doorstep?"

"Someone who wants to get paid for his trouble," Urion said.

Vinton's head tilted. "Guards." The additional imps fanned out to surround them. Vinton came forward and took his dagger from Urion's unresisting fingers. "Thank you for returning this. It belongs to a matched set." He touched the point of the dagger to the tip of his finger. "However, I'm afraid there will be no reward. I received a message from one of my magicians. Lord Smew made the acquaintance of a rather dismayed young man in Farrago. This Kaidence was on the trail of a half-breed who besmirched his betrothed. That halfling escaped with the help of a girl and her dragon. Not once, but twice. The second time, the girl called down lightning to get away."

The corners of Urion's mouth turned down as he shook his head. "Doesn't ring a bell."

Vinton smashed his fist into Urion's stomach.

The halfling doubled over then fell to his knees.

Moira stepped forward, but the armored imp grabbed her arm and held her back. She struggled, but there wasn't much she could do.

"Urion, isn't it?" Vinton flicked Urion's hair aside to reveal the points of his ears. "He described you very well." Vinton stuck the dagger in his belt. "Show them to their cells."

He turned to Moira. "I'm glad you survived. Although I had hoped for your death at the river, now I see you are much more valuable to me alive. I have plans for you. And for your dragon."

The imp pulled at her arm with such force she knew her choices were to walk or get dragged. With haste, she turned to Zephyr. His expressive eyes, set in an impassive face, comforted her. Their connection flashed unspoken emotions between them. She twisted back. Urion lay on the floor, his face hidden. Ansel looked down.

Aaron, however, met her gaze. With her eyes, she tried to tell him it was going to be okay.

In answer, Aaron's lips pressed into a firm line, his posture rigid.

Moira couldn't blame him. She would have been skeptical too if she saw her only chance for aid being dragged away from the hall, hands tied, to be thrown into a cell.

39

They stopped at the bottom of a long flight of stairs.

The imp standing guard snapped to attention. "General?"

Her metal-plated escort released her arm. "Another one."

Moira's eyebrows drew together. *Another what?*

"There's room near the end." The guard lifted a set of keys from his belt and they started down a long corridor with barred rooms on either side.

The imp general pulled her along beside him down the torch-lined hallway with the guard on her other side. Light spilled from all but the last cell. Doors of crisscrossed, rigid iron bars lined both sides of the corridor. Each cell's door had a panel with a locking mechanism. Solid walls separated the individual cells. As they passed, she glimpsed the faces of several women who watched in silence as the imps led Moira past them. The prisoners appeared clean and well cared for aside from their middles, which were all in various stages of being swollen with child.

Inside, Moira seethed, her muscles tense, but she continued to allow herself to be led. She had found the women of Councy Forest and who knew how many more beside.

The guard had the key out and ready by the time they reached the cell next to the darkened one at the very end.

Moira did her best to take a mental picture of the key and paid careful attention to how the imp opened the door. It swung inward. The general pushed her inside. The jailer slammed it behind her. She got a quick impression of three beds, one pressed against each wall, two of them occupied, before she faced the door from the inside.

"Behave and there'll be food and drink, time for exercise, and candles. Don't, and it'll all get taken away," said the jailer.

Moira made no comment.

"That will be all." The general waited for the guard to return to his post at the other end of the hall before stepping over to the darkened cell adjacent. His hand rose to rest on the handle of his sword as he stepped in close to the door, his head turning to search the cell. Light from the torches along the wall bounced off the dark blue gemstone set in the hilt.

Moira drew in a breath. The artfully crafted handle could only be Brixton's work; thus, the stone could only be the soul sapphire he had described.

Nothing stirred within the cell. After a minute the general backed away from the door and left, his footsteps fading.

"It's kind of sad," said a voice over her shoulder.

Moira jumped.

A young woman stood behind her, one hand on her hip, the other cradling the bump in front of her. Her hair was a sunny yellow, tied back from her face, but clean and lustrous even in the low light.

"What is?" asked Moira.

The woman tilted her head toward the darkened cell. "That's his mother." She grimaced in sympathy. "I'm Leeza. Do you want me to untie you?" She moved behind Moira. "Where did you come from? Are there any more women, or is it just you?"

"Would you stop?" Exasperation filled the fresh voice. "She's going to be here a while. There's no need to bombard her with questions as soon as she arrives." The other woman spoke from her bunk where she sat with a blanket wrapped around her shoulders. Older than Leeza, with dark hair, lines of worry etched into her face, she wore a pair of spectacles perched on the bridge of her nose.

"That's Carina. We've been here a while. She's tired of listening to me talk, but I was just curious. They don't usually bring the women in one at a time, that's all," Leeza prattled on.

Moira didn't mind the talking, especially because Leeza was good with knots.

The ropes parted and Moira's hands were free. She sighed and rolled her shoulders. "Thank you. I'm Moira." She rubbed at her abused wrists. The troll had tied her hands together much tighter than they had been before. "They brought me here with a friend and my dragon."

"A dragoneer?" Leeza asked. "Does that mean there are others coming? Are they going to get us out of here?"

"Don't be ridiculous, Lee," Carina said. "No one is coming to rescue us. No one cares. We're on our own. Don't listen to her," she told Moira. "She still thinks she's going to get out of here, go home, and raise her—baby."

Carina clearly had replaced the word "imp" at the last second. It seemed to be a conversation they'd had before.

Leeza sat on the bed across from Carina. "Well, look at the general. He comes to visit his mother even if she wants nothing to do with him. I don't blame her, but it gives me hope. If we could just get away from here, I could raise him right."

Carina leaned forward. "Keep your voice down. You upset the others when they hear you talk like that."

Moira rubbed her wrists. "How do you know it's a boy?"

"All imps are boys. Everyone knows that." Leeza yawned. "Anyway, time to sleep." With that, she covered up with a blanket and laid down with her back to them.

Carina stood and unrolled the thin mattress on the unoccupied bed at the back of the cell. "This is yours." She pulled out a blanket stored underneath to set on top.

Moira sat on the edge of her bunk. "Thank you." Her gaze came to rest on Carina's middle.

"They take you away, give you a foul drink, and you wake up pregnant."

Moira rested her forehead in her hand. "Is that how..."

Carina sat on her own bed. "Yes, it's all very..." Her voice trailed off. "It doesn't change what it is though. Not to us. Lee's the exception. The rest of us ignore the pregnancies as much as we can and would do just about anything to get out of here." She shook her head. "But it's impossible."

Moira chewed the inside of her lip. "I used to think dragons were impossible."

Carina huffed out a small laugh, her lips settling into a small smile. "You're a dragoneer."

"I know. Sometimes the big things are so ridiculous, so hard to believe, the smaller things seem like a miracle and the impossible becomes possible. You just have to be ready." Moira was afraid to say more than that. She didn't want to offer Carina, Leeza, or any of the other women hope and then snatch it away.

Carina offered her a tight smile. "How old are you?"

"I turned fifteen on my last birthday."

"Ah. Okay. Well, the water bucket is by the door if you're thirsty and the toilet's over there," she tipped her head toward another bucket in the opposite corner. "Don't get confused. I'm going to bed. Sleep well, Moira. Mornings come early around here." Instead of lying down, Carina leaned back against the wall behind her, tilted her head back, and closed her eyes.

Moira spread out the blanket and laid down on top of it to wait.

40

Moira did not go to sleep. When the quiet was only interrupted by a random cough or snuffle she stood and slipped quietly to the door of the cell.

She cursed the loss of the lock picking tools. They would have come in handy. She'd never picked a lock before, but she had counted on being able to figure it out. Without the tools, she was left with one alternative. Reaching up, she pulled the blade out of the comb Princess Day had given her. Her arms through the door, she slipped the small knife into the keyhole and wiggled it around.

She didn't know how long she fussed with it before she knew it wasn't going to work. In resignation, she slipped the knife into the waistband of her pants at the small of her back.

In her mind's eye, she recalled the cut of the jailor's key. She knew how locks worked, how the pins lined up with the tumblers so the key could turn. This was no arrow, rock, or dagger. This was subtle work that required all of her concentration. When she thought she had the image focused in her mind, she carefully pressed her hand to the metal plate containing the door's lock and closed her eyes. She released a pinch of her will.

Nothing happened.

Moira opened her eyes. The faintest *snick* of metal against metal reached her ears. She pulled on the door. It moved. Moira opened it just enough to unlatch the door and waited. Nothing stirred.

Now for the hard part.

Zephyr could camouflage himself at will, not just when they were outside in the woods, but anywhere. A rare talent, or so everyone told her. Urion and Rasti thought they should have been in the Light Legion, not because of his ability to fight, but because of his aptitude to bend light and make himself invisible.

However, Moira could always see him even when others couldn't. She suspected she shared this talent, which meant she should be able to make herself disappear. Thinking back, she had probably done it in the school library when Ms. Haven had come out of her office. Now she needed to do it again. And if she could see Zephyr when he was camouflaged, she would probably be able to see herself, which didn't help. How would she know if she had gotten it right?

Moira stood there, chewing the inside of her lip. Light glinted off the water in the bucket by the door from a torch outside. She waved her hand over the bucket and the movement reflected on the water's surface, her hand blocking the light from the torches outside. She closed her eyes and summoned her will, not to block the light, but to wrap herself in it. Tapping into her will, she let it trickle out, unsure if she would remain invisible once she released her intention.

Exhaling, she released her will, and opened her eyes. She waved her hand over the bucket.

No reflection.

She made a fist and pumped it in the air, happy no one could see her.

Moira pulled the door of the cell open enough to slip through the opening. The hinges squealed loudly to her ears, but no one sent up an alarm. She pulled the unlocked door closed behind her. As quietly as she could, she raced to the end of the hallway toward the jailor. She didn't know if she could unlock the other cells as she had hers, but if she had the jailor's keys, she didn't have to worry about it. Wondering how she was going to get the keys away from him, she didn't need to bother. The jailor, slumped asleep in a chair, proved an easy target. She freed the key ring from his belt without disturbing him.

A pinch in her side told her the keys were now invisible too. Her will had drawn on her strength to include them in her light bending. She hurried back along the corridor, holding the keys so they wouldn't jingle. Back and forth down the hall, she unlocked cell doors as quietly as she could. Some cells were larger than others. Moira tried not to focus on the women inside. Most slept. Some stared off into space, oblivious. Outside the last cell door at the end, she hesitated. Much like the imp general had done, she searched the darkness for the cell's inhabitant but found no one. Regardless, she found the right key and unlocked the door.

When she glanced up again, she jumped. Without making a sound, a young woman now stood on the other side. Her hair hung in a limp curtain around a pale, oval face, while her eyes seemed to stare straight at her.

Moira wondered if her spell had weakened so she backed up, but the other woman's eyes didn't follow her.

Moira squinted. The woman in the cell had the same eyes as Heather Ann, in shape and color, but with a harsh gleam to them. *Is this her sister? What was her name? Jeanette.*

On the other side of the door, Jeanette blinked and glanced down at the lock.

Convinced she remained invisible, Moira did not stick around to see Jeanette's reaction to the unlocked door.

With a tight grip on the keys, Moira ran down the hallway and past the sleeping guard. She'd paid careful attention earlier when the imp general led her downstairs. Quietly retracing her steps, she came to where the soldiers escorting Urion had turned. She headed that way, passing imps and guards, though not one of them saw her. She checked for her reflection when passing shiny surfaces. Nothing showed. At the bottom of another set of stairs, she came across a cluster of fetid cells. The imp on duty's lips rippled with his snores. Urion sat huddled in his cloak with his back pressed to the wall of the nearest cell.

How many different locks could one keep have? She started with the keys she'd used to open the other cells. The second one she tried worked. Urion's head lifted and turned toward the sound. Afraid to give herself away, Moira backed away from the door without a sound.

Urion stood and tried the cell door. It opened. He smiled. Then his eyes narrowed, and he scanned the space where she stood. His lips mouthed her name.

She didn't answer. Instead, she turned around and headed back the way she had come. Now that he was free, Urion would return to their plan and get Zephyr so they could open the gate for Prince Owen's army. Moira's part of the plan remained the same. Find Aaron and Ansel.

She slipped through the rest of the castle like a light-footed shadow, retracing her steps through the heavily-guarded foyer back into the throne room. Inside the long hall, it was quiet. A moment later, she saw why. To the left of the throne, Kingkiller lay asleep. Hedrick was nowhere to be seen.

Her heart pinched with an unexpected sadness. How could Hedrick leave his dragon all on his own to sleep on a cold stone floor? *That's no way for a dragoneer to treat their dragon.* Her heart ached for Kingkiller, which she hadn't expected. Maybe that was the way things had to be, like at home with Zephyr in his cave and Moira at the house, but she didn't think so. Something was seriously off between the dragon and dragoneer. She couldn't tell what it was, but she didn't have time to fix it, even if she knew how.

Moira moved with caution to the side door Aaron and Ansel had first emerged from, and slipped through it into a corridor with doors on either side. With care, she checked each one. The unlocked doors led to a variety of rooms, some with furniture, others without, but none with occupants.

Halfway down, the door opened to a joyless little room with one small window high on the wall, two cots, and a large flat desk with a single lit candle. One cot held a sleeping form. Aaron sat at the desk, his head buried in his hands.

Moira slipped into the room and closed the door behind her. She closed her eyes to slough off her spell now that she wanted to be seen. Something that had been tense inside of her relaxed. She didn't know if it worked, but she would find out soon. She whispered, "Aaron?"

At the desk, Aaron jumped to his feet, startled. The chair fell over behind him, raising a racket, but his gaze went right to her face and not through her. "Moira?"

Moira raised a finger to her lips.

Ansel mumbled where he lay on his side, facing the room. Moira crossed to the side of his cot and dropped to her knees beside him. What she'd seen of him earlier had disturbed her. From their brief encounter, she knew Ansel was not well but she didn't know how bad it was. Her hand settled on his shoulder.

"Don't wake him. They give him something to help him sleep. Otherwise, he doesn't," Aaron said. "What are you doing here?"

Moira's gaze snapped to Aaron, who stood with his shoulders squared and jaw clenched. She got to her feet. "I'm here to get you out of here and go home."

His head tilted in the direction of the throne room. "Was that… was that your dragon?"

"Yes. That's Zephyr."

Aaron nodded, his teeth grinding together. "I didn't know what the magician was talking about. I never knew. But he did." He tipped his head at Ansel. "Do you know what that magician did to him? Ansel tried to fight him. At first. But the magician was too strong. One day he couldn't fight anymore."

Moira flinched. *I've got a pretty good idea.* A lump formed in her throat as she viewed Ansel's sleeping form. Her eyes gritty from lack of sleep, she thought it best to remain silent.

"Do you have any idea what kind of hell we've been through?" Aaron asked, his tone scathing. "Do you know what we've had to do to survive since we got here? If it weren't for me, we'd be dead. I've had to do terrible things for them."

She heard the catch in his voice and winced.

"And it's all because of you. We wouldn't *be* here if you hadn't told my brother what happened to you and invited him along on some crazy adventure you two kept to yourselves."

He was right. Moira couldn't deny her part in their being where they were. It was why she was there. Her voice cracked when she spoke. "I'm sorry."

"You're sorry?"

Moira faced him. "That's what I said. I am. Sorry. I never wanted this. We came as soon as we could, but time doesn't run the same way here as it does at home."

Aaron shook his head, his face and neck turning a mottled red. "What are you talking about? Who cares about time? We don't have any. It's too late for apologies." His voice grew louder and firmer as he spoke until he yelled. "Guards!"

Moira dropped the ring of keys from nerveless fingers. "What are you doing?"

"What I should have done as soon as I saw you. Guards!"

The tread of heavy footsteps sounded from the hall. She speared both hands through her hair. No time. No time to run, hide, or turn invisible. As she turned to face the door, her foot kicked the keys under Ansel's cot. She was out of time, but the others weren't.

Moira shook her head, her mouth a wry twist. She'd had it all wrong. Aaron and Ansel weren't prisoners.

41

Once the guards collected her, they tied her hands behind her back and unceremoniously deposited her in the throne room. While someone checked the cells, and others roused everyone who wasn't already awake, Moira stood in the middle of the hall contemplating her fate.

Things did not look good.

Aaron had turned against her. Could she blame him? Back before Vinton abducted him, they had only recently rekindled their relationship , punctuated with a singular kiss the night of Homecoming. Whatever they'd had, it wasn't enough for him to stay loyal to her. Not when the High Magician terrorized them for so long. Their subordination shouldn't have been a surprise. And it wasn't. How many times had she hoped they would make themselves useful and tell the High Magician whatever he wanted? As long as they stayed alive, it didn't matter. She would do everything she could to get them back and take them home. That part of the plan hadn't changed. Not for her.

Now she understood the twins' door had been unlocked because Vinton knew they wouldn't try to run. Aaron might hide his fear behind his newfound loathing for her, but Vinton had tormented him into terrified compliance. The alternative, his brother Ansel, served as a clear warning. Before all of this Ansel had been her best friend. He'd been upset about her going out with Aaron, but it was something they would have moved past eventually. Now Vinton left him a shell of his former self. She didn't know if she could bring Ansel back the way she had Bertram. They needed to get away from here to find out.

But at least they hadn't searched her.

The breath shuddered out of Moira with a heaviness that did not go unnoticed.

Her exhalation drew the attention of Kingkiller, awakened by all the noise. His electric blue gaze focused on her. If she hadn't spent so much time around Zephyr, his staring might have unnerved her. Aside from the imps left to guard her with their swords and pikes, there was no one else around.

He was a gorgeous specimen of dragon. Not as awesome as Zephyr, obviously, but handsome. She didn't wish to engage with the enemy, but she saw an opportunity and took it.

Moira bent deeply from the waist. Deep enough to reach for the knife she'd stuck in the waistband of her pants at the small of her back. "It is a pleasure to make your acquaintance, Master Wyvern." She couldn't bring herself to call him by his given name, but the greeting sounded fine to her. Kingkiller must have thought so, too, because he came away from his place beside the throne to approach her.

She palmed the knife and straightened.

Kingkiller walked a circle around her, his talons clicking against the stone floor, and stopped in front of her. The imps guarding her pulled back. "Well met, Dragoneer Moira." His voice was low but melodious. He inhaled, his nostrils flaring as if he were taking in her scent. His lids drifted shut. His shoulders drooped with a sigh as he walked back to his place beside the throne.

Did she smell bad? Moira didn't think so. She lowered her nose to her shoulder. There had been some cause for perspiration since her arrival, but she didn't think she smelled awful. She still smelled of whatever flowers and spices Princess Day's ladies-in-waiting had scented the bathwater with. Kingkiller's pupils were wide. She didn't get the sense she was in danger. At least, not from him. Moira had already surmised he was a sulky dragon, but now he struck her as downright unhappy. Despondent even. She pulled her thoughts away from his predicament. Given how much trouble she found herself in, maybe she was just trying to distract herself by reading too much into the wyvern's reaction.

She sighed, weary to her soul, tired of the machinations that had brought her there. Not just the plans she'd made, but the events set in motion that caused Zephyr to find her and bite her in the first place. She didn't regret that bite, but if he hadn't, none of this would be happening. She could hold the two thoughts inside herself and not explode, which was a kind of magic all its own.

What had happened was done. She had reacted and now she was acting. She simply had to remember that waiting was also an act and to not lose hope even though they had come so far only to be stymied so close to the goal of freeing her friends.

When the sound of footsteps reached her, Moira rolled her shoulders and stood up straight, working all the while at her bonds. Hedrick strode past her, up the steps to the throne. He didn't even glance in Kingkiller's direction. Vinton came in with his retinue of soldiers, minus the imp general. Archers filled the balcony above her at regular intervals, all of their arrows trained on her. It seemed excessive, in a flattering way.

Vinton stopped in front of her. "Where is the co-conspirator halfling known as Urion?"

Moira's eyebrows lifted. "I have no idea."

"Where is your dragon?"

Her brows lowered. "You *lost* my dragon?"

Vinton glowered. "Where is he?"

"I don't know." That was not entirely true. She sensed Zephyr's direction, but not his exact whereabouts.

"Several of my guards are dead. I suppose you know nothing about that, either?"

"I haven't killed anyone, if that's what you're asking."

"How did you get out of your cell?"

"Through the door." The less she said, the better. He didn't have a clue what dragons were capable of. Strange, considering one was sleeping next to the throne.

The imp general came through the side door with Aaron and Ansel, who looked no better off than before, arms wrapped tight around his middle. Aaron appeared no different either, glaring daggers at her.

"Did you have a good late-night rendezvous with your friends?" Vinton asked. He went to them and seized each one roughly by an arm.

Ansel whimpered.

Aaron's eyes widened.

Vinton dragged them forward about halfway between her and the steps to the throne. He left them there and slunk toward Moira. "Did he tell you?" Vinton asked as he circled her.

Moira frowned, not following.

Vinton pointed to Aaron with a tilt of his head. "Did he tell you what he's done?"

Her eyes narrowed.

"He didn't, did he? For shame! He should be proud of his accomplishments."

Aaron paled and lowered his gaze to the floor.

Moira's stomach fluttered with unease.

Vinton stopped in front of her. "I couldn't have done it without him. He's such a clever boy. Once my scouts discovered a legion of dragons in our midst, they had to be taken care of. Your friend helped me build the most wonderful devices. Then my men took them and placed them all around the dragon's camp. It only took a bit of magic to touch them off. And then boom. No more dragons. No more dragoneers. And no more Light Legion. I'm impressed with your world and its use of, what is it? Oh, yes, fireworks."

Nausea rolled through her. She knew Aaron had done it to save himself and Ansel, but it made the backs of her eyes prickle. If her arms were free, she might have buried her face in her hands and wept. But with Vinton in her face, his attention on her, she couldn't afford the tears. She blinked rapidly and sniffed loudly one time, letting her sadness morph into anger.

Vinton practically cooed, "Your friend killed all those people. All those dragons."

Moira's teeth ground together. When she spoke, she did so softly, rage causing her voice to waver. "No. He didn't. You did. Don't blame it on him, you coward!"

Aaron had been at the top of their chemistry class. He had the knowledge. Vinton had been the one to exploit it. Aaron never would have done something like this on his own. The problem was, Vinton should never have had access to Aaron. Her hands balled into fists behind her back, working as hard as she could undetected.

A ruckus at the back of the hall pulled Vinton's attention away from her. "What is it? Have you found the dragon?"

"No, Master, we found this one instead, skulking around the north gate."

Moira looked over her shoulder. And then she did a double-take. The large purple-grey troll escorted Princess Day into the throne room with one hand wrapped around her upper arm. Day wore the same clothes Moira had last seen her wearing as they left Prince Owen's camp, but she'd added a black cloak. The troll deposited her beside Moira with about three feet of space between them. Day's eyes caught hers, but the princess's expression was so inscrutable, Moira couldn't make out what she might have been trying to tell her.

This was not good. Moira couldn't stop the frown forming on her face.

How could they have captured Day? Where were Zephyr and Urion if they weren't with her? They were supposed to find Day and get their weapons back. What was she doing here?

"How lovely of you to join us, Day. Have you come to negotiate on your brother's behalf?" Vinton's laughter rolled through the hall.

"She had these." The troll threw Moira's bow and quiver on the floor at the princess' feet along with her sword, another sword, and a dagger.

"My goodness!" Vinton said. "It would appear not. Send extra men to the north gate. I can't imagine Owen letting his dear sister wander far from his sight."

Day ignored him. Her gaze had lifted to take in the throne and who was sitting on it. Her brows drew together at the sight. "Lord Hedrick."

Hedrick didn't bother to get up. "King. It's King Hedrick."

Day blinked rapidly, her gaze floating downward.

Hedrick lifted his right hand. "This is my dragon, Kingkiller."

Far from sulking now, the dragon stepped forward, smoothing the scales across his belly, his blue eyes fixed on Day. He stopped at the bottom of the stairs leading to the throne and leaned forward, his posture stiff as if he were ready and waiting for something to happen.

Day inhaled swiftly, taking him in. "He's... he's beautiful."

"Beautiful?" Hedrick asked. His laughter rang out. "A beautiful killer."

"And allow me to introduce the dragoneer Moira." Vinton nodded to her. "She calls herself noble, but she's got nothing on you, Princess." He crossed the floor to come up behind Aaron and Ansel, wrapping his arms around them and clasping each one on the shoulder. They both flinched. "Poor little orphan Moira came all the way here to steal her friends back, but she's not as smart as she thinks she is. And now she'll have to choose."

Moira swallowed, her throat tight and her mouth dry. "Choose what?"

A cruel twist turned Vinton's lips. "Which brother you want to live and which brother you want to die." He let go of Aaron and Ansel, brushing at his hands. "The two are such a bother. I only need one. Will it be the weak-minded brother? Or the mass murderer? I know which one I would choose." He jerked his head. ordering his guards forward.

Ansel shuddered and rocked back and forth while he held himself. Aaron shook from head to toe, his eyes darting every which way, looking for an escape until his gaze landed on his brother. Then he seemed to focus, though his chest heaved.

Vinton strode toward her. "You haven't even heard the best part yet." He pulled a small stoppered glass vial from inside his cloak. "Do you know what this is? Hmm? It's dragon venom. That's how your friend will die. The very thing injected into your veins to make you so special will make one of your friends writhe on the floor in agony until they perish. Now... which one will it be?"

He didn't have to do this. He chose to. For entertainment. Moira knew a bully when saw one, and there would be no reasoning with one as powerful as him. In ordinary everyday life, she steered clear of people like him—but that wasn't an option here.

"You're out of your mind," Moira said.

Vinton laughed at her. "You don't get to judge me. Once I put down this foolish rebellion, I'll control all the lands west of the river. From here, we invade the east until I unite everyone under the banner of the Fells. No dragon-bit soul of noble blood is going to stop me. No one is coming to help you. Even your dragon has abandoned you. Now choose, or I'll choose for you."

Moira stared past Vinton. Past her friends. Past Kingkiller, the throne, everything.

The world blurred as his words pressed against her ears. This couldn't be happening. This was the worst ending possible. It didn't even deserve to begin with 'Once upon a time...'.

Once upon a time, two dragons bit twin brothers.

The world flickered, the edges of her vision dimming until the center resolved into a picture of stunning clarity. It couldn't be. She remembered the day she met Zephyr. Her heart leapt in her chest and she knew what had to happen. It all made sense to her at that moment.

Unfortunately, the High Magician still stood between her and what she needed to happen, and he played with people's lives as if it were a game.

She had no option but to play along.

Moira blinked and refocused on Aaron and Ansel. "I can't. I can't choose." She knew Vinton was going to give the dragon venom to either Ansel or Aaron. She had to make sure he gave it to the right one; otherwise, this really would be the end.

Vinton chuckled, low and soft. "I know. It's a tough choice. They've both been so useful in their way." He spun to face her friends, putting himself beside her. "That one's mind was sound, but it eventually broke. They all do. I didn't have to work so hard. Your murderous friend there was more than willing to tell me all about you if I would just stop hurting his brother, but by then it was too late. I understand how difficult this must be for you. Maybe I should help. After all, as soon as this is over, we can get down to the business of what I have in store for you." He strode forward and raised his arms. "Which one will it be?" He faced her. "Which one gets a taste of dragon venom?"

Moira's lips trembled. She didn't want to choose, but she already had. She knew who she wanted to drink the poison, but she had to make sure Vinton gave it to the right brother. Vinton would never do the thing she needed him to. Her eyes stung, and she allowed her tears to fall. "I'm so sorry," she cried. Then she lifted her head and stared at Ansel.

Vinton smiled a malicious grin. "Yes. She's so sorry to kill your brother. Hold him."

Two guards grabbed Aaron by the arms. He struggled.

I have to make this look good. Moira stepped forward. "No! What are you doing? Stop!" The troll grabbed her by one arm, still held behind her back.

Vinton took the stopper out of the bottle of dragon venom. Then he gripped Aaron's chin in one hand, forcing his mouth open. He upended the bottle of poison into it and slammed his jaw shut, holding his mouth closed.

Aaron gasped and choked, but there was no way he could have avoided swallowing at least some. Satisfied the poison would soon have the intended result, Vinton ordered the guards to release him.

Aaron dropped to his hands and knees on the ground, his back arching high.

42

Moira's heart raced as her friend coughed and gagged on the floor of the throne room.

What effect would the dragon venom have on Aaron? Had she guess right? When Lord Q poisoned her, she'd ended up having a meet and greet with the book in her head as Cal. She didn't think that would happen to Aaron, but maybe something else just as profound would.

The troll, with his hand around her arm, entranced by the scene being played out like the rest of the room, loosened his grip. Moira faked a sob and pulled her arm free, but instead of moving toward Aaron, she stepped over to Princess Day.

A moment later, she had finished sawing through the ropes around her wrists.

Aaron took huge gasping breaths, but there was no writhing to be seen.

The entire room's attention was focused on Aaron—except for Kingkiller, who only had eyes for Princess Day.

And Moira knew why. With her hands free, she returned the knife to her waistband and retrieved her sword from the ground. Day, who had been watching her, scooped up the rest of their weapons.

Aaron sat back on his heels, breathing hard, and still very much alive. He didn't even vomit.

Vinton looked at the glass vial in his hand with a frown.

Moira grabbed Day by the arm. She pulled the princess around in front of her and gestured to Kingkiller. "Name him."

Day frowned at her, confused. "What?"

Kingkiller leaned toward Moira and the Princess.

Moira took Day's bandaged wrist and squeezed it lightly. "I know you don't remember, but look at him. He's your dragon. He wants you to name him. Please! Give him a name!"

Moira expected Day to stammer, but she didn't. Instead, she faced Kingkiller, meeting his fiery blue gaze with one to match.

Day inhaled, opened her mouth, and shouted, "Tahmoh!"

A brief smile crossed Tahmoh's face. Every scale on the dragon's hide rippled in an invisible rush of air from face to tail.

A second later, the sounds of battle reached the throne room as the front doors of the castle keep crashed open. Shouts and the clash of steel on steel echoed from the antechamber.

Prince Owen sure knows how to make an entrance.

Vinton dashed the empty bottle of dragon venom against the stone floor. It shattered into a million crystal shards. "Archers!" His face screwed up in a rage, he turned to where Moira had been standing, then had to stop and point to where she and Day now stood. "Fire!"

Moira had stopped arrows once before. She could do it again. She raised her free hand. Her gaze darted to the balcony. Ten archers were taking aim. It had been easier with the goblins. All the arrows had been coming from one direction. Even then, the effort had worn her to a nub. She didn't know how she would have the strength afterward to keep her friends safe, but she would never know if she didn't survive the forthcoming onslaught.

The archers fired.

Moira visualized a protective dome over herself and Day, but Tahmoh lunged forward, sweeping Day and herself into his arms, shielding them. The arrows bounced off his dragon's hide and clattered to the floor.

Unfortunately, Day's hand grazed Tahmoh's for the first time and she hissed in pain a second before her eyes rolled back in her head and she passed out. Tahmoh sucked in a breath, his head lowered over his unresponsive dragoneer.

Moira reassured him. "She'll be fine, Tahmoh. It happened to me too, the first time I touched Zephyr. She'll probably come up swinging." Moira took her bow and quiver from Day's slackened grip. "Go. Keep her safe." She ducked out from under his protective crouch, sheathing her sword and strapping it around her waist.

The fight came to them, spilling into the throne room.

Moira's spirits rose to see Aaron back on his feet, none the worse for being poisoned, and at his brother's side. She got them behind her and backed toward the throne away from Vinton, who had turned to the fight at the other end of the hall.

Behind them, Lord Hedrick had risen. He stared, his jaw slack, at what used to be his dragon. "Kingkiller?"

Tahmoh lifted his head with a snap of his jaws. "That is not my name."

Hedrick fell back against the throne, devastation plain on his face. *Imagine if Zephyr said that to me...* Unsure of what Hedrick was capable of in his current state, she got Aaron's attention. "Keep an eye on him."

Aaron coughed. "Sure."

A distinctive roar made her heart lift. She looked toward the entrance. No sign of Zephyr fighting the imp army, but mixed in with the soldiers, a group of women hacked and slashed. At the vanguard, Jeanette wielded her sword with ferociousness, carving a path through the imps to meet the trolls head on.

Vinton unsheathed his sword. "Archers!" He pointed his blade at the front of the hall, where more men and imps spilled inside. "Fire at will!"

They fired one volley in the time it took Moira to get an arrow nocked and ready. Men and women screamed at the front of the hall. Moira's position was terrible. The imps had the higher ground.

But I have magic. Pouring her will into each arrow, she fired ten times in quick succession, aiming high. She visualized each one finding their targets with finality. By the time one archer noticed his fellow had fallen, he was the next to be struck down.

The attack from the balcony ceased.

Moira bent double, winded.

"Moira?" Aaron called her name.

She waved at him to let him know she was okay. Another roar came from the front of the hall, but this one was different. The sound went through her with a hot rush from the top of her head to the soles of her feet. She'd never intentionally drawn on Zephyr's strength before, unwilling to put him at risk.

She didn't do it now either. Not in the middle of a fight: Rasti had said it could be dangerous.

Somewhere nearby, Zephyr must have known she was hurting and decided differently. By the time the sound of his roar faded, her tiredness vanished. She stood up straight, scanning the room. Still no sign of her dragon.

Behind her, Ansel huddled against Aaron's side. The dragon-deprived Hedrick had slid to his knees and didn't appear to be a danger to anyone, while Tahmoh carried the unconscious Day to his space at the left of the throne. Moira ushered Aaron and Ansel toward Tahmoh. They would be safer with him. She noted Tahmoh had placed Day on a mat where he watched over her anxiously. Moira also got a good look at the area where the dragon seemed to spend most of his time. A collection of daggers lay on another mat on that side of the throne. The unsheathed blades glittered, the light bouncing off of their points. Tahmoh must have collected them as soon as he could.

"You and Day are going to get along great," Moira said before she could stop herself.

Tahmoh spared her a glance.

"I'm leaving my friends with you, Master Tahmoh. Please keep watch over them." She didn't wait for a response, but turned back to the fray.

Across the room, Jeanette dispatched one troll, then searched the hall, her gaze landing on the imp general who fought beside Vinton. She headed straight for him, teeth bared. Another imp made the mistake of getting in her way. She cut him down with a savage slice. Then another troll stepped between Jeanette and her target. That slowed her down. An imp tried to stab Jeanette from behind. Moira stopped him with an arrow.

Moira helped where she could until her ammunition ran dry. Then she dropped her bow and got rid of her empty quiver. She unsheathed her sword as her breath caught. She swung toward the opposite end of the hall.

Zephyr entered, dragon sword drawn, flanked by two other battle dragons, a couple of humans, and one halfling. Moira recognized the green dragon, Sorrence, from Prince Owen's camp. Next to him was the blond soldier, Cale. Urion stood on the other side of Zephyr, splattered in mud, and beside him another dragon she thought looked familiar. She squinted. The dragon was older, his brown scales not as vibrant, but he was the only one who wore a large metal breastplate. She'd only seen one dragon wear something similar. It had to be Constable Belcrief and beside him, Sergeant Levin, all the way from Farrago.

In the space between, Jeanette had fought off the other troll. Now there was nothing between her and the imp general. She ran straight at him and rained down a flurry of blows. The imp general defended himself, but, Moira noticed, he didn't attack. He just kept deflecting her blows as if he didn't want to hurt her.

Vinton had no such qualms. His general was under attack. He waited for the right moment and drove his sword through Jeanette's side.

Moira screamed, but her voice got lost in the din of combat.

Zephyr alone looked to see what had happened. Without a word, he and the other two dragons stormed forward, cutting wide swaths through the enemy.

Vinton pulled his sword free.

The imp general stood for a moment, stunned. Then he dropped his sword and caught Jeanette before she could hit the floor, falling to his knees under the added weight. He stared at her and she at him. Jeanette's lips moved. The imp general bent closer, putting his ear next to his mother's lips. A moment later, he sat up to reach for the sword he had dropped. He picked it up by the blade and wrapped his mother's hand around the hilt. Jeanette's fingers grazed the soul sapphire as she breathed her last and her body went limp.

The imp general rocked in place, the lifeless body of his mother sprawled across his lap.

Vinton yelled at him.

The general ignored him.

With battle dragons bearing down on him and his retinue of imps in tatters, Vinton must have decided it was time to retreat. He dashed toward the side door of the throne room, no doubt planning to slip out and disappear. Moira stepped into his path and blocked his way.

Vinton slid to a stop. He raised his sword.

Moira had no illusions about her sword-fighting skills. Vinton was probably the superior swordsman, but she didn't have to beat him. She just had to keep him busy until enough dragons surrounded him to make him realize he couldn't get away.

He attacked and she defended, keeping herself between him and his escape route. He lowered his sword, as if considering his options, until his lips curled into a cruel smile. Vinton attacked again, putting all his strength into knocking Moira's blade aside. As he did, he dropped his sword, stepped in close, and took her head in both his hands.

The last thing she heard was Zephyr roaring her name.

43

The roaring that filled Moira's head ceased.

"Finally," Vinton said. "Just the two of us."

She blinked. She still stood in the throne room, yet every stick of furniture and every other person, except for her and Vinton, had vanished. They faced each other in the middle of the open floor.

He smiled, a vulpine curve to his lips.

This throne room differed from the real one. The walls were solids. No exits. No way out. Her brow furrowed.

Vinton waved a hand. "You need not worry. No one will disturb us."

Moira got a flash of the two of them locked in a terrible embrace, Vinton's hands pressed to either side of her head.

He waved a hand at their surroundings. "They'll be too afraid of what will happen to you if they try to interrupt." He lowered his hand. "Why didn't your friend succumb to the dragon venom?"

Moira glanced around the room again. Everything was the same right down to the balcony above her, the one the archers had fired from. Wait, had that been there a moment before?

Vinton's chin lowered as he stared at her. "Tell me."

The lights brightened.

She ignored the room changing around them.

"Dragon venom doesn't affect those who are dragon-bit," she said.

"Kingkiller never laid a tooth on him."

"You're right. Tahmoh didn't bite him." Moira turned in a circle, peering up at the ceiling. The move also allowed her to pause for dramatic effect. "But Zephyr did."

"Zephyr...?"

Moira lowered her head. "My dragon bit Aaron. A long time ago. I never realized it until today."

Aaron running through the woods and getting creeped out. His visceral reaction to Ansel's portrait of Zephyr. Perhaps even his somewhat sudden need to rekindle his friendship with Moira. And then there was Zephyr's reaction. Moira doubted if he remembered biting Aaron in the first place, having been under the influence of his wyvern senses, but he'd recognized Ansel when they'd first met. Well, he'd recognized Aaron in the features that they shared. Maybe that was another reason Zephyr had revealed himself to Ansel. Not just because Moira had wanted someone she could talk to about what was going on.

She faced Vinton. "It's like a story. Once upon a time, two dragons bit two brothers..."

He scoffed. "Fairy tale nonsense."

"No. It isn't. The way it's written, you think each dragon bit one brother, leading to a terrible rivalry where horrible things happened. So horrible that now, if two dragons have to bite someone, they know not to bite people who are related." She squinted and tipped her head from side to side. "Which is strange. How would a dragon know your cousin already got bit by another dragon? Maybe cousins are a great enough distance? The point is, they definitely wouldn't bite two people from the same family, especially not siblings. Not anymore."

Vinton frowned at her, but he let her talk.

Moira continued. "What really happened was, once upon a time, two dragons each bit two brothers, because dragons are compelled to bite two different people when they have to bite anyone at all. After Zephyr bit Aaron, he had to find someone else, even though Ansel was right there because he couldn't bite someone from the same immediate family, especially not his twin brother.

"That's what happened in the story. A dragon hatched and was compelled to bite a boy, and, perhaps due to a lack of suitable candidates, had to bite his brother, who also happened to be his twin. Another dragon hatched not long after, and, don't ask me how, bit the same pair of twin brothers. Because the brothers were also twins, it messed with the connection between dragon and dragoneer. They couldn't make it work. They tore themselves apart." She chewed the inside of her lip, speculating on what could have gone wrong. "As a result, dragons adopted the custom of not biting anyone from the same immediate family. So once upon a time, Zephyr bit Aaron and then he bit me. Just like Tahmoh bit Hedrick and then he bit Princess Day."

Vinton's mouth turned down at the corners. "Impossible."

"I believe I've just explained how *not* impossible it is. Were you not listening?"

"We took every precaution with Kingkiller—"

"Not his name."

"He bit Lord Hedrick alone. No one else." Vinton made a slashing motion with his hand.

A huff of laughter escaped Moira. "Obviously not." She tilted her head back. The ceiling glowed white, but she longed to see the sky overhead. "Let me ask you this: How excited were you when your plan to ensure a dragon bit Hedrick succeeded? I bet you were pretty excited. After that, you probably didn't care what happened to Tahmoh." The ceiling changed to a calm cerulean. Moira looked back at Vinton. "Your arrogance led you to let him out of your sight and that's when he bit Princess Day."

Vinton's nostrils flared. "He could not have gotten out of the castle, found the princess, bitten her, and returned with no one knowing."

Moira's gaze returned to the ceiling. "It wouldn't surprise me at this point if dragons could walk through walls."

Speaking of walls, Moira pushed at the throne room's walls with her thoughts. They split at the corners and fell away from each other, dissolving outward into rolling mist before they hit the ground. Now she and Vinton were outside, in a clearing surrounded by trees with a lush carpet of grass underfoot.

Vinton acknowledged the change of venue with a cursory glance. "How did you know the dragon bit Princess Day?"

If I have to answer more questions, I might as well be comfortable. Moira closed her eyes and thought of a chair. When she opened her eyes, a chair had appeared. It may have resembled the throne, but certainly it was less ostentatious. She sat down. "How did I know Tahmoh bit Day? Was that the question? I've lived it." She lifted both shoulders in a 'What can I say?' shrug. "It still took me a while to figure it out. You helped." She deepened her voice, mocking him. "No dragon-bit soul of noble blood is going to stop me." She coughed. "What was all that about?"

Vinton blinked. "That doesn't concern you."

Moira laughed. Didn't concern her? She laughed harder. Finally, she sat up straight, a knuckle wiping a tear from one eye. "It's just my name, but when you said it, things started clicking into place. I think the last piece of the puzzle came when the princess showed up out of nowhere. That was not part of the plan." To Moira, it meant the princess had been drawn there, similar to how she had been drawn to the cave when she first met Zephyr.

"What plan?" Vinton asked.

"The plan to rescue my friends and go home. It's undergone some revision since then." She couldn't stop anger from creeping into her tone. "First, when you tried to kill us with the river. Then, when we found out what you've been doing to women, and again when I saw what you did to Ansel. It's pretty fluid."

"And what's your plan now?"

"To keep you from hurting anyone else ever again."

Vinton shook his head. "Foolish girl. Once I crush Prince Owen, my army will push east. I'll take over every town from here to Farrago. No tyrant or anyone else will stop me from reaching the Outer Isles and uniting this land to form a single nation. Don't you see? I'm bringing the people and the land together under one rule."

"How many more women will you steal away from their families? How many more legions of dragons will die?"

"Sacrifices have to be made."

"No. Not anymore they don't."

"You—" Vinton spat the word— "have no say in it!"

The chair disappeared from under her. She fell on her backside. The sky blackened and the trees faded away. The grass was gone, replaced by smooth black rock. She tried to bring everything back. Nothing changed.

"There's something I've wanted to share with you for a long time," Vinton said.

A sharp pain arced through her head. Moira's hand flew to her brow. It felt as if shards of glass had lodged themselves inside her temples. Then, apart from the pain in her head, something tore through her like fire. She gasped with the icy shock of it and looked down. The shaft of an arrow erupted from the middle of her chest, piercing her leather armor. It wasn't her chest the arrow had cleaved, but it was her arrow that had done the damage. This was Vinton, sharing his memory of her shooting him. As soon as she realized what it was, the pain in her chest dialed back to a dull ache, but her head still pounded.

"What's your biggest fear, Moira Noble?" Vinton said. "What's your worst memory? I can make you relive it. Over and over again."

Her head throbbed and she was back in the riverbed. Her last glimpse of Rasti facing the wall of water that would take his life. The wave crashing into her.

A moment later, it happened again.

"Show me everything," Vinton said.

Her brain was on fire. She couldn't take it. He wanted her to show him everything?

She did.

Moira didn't hold back. She had no secrets. If Vinton wanted to know what she thought, all he had to do was ask. The pain eased, but the shards of glass remained, foreign bodies introduced to places where they should never be. If Bertram and Ansel hadn't been trying to keep her secrets, might they not have suffered as much as they did?

Vinton made a disgusted noise at the back of his throat. "How dull. I expected more. A lot more. Where are the memories of your dear departed father?"

Moira gasped as the pain increased. Aaron or Ansel must have told him her father was dead.

But she couldn't share what she didn't have. He could search all he wanted for the memories of her father, but he wouldn't find them. The pain grew. Her stomach roiled with nausea. She spoke through gritted teeth. "They're gone."

Vinton scoffed. He didn't believe her, and she realized he would not stop until he had scoured every molecule of her essence in search of what he was after. If it tore her mind asunder, it wouldn't bother him. He wanted memories of her father? The picture above her desk flashed through her mind. The last time she'd seen his face had been across a campfire.

"Stop," a voice said.

Immediate relief. Moira breathed through her mouth, the need to throw up subsiding. Cal stood beside her in his umber robes. It took everything she had to climb to her feet.

Vinton frowned, his eyes widening. "Who are you?"

Cal offered Moira a small smile and faced Vinton. "I... am the least of your worries."

The surrounding darkness grew lighter, and Moira got the sense someone was coming. Oh, Vinton had done it now. When the Librarian materialized out of thin air beside her, for the first time his sudden appearance didn't surprise her.

Vinton recoiled and stumbled back a step. "What is going on? No one else should be here."

The Librarian gave Vinton a glare so cold she imagined the temperature dropped several degrees.

That or she was going into shock. No way to tell.

She pursed her lips. "*You're* the one who shouldn't be here." As their surroundings lightened further, a movement behind Vinton caught her eye. "Leave. Now."

"I'm not done with you yet. I'm not going anywhere."

The part of Zephyr that was always with her spoke from behind him. "Oh, yes, you are."

Vinton barely had time to look over his shoulder before Zephyr's tail whipped around him, trapping his arms at his sides. With a great spin, Zephyr unfurled his tail and flung Vinton into the darkness and out of Moira's mind.

44

Moira came back to herself with a gasp, her knees weak, the world spinning. Her hands hung limp. She must have dropped her sword. Zephyr's leathery palm under her arm was the only thing keeping her upright.

"What took you so long?" she said.

"I would have been here sooner," Zephyr said, "but I had to pay a few trolls along the way."

A watery "Ha!" escaped her.

Vinton stood six feet away, empty hands raised, gaze unfocused

Fighting inside the throne room had ceased, but the commotion continued outside. Across the room, the imp general had been dispatched. His body slumped over his mother's as if even in death he couldn't bear to be far from her. Urion, next to the throne, kept the crestfallen Hedrick under guard while Princess Day, awake, spoke with Tahmoh. Ansel stood nearby, slowly blinking, his gaze unfocused, while Aaron stood next to him surveying the carnage with eyes wide.

Across from her, Vinton's expression sharpened until he stood staring at his empty palms with a ferocious glower, as if they'd failed him. His fingers curled into claws. As he lowered them, he raised his gaze to meet hers, his face a rictus of loathing. His lips moved in a silent chant as he turned toward the throne.

Moira stiffened. "Don't! Don't do it!" Her sword, laying on the floor, seemed miles away.

Vinton's silent chant continued as he unsheathed a dagger, muscles coiling. Light flared along its edge.

Moira sprang forward, pulling the knife from her waistband, hurling herself at Vinton as the dagger flew from his fingers. She drove the blade into Vinton's gut below the edge of his breastplate, thrusting upward. With a shove, she pushed him away.

Vinton groped at his belly, the hate draining away from his face along with his life's blood. He stumbled backward, tripped, and fell. He stayed down.

Moira turned away from the gruesome sight to one more horrifying.

The handle of Vinton's dagger protruded from Aaron's back. The knife must have been headed straight for Ansel's heart before Aaron turned to put himself in front of his brother. Ansel's gaze flickered from side to side, barely registering what was happening.

"No." The denial flew from her lips before she could stop it.

Moira rushed to Aaron as he stumbled to his knees. She wrapped an arm around him and grabbed his hand as he slumped to the side. His lips parted.

"No, no, don't talk." Moira's vision blurred. "Zephyr!"

He was right there.

"Do something. Help him. Please!" Her voice rose with her panic. She couldn't see very well, but she could make out Zephyr's head as he shook it from side to side.

"Moira," Aaron said her name.

"Yes. I'm here." She sniffed, wetness crawling down her cheeks.

"Take me... take me home." Aaron gasped, shuddering to get the words out.

Moira's face crumpled. "Yes. I will. I promise." She didn't know how, but she would see it done.

Her tears flowed freely as her gaze fell on Ansel who stood by, unaware of what was happening. For a brief moment, she wanted to go and stab Vinton again. The rage burned through her and brought a rush of sense with it. Moira wiped her face on her shoulder and cleared her throat. She didn't yell, and she didn't rage. She simply spoke his name. "Librarian."

Her call summoned him into being.

Several people gasped.

The Librarian stood over her in the same black clothing she'd seen him wear in her head, the same dark tunic and cloak he'd worn after he pulled her from the river.

"Can you help him?" she asked

The Librarian's lips pursed as he assessed the situation. "I cannot save his life, but I may save his mind." His gaze shifted to Ansel. "They're twins. Their natural state is to be together," the Librarian said. "We must hurry."

"Zephyr, take him," Moira said.

The Librarian gave them space and Zephyr eased Aaron from her grip, holding him steady.

Moira got to her feet and went to Ansel, who jumped and shied away from her.

"Ansel," Moira said, and she had to stop, her voice choked by tears. "Ansel," she tried again. "Aaron needs your help."

"Aaron?" Ansel's voice sounded scratchy and unused, as if he didn't speak often.

"Yes. Aaron needs your help. Will you help him?"

Ansel's eyes met hers for a split second. No spark of recognition brightened his eyes and Moira realized just how little remained of the Ansel she knew. But Ansel knew who Aaron was. That was the important thing. He rolled his lips between his teeth and nodded.

"Thank you," Moira said. She took him gently by the hand and led him to his brother's side. When she kneeled across from Zephyr next to Aaron, Ansel shadowed her movements and lowered himself to his knees beside her.

The Librarian, crouched at Aaron's head, got to work as soon as Ansel was in place.

Moira thought Ansel might have balked at the Librarian's touch, but his focus was on Aaron, whose eyelids fluttered with the last of his strength. With a hand on the head of each brother, the Librarian closed his eyes. Minutes passed. She rubbed her forehead, her gaze bouncing between the three of them. With a rush, Aaron's final breath left him, his body going lax. The Librarian didn't budge. A moment later, Ansel collapsed, unconscious. She caught him before he hit the floor.

The Librarian stood, his eyes as black as pools of spilled ink. "I've done what I can. Your friend will need time to recover." He turned away but stopped. "I am sorry for your loss." With that, the Librarian turned and left as she had never seen him go. He walked out, soldiers and dragons jumping out of his way as he did.

Moira's sobs filled the quiet that followed his departure.

45

Princess Day drew her away from Aaron and Ansel's sides when, eventually, numbness dulled her anguish from a burn to a throb. The princess promised to have someone see to Aaron's body while they found Ansel a proper room. Trusted servants would keep watch until he awoke. Day led them through the keep until she found a room large enough for her and Zephyr. The last thing she remembered was Day insisting she lay down and rest.

When she awoke, Moira had one blissful moment of ignorance before what happened came rushing back to kick her in the gut, causing fresh tears to flow anew. Grief sprang upon her like an enemy, but there was nothing to fight and nowhere to run. She lay there, frozen. Aaron was dead. So was Ansel, in a way. She wouldn't know if the Librarian had succeeded until Ansel woke. Moira had failed to save her friends. Yet one thing remained for her to do. *I have to get them home.*

Never had she felt so far from the place she was trying to get back to. The thought tore a sob from her throat, the noise rousing Zephyr from where he lay curled up on the rug next to the bed.

Zephyr shifted his bulk from the floor where he had slept to sit up and envelop her in a massive hug. He patted her back and rumbled words of reassurance too low for her to understand. At one point he hummed a simple slow four-note tune that made his chest vibrate against her cheek and brought her a breathless solace.

After a while, Zephyr encouraged her to go downstairs with him. The thought of food turned her stomach, but she knew Zephyr had to be hungry. When they passed the throne room, the voices of Day and Owen drew her inside. Workers had cleared away the bodies from the battle, but a great number of weapons lay scattered across the floor.

At the front of the hall, Prince Owen stood alongside General Hill as they spoke to Day and Tahmoh. The prince's arm hung in a sling, but he appeared otherwise unhurt. The general had a bloody bandage wrapped around his head and kept sneaking glances up at the dragon, who stood twice as tall as him.

The princess spotted them and called out.

Moira and Zephyr came forward.

"Did you rest?" Princess Day asked.

Moira nodded. "What's happening?" Her voice came out low and croaky.

"A total rout," Prince Owen said. "Without Vinton or the imp general, the trolls and imps have scattered. My army hunts them as we speak. *Lord* Hedrick is under arrest, as will be any traitorous members of his court once we find them. There is much to do." His eyes darkened for the briefest of moments. As his jaw tightened, his eyes cleared

Moira didn't miss the emphasis Prince Owen put on saying 'Lord,' which no doubt pleased him. Moira believed him. More than that, Moira wished to relieve Owen of a small portion of his duties. "I have a request."

The prince didn't hesitate. "Anything that is within my power will be yours." He bowed forward slightly from the waist.

"The women Vinton had kidnapped from their villages, those the fae raped and impregnated, I want them released to my care." She didn't have it in her to use pretty or passive words for what happened.

"I am curious as to why."

"I promised the people of Councy Forest that I would return their women if I could. Why not help all of them? I'd like to ask each of them what they want to do."

Hill spoke up. "Some of those women are pregnant. They can't leave."

Moira turned a cold eye on the prince's most trusted advisor. "And why is that?"

Prince Owen raised his brows as he, too, turned to Hill, waiting for an answer.

Hill sputtered. "It would be safer for them to stay here until they give birth. Then we can see them safely home."

Moira's eyes narrowed in suspicion. "With or without their children?"

"You mean their imp bastards?"

Moira was glad she didn't have any weapons on her. Her teeth ground together as her chin lifted. "They should decide what happens to them and to their offspring. All women should, but especially these women, after Vinton took that away from them."

Hill glowered. "Imps are an abomination and should be killed on sight."

All she could see was the imp general refusing to leave his dead mother's side. Her eyes narrowed. "Where are they?"

"The women?" Princess Day asked.

"No," Moira said. "The imps who weren't old enough to fight yet. They aren't inherently evil. If raised well, they can serve Prince Owen just as easily as they could have served Vinton."

Princess Day shook her head. Moira could tell by Prince Owen's puzzled expression that he didn't know either. Hill's mouth turned down at the corners. His insolent shrug told her he knew where the younger imps were and that he would not tell her.

The answer came from an unlikely source. "Near the stables," Zephyr said. "Where they kept me."

Hill sniffed. "What does it matter? All the women you want released into your care would agree with me."

"You're wrong." Moira turned her back and faced the prince for his answer.

Prince Owen didn't keep her waiting. "Granted."

Hill's jaw shut with a snap. He looked as if they had made him swallow something unpleasant—but not as life-threatening as dragon venom. Moira dug deep, trying to give Hill the benefit of the doubt. She imagined he was trying to protect Prince Owen and Castle Tern from future imp attacks. Her concern, however, remained in the present with what was to be done now.

"I'll take you," Day said, stepping forward to thread her arm through Moira's. Her show of solidarity accomplished two things. With the princess on her side, it seemed less likely Hill would try to convince Owen to change his mind. Second, with their arms entwined, Day could steer Moira from the room in the direction they needed to go.

Outside, the sun had passed its zenith. Day let go of her arm with a quick squeeze.

Moira looked over her shoulder. Zephyr and Tahmoh trailed behind them. The two dragons eyed each other, but when Zephyr saw her watching, he winked.

Away from the throne room and the keep, Day remained quiet, though she greeted anyone who called out to her. They didn't rush, but they weren't exactly out for a stroll, either.

As they approached the stable yard, they passed the burned-out shell of a wagon and their surroundings took on an unearthly hush. It reminded her of when they had come across the dead horse before they made their way to Prince Owen's camp. Her guts seized with dread.

"There." Zephyr pointed to the far end of the yard. A large, low structure stood on its own, not connected to the actual stables.

Their footsteps slowed as they approached the barracks. The door was open, light streaming through it. However, the inside remained sullen, shadows unwilling to reveal the interior.

They stopped.

Moira breathed deep and took a step forward. The link between her and Zephyr drew taut, keeping her from going any farther. She could have kept moving. There was nothing physically holding her back, but Zephyr was trying to tell her something. She turned to peer at him over her shoulder, brows raised.

Zephyr's gaze was on the door. "Perhaps this is not wise."

She blinked. An image of the dead horse rose unbidden in her mind's eye once more. The Light Legion. Zephyr and she had not witnessed their decimated ranks, only one dead horse. However, her mind filled in the gaps with scenes as awful and obscene as if she had been there. She watched Zephyr wince and cleared her mind.

I have to look. I'm not going to hide from the truth.

Without a word, Moira continued toward the open door. It was too small for Zephyr to enter, but she didn't plan on going inside. She stopped at the threshold and let her eyes adjust to the gloom.

Inside hung a tableau of awfulness, bodies strewn lifeless where they had fallen, bunks and tables smashed or otherwise knocked askew. Moira couldn't help but notice how very small some of the bunks were.

Footsteps sounded behind her as Day came to stand next to her. A moment later, the princess covered her mouth as she choked back a strangled gasp. Behind them, Tahmoh hissed. Day shuddered and turned away, going to her dragon.

Moira stayed.

A minute later, more footsteps approached, these larger and heavier, though she knew Zephyr could move without making a sound when he chose to. He stopped, ducking his head to stare into the room. He didn't say anything at first, but after a while he asked. "How long will we stay?"

An insect buzzed past her ear as Moira searched the abattoir before her, seeking out all its secrets, willing it to tell her everything that had happened there. "Until the sight no longer bothers me."

They stood there together for a very long time.

46

Once Moira had seen enough, she followed Day and Tahmoh back to the keep without a word. They found Urion sitting on a barrel outside the kitchens. He stared at the ground between his feet as he absentmindedly rubbed an apple against the sleeve of his tunic. He'd washed his face sometime since Moira had last seen him last, but his clothes remained soiled from the battle, as were hers.

"You're going to get that apple dirty," Moira said.

Urion started. "You're awake." He saw Day and jumped to his feet.

The princess stepped forward. "Why don't I see about something to eat? I want to make certain there's enough for the dragons." She headed inside the kitchens through a human-sized door. Moira wondered how soon the castle would undergo renovations to make it more dragon friendly. Behind her, Zephyr and Tahmoh spoke quietly off to the side in low rumbles.

As soon as Day was out of sight, Urion hugged Moira.

Moira squeezed him tight in return. When they parted, Moira reached into her tunic and grabbed the gold coin Urion had looped around her neck the night before. She lifted it free of her shirt and pulled the chain over her head. "I don't want to forget to give this back to you. It's so light, I forgot I was wearing it until just now. Thank you for loaning it to me."

"Thank you for letting me out of my cell," Urion said.

Moira lifted one shoulder. "That could have been anyone."

"Right. An invisible someone just happens to unlock my cell door and no one else's in the middle of the night?" He raised one brow. "In any case, I freed Zephyr with a small diversion and we made it to the south gate."

Moira squinted. "Did I see Constable Belcrief?"

"You did. It seems Lord Quintillius was not as impartial as he stated. I recognized several members of the city Sentinels. He also engaged the services of more than a few retired battle dragons. I'm not sure things would have gone our way without them. Do you know who else was there?"

"Who?"

"Remember the goblins? They heard there was going to be a fight and joined whatever side the trolls weren't on."

Moira shook her head with a grin.

Urion cleared his throat, growing serious. "I'm sorry about your friend."

She sucked in a noisy breath. "Me too."

"Was that the Librarian? The one who pulled you from the river?"

"That was him."

"A powerful ally."

Moira tilted her head. "Hopefully. Maybe."

"So, what's next?"

"I'm headed back to Councy Forest, like I promised, with anyone who wants to go. From there, I'm taking Zephyr and my friends and going home. As soon as I figure out how."

"I'll come with you. To Councy Forest, I mean. I found something Brixton might like to have." Urion checked behind the barrel where he'd been sitting and pulled out a long parcel. He folded back the end of it so she could see what was inside. She recognized the craftsmanship in an instant. The last time she'd seen the sword, it lay across the chest of the dying Jeanette. The blue sapphire winked at her.

Moira stared at it, the backs of her eyes burning. "I think you're right." She blinked rapidly. "When you're done here, can you do something for me?"

After a quick meal of bread, cheese and apples, Day led Moira to where the women were waiting. Out of their cells, they waited at one end of a large hall made into a makeshift infirmary. A good number of them had been injured. Moira never expected the women to take up arms and fight. However, held prisoner for so long, she suspected the women couldn't let the opportunity to strike out against their abusers and tormentors pass. Once Jeanette was out of her cell, she had killed the jailor and taken his sword, waking the others. Many of the women followed the fierce mother of the imp general into battle after that, but not all.

Just under a hundred women had survived. She wished more had lived.

Moira and Day pulled up a couple of chairs and got to work. Most of the women spoke with them. Few refused to talk of how they came to be there and what had happened to them. The experience struck some mute, and those women could not speak of what had happened to them or of anything else. The women who found their voices watched over the ones who hadn't yet. Of the women who talked, their stories spilled from them like water over a dam, a little at first and then much more, similar, but unique. The women offered each other what comfort they could: a squeeze of a hand here, a shared look of understanding there.

Day sent for pen and paper so they didn't forget anyone's name. They sat and listened. It took time. After they'd heard from the women, Moira spoke with Day privately about what means were in place to help them. Day assured her that there was a way to avoid a scene such as had happened in the barracks, and promised Moira she would take care of any arrangements needed. Moira didn't know what Day had in mind, but it was obvious what the princess saw in the building had affected her deeply, and that she wanted to avoid anything like it ever again.

After supper, they came together once more. Moira explained the women's options, letting them know they had choices available, and that they could do whatever they wished. Then she explained she would return to Councy Forest as soon as possible and the people there would welcome anyone who wished to travel with her and Zephyr, regardless whether they were still pregnant or not. This sent a murmur through the crowd. Some expectant mothers didn't think they could leave. Others had no plans to go anywhere until their pregnancies were complete.

The women who were able talked it over, deciding swiftly. Moira and Day met briefly with each one again. Two uneven groups emerged, those who would travel with

Moira and those who had other plans and would stay with Day to work out what they would do.

Moira did a tally. Eleven women wanted to travel with her. Seven were originally from the Councy Forest area. Three other women who wanted to keep their imp children would join them. One was Leeza, who had stayed behind when the fighting broke out, afraid for her child's life. The last was Leeza's cellmate Carina, who had suffered a nasty gash to her forearm, requiring stitches. Carina had no ties to the area, but she told Moira that wherever Leeza went, she would travel as well.

Day took the list, saying she had some tallying of her own to do.

By then, night had fallen. Day promised to seek transportation and begin planning with the rest of the women the next morning. By the time they finished, the pall of despair had lifted and there was a relief in the air, if not exactly lightness. A few women chatted quietly, and some even laughed amongst themselves.

They asked Moira to join them, but she declined. She made sure Zephyr ate, thankful for noodles and hapshulyc, and asked Day to show her to Ansel's room.

Day and Tahmoh led them to a space similar to the room Moira and Zephyr had shared.

Urion sat next to the bed. She knew Day had promised to have someone watch over Ansel, but it put her mind at ease to know he was there.

"Anything?" she asked.

Urion stood with a stretch. "Not yet."

Moira thanked him and relieved him for the night. Day asked her if she needed anything, but Moira shook her head. Day, Tahmoh, and Urion left her and Zephyr alone with Ansel. The room was large enough for Zephyr to curl up on the floor, his head resting on the foot of the bed

Ansel lay on. The chair Urion had vacated was comfortable and wide. She crossed her arms and drifted off, certain she would hear Ansel if he awoke.

Ansel didn't stir in the night or wake when light streamed in through the narrow window. If she hadn't heard him breathing, she might have been more worried. Urion returned in the morning and offered to again keep vigil. Moira took him up on his proposal and went to find Zephyr something to eat. Afterward, she asked where she could find Aaron's body.

The crypt was below ground, through a warren of narrow passages Zephyr couldn't navigate. He had to wait outside. Covered by a white shroud, Aaron's body lay on a stone slab. The air was cool, but it could have been colder.

A bucket of water nearby gave her an idea. She brought it closer. Then she bent down to press one hand to the stone slab supporting her friend's body while the other dipped below the surface of the water in the bucket. She willed the heat from the stone into the water, acting as a kind of conduit. The sensation trickled through her and she grunted with the effort, but she didn't stop until a thin layer of ice crusted under her palm against the stone, while half the water in the bucket steamed away to nothing. Satisfied she'd done what she could for the moment, she found her way back to Zephyr.

There was a lot to be done when a pretender's regime got overthrown, but a dragon could make quick work of any task. There were numerous requests for Zephyr's assistance. Moira found herself of most use when she helped Zephyr. After helping at the stables, they cut wood, which Zephyr agreed to because they had experience. He still wouldn't let her help chop down trees, though, so she ended up sharpening axes.

Moira didn't mind. Day and Tahmoh joined them and Day relayed how her brother was trying to decide what to do with the people who remained at Castle Tern after the Regent died instead of joining his fledgling army outside the castle walls. Her brother decided no one would face execution. Such extreme measures would be unwise with his forces so depleted. His decision was made easier because the battle at the south gate had been a little one. When the soldiers recognized the true heir to the throne, they welcomed him home with a cheer. The only resistance had been at the castle keep.

Zephyr brought her a dull axe, trading it for a sharp one, and said hello to Day.

Moira continued sharpening the axe she was working on. "What were you doing at the north gate? That wasn't the plan."

Day grew quiet.

Moira looked over at her.

Day frowned at the stone she used to sharpen the axe, as if she had forgotten what it was for. "I don't know. We used to play outside these walls growing up. I knew the fastest way to get to the north gate. At first I thought I could draw the High Magician's men away from my brother. Become a diversion to the diversion? But I wanted them to catch me. That's strange, isn't it?"

Her gaze went straight to Tahmoh.

"Not at all," Moira said. "Considering."

Day's brow relaxed as her eyes met Moira's. "How did you know?"

"I didn't. Not for a long time. It started with a story." Of course, Day had heard about the two brothers bitten by two dragons, but, like everyone else, she had assumed one dragon had bitten one brother, when, in fact, each dragon had bitten both brothers. That was what led to their downfall. Ever since then, anytime a dragon had to bite someone, they still had to bite two people, but they could not be related. Then it became a matter of naming the dragon and the dragon choosing the dragoneer.

"I still can't believe he chose me," Day said, her words laced with wonder.

"Really? I would think after getting a taste of Hedrick and being named Kingkiller, he might want to find someone completely different."

Day's brows brew together. "Are Hedrick and I really so different, though?"

Moira thought so, but she wasn't sure how to express those differences in words.

Then Day surprised her by saying, "Come to think of it, are you and I so different?"

Moira smiled as she shook her head. "That you would even ask that question does a better job of explaining how unalike you and Hedrick are than I could ever say."

The sound of running feet brought Moira's head around. Urion skidded to a stop when he saw she'd spotted him. She set the axe she'd been sharpening aside and shot to her feet. Zephyr pulled up mid swing from where he was about to fell another tree, his head snapping around in her direction.

Urion's appearance in the middle of the day could only mean one thing: Ansel was awake.

47

Ansel sat on the bed with his back to the door. He held up both hands in front of himself, running them through the light as if he were seeing them for the first time.

Moira exchanged a look with Zephyr. "Ansel?"

No response.

She took one halting step forward. "Aaron?"

He didn't turn around, but he lowered his hands. "Yes. And yes."

Moira inched forward around the end of the bed. Zephyr crossed the threshold but waited near the door.

A slight frown furrowed her friend's brow, but he didn't appear upset. He looked like Ansel, but when his eyes met hers, there was a wariness in their depths that made her think he'd aged a lifetime since her gaze last met his. It took everything she had not to move away.

He blinked. "We have a problem."

Moira swallowed. "What is it?"

"We know what happened. We understand what had to be done, but we're having a little trouble… adjusting."

"I assume you don't mean 'we' in the royal sense?"

He shook his head slowly. "We as in the two of us. We're both here, together, in the same… space. It's very disconcerting. We can't use our old names anymore. It's not fair. Not to either of us. We don't like it." He stopped, his face reddening. "*I* don't like it. I want to be called something different."

"What do you want to be called?"

"Sinjin."

Moira's brows inched upward. "Sinjin?"

"We like the sound of it."

Moira stared at him. "What are we going to tell your parents?"

Sinjin looked toward the window. "That assumes you can get us home."

Well, that sounded like Aaron, though he spoke the words without heat, so perhaps Ansel tempered his speech. No, she couldn't think of him in terms of one or the other anymore. Sinjin's lack of faith may have stung, but he, more than anyone, had a right to doubt her.

"Can you take me to our... the... body?" he asked.

That she could do. Zephyr waited outside as Moira led Sinjin through the castle to where Aaron's body lay.

Sinjin pulled back the shroud and stood there, staring. "We—*I*—had to see. Do you think it's strange that I had to see for myself?"

"No, I don't." While they were there, Moira performed the same cooling act on the stone as she had that morning.

Sinjin watched as ice crystals formed on the stone slab around her hand. "That's new."

"Something I just figured out."

Sinjin said nothing else. A few minutes later, he replaced the shroud, and they left. He led the way back to Zephyr, but didn't stop there. He just kept walking.

Moira and Zephyr shared a questioning glance, but followed him back into the castle to the throne room. It was empty of people.

Sinjin marched straight to the door at the side of the room and threw it open. Moira followed. Zephyr squeezed through after her, leaving scrape marks on the wood and stone work. Sinjin stopped halfway down the hall and went into the room where Moira had found Aaron and Ansel. No way would Zephyr fit through there. They hurried to catch up.

Moira found Sinjin kneeling in front of an open trunk he'd pulled from beneath one cot. He pulled out the clothes Aaron and Ansel had been wearing the night they disappeared, clean and folded. On top was a set of keys. He set the clothes on the cot and picked up the keys, sliding the key ring down his middle finger, gripping them in a tight fist. He knocked the lid of the trunk shut and kicked it back under the cot. In what Moira could only describe as a frenzy, he turned to the desk and attacked it, picking up the papers on top and ripping them apart. The sound of tearing paper filled the air. He tore every piece into unreadable shreds on the floor before he opened the drawers, drew out what was inside, and the ripping began again. By the time he was done, his chest heaved. He turned to Moira with wild eyes. "Do you have a match?"

She did not. She left Zephyr to watch him from outside the door and sought one out. There weren't any matches, but she tracked down a fire going in a grate in another room. As soon as she returned with an ember on a fireplace shovel, he tossed it on the pile of paper. It caught without trouble. There was no rug beneath it to burn, just bare stone. Before the smoke drifted up and out the one small window, it filled the room, making them both cough. It didn't stop Sinjin from seeing that everything in the pile became charred and unreadable, his eyes watering. His expression, at first tense, relaxed as the papers burned to nothing. Then Sinjin grabbed a blanket from one cot and tossed it over the smoldering remains, stepping on it to kill the flames.

"We feel better now."

48

That night, the prince summoned Moira and Zephyr to the throne room. Day and Tahmoh joined them. Prince Owen and General Hill were already there. Upon their arrival, the guards ushered everyone else out. The throne, Moira noticed, sat empty, the prince keeping to the same level as the general, his sister, and Moira herself.

Prince Owen wore a clean tunic, his arm no longer in a sling, though he kept it bent and close to his side. "I understand you'll be leaving us tomorrow."

"I'm taking eleven women to Councy Forest, along with Urion, Sinjin, and Zephyr. Princess Day has promised to see the rest home in due time. " Her words faded as she noted his impassive response. *Something's wrong.*

The prince drew a long breath. "I was fighting elsewhere, but my sister states she saw you slay the High Magician."

Moira's brows arched. "I stabbed him. In the stomach. He went down and didn't get back up." She recalled the blade slipping into his gut, shuddering in her hand, blood flowing from the wound. Her hand tightened into a fist.

"After the battle, our people collected and sorted the bodies. They could not find his."

The pit of Moira's stomach sank. "You don't think he's dead."

"It is possible they somehow overlooked his remains, but that is unlikely. General Hill personally searched as well—a rather gruesome endeavor. We don't know what foul methods Vinton may have had in place to ensure his survival."

Moira knew what he meant. "He'll be back. Someday." The knowledge settled around her like an invisible mantle, but she didn't let it show. "Thank you for telling me."

Prince Owen tipped his head forward. "Know that if he returns to my kingdom, I will see to it he does not cheat death a second time."

If Vinton was not, in fact, dead, how long would it take him to regain his strength? Would he be in a vengeful mood? Moira had to be at the top of his list. If they were to face off again, he'd probably just try to kill her. No more fooling around. "We'll do the same."

The thought of Vinton out there, plotting his revenge, made Moira even more eager to hit the road. She and Zephyr shared the news with Sinjin and Urion in the privacy of the former's room.

Urion acknowledged the news with a squint. "Magicians are hard to kill."

Sinjin, too, took the news in stride. "I'm not surprised. Not after everything I saw him do." He lifted his hand. His fingertips grazed his temple as he stared at the ground.

Day and Tahmoh came to see them off early the next morning.

"Are you sure you don't want to stay for the coronation?" the princess asked, her breath misting in the chill air. "Truth be told, I wish we had more time together. I have so many questions to ask."

"I know, but we have to get home. Or try anyway." Moira motioned to the wagons loaded with supplies. "Thank you for this."

"We should be holding feasts in your honor."

Her history teacher would have described their victory as Pyrrhic, the costs so heavy it seemed more like a defeat. "No, thanks." Getting home would be another challenge.

Day's mouth curled in understanding as she clasped one of Moira's hands between hers. She slipped a leather pouch into it. "Split this equally among the women. Reparations. I'll see to it the rest receive their share."

Moira frowned at the clinking bag of coins. "Where..."

"We are not a rich kingdom. Much has been squandered or pilfered, but this is at least we can do." She smiled. "As a dragoneer, I will not want for much. With Tahmoh by my side, we may go wherever we wish." A strange look passed over her features that made the hair stand up on Moira's arm. She suspected the money came out of Day's own pocket and that wherever the princess wanted to go, money wouldn't be of use.

Moira accepted the bag of coins. "And where is that, Princess?"

Day inhaled, then shook her head with a little smile. "That story... of the two dragons and the brothers. I think I know where it might have happened and I want to go there. I want to find out more."

She'd already said it, but Moira had to agree that with Tahmoh beside her, Day could do whatever she liked. If she wanted to delve into dragon lore, there was no one to stop her. "Have dragon, will travel."

Day laughed. "Indeed."

"Could you use some help?" Moira asked.

Day lifted her brows in silent enquiry.

"Not me," Moira said. Well, not unless she couldn't figure out how to get herself, Zephyr, and Sinjin back home. "I was thinking of Urion."

Day tipped her head to the side in a considering manner, before saying, "I think I would be happy to have all the help I could get." She took Moira's hand again. "Thank you for suggesting it."

Moira squeezed her fingers in return before letting go to bow low to Tahmoh. They were ready to go.

Urion drove the first wagon. Sinjin sat in the back with the supplies and Aaron's shrouded body. Carina drove the other wagon with the women in it while Moira and Zephyr brought up the rear. They departed the grounds via the south gate without fanfare, though many of the people they passed stopped to lift a hand in silent farewell.

The first day was a long, hard day of traveling. When Moira got tired, she hopped on the wagon with the women. The more distance they put between themselves and Castle Tern, the chattier the women became, talking, laughing, their relief at being away palpable. They asked her about Zephyr, and then Urion and Sinjin. Moira was grateful the wagons were loud, but couldn't imagine the women's voices didn't cut through some of the noise. She also guessed they were tired of talking to one another, wishing to avoid the topic of their imprisonment, and that was why they were grilling her. Moira told them what she could of her story, stopping to drink from a waterskin several times, her throat parched from talking so much. She told them how she'd met Urion and what had happened since they left Farrago. How they lost Rasti and found themselves among the men and children of Councy Forest helping cut down trees. Traveling to meet Prince Owen and how she'd ended up in the cell with Carina and Leeza.

"I knew there was something different about you," Leeza said.

"Was it the dragon?" Carina called over her shoulder, and everyone laughed.

They found a place to make camp late in the day to cook—what else—noodles. They supplemented the pasta with fresh vegetables and hard cheese from their supplies. Then most of the women huddled down together on one side of the fire. The three pregnant women slept off the ground in the back of a wagon.

Moira and Zephyr agreed to take the first shift, and Urion the second. Moira suspected the women would be up early so there would be no need for a third.

Urion turned his back to the fire and immediately went to sleep in his very annoying way.

Sinjin sat on the other side of Zephyr, lips pursed in thought. He stared into the flames. "There's something that's been bothering us—me." His voice barely carried above the crackling of the fire.

Moira fed a few more pieces of wood to the flames and waited.

"Did you know what the dragon venom would do to me?"

"No, but I had a strong suspicion. I couldn't stop Vinton from giving the venom to either Aaron or Ansel. I had a split-second decision to make. Everything fit. I realized Zephyr must have bitten Aaron. Probably before he bit me."

Zephyr leaned forward between them. "Did I?"

"You did, Zeph." Moira leaned back to look up at him. "But I understand why you don't remember. You said you were driven to bite me. Now we know you were driven to bite two people, like the two dragons who bit the two brothers. Kind of like a safety net. That's why I think you bit me after you bit Aaron. Your wyvern senses kept you from biting his brother, so you had to find someone else. You found me. Like Tahmoh. He had to bite Hedrick because he was there and he didn't have a choice. But then he bit Day. When she showed up and named him, he chose Day to be his dragoneer."

Sinjin sat back, silent for a handful of seconds. "So… I could have been the dragoneer."

"No," Moira said at the same time as Zephyr. Understanding flowed along their connection.

"What's that supposed to mean?" Sinjin asked.

"I named him. He's my dragon. Sorry."

Sinjin didn't let it go. "So, just to be clear, there was no way I could have been the dragoneer? Not even if I had found Zephyr first, and named him, I don't know, Edmund or something?"

Moira hesitated. "If I had died, maybe? I did get very sick. I don't know. Ultimately, I think the dragon chooses. It's hard to explain."

Zephyr hummed. "Edmund…" He tilted his head to the side. "Has a nice sound to it."

Moira slowly blinked as she turned her head to look up at Zephyr. "It's a little late to change your mind now."

Zephyr cracked, laughing low. Beside him, Sinjin shook his head, the corner of his mouth lifted in silent mirth.

Moira crossed her arms and stared into the flames.

49

The next day, as they drew closer and closer to their destination, the women grew more restless. Half of them jumped down to walk beside the wagons until they came to the last hill. At that point, they started running. Moira and Zephyr hurried to follow.

The women started shouting out names as they ran to greet the men and children spilling out of the long, low building that served as their schoolhouse and meeting hall. More shouts, cries, laughter, and tears followed as they came together.

By the time both wagons rolled to a stop in the middle of the small hamlet of Councy Forest, every building's door was open.

Brixton emerged from his forge and scanned the reunited families around him with hopeful eyes. His expression turned to disappointment as Moira and Urion presented him with the bundled sword.

The blacksmith folded back the wrappings to reveal the prize Jeanette had fought so hard to regain before she died. His face crumpled as he accepted the sword. He knew his daughter wasn't coming back.

"She chose to fight," Moira said. "As did others."

The blacksmith cleared his throat. "Aye, she would." He lifted his gaze from the sword. "I don't see all the faces that were taken from us, yet I see new ones?" He nodded toward the wagon with the four new women, three of them sporting rounded middles.

Moira told him.

Brixton blinked. Then he swallowed. "What will we do with the… the babies when they come?"

"I don't think you'll have to do much of anything, but you've got the opportunity to do something great. These women came here because they want their children to have a future. Each baby will have a mother who wants them, but they're going to need help. You can see to it they get that help and that they get it free of judgment."

The blacksmith stared at the women. Then he nodded.

Heather Ann swooped in from the side, her arms going around her father's waist as she hugged him tightly. She pressed her face to her father's shirt a moment before she turned red-rimmed eyes to Moira. Heather Ann must have also realized her sister was not amongst the returned and would never come home. "Did you rescue your friends?" she asked.

Moira glanced at Sinjin. He sat alone in the wagon, watching the reunions going on around him without focusing on anyone in particular. Yes. She'd found her friends, lost one, and then found him again. How could she tell Heather Ann any of that?

"In a way," Moira said, and left it at that.

Brixton wrapped his free arm around his daughter's shoulders. "Let's welcome our new neighbors."

Heather Ann nodded but didn't let go of her father's waist. Brixton didn't seem to mind. They walked in a three-legged way over to the wagon and Brixton raised his hand to clasp each woman's hand in turn.

Afterward, a few of the men told them where they could park the wagons and where they could stable the horses. Moira, Zephyr, Urion, and Sinjin took care of everything. Then Moira grabbed a waterskin and sat in the shade of a tree out of the way with Zephyr curled up next to her, watching the town come together to sort itself out. Urion chatted with a group of men and women. Sinjin stuck close to the wagons, straightening and organizing. Having observed him the past couple of days, she knew he looked like Ansel, but his mannerisms and the way he spoke were pure Aaron. Not that she would ever tell him that.

Moira and Zephyr had been under their tree for a little while when Heather Ann approached them with a sketch pad in hand.

Moira smiled. "Hello."

Heather Ann ducked her head. "I've finished my book."

"May I see it?"

The young artist handed over the completed sketchbook. The last pages were full of more sketches of Zephyr plus a few of Moira and Urion.

Brixton called for Heather Ann, who rushed away, leaving the book with Moira. She flipped back to the front to start over when a prickling sensation swept across her. She glanced around, but there was no one there. At the moment.

A second later, the Librarian stepped out from behind the tree and sat down next to her in the grass.

Moira didn't jump. "You're losing your touch. I knew you were there. Or about to be."

Zephyr stirred, saw who she was talking to, and put his head back down.

Moira was surprised that the Librarian would physically lower himself to her level, but at least she didn't have to crane her neck to look at him. "Thank you. For what you did."

"You're welcome."

He looked much less surreal than he usually did. Much more approachable. "I like the beard."

He stretched his neck. "I'm shaving, then."

Moira chuckled. "Is that why you're here? To keep me informed of your grooming habits?"

His black eyes met hers, a smile curving his lips. "I'm here because I thought you'd like to get that book out of your head."

She scoffed. "I would, but you said I had to have the original."

The Librarian slowly pivoted his gaze to her lap.

Moira looked down at Heather Ann's sketchbook. An icy rush flushed through her veins. She stared back up at the Librarian.

He held out his hand. "I told you the physical copy of the book would want to be reunited with its content."

Moira lifted the book, seeing it in a new light. Was she imagining it, or did the book feel warmer in her hands than it did a moment before? *I never thought I'd find the original text.* She'd certainly never expected *The Book of Wyverns* to look like a sketchpad. She carefully handed the book over. "What do we do?"

"You sit there quietly while I put the book back where it belongs."

"Oh. Right." She closed her eyes. Fingertips brushed her temple. "Goodbye, Cal," she whispered.

A breeze stirred the trees behind them. Or maybe it was just the blood rushing to her head at the prospect of having her brain back to herself. A rush of wind whooshed past her ears and then stopped.

When she opened her eyes, the Librarian held the book in his hands, his eyes completely normal.

"May I?" She held out her hand.

The Librarian gave her the book. Heather Ann's pictures were still inside, but now there was a flowery, flowing script underneath the drawings.

Moira smiled, closed the book, and handed it back. "You wouldn't have a new sketchbook on you by any chance, would you?"

He frowned. "Who do you think I am?"

"The Librarian."

He gave her a very put-upon glare, then reached under his black cloak and withdrew a brand-new sketchbook, which he held out to her. "I am. Don't forget it."

Moira wouldn't. She'd already had to sacrifice a part of her memory to carry the book around in her head without suffering the same troubles as Bertram. She'd never thought to ask if she would get her memories back; she had just assumed they were gone. Her father...

Moira stiffened with a gasp as if electrocuted.

Zephyr jerked and sat up. "Moira?"

She stared into the distance, not focusing on any one thing, her eyes welling as Zephyr's irritation with the Librarian grew. "Shh, it's okay. I just... I just... remembered."

Zephyr looked confused. "Remembered what?"

A small noise escaped her. *"Everything."* The tears spilled over as her mind raced through all the memories she'd handed over without hesitation and without the guarantee she would get them back. Bike rides. Boat trips. Camping and hiking. Bird watching with Dad. Aunt Paige's sugar cookies. The faintest trace of freesia from her mother's jewelry box. All came back in a bittersweet rush. "It's okay. I'm okay. I just wasn't... expecting that." She wiped the wetness from her cheeks. "That night you pulled me out of the river..."

"Yes?" the Librarian said.

"Cal already looked like my dad, but that night I could have sworn it was really him. It couldn't have been, though, because I traded away all of my memories of him. If you held on to them, though—"

The Librarian cleared his throat. His reluctance to meet her eyes told her she was correct. The Librarian had held onto her memories for her when he didn't have to. It had never been part of their deal. But because he had, she'd seen her father again, the memory of him, all mixed up with the book in her head somehow. When she thought she'd never get her memories back, she hadn't worried. She'd just thought she'd make more.

And she had, but now she remembered all of it.

"Thank you," she said again.

The Librarian wouldn't meet her eyes, but his cheeks bloomed with color, which she had never seen. She wouldn't have thought he could have such a reaction. It seemed beneath him. If she hadn't seen it with her own eyes, she might not have believed it, as the color was already fading.

"Ready to go home?" the Librarian asked.

50

Moira reared back, her mouth falling open. "What? Now?"

Again the Librarian refused to meet her gaze. "If you have a key, I... might be going that way."

Her head spun. She hadn't expected to return home so quickly once they reached Councy Forest. But that was no reason to delay. "A key?" Moira turned to Zephyr. "A key from home. We have a key. More than one. Just give me a few minutes, okay?" She jumped to her feet. "Don't go anywhere. Zephyr, come on." She backed away until she was relatively certain the Librarian wouldn't leave without them and then rushed to Sinjin's side.

He'd left the wagon but stood beside it. "Who is that? He looks familiar." He stared past her at the Librarian.

"He's our ticket home. Get your stuff together. We're leaving."

Sinjin snapped to attention. "Home? Right now?"

"Yes." Moira grabbed her backpack. She asked Zephyr to carry Aaron's body. Their movements attracted the attention of Urion and Brixton, who headed toward them.

"What's going on?" Urion asked.

"It's time for us to go," Moira said.

"Now?"

"Yes." Moira pointed to the Librarian, who still sat under the tree. Urion followed her finger and understanding dawned. His shoulders slumped.

Moira turned to Brixton and gave him the blank sketchbook. "This is for Heather Ann. Can you make sure she gets it? Tell her I'm sorry about the other one. It… kind of got ruined. Someone spilled ink on all of her beautiful pictures."

"I will." The blacksmith stared down at the book. "And this is for you." He held out the sword they'd carried home to him.

Moira stopped, her gaze going from Brixton to the sword and back. "I... I can't accept this."

"You can and you will, dragoneer. It's a fine blade. It wants to go with you. Please take it. And... thank you for helping us."

Moira didn't know what to say. Words failed her. She accepted the sword and held it close to her middle.

Brixton clasped her shoulder. "Safe travels." Then he let go and strode away.

Urion stood, hands on his hips, his face a picture of confusion. "You know you can't leave, right? I'm pretty sure I still owe one or the other of you a life debt, so..."

Moira swallowed back tears. "I'm pretty sure we're the ones who owe you."

He shook his head and raised his arms. Moira launched herself into him. A second later, Zephyr's massive arms were around them both, squeezing them. The three of them stood that way for a long minute before breaking apart.

Moira wiped her eyes. "What will you do next? Where will you go?"

Urion smiled, though his eyes were bright. "Wherever my fortune leads me." His tone sounded as if he'd already accepted defeat.

Moira worried about him having a sense of purpose. "Can I make a suggestion?"

"By all means. It won't make a lick of difference, but go ahead."

"I think Day could use some help."

Urion leaned back. "Princess Day? I'm fairly certain she doesn't need anyone's help now that she has an enormous dragon."

Moira's gaze didn't waver. "Zephyr and I never would have made it this far without you, and Princess Day said she'd love to have your help."

Urion smiled. "She really said that?" He raised his chin high and scratched his neck. "Well, I do have some experience with dragon-bit dragoneers and their wyverns, don't I?" He stood up tall. "I'll do it."

Moira grinned. "I won't wish you luck. But I will wish you peace."

He laughed. "I could use some of that." Then he sniffled. "Take—take care of each other." He blinked rapidly and stepped away.

Moira turned away too. Zephyr laid an arm across her shoulders. She leaned into him for a moment. She had known they would have to say goodbye at some point, but now that the moment had come her heart ached.

She looked upward into his bright, citrine-colored eyes. "This is it, Zeph. This is your last chance. Let's be honest... I have no idea what I'm doing. You should stay here. You have other dragons and dragoneers here." She inhaled shakily. "You know what my world has."

Zephyr faced her. His big hand chucked her under the chin, raising it so that he could peer directly into her eyes. "Your world has you."

As soon as he said the words, she knew there would be no persuading him otherwise.

He released her. "Besides. They do not have spicy chips here."

"You should have stopped after the first thing."

"That is true. And you should keep silly thoughts to yourself."

Moira shook her head. Zephyr gathered Aaron's body in his arms. Sinjin joined them.

The Librarian climbed to his feet as they approached. "Keys?"

Moira dug through her new backpack for her old backpack and the rock pick she had carried since the day she and Zephyr first arrived. The hammer and the backpack with her dead cell phone were the only things she had left. Sinjin rifled through the bag that held his belongings and came up with an actual set of keys. Zephyr hefted his important burden.

"Okay," said the Librarian.

"Wait," Moira said. "How much time has passed since we left?"

The Librarian's head tilted in thought. "About six hours."

They would arrive back in the wee hours of the morning. Moira chewed the inside of her lip, her eyes on the body Zephyr carried.

Sinjin touched her wrist. "I have an idea. We hate it, but I have an idea." He spun the car keys around his finger.

"Everyone ready?" The Librarian asked.

"Wait," Moira said. "Together." She linked arms with Zephyr. Sinjin linked arms with her. "Ready."

Moira leaned forward. Then she felt a tug somewhere behind her navel that pulled her, tumbling forward into an abyss.

EPILOGUE

The funeral was the following weekend.

Mr. Bertram would have been there, but he was still in the hospital, weak from his ordeal with Vinton, though he insisted he was getting stronger. Moira had visited him, offering an edited version of events concerning what happened after she fled his hospital room. He knew she'd lived weeks outside their world, but he still didn't know everything that had happened. However, he knew Aaron had died.

He didn't take the news well. Nobody did.

The accident had been Sinjin's idea. It pained him to do it, but the Chevelle had met with an unfortunate mishap involving a sharp curve and a defective guard rail. The accident turned the car into a twisted piece of wreckage, Aaron's mangled body inside. She and Zephyr had helped, because when the call came, Sinjin's parents found him pretending to be asleep in Ansel's room.

After separating from Zephyr, Moira slipped into her house, not knowing if her aunt was home or not. A quick check told her Aunt Paige had returned to the hospital to sit up with Bertram that night, as she said she might. Moira dug out her phone. It had dried out enough to plug in and to her surprise, it turned on. She couldn't help wondering if it was the last bit of Urion's luck that might have rubbed off on her.

Upstairs in her room, Moira shredded the note she'd left for her aunt and threw the pieces away. The walls and furnishings were familiar and yet alien to her. She took the clothes she was wearing and folded them away into the back of her closet. After a quick shower, she was climbing into bed as the sky turned pink, convinced she would never sleep.

As soon as she closed her eyes, she was out.

Having set her alarm, she came downstairs a few hours later to find Aunt Paige staring out the kitchen window with reddened eyes and an anxious expression. Aaron and Ansel's parents had called. There had been an accident after Aaron dropped her off.

That was the story she and Sinjin had come up with. It was the story she would stick to.

It hadn't been hard to produce tears for Aunt Paige. Not hard at all.

Moira stood next to Aunt Paige in the middle of a sea of mourners. So many people from school were there. It was like someone had pulled the fire alarm, except everyone wore black. That a serious car wreck had ended the life of one of the school's best and brightest stunned everyone out of their passive day-to-day existence and reminded them, even teenagers, how finite life could be. One day you have ten thousand tomorrows together. The next day you don't.

Sinjin stood with his parents at the graveside. Black sunglasses protected his eyes from the late morning sun. The trees were in full color and there was a chill in the air, but it wasn't windy. His mother cried openly with his father's arm wrapped around her. Beside them, Sinjin shoved his hands deep into the pockets of his black coat.

How strange it must be to attend your own funeral.

Moira hadn't spoken with Sinjin since the night of their return. He hadn't been in school and he didn't answer her texts or voicemails. She didn't want to think he was avoiding her, but there was no other explanation. Perhaps being around her was too painful for him.

She'd gone back to school on Monday. It was strange to be back, listening for a bell to ring telling her where to go. She had a hard time focusing, drifting through the halls between classes. After school, she went to see Zephyr and stayed with him until she knew her aunt expected her home. Sometimes they trained. Other times, they talked about what happened. And sometimes they didn't say much at all. They didn't need to.

The service finished. Mrs. Idlewild cried harder. Sinjin spoke in her ear. She calmed down a little after that, and the crowd dispersed.

Sinjin raised his head, looked straight at Moira, and came toward her.

Moira met him halfway, trying to read his expression behind the sunglasses without success. "Sinjin, I–"

"We've been thinking." Sinjin paused. "You should have let one of us die, instead of killing us both."

Her mouth fell open.

"Now my parents are suffering and everyone looks at me like I'm broken. Which I am. In no small part thanks to you. You never should have dragged us into what happened. Now, stay away from us and my family." With that, he turned and rejoined his parents.

Aunt Paige came up behind her and squeezed her arm. Moira blinked, looking away from Sinjin. Breathing hard, she had to work not to burst into tears.

Aunt Paige turned to leave and Moira took a deep breath and followed her. She had two tests to study for in the coming week. She'd survived going up against a High Magician, a royal pretender, trolls, goblins, and an army of imps.

Now she just had to survive high school.

Acknowledgments

Here are a few of the people who have made this work possible.

Thank you to the members of my long-time writing group Tuesdays With Story for their critiques and insights. They read this book two to three chapters at a time, sometimes more, over the course of a year in the middle of a pandemic. Let's continue to lift one another while making efforts to preserve digital ink.

My appreciation swells for anyone who was willing to read the entire book at once, my beta readers, Diane Boles, Marianne Flynn Statz, Becky Crookham, and August Crass.

A special thanks to the beta reader who has to live with me, my husband, Armand. Talking over ideas with you always helps make things clearer, even if there is some yelling involved. In return, I'm always happy to hear about your latest D&D session. Perhaps one day I'll make a guest appearance. Maybe. In addition, I have to thank my kids for doing something every day that reminds me, yes; they are mine. You are beautiful.

Thank you to Dragon Street Press and the people there who helped put the final polish on this prose. Your enthusiasm and willingness to work together have been a delight.

Last but not least, thank you, the reader, for picking up this book and coming on this journey with me. I'd love to hear about it. Let's see if we can decide what Zephyr's favorite color is. You can find me on Facebook, Twitter, and Instagram at **@AnAmberAuthor.**

About the Author

Amber Boudreau has a background in geology. In between household projects and parenting, she writes youth and adult fantasy. A native of northwest Indiana, she currently lives in Madison, Wisconsin with her husband and two children.

THE DRAGONEER AND THE PRETENDER is her third novel.

She can be reached on Facebook, Instagram, or Twitter at **@AnAmberAuthor** or at **authoramberboudreau.com**.

AN IMPORTANT MESSAGE FOR YOU
FROM AMBER BOUDREAU

I need your help. Independent press books like this one depend on people like you to spread the word. Reviews are the lifeblood of books, their authors and their publishers to gain the notice of booksellers and readers.

I don't know how this book came to be in your hands, but if you enjoyed it at all, then please consider dropping some stars and/or writing a review of The Dragoneer and the Pretender.

I look forward to reading what you have to share.

Amazon Review:

www.amazon.com/Amber-Boudreau/e/B08HSJXPNM

Goodreads Review:

www.goodreads.com/author/show/19755760